"**I**'m here," Nils said, painfully aware of how little that might mean to her. He tried again. "You're not alone in this anymore, Meg."

She clung to him, and he held her just as tightly, stroking her hair, kissing the top of her head, wishing . . . Christ, he didn't know what he wished.

Maybe he wished that she could've been in his arms any place else in the world and at any other time but right here and right now.

He could feel Lt. Paoletti standing off to the side, giving them both some space. But they didn't have much time.

"I need you to be tough for just a little bit longer," he told her. "Can you do that for me, Meg? We've got a lot of questions that only you can answer."

She was trembling, but somehow managed to nod, yes. She released her death grip on his neck and pulled back to look at him, wiping her eyes with one shaky hand.

"They kidnapped Amy and my grandmother," she said. "They said they were Kazbekistani Extremists, and that, and that if I didn't come here and abduct or kill the new Ambassador—they didn't really care which—they'd kill them."

Her eyes welled with tears again, but she wiped them fiercely away. "But then I thought of you. I thought if anyone could get me out of this . . ."

"You did the right thing," he reassured her. "Calling me—asking for me—was the right thing."

Books published by The Random House Ballantine Publishing Group are available at quantity discounts on bulk purchases for premium, educational, fund-raising, and special sales use. For details, please call 1-800-733-3000.

THE DEFIANT HERO

SUZANNE BROCKMANN

IVY BOOKS • NEW YORK

An Ivy Book
Published by The Random House Ballantine Publishing Group
Copyright © 2001 by Suzanne Brockmann
Excerpt from *Gone Too Far* copyright © 2003 by Suzanne Brockmann

This book contains an excerpt from the forthcoming book *Gone Too Far* by Suzanne Brockmann. This excerpt has been set for this edition only and may not reflect the final content of the forthcoming edition.

www.ballantinebooks.com

ISBN 0-345-46340-4

Manufactured in the United States of America

First Edition: March 2001

10 9 8 7 6 5 4 3 2 1

For the brave men and women who fought for freedom during the Second World War. My most sincere and humble thanks.

ACKNOWLEDGMENTS

Special thanks to Lyssa Davis who sent me a hard to find, out of print copy of *We Remember Dunkirk* (all the way from Australia!), and to Joyce Mullan and Cris Martins and all the other wonderful people on my email newsletter list for providing me with contacts and/or information on England in the late 1930s and early 1940s.

Thanks as always to Deede Bergeron, Lee Brockman, and Patricia McMahon—my personal support staff and early draft readers. More thanks than is humanly possible to Ed, whose patience and love are limitless and desperately appreciated.

Any mistakes that I've made or liberties that I've taken are completely my own.

THE DEFIANT HERO

One

∞ ∞

MEG DIDN'T UNDERSTAND at first.

The man was smiling, and his pleasant expression and tone of voice didn't match his words. "We've taken your daughter hostage."

She was in the parking garage beneath her condo, hauling a box of files from the back of her car, when he approached her. She wasn't even a hundred feet away from Ramon, the building's security guard.

The smiling man must've seen the confusion in her eyes, because he said it again. In a Kazbekistani dialect. "We have your daughter, and if you don't follow our orders, we'll kill her."

And this time, Meg understood. *Amy.* She dropped the box.

"Everything okay over there, Ms. Moore?" Ramon was down off his stool, starting toward them. There'd recently been a rape in another parking garage in this part of Washington, DC.

"Tell him yes," the smiling man murmured, opening his baseball jacket, giving her a flash of a very deadly looking gun.

Oh, God. "Where is she?"

"If I don't make a phone call to my associates within the next hour, she's dead," he told her as he bent down to pick up the box. "My associates are Kazbekistani Extremists."

Terrorists. But not just regular terrorists. The Extremists were religious zealots, capable of terrible violence and cruelty, all in the name of their god. And they had Amy.

Oh, God.

"Everything's fine," Meg called to the guard, her voice shaking only slightly.

1

"We're old college friends." The man turned his friendly smile on Ramon. "I thought I recognized Meggie. I didn't mean to appear before her like the ghost of Christmas past, though, and scare her half to death."

Ramon's hand was on the gun holstered at his waist. He smiled politely, but his dark brown gaze was on Meg. "Ms. Moore?"

Help.

She'd prepared for situations like this, back when she was working at the American embassy in Kazbekistan, an Eastern European country also know as K-stan or "the Pit" to the Americans who served time there. During her stay, she was reminded regularly that the United States didn't negotiate with terrorists. The best solution was preventive—stay safe, stay secure, stay away from dangerous persons and situations.

It was a little late for that now—although who would have thought a K-stani terrorist would show up here in Washington, all these years later?

Meg knew what she *should* do in this situation. She should enlist Ramon's help while this man held her box of files, while his hands were full and he couldn't easily reach for his gun. She should be a strong American and refuse to negotiate with terrorists. She should seek help from the FBI.

Who, no matter how good they were, wouldn't be able to find her ten-year-old daughter within the next sixty minutes.

After which time Amy would be killed.

Meg forced a smile. American be damned. She was playing this one out as Amy's very frightened mother. "It's all right, Ramon," she lied. "We're . . . old friends."

"How about I carry this upstairs for you?" The man continued the charade. His English was remarkably good—he had only the faintest of accents. "We could talk about old times over a cup of coffee."

"Great." She smiled again at Ramon, who watched them all the way over to the elevators.

"Where is she?" Meg hissed from behind her frozen smile. "Where's Amy? And what about my grandmother?" Amy had planned to take her great-grandmother, Eve, to the Smithsonian while Meg picked up these files she'd been hired to translate. Meg hadn't been sure exactly who was the baby-sitter—the ten-year-old or the seventy-five-year-old.

"The old lady's your *grand*mother." He nodded as he pressed the elevator's call button. "I *thought* she was too old to be your mother. We've got her, too."

Meg felt a rush of relief. At least Eve was with Amy. At least Amy wasn't alone and terrified and . . . "I don't understand. I'm not rich, and—"

"We don't want your money." The elevator doors opened and he stood back, politely letting her on first—the perfect terrorist gentleman. "We want you to do us a little favor."

Oh, God.

"You frequently do business at the Kazbekistani embassy across town, right?"

Oh, mighty God. The doors slid closed, but she kept her smile in place. Ramon would be watching through the security cameras.

"I only work as a consultant, a translator. It's never, I never . . ."

He pushed the button for twelve. Somehow this man she'd never seen before knew she and Amy lived on the twelfth floor.

Meg took a deep breath and tried again. "Look, I'm not allowed into any areas inside the embassy that contain confidential information or—"

"We don't want you to spy for us. We already have an agent in place inside the embassy for that purpose." He laughed and it wasn't purely for the cameras. This man was enjoying himself, amused by her fear.

A fear that morphed hotly into anger as she turned her back to the security camera. "Then what *do* you want, damn it? How do I even know you've got Amy and Eve?"

The elevator doors opened at the twelfth floor. He stepped back, again to let her go first. "If you like, we'll send you the old lady's head in a box—"

"No!" Oh, *God.*

He laughed again. "Then I guess you've just got to trust me, don't you, Meggie?"

Meg's hands were shaking so badly, she couldn't get her key into the lock.

He shifted the box to one arm and a hip as he gently took her key ring from her, opened the door, and pushed her inside, following her into her living room. "I'm afraid I can't be as trusting," he continued, setting her box next to the couch. "After we discuss strategy and negotiate terms, I'm going to drive with you over to the embassy. I know it's after five, but there's a function tonight. Nothing formal. You can wear jeans. In fact, I *want* you to wear jeans. With those boots you have. What are they called? *Cowboy* boots. Or should it be cow*girl* boots?"

"Negotiate terms?" Meg didn't give a damn what she wore. "What terms?"

"Well, it's actually a pretty simple negotiation with only one or two minor points. But the bottom line is that if you want to see your daughter and grandmother again, you'll do what we tell you to do. If you don't . . ."

"I *do*."

"Good." He crossed to the windows, pulled the curtains. "Once you're in the embassy, our inside agent will keep an eye on you. If you make any attempt to get help or to contact the authorities at any time, we *will* kill your daughter. Have absolutely no doubt about that."

His smile was gone.

Meg nodded. She didn't doubt him. After living and working in Kazbekistan for years, she knew quite well what the Extremists were capable of.

"What do you want me to do?"

Eve was certainly old enough to recognize real trouble when she found herself in it up to her hips.

And regaining consciousness on the hard metal floor in the back of a moving cargo van with her hands and feet tied was something of a clue that this day had taken a real turn for the worse.

It hadn't started out as a real swell day anyway, considering it was her seventy-fifth birthday and she'd long since given up celebrating the fact that she was continuing to get older. A faceful of wrinkles, sagging breasts, thin gray hair, loose skin, brittle bones, failing memory—wah-hoo! Let's have a party!

She hadn't minded so much while her husband was alive. He'd always managed to make her feel twenty years old and impossibly beautiful. But he'd been gone for two years now, and for two years, all she'd felt was old.

She could smell cigarette smoke, hear the hum of low voices drifting back from up front.

When she'd first awakened, she'd thrashed about a bit, searching desperately in the dimness for her great-granddaughter. She'd found the little girl right away. Amy was still unconscious—knocked out from whatever drug they'd been given, there on the sidewalk outside the Smithsonian.

Eve had made sure the girl was breathing, made certain her pulse was clear and strong, then had sunk back onto the floor, the rope digging into her wrists and ankles, the cold metal biting into her tender hips.

They were moving steadily forward, without any radical turns. The van was on the highway, Eve decided. Lifting her head slightly, she caught the final glow of the sunset out the front windows, to the right. They were heading south, probably on Route 95.

How had this happened?

Eve closed her eyes, struggling to remember.

She and Amy had been headed to the Smithsonian, ready to spend the day taking it all in. They'd packed a picnic lunch as Meg had rushed out the door, promising a birthday that Eve would never forget.

Eve doubted that this was what her favorite granddaughter had meant.

She and Amy had just gotten out of a cab and were there on the sidewalk in front of the museum when a man had approached them, hopelessly lost, asking for directions.

He had a map, and as Eve had leaned over it, trying to read the tiny street names, she hadn't noticed someone else coming up behind them until it was too late. Until they'd grabbed her, grabbed Amy.

She could remember Amy screaming. She could remember her own struggles to reach the little girl, and the sharp stab of a needle that made the world wobble and waver and finally just plain disappear.

There was no doubt about it. She and Amy had been kidnapped.

She had to find Osman Razeen.

Meg could feel a bead of perspiration trickle down her back as she tried to move purposefully up the stairs toward the new Kazbekistani ambassador's office. She tried to look as if she had a real reason to be here, tried to look as if she couldn't feel the gun in her boot, hard and cold against her leg. She tried to look as if her insides weren't tied in a knot of fear for Amy. Please God, don't let them hurt her . . .

This was impossible.

Ridiculous.

Although it *had* been absurdly easy getting into the embassy with a loaded gun. The decorative chains on her cowboy boots had set off the metal detector at the front entrance—the way they'd done many times in the past. She knew the guard on duty—Baltabek was his name—and he just rolled his eyes, laughed, and waved her through.

Obviously the Extremists had been watching her for a while. Obviously they'd targeted her specifically for this because they knew she could get into the embassy unquestioned.

What else did they know about her?

They knew that she'd do anything—*any*thing—including give her life to keep Amy safe.

Including smuggle weapons into the Kazbekistani embassy, intending to kidnap or—if it looked as if she couldn't get her target out—to kill.

That target was a man named Osman Razeen, the leader of a rival terrorist group known as the GIK—the Islamic Guard of Kazbekistan. The Extremists hated the GIK and thought Razeen disloyal to their cause and deserving of death. They wanted to bring him back to K-stan for a public execution. But they'd settle for his assassination right here, right now.

And the Extremists seemed confident that Meg, in order to protect her daughter, would be capable—if she had to—of pulling that trigger and ending his life.

Meg didn't know for sure that this Osman Razeen was really here, inside the embassy. But the thought that he *could* be here, that the leader of the GIK might have worked his way so thoroughly into the political trappings of his country's government, was mind-boggling.

Still, at this moment, she didn't give a damn if the K-stani government had been penetrated by spies or terrorists or even the Easter Bunny himself.

At this moment, she wanted only to save Amy and Eve.

And to do that, she had to find Osman Razeen.

She couldn't get help without the Extremists finding out. There was no one inside the embassy that she could speak to, no one she could trust.

She couldn't even dare to approach the Americans that were here at the embassy on business. One of them could just as well be the Extremists' inside man.

Meg looked back at the K-stani guards standing at the foot of the stairs in their ornate formal uniforms. Despite the bright colors and the flash of gold braids, those uniforms weren't half as resplendent as the U.S. Navy's dress whites.

No, there was no one and nothing that could compare to an officer of the U.S. Navy when he was dressed to shine. . . .

Meg gripped the banister, stopping short at the top of the stairs. She needed help—there was no doubt about that. There was no way in hell she could do this alone. And in a flash of clarity, she realized exactly whose help she needed, and how she just might be able to get it.

But first she had to find Osman Razeen.

He was believed to be a tall man, about six-one or -two, dark hair, brown eyes, about forty years old. The Happy Terrorist from the parking garage had shown Meg a blurred and faded photograph taken a good fifteen years ago. It was apparently the only picture in existence of the elusive Razeen.

She'd studied the photo, memorizing his chin, his nose, his light brown eyes and his rather unremarkable face, praying that she'd recognize this man when she saw him.

In the picture, he didn't glare the way a terrorist was supposed to glare. He didn't have a heavy, furrowed brow or thin, cruel lips. In fact, his lips were rather full, and he smiled crookedly, charmingly, at whomever was taking the photograph.

And now he was fifteen years older. His hair might be

gray. It might be gone. He might've gained fifty pounds, might've aged into someone unrecognizable.

And to add to her problem, Razeen could be virtually anywhere. He could be in the kitchen, disguised as part of the serving staff, cutting lamb into cubes for shish kebab for tonight's dinner. He could be the aide to the ambassador. God, he could *be* the new ambassador. . . .

Then Meg saw him. It had to be him, didn't it? Osman Razeen, only slightly heavier than the man in the photo, dressed in a dark business suit, deep in conversation with three other men as they headed together down the hall. But she wasn't sure. How could she possibly be one hundred percent certain it was him?

He was about the right age, the right height, the right coloring.

His companions were speaking in Russian as they passed, one of the men, heavyset and balding, making a cruel joke about Putin.

All four men laughed, and it was the smile, that same slightly crooked smile that was in that photo, that convinced Meg.

She'd found Razeen.

As she watched, he went into the men's room with the other three men. And she knew. It was now or never. She couldn't have asked for a better location.

Meg crossed the hall, heading directly for the ladies' room, right next to the men's. She pushed open the door and went into a stall, where she pulled up her pant leg and reached into her boot for the gun.

She took off the safety the way the Extremist had shown her, slipped the compact weapon into her jacket pocket, finger wrapped around the trigger.

Pushing her way back out of the stall, Meg purposely didn't look at the big mirror above the sinks. She refused to look at the reflection of her face, pale and grim, refused to think about the fact that these next few moments could well be her last. By pulling out that gun, she would be making herself a target, damn near begging to get herself shot and killed.

But she'd do it. She'd kill Razeen if she had to. And if and when it came down to it, she'd even die herself. For Amy.

Yes, the Extremists knew quite a lot about her.

But they didn't know everything.

They didn't know about John Nilsson.

She yanked open the door, hung a sharp left, and went directly into the men's room.

Alyssa Locke missed her uniform.

She hated waking up each day and staring into her closet. She despised having to decide which pants to wear with which blouse and which blazer.

And then there was the matter of accessories. Locke wished she could wear a tie, but unfortunately the Annie Hall look had come and gone before she was out of grade school. So she also had to worry about whether or not to tie a scarf around her neck for a splash of color. Would that make her look too feminine, or would it counteract the message sent by her extremely sensible, flat-heeled shoes?

Yes, she missed her uniform.

She also missed the order and regulations, and the inherent respect that was so often absent in the civilian sector.

But that was about all that Locke missed since resigning her commission as an officer in the U.S. Navy.

What she *didn't* miss was the frustration. Frustration caused by the knowledge that despite her talents and skills, despite the fact that she was the best sharpshooter in the entire U.S. military, she was destined to be kept far from the real action. Despite the fact that she could meet the fitness requirements, there was no chance in hell she'd ever be welcomed into the hallowed ranks of a spec-op group like the U.S. Navy SEALs.

Simply because she'd been born without a penis.

Not that she particularly wanted one.

Locke smiled as she got into the elevator and headed skyward toward her office. Now, *that* wasn't entirely true. She did happen to want one. At times, she wanted one quite badly, in fact. Unfortunately, though, penises came attached to men. And therein lay one of her biggest problems.

Men wanted to own her.

Alyssa Locke was a beautiful woman. She could state that without any ego involved. Why should her ego have anything to do with it? It was pure genetics that gave her green eyes, flawlessly smooth mocha-colored skin, and a face that combined the best features from all of her various African American, Hispanic, and white parents and grandparents.

Sure, maybe she worked out to keep the body God gave her trim and in shape, but the basics were there to start with.

Now, her skills as a shooter . . . *That* was something about which she could be extremely egotistical. And rightly so, because she was as good as it got. She'd honed that skill with hard work and endless practice, until hitting a target dead-on became as natural and effortless as taking a breath.

Yeah, when it came to shooting, she was all that, and more.

The FBI wouldn't have sought her out for their top counterterrorist unit if they didn't think as much, too.

And when the FBI recruiter said the magic words *field work*, Locke shook hands on the deal, resigned her commission, and went out shopping for black business suits and a pair of dark sunglasses.

The elevator opened onto her floor, and she moved briskly down the hall, keeping eye contact with the mostly male agents to a minimum. She'd give a nod of acknowledgment if she knew them on a first-name basis. But God forbid she smile. The male interpretation of a friendly smile in the hall was somewhere between "I'm extremely interested, let's have a drink after work" and "I want to jump your bones right here, right now."

She'd stopped smiling at a man—unless he was a close friend—right about the time she'd turned fifteen.

She breezed into her office, opened the drawer of her desk, and dropped her fanny pack inside.

Jules was already in. He'd poured her a cup of coffee and left it steaming in a mug atop her desk, bless his strange little soul. Even though it wasn't morning, their day had just begun.

He stuck his head in the door, and today it was quite a head. FBI Agent Jules Cassidy had gone blond. Garishly, glaringly blond, with dark brown roots.

The dye job and the new cut made him look about seventeen years old, which was exactly the idea. With his handsome baby face and vertically challenged stature, he could gain access to places more traditional FBI suits could never get into.

"Any word?" he asked.

Locke shook her head, settling behind her desk. "Nothing yet." And she didn't want to talk about it. "That nose ring real or—"

"Nah. You think I would risk scarring this face?" He took it off as he came all the way into her office. He was wearing a silk shirt and leather pants that were impossibly tight. Amazingly tight. If she had a thing for gay seventeen-year-olds, she'd be in big trouble. "I was doing the club circuit—the early happy hour crawl—searching for Tony Ghilotti. I forgot I had it on."

"Find him?" she asked.

"Nah. Son of a bitch's long gone. I'm sure of it. But try telling that to the boss. . . ." He gazed at her, his brown eyes concerned. "I'm the one doing double shifts, but you're the one looks like shit. Sleep much lately, girlfriend?"

With anyone else, she would've lied. But this was Jules, so she shook her head. Over the past few months, they'd worked too closely together too often to keep any secrets.

He watched as she took a sip of her coffee. "You know, it's got to happen soon. And your sister's going to be all right."

Locke nodded and smiled because he wanted her to nod and smile. "It's the waiting that's killing me," she admitted.

"Maybe you should take some time off," Jules suggested. "Go hang out with her—"

"Bad idea."

He shrugged. "Suit yourself." He ran his hand across the top of his head. "So. You hate the hair."

Locke had to laugh. "You are so vain," she told him. "You know exactly how gorgeous you look, Mr. Fishing-for-a-compliment."

He grinned, turning to give her a view of his backside. "Check out my ass in these pants."

"Already did, thanks."

"And . . . ?"

"Thanks for the coffee," she said. "Get out of my office."

"Hands up! Move it! Come on, hands high—up where I can see 'em!"

Two of the men were standing by the sinks, two—Osman Razeen and the heavyset man—were still over by the urinals. They all looked up in surprise as Meg burst into the men's room.

"What *is* this—"

"Freeze!" she shouted, holding the gun in both hands, the way she'd seen on cop shows on TV, shifting her aim from one group of men to the other. "Don't move, don't talk, don't do anything but put your hands in the air! *Now!*"

Oh, God, was she really saying this, really doing this?

It worked. Four pairs of hands went up, and the heavyset man peed on his shoe.

His pants were unzipped and . . .

Oh, this was just perfect.

She waved her gun at the men over by the sinks. First things first, then she'd deal with . . . other issues. "Get over with the others. Move it, let's *go!*"

They moved.

The K-stani embassy men's room was much larger—at least five times more so—than the women's room. The walls were covered with blue tile, the floor a paler shade. Urinals lined one wall, the stalls were across from the sinks. There were no windows and only that one door.

It was the perfect location for holding off a siege.

"Keep your hands high." Meg quickly checked to make sure there was no one else in the room, no one hidden in one of the stalls.

"Do you mind if I—"

"Yes." She cut the heavy man off. "Keep your hands up."

She wanted to apologize. *So sorry for the humiliation but I can't let you lower your hands, not even for that. . . .* But she knew she couldn't risk coming across as weak. She had to keep them believing that she knew how to use this gun, that she *would* use this gun if they threatened her.

And she couldn't let them lower their hands. Not if she wanted to stay alive.

Sure, the ambassador's staff weren't supposed to carry weapons in the embassy. But there was also a rule stating that *she* wasn't supposed to have a gun, either. And here she was. Fully armed and dangerous.

"Do you honestly think you can take the Kazbekistani ambassador hostage inside his own embassy?" the heavy man asked. He was sweating, and Meg realized that he didn't fear a hostage situation. He was afraid she had come here on a suicide mission, to gun them all down. Such were the ways of the violent world from which he'd come.

Razeen was silent, just watching her, his dark gaze impossible to read, but another man spoke up. "Perhaps we could negotiate. If you would tell us what it is that you want . . . ?"

"I want *silence*," Meg told them sharply. "I want your hands in the air. I want *you*—" She pointed with her gun at the heavyset man in all his unzipped glory. "—to take a message to both your government and mine. I want all guards and police to stay far away, I want this entire floor cleared. If someone so much as *touches* this door, I'll start shooting. You make sure they understand that—they breathe funny on the door, and these men are dead."

He nodded his understanding, his double chins wobbling.

"Tell them," Meg continued, "that I have a list of demands, but the only person I'll consider negotiating with is Ensign John Nilsson of the U.S. Navy SEALs. Tell them to find him and bring him here, and then I'll talk."

Please God, let John be somewhere close by . . .

"Do you understand?" she asked.

He nodded. "John Nilsson. U.S. Navy."

"He's a SEAL. Make sure you tell them that."

"A SEAL," he repeated obediently, his eyes longingly on the door.

"Go."

Hands still high, the heavyset man took his various exposed parts and lunged for the door.

And Meg sat down, her back to the tile wall, her gun on her remaining hostages.

Waiting for John Nilsson to come and save the day.

Two

LIEUTENANT JUNIOR GRADE John Nilsson was on a mission. Under his leadership, a six-man team of SEALs had been ordered to break into an Iraqi compound and rescue Captain Andy Chang, a downed American fighter pilot.

Getting inside would be easy. It was getting back out after their presence had been detected and an alarm had been raised that was going to be the hard part.

Nils's original plan had been to insert and extract without waking even the lightest sleeping Iraqi soldier. But—what a surprise—there were ten times as many soldiers in this compound as intel reports had indicated, and what was described as a sleepy little ill-equipped and poorly manned outpost was in truth a brightly lit, teeming center of activity, even at 0300.

Going in after that pilot with only a six-man team would be little more than suicide.

Still, he'd sent Ensign Sam Starrett and Petty Officer WildCard Karmody in to verify that the pilot was being held at this location. And at least naval intelligence had *that* much right. Sam and WildCard returned in short order with a report that Chang was indeed there. And, overachievers that they were, the SEALs Nils thought of as his best friends also came back with the complete layout of the compound.

Nils lay just behind the scrub brush growing on a small rise and gazed at the roof of the two-story building through night vision glasses. That roof was the way Sam and Wild-Card had gotten inside undetected. It was the route his team would take, too.

If this didn't work, he was going to get hammered. He knew damn well that his correct response to the additional security was to accept failure. He should cut his losses, turn his team around, and slip back over the border.

But he'd never been fond of losing. And accepting failure wasn't the only option. Not when he'd prepared for exactly this possibility.

Nils felt more than heard Senior Chief Petty Officer Wolchonok move beside him, and he glanced at the older man. Even clean of the camouflage greasepaint he currently wore, Stanley Wolchonok had a face only a mother could love—a mother, and an entire team of SEALs, who'd come to trust the senior chief with their very lives. There wasn't a single man in SEAL Team Sixteen—including their CO, Lieutenant Tom Paoletti—who wouldn't jump off the edge of the Grand Canyon without hesitation if the senior chief assured them they'd sprout wings midair and be able to fly safely to the other side.

But right now Wolchonok was shaking his head. "Don't even think about it, Lieutenant."

"I can get Chang out of there."

"No, you can't."

Nils always thought God would have a voice like the senior chief's. Deep and resonant and filled with such absolute certainty. And with just a hint of a Chicago accent. "As always, I appreciate your opinion, Senior Chief. But if it's all the same to you, I'm going to try."

Wolchonok leaned closer, lowering his voice even more, speaking not as a senior chief to his commanding officer, but as an older, more experienced man to one much younger. "Johnny, come on, you know what this is. It's the no-win scenario. You know as well as I do that you win by admitting defeat. Don't screw this up for yourself."

Nils knew the senior chief was right. An officer needed to assess a situation and make decisions based on what was best for his men. But they were SEALs, and being SEALs meant that sometimes they had to take risks. It also meant that sometimes they had to cheat the rules. He looked back through the NVs. "I'm not ready to admit defeat."

Wolchonok gave him a look designed to make men squirm—men with far higher rank than Nilsson. "Cut the Hollywood heroics, Lieutenant. This is only a training op, and today's lesson is all about backing down. You lose Chang, yeah, but you avoid a total goatfuck—and a little black mark next to your name. By walking away, you keep the Iraqis from getting their hands on six more hostages—a situation that would be politically damaging to the United States. Need I remind you that we're undermanned and—"

"How many more men do you figure we'll need?" Nils put down the NVs and met Wolchonok's evil eye. He knew damn well that this was only a training op, that this was, indeed, the no-win scenario that, as SEALs, as officers, as human beings, they were forced to come up against again and again out in the real world.

However, none of *this* was real.

They were in the California desert, not the Middle East. Those weren't real Iraqis he'd been watching through his night vision glasses, they were jarheads—Marines— assigned to participate in this exercise in futility. The assault weapons they were all using didn't fire bullets. Instead they fired lasers and were hooked into an intricate computer system. If a soldier was "killed" by a laser "bullet," he'd get a small jolt and his weapon would be disabled by the computer and would no longer fire.

Captain Andy Chang of the U.S. Air Force was really Captain Andy Chang, but after they finished here tonight, whether Nils and his SEALs managed to rescue him or not, he was going to grab a beer with the rest of the guys before heading home to his pregnant wife.

The most real thing about this entire scenario was that black mark Wolchonok had mentioned—the one that would show up on Nilsson's fitness report if he tried this and failed.

He had, however, absolutely no intention of failing.

"I think six more men will do it," Nils continued, still holding the senior chief's gaze. "Four to create some well-placed diversions and a couple of snipers to even up the odds if and when the shooting starts." He switched on his radio, pulling the lip mike closer to his mouth. "Team Bravo, stand ready."

Wolchonok blinked. And then he laughed—just a short burst of disbelief as his eyes narrowed and he tried to see inside Nilsson's head.

As Nils gazed back at him, he couldn't keep a smile from escaping.

And then Wolchonok smiled, too. Senior Chief Stan Wolchonok had a smile about as bright as a sunrise after a solid week of rain. It transformed his butt-ugly, weathered face into a thing of true beauty.

"What have you done?" Wolchonok asked.

"It's not what I *have* done, Senior Chief," Nils told him. "It's what I'm *going* to do."

He was going to win the no-win scenario.

Johnny Nilsson was one of those guys who was going to make admiral some day.

It was more than just his fancy degree from Yale and his silver spoon "mumsie's playing tennis at the yacht club today" childhood that had Sam Starrett convinced of that fact. There was something he could see in Nils's eyes, even when his friend was shit-faced, even when he was puking and feverish with the flu, even when he was half asleep and muttering in Zamboorian or Chinese or God knows what languages.

It was in the way Nils walked, the way he smiled, the way he took a piss. It surrounded him at all times, hanging about him like some freaky-deak aura that was so powerful, even mere mortals like Sam could see it.

And Sam could see it super clear tonight, as Nils outlined his revised strategy for getting them in and back out of the compound with Captain Chang in tow.

Somehow Nils had found out that tonight was no ordinary training op. Tonight he was in command of a no-win scenario, and knowing that, he'd not only restacked the deck in his favor, but he'd reshuffled and redealt the damn thing as well, making arrangements for six additional SEALs to join in on the op.

And now Sam had the point, leading the team stealthily through the corridor, toward the room where the jarheads were holding Chang. There were no booby traps here, no alarm systems, not even any guards in the hallway, which was typical brute-strength thinking. Figuring no one could penetrate their densely guarded perimeter, the Marines had left their vulnerable interior unprotected.

He knew from his earlier visit that there were only two guards in with Chang. The SEALs would take 'em out fast, kicking open the door at the exact moment Team Bravo set off the first of their diversionary explosions.

Sam checked his watch as they silently moved into position outside the door. He glanced at Nils, who gave him a nod and something that looked a hell of a lot like a smile. The son of a bitch was enjoying himself.

He was enjoying himself, too, Sam realized as he nodded back at Nils. Of course, it helped knowing that the bullets weren't real. Ever since last summer when he'd felt firsthand what it was like to be a target, his hands got sweaty at the prospect of getting shot again.

Not that he'd ever mention that to the shrink he still met with, although far less frequently these days. God, no. He'd lie through his teeth first, without any guilt. Because Sam knew a truth no shrink would be able to understand. Yes, he understood that being scared was part of being alive. But *admitting* that fear was something he simply could not do, not to a shrink, not to a girlfriend, not to his mother, not even to John Nilsson, his teammate and best friend.

Lieutenant Jazz Jacquette was gently turning the knob so that the door was unlatched. As Jazz nodded at Nils, Sam could see his full lips twitch. From another man, it wouldn't have meant anything, but from SEAL Team Sixteen's grim-faced executive officer, it was the equivalent of an all-out grin.

The Marines were expecting an easy victory. They were expecting that the SEALs would back down and go home. But in approximately seventeen seconds, Nils and his men were going to kick some serious Marine butt.

Nils gave a hand signal. Stand by.

Sam held up fingers as he watched the seconds tick down. Four. Three. Two . . .

He used all of his weight to kick the door open, and it went like clockwork. He and Jazz went in first, moving fast, in sync, shoulder to shoulder to stay out of each other's firing range. He saw the absolute surprise on the guards' faces, saw the weapon down on the table, saw Chang safely off to the side.

Sam's weapon was already up, and he fired, neatly taking out the guard on the right as easily as Jazz handled the guard on the left.

It was over in less than two seconds.

Nils moved toward Chang—he and WildCard cut the captain free.

"You're badly outnumbered," Sam heard Chang say.

"Just stay close, stay down, and we'll get you out of here, Captain." When the light hit Nils a certain way, he looked a little like that movie star, Ben something. The one who'd dated Gwyneth Paltrow. Except Nils could play earnest and sincere better than any Hollywood actor Sam had ever seen.

And they were off, back out into the hall, moving swiftly toward the front entrance.

Sam could hear the sound of explosions, more of them now, one right after the other, rapid-fire. It sounded like an all-out frontal assault. And knowing the Marines, they would *respond* to it as if it were an all-out frontal assault, sending their men out in force to meet the threat.

Except the threat was already behind them. Within them. Inside them.

Team Bravo had set off smoke grenades in the lobby, bless their devious little hearts. It made it impossible to see—or to be seen.

They led Chang right out the front door, pretending to cough and choke along with the Marines, hiding amidst the chaos.

The area around the compound was thick with smoke as well. And all of the big floodlights had gone dark—Chief Frank O'Leary's handiwork, no doubt.

There was only one sharpshooter in all of the U.S. military who was better than O'Leary, and that was Lieutenant Junior Grade Alyssa Locke. Who, rumor had it, had resigned her commission as an officer in the Navy just shortly after she and Sam did an op together up in New England, last summer. Was it something he'd said? Was it *every*thing he'd said? God knows they hadn't hit it off the way Sam had wanted them to. . . .

Focus, he ordered himself. This was neither the time nor place to devote even the smallest percentage of his concentration to Alyssa Locke.

The coldhearted ice bitch.

The coldhearted, drop dead gorgeous, impossibly beautiful, achingly exquisite ice bitch. With her eyes that were the color of the ocean, a startling contrast to her smooth, light brown skin, and that mouth. That incredible mouth. Lord have mercy, Alyssa Locke had the kind of lips that would have sparked erotic fantasies in a Puritan.

Sam had a recurring dream in which Locke would turn to him and smile that certain kind of smile that meant heaven was just a heartbeat away. She'd moisten her lips with just the very tip of her tongue and . . .

"Watch it, Starrett!"

Oh, Jesus, he'd stepped on Lopez.

"Sam, we're almost there, but I need you with me," Nils said softly.

Crap. Scolded out by his best friend.

Damn Alyssa Locke.

Nils did a quick head count as he approached the extraction point, the men around him barking like seals to let the Marines know who'd bested them.

Chief O'Leary, Ensign Mike Muldoon, Jenk, Rick, Steve, and Junior. His Team Bravo was all there, as were the trucks that would take them back to the base.

Nils had done it. He'd fucking *won* the no-win scenario.

There was a helo there as well, he realized. A puddle jumper.

And—surprise, surprise—Lieutenant Tom Paoletti, commanding officer of SEAL Team Sixteen, was standing beside it, arms crossed. Nils hadn't expected to see his CO tonight. Not out here, anyway. And there was another man next to Paoletti, but he was even farther in the shadows and Nils couldn't make out his face.

Was the CO mad or was he merely cold? It was too dark to see his eyes, but there *was* something of a chill in the desert air.

Petty Officer Second Class Mark Jenkins more than made

up for Paoletti's seeming lack of enthusiasm. Jenk practically did a cartwheel. "You did it, Lieutenant! You beat the no-win scenario!" He started another round of barking among the men.

"By cheating." The man beside the CO stepped into the light, raising his voice to be heard over the din.

Shit. It was Admiral Larry Tucker. What was he doing here?

Senior Chief Wolchonok came and planted himself beside Nilsson, an unmovable rock, ready to go into battle with him for a second time that night. And the rest of the team fell right in behind him—including Captain Chang. Nils nearly laughed aloud. The elation he'd felt at winning was nothing compared to this show of support from his teammates. He looked Tucker straight in the eye. Come on, dickhead, give it your best shot.

"There was a security breach of the computer system last night." Tucker glared at Nils. "I assume you're behind that, Lieutenant? Or maybe you'd like to go back to being an ensign again? Maybe three years wasn't enough."

Ah, Christ. Bring *that* up, why don't you?

But from behind him, Nils heard Sam Starrett cough into his hand, "Asshole," and he had to struggle not to laugh.

Lieutenant Paoletti stepped forward. "Admiral Tucker—"

But Tucker had fixed his death-ray gaze on WildCard, who was doing his best to look angelic—not an easy task for a guy who looked an awful lot like the devil incarnate. "This smells like one of *your* stupid tricks, Mr. Karmody. Before this is over, we're going to find that you're involved, aren't we?"

"No, sir," WildCard said.

Nils knew he meant "No, sir, you're not going to find anything." WildCard was a hacker extraordinaire. He didn't leave calling cards. At least none that Tucker or his staff would be able to find.

"Personally, Admiral," Paoletti said mildly, "I'm of the opinion that if Lieutenant Nilsson and Petty Officer Karmody *did* hack into the computer to gain knowledge of tonight's training op, they should be commended for their attempt to go into this mission as fully prepared as possible. If this situation were real, and that was an Iraqi computer they'd compromised—"

"But it wasn't an Iraqi computer. It was a U.S. Navy—"

"I really don't see the difference." The CO had the balls to interrupt the admiral. "SEALs are trained to seek unconventional alternatives and options for every given situation. Lieutenant Nilsson should be commended for his initiative."

Nils realized that while he was speaking, Paoletti had managed to move so that he, too, was standing beside him, with the team. "Good job, Lieutenant," Paoletti said. He held out his hand.

Nils shook it. "Thank you, sir."

From over on his left, Wolchonok let out a resounding, "Hoo-yah!" It was a cry that the rest of the men, both officers and enlisted, echoed.

The senior was grinning at him, and Nils smiled back, knowing he'd remember this moment for the rest of his life.

A vein stood out on Tucker's forehead. "Lieutenant Paoletti, are you—"

"Going to have a beer with Lieutenant Nilsson and my men? Definitely." Paoletti cut him off again, turning this time to the men in Nils's Bravo Team. "What, do you guys have tomorrow off or something, staying out like this all night?"

They shrugged, and Jenk answered for them. "No, sir, muster's at oh-five hundred. We'll be there."

"Let's see if we can't spell this out so Admiral Tucker will be sure to understand," Paoletti said. "We have here an ensign, a chief, and four petty officers who—even though I didn't hand out this assignment, even though this was their time off, including their time to *sleep*—have spent an entire night participating in a training op. And the reason they've done this is . . ." He looked at O'Leary. "Can you help me out here, Chief?"

The taciturn chief shrugged. "Because Nils—Lieutenant Nilsson—asked." The other SEALs nodded.

"Because Lieutenant Nilsson asked," the CO repeated.

Tucker was finally silent, and Nils actually felt sorry for the SOB. When was the last time anyone did anything for him simply because he asked instead of ordered?

"You guys have tomorrow off," Paoletti told them. "Good

job tonight. All of you. Lieutenant Howe," he called to the waiting helo pilot, "I think the admiral's ready to return to the base. I'll be driving back with my men."

Poor Teri Howe. She had to fly back to Coronado with only Admiral Tucker for company. She sent a longing glance in Mike Muldoon's direction, but as usual, the newest member of Team Sixteen was oblivious. He was already in deep discussion with the senior chief.

Nils held his breath until Tucker was safely on the helo and off the ground.

Lieutenant Paoletti turned to Nils and sighed. "What am I going to do with you, Johnny?"

"Just promote him to admiral, L.T., and get it over with," Sam Starrett drawled. "Then he can fight it out with Tucker himself."

"Let's get moving." Wolchonok began herding the team.

"I support your creativity, Lieutenant," Paoletti said to Nils as they headed for the trucks. "You know I do. But we're going to have to have a talk. Tomorrow. Fifteen hundred. My office. This stunt's going to get some attention, and not just from Admiral Tucker."

Nils shook his head. "Please don't ask me to apologize for winning, L.T."

"I'm not going to do that. But we might need to do some explaining." Paoletti's cell phone shrilled. He glanced at his watch, and Nils automatically checked his own timepiece.

It was 0343. Who was calling the CO at this hour? Was it possible Tucker was so determined to crucify him that he'd already started spreading the word?

Paoletti found the pocket that held his phone as it rang again. "This can't be good."

"Oh, Tommy," WildCard singsonged obnoxiously. "It's your wife!"

As Paoletti opened his phone and stepped aside to take the call, Nils quickly moved to intercept WildCard. He wasn't the only one. Wolchonok and Jazz Jacquette also made a beeline for the gangly SEAL.

"She's not his wife," Wolchonok said bluntly. "So shut the fuck up."

"Whoa," WildCard said, blinking. "I was just kidding, Senior. I was—"

"It's becoming something of an issue for L.T.," Nils explained, his voice low. "He wants to get married, and she keeps putting it off."

"Who, Kelly?" WildCard was genuinely surprised. It was obvious that for once he hadn't meant to be an asshole.

"Yes, Kelly," Jazz told him. "Every time L.T. tries to pin her down to a wedding date, her pager conveniently goes off."

WildCard laughed. "No way. She's crazy about him. Whenever she comes to see him at the base, I swear, it's not even five minutes before he locks the door to his office and—"

Jazz gave him a silencing look as Lieutenant Paoletti shut his phone with a snap and approached them.

"Problem, sir?" Wolchonok asked.

"That day off's going to have to wait," the CO announced. "That was Admiral Crowley on the phone. He wanted to know if I knew where Lt. John Nilsson was."

Oh, shit. Nils had always thought of Crowley as one of the good guys. The admiral was a SEAL himself. If *he* was pissed about this . . .

"We've got to move," the CO continued. He was talking to Jazz and Wolchonok now, but the rest of the team had stopped to listen, too. "The entire team's going wheels up ASAP. We've been ordered to provide assistance to an FBI counter-terrorist team in DC. There's a hostage situation in the Kazbekistani embassy." He turned and looked at Nils. "And the hostage taker will only negotiate with Johnny Nilsson."

Three

$\backsim \sigma$

MEG HELD ON tightly to her gun as she stared across the men's room at Osman Razeen.

All three of her hostages sat on the floor, their hands carefully on their knees. But only Razeen's eyes were open. He stared back at her, watching her as intently as she watched him.

Did he know why she was here? Could he tell just by looking into her eyes that she would kill him, ruthlessly, if she had to? Did he even suspect that she might well be his assigned executioner?

It had been ten hours since she'd sent the fat man out of the room, and there was only silence in the hall outside. Ten hours—and she was completely exhausted. Who would've guessed sitting on a bathroom floor could be so completely draining?

It was definitely time to check in.

Ten hours was plenty of time for the FBI or the Mission: Impossible team or whoever the heck was out there to rig their miniature cameras and high-powered microphones, running them into this room through the air vents, or up through the plumbing in the sinks and—why not?—even the toilets.

Meg cleared her throat and spoke for the first time in all those hours. "I want to know if Ens. John Nilsson has been contacted."

The two other hostages opened their eyes. They glanced at each other, and one of them opened his mouth to speak.

Meg cut him off. "I wasn't talking to you." She raised her voice only slightly. "I know you can hear me. I'd like my question answered, please."

From the bottom of her handbag, her cell phone rang.

She'd imagined them yelling the answers to her questions right through the closed bathroom door. She'd feel right at home—that was one of Amy's favorite forms of communication.

Oh, God, she wanted Amy.

She let the phone ring until she was sure she could answer it without her voice wavering. She couldn't sound weak. She couldn't let them think they could just walk in here and take the gun away from her.

Even if that was the truth.

Taking a deep breath and holding the gun with her right hand, she reached into her bag with her left, her eyes never leaving her hostages. She flipped the phone open.

"Guess you figured out who I am, huh?" She tried her best to sound flip, casual. As if she were a hardened terrorist who'd taken hostages a dozen, no, a *hundred* times before.

"Ms. Moore, my name is Max Bhagat and I'm—"

"Has John Nilsson been found?" All those relentless sales calls from AT&T and MCI were finally paying off. After years of practice, Meg didn't even feel compelled to wait until he took a breath before she cut him off.

"Ms. Moore, it would help a great deal if we knew—"

Meg hung up the phone. She couldn't talk to him. She couldn't listen. Max Bhagat was an FBI negotiator. A professional. He had to be. And she couldn't afford to let him distract or confuse her. It had to be John she spoke to. *Only* John.

The phone rang again, and she let it go for six long rings before answering.

"That was a yes/no question," she said. No hello. Right to the point. She'd never been so rude in all her life. "Let's try it again. Has John Nilsson been found?"

There was only the slightest pause before Bhagat replied. "Yes."

"Is he coming?"

"Yes."

"His ETA?"

"We just located him. It's hard to know exactly—"

"Guess."

"Six or seven hours?"

Oh, God. "Six hours. Make it six," she said, and hung up the phone. Six more hours. Dear, sweet Jesus, help her. Another six hours and she would be dead.

Tired, she corrected herself. Please, God, only dead *tired.* Dead would no doubt come later.

When they were pulled out of the back of the van by a man who wasn't wearing a mask, Eve knew that she and Amy wouldn't be left alive.

It was almost absurd, after the life she'd led, that it should all end here.

She'd survived the tragic death of both her parents at age fifteen.

She'd survived moving from her beloved southern California all the way across the Atlantic Ocean to England, a country where the drizzle seemed relentless and the sun never shone quite as strong—a country she'd learned to love with all her heart.

She'd survived the War. The terrible war with Nazi Germany. She'd lived through the Battle of Britain, as the German Luftwaffe bombed the English coast night after excruciatingly endless night.

And—speaking of excruciating—she'd survived the disco era, too. She mustn't forget about *that.*

The thought would've been ridiculous enough to make her smile even as she was roughly dragged up the overgrown path to a ramshackle two-story house, if it hadn't been for Amy.

Face it. Eve had lived darn near forever. Three quarters of a century was a long time. And while she wasn't eager for it to be over, she'd lived a full life and could gracefully accept whatever fate had in store for her.

But she could accept no such thing for Amy.

The girl was still almost completely out of it from whatever drug they'd both been given to knock them out. Eve carried her awkwardly, with her hands tied in front of her, even though her bones creaked from sitting still for so many hours, even though she barely limped along.

The thought that Amy's life was about to end was obscene. Meg's daughter was so young, so beautiful. She had

Meg's glorious dark eyes. And even though she had her perfidious father's hair, on Amy it was gorgeous—thick and dark, a tumble of curls down her back.

Eve had longed for such hair when she was younger. She'd been born with straight, baby fine, wispy blond hair.

Amy whimpered like a child half her age and clung to Eve's neck, and Eve glared at the man who had such a tight hold on her arm. She would have finger-shaped bruises there come the morning.

"I'm seventy-five years old," she told him. "If you push me again, I might fall and break my already too-painful hip. And then where would we be?"

Spending her last few moments on earth in serious pain, unable to comfort Amy. Eve could see that answer in the man's eyes.

God help them.

She limped up the stairs and into the house where another man and a woman, both carrying enormous guns, looking like commandos from a bad movie, pushed her into a room with no furnishings.

She shifted Amy higher up, her muscles screaming from carrying a ten-year-old girl, as she looked around.

The room was completely bare, save for the balls of dust on the floor.

The walls were dull, the dingy shades were pulled tightly down. French doors with smudgy glass opened into another room—a dining room. It held a rickety card table and some gray metal folding chairs. Beyond that, through an open door, Eve could see a glimpse of a kitchen, decorated in what she knew had once been cheery oranges and avocado greens, but both had aged to a very similar shade of putrid brown.

One of the men—there were four, and one woman—closed the French doors with a rattle that made Amy lift her head.

Where are we? Who are you? Why are we here?

Eve had tried those questions when they pulled off the highway to take a very public personal hygiene break by the side of a deserted road. She'd persisted after they'd been tied back up and unceremoniously loaded back into the van.

That and Amy's crying had gotten them another set of needles in their arms, and more of that mind numbing unconsciousness. She'd dreamed about running. The five-kilometer Dover Dash that she'd first entered when she turned fifty. Only, in her dream, she was being chased by Nazis. If they caught her, she was dead.

Eve wasn't going to risk another dose of drugs, or an even more permanent solution, so this time she kept her mouth firmly shut.

"Sit," she was ordered, so she sat. Lowering Amy to the hard floor first, then creakily joining her, she took the child back into her arms as her captors spoke quietly in a language she didn't understand.

The man who had spoken wanted to be the leader. He'd been one of the two men in the van. He was shorter than the other men, but he clearly wanted to be in charge.

The other one who'd been in the van, Mr. Push-the-old-lady-up-the-stairs, was full of complaints. That was obvious even though Eve couldn't understand a word of what they were saying. But he gestured, he pouted, he whined. And a whine was a whine, whatever the language.

The other men were silent. One of them was enormous, a great huge bear of a young man.

They were all young, barely more than children. The oldest couldn't have been more than twenty-five.

The oldest was the woman. She had dark hair pulled severely back from her face in a ponytail and eyes that were already dead. All five of them had those enormous guns, but the woman held hers as if it were a natural extension of her arms. *She* was the one who was in charge. Eve could tell that with one look.

Eve saw from Amy's ragged breathing that she was very close to tears. As a sob escaped, the woman looked over at them sharply. Best not to get that one angry. It wouldn't take much to push her over the edge.

Eve held Amy more tightly, hushing her, murmuring words of reassurance that she didn't quite believe. "It'll be all right." She rocked Amy gently in her arms, like she'd done when the little girl was just a baby. Her eyelids drooped,

and she sagged against Eve, giving in to the last remaining
vestiges of the drug. Thank God.

Thank God.

Eve had never been one to spend a lot of time in prayer,
begging for miracles. She was far more a student of the
"God helps those who help themselves" school. But if there
were ever a time she could use a little deus ex machina, it
was now.

It didn't have to be much, God. It didn't have to be a black
helicopter filled with those U.S. Navy SEALs that Meg had
spoken of so many times, with such admiration in her voice.

A sudden, intense fatigue that all five of their kidnappers
came down with at once would certainly do it. Eve could
haul Amy into her arms and steal away with her into the
darkness of the woods and swamp that seemed to surround
this run-down old house on three sides.

Please, God, don't let Amy's life end here.

Eve could remember when she herself was nearly as
young as Amy, when her own life was stretching out in front
of her with such limitless possibilities. She could remember
1939, the year she was fifteen. She hadn't been quite so innocent and sweet as Amy was at ten, but still, she'd been
filled with such hope despite the fact that Hitler was terrifying people in England with the threat of war.

She'd been fifteen and still a child, but all grown-up as
well. She'd been both mother and father to Nick, her little
brother. He'd been Amy's age that year—ten—and so like
Amy in so many ways, so furiously, joyfully *alive* despite all
the hurdles life had sent their way.

Eve closed her eyes, remembering the hurdle she and
Nick had been so afraid of—a hurdle named Ralph Grayson. He'd been hired on as Nicky's tutor—a young Englishman sent to spend the summer with them in Ramsgate, to
teach Nick the impossible—to teach him to read.

She could see Ralph's face as clearly as if it were yesterday. He had a beautiful face, although clearly he didn't think
so, with a long English nose, exquisite cheekbones, and a
high forehead. He had wavy brown hair and hazel eyes that
twinkled with good humor when he was amused, and glowed
with such intensity when he was passionate.

And it didn't take much to make him passionate. Shakespeare. Wilde. Shaw. Higher mathematics. Science. History. Oh, history could make the man forget propriety—no small thing for an Englishman—and turn literal cartwheels across the estate lawn.

He'd captivated Nicky. And Eve as well. No, it wasn't long before he became everything to her. Best friend, confidant, teacher, hero.

Lover. But only in the purest sense of the word.

God, she missed him. It had been years, and she still missed him so much. . . .

Meg Moore.

Holy shit.

The gunman who had taken over the Kazbekistani embassy was a woman. And not just any woman. She was Margaret Delancy Moore.

As Nils stared at the pictures coming onto the transport plane's video monitor through satellite transmission, he was stunned. If someone had asked him to make a list of all the women he'd met in his twenty-eight years of life, with number one being the woman most likely to take hostages in the Kazbekistani men's room, Meg Moore would have come in dead last.

On the screen, Meg sat on the floor of that elaborately tiled bathroom, weapon held unwaveringly in her hand. She was wearing jeans and a fancy pair of cowboy boots, a dark blue shirt, and a denim jacket. Her straight dark hair was cut short around her face, making her pretty features appear even more delicate. Her brown eyes had dark smudges beneath them, as if she were sick or at least exhausted, her mouth a grim line.

What did he expect, though? That she'd be smiling? The woman had taken hostage the K-stani ambassador and two of his staff. There wasn't much to smile about.

But, God, he'd always loved Meg's smile. . . .

What the *hell* was she doing on the nonhostage side of a handgun?

"One gunman—or woman, in this case," Jazz reported,

"and three hostages. In a room with a single door and no windows. She chose her location well."

"According to Admiral Crowley, the K-stani government is pushing for immediate action," Tom Paoletti added. "The FBI counterterrorist group called onto the scene is considering letting a local SWAT team kick down the door and take her out."

Nils finally found his voice. "Oh, Christ, no," he said, and Jazz, Paoletti, and Wolchonok all turned to look at him. "L.T., Jesus, please—don't let them do that."

"Who is she, Johnny?" Lieutenant Paoletti asked.

"L.T., really," Nils said. "You've got to call the admiral *now*, and tell him to ask the FBI to wait. They've got to let me go in there first and talk to Meg—her name's Meg Moore. Seriously, sir, I doubt she's ever even *held* a weapon before, let alone fired one. I don't know what this is about, but there's definitely something going on here that we don't know. This is a woman who has a young daughter. I'm telling you, Meg's probably never even had a speeding ticket in her entire life. Please, Tom, God, don't let them send in a SWAT team."

Tom Paoletti was already dialing the phone. "I'll talk to Crowley."

Nils felt almost lightheaded with relief.

"Shit, Johnny." Wolchonok was looking at him with sympathy. "Is this some kind of girlfriend-gone-crazy situation?"

"Oh, no way, Senior Chief," Nils said. "Not even close. She's not my girlfriend. I haven't seen this woman in years."

"Jesus Christ, is that Meg Moore?" Sam had been in the back of the transport plane with the rest of the team, but now he stood squinting at the slightly blurred pictures on the video screen. He looked at Nils. "It is, isn't it? Hey, Karmody, come check this out."

"You know her, too?" Jazz asked.

Sam glanced over at the stone-faced XO. "Yeah, she worked at the American embassy in the Pit back in '97. Me and Nils and WildCard played hide-the-refugee there with that CIA spook—what was his name?"

"What's the Pit?" Ensign Mike Muldoon was green and hadn't had the chance to visit many of the world's more choice garden spots like Beirut, or Algeria, or the crème de la crème, Kazbekistan.

Mike was one of those digustingly gorgeous guys that women drooled over. He looked like a Hollywood action-adventure hero, hard bodied, with a face that would adorn the bedrooms of teenage girls across the country. But unlike many too-handsome men, he was completely clueless about his good looks. Apparently he'd been overweight as a kid, and when he looked into his mirror, he still saw eight-year-old Tubby Muldoon.

He was a damn nice guy—one of the nicest in the teams, and sharp as hell, as well. If there was something he didn't understand, he wasn't afraid to ask questions. He'd hit it off with the senior chief the moment he joined Team Six-teen, and now, as usual, he looked to Wolchonok for an explanation.

"Kazbekistan—" Wolchonok gave the kid his best professor voice. "—is also known as K-stan or the Pit. And for good reason. It's an oil-rich country, but it looks like the surface of the moon. About four thousand K-stanis are filthy rich; the other millions are piss poor, starving, and angry about it. The government's allegedly a democracy since the breakup of the Soviet bloc, but the hundreds of thousands of Muslims they oppress probably wouldn't agree. Every other hovel hides a terrorist cell; Americans can't travel from the airport to the embassy without armed escort. If it's ever a choice between K-stan and the Cayman Islands for your vacation, Muldoon, I'd go with the Islands."

Sam looked at Nils. "What *was* the name of that guy we went in to rescue? It was some kind of Arab handle. . . ."

"Abdelaziz," Nils told his friend. He was never going to forget that name, nor the CIA operative it belonged to, not if he lived to be four hundred years old.

WildCard unplugged himself from his laptop long enough to take a quick look at the video monitor. "I remember that. *And* I remember Meg Moore. That's definitely her. She was hot."

"She was also married—to that asshole foreign service officer," Sam said. Nils could feel his friend's eyes on him and he carefully didn't meet his gaze. "That prick who thought he was God's gift to the world—remember him?"

Oh, yeah, Nils remembered Daniel Moore. He was older than Meg by at least ten years, with a hint of gray at his distinguished temples. He was one of those guys who'd spent so many years lying, he would no longer recognize the truth if it came up and bit him on the ass.

Of course, Nils should talk. It took one to know one.

Both Sam and WildCard were gazing at him with unabashed interest. And Nils knew what they were thinking. All this had taken place three years ago. And now, from out of the blue, Meg had reappeared, asking for Nils by name. Or *was* it from out of the blue?

"Just how friendly did you get with her, Johnny boy?" WildCard voiced the question that was in Sam's eyes, too. "I thought messing around with married women was a relatively new hobby for you."

Nils could feel Wolchonok watching him, and felt a flash of shame. And then anger—at himself. It was stupid. Why did he go into bars, his sixth sense tuned in and adept at finding married women looking for a little clandestine recreational activity, if he was going to feel crappy when someone like the senior chief found out? He wasn't guilty of any real wrongdoing. All he did was smile, and these women approached him. It wasn't as if he trolled Navy bases, targeting the sweet young things whose husbands had just left for a six month WESTPAC cruise.

And as for Meg . . .

"It wasn't anything like that," he told WildCard, giving him his best earnest face. "She was in DC later that same year, you know, when I was there, too, for the inquiry? We were friends. That's all it ever was."

They weren't buying it.

"You never told me that Meg was in DC that summer," Sam said. "I remember you were there a long time. The inquiry kept getting postponed or something."

"It was just a couple weeks. And we were friends," Nils repeated. "It was no big deal. There was nothing to tell."

"You hit on her, and she turned you down," WildCard interpreted. "Either that or you slept with her, fell completely in love, and she broke your heart by kicking you out when her husband came home."

"Look, I didn't hit on her, I didn't sleep with her," Nils said.

"It's the ones they *don't* talk about that you have to watch out for," Sam agreed with WildCard.

Nils shook his head. "Believe what you want, assholes. But we were just friends."

But even Mike Muldoon was skeptical as he stared at the video screen. "John Nilsson was *friends* with a woman as good-looking as this one?"

Nils gave up and went to where Jazz was monitoring information coming in via fax. He glanced through the pages they'd already received—background on the suspect.

On Meg.

WildCard had plugged himself back into his laptop computer. Which didn't mean he wasn't up for conversation. Sam had once seen WildCard take a phone call from a rear admiral while writing code *and* maintaining seven different instant message conversations on America Online.

WildCard called it multitasking. Sam called it crazy. It was one thing to spread your attention thin when talking to your girlfriend, but a rear admiral . . . ?

Of course, WildCard was one of those guys with no social skills, and not a whole hell of a lot of common sense. Like, when he went out drinking, he went out *drinking*. He didn't go to a bar to meet women, he went to get completely wild-assed and shit-faced.

Part of that might've had something to do with the fact that up until about four months ago, WildCard had been all but engaged to his high school girlfriend, Adele Zakashansky.

She'd broken up with him via email, and ever since then he'd been spending all of his free time almost grimly focused on developing a long-distance tracking device that utilized the cell phone satellite system. It was a project he and Adele—also a computer geek—had dreamed up, and he was determined to get rich off it without her.

Sam sat down next to him now. "What do you think really went on between Nils and Meg?"

WildCard didn't look up. "If he wasn't banging her, he wanted to. Still wants to. Badly. Personally, I think he had a taste of what she had to offer. Of course I could be wrong. Maybe he only spent a lot of time imagining it."

Sam dug into his pockets as he nodded. You could always count on Karmody to express himself dead honestly. He found a bag of peanut M&M's and tore it open, popping three into his mouth at once, holding it out to WildCard.

"Warm chocolate sucks," WildCard said. "You know, there's a reason people store 3 Musketeers Bars in the freezer. That way it doesn't suck because it's all melty and shit. Personally, I'd think a guy who's an officer in the Navy might recognize the fact that carrying chocolate in his pockets is like the direct opposite of storing it in a freezer."

"Yeah, but these are M&M's. You know, they melt in your mouth . . . ?"

"They melt in your pocket, too. It's disgusting. It's like sucking on a warm turd."

Sam tossed another small handful into his mouth to test that theory. "No, it's not."

"Oh, yes it is."

"So is that a no?"

"It's a *shit*, *no*! Get 'em outta my face. Sir."

Sam shrugged. "More for me." He chewed for a moment in silence. "How's the project going?"

WildCard finally looked up. "It's going well. You want to help me beta test?"

He'd been wrecked by Adele's rejection, running on anger and the thought of financial revenge for the past four months. Sam could see it in his eyes. And he knew that even if Wild-Card made five million dollars from this thing, he still wasn't going to have what he really wanted, poor bastard.

Sam nodded. "Yeah, I can help. What do you need me to do?"

WildCard dug into his own pocket and pulled out a small envelope. He shook its contents into his hand.

"Take these," he commanded as he dropped two tiny metal balls into Sam's open palm. They were about half the size of ball bearings, but they weren't smooth. Instead they were rough to the touch, almost sharp—like techo-burrs. "Attach 'em to someone's clothing. Don't tell me whose. I want to see, number one, if I can track 'em, and number two, how far they get before they're dislodged."

"Some people actually wash their clothes," Sam felt compelled to point out.

"Yeah, well, the world's full of danger, isn't it?"

"Where's Meg's husband?" Nils asked the team's executive officer, Lt. Jazz Jacquette, as he began sifting through the piles of faxed information. "Is he out of the country again? Any details on whether he's been notified?"

Jazz shook his head. "There's no husband."

"Yeah, there is, XO. His name is Daniel Moore and he—"

"He's dead."

Nils felt himself go very, very still. "Excuse me?"

"It says it right here." Jazz pulled a page free and handed it to him. "Daniel Moore was killed in a car accident in Paris over eighteen months ago. Margaret Moore's a widow."

Nils looked at the report, saw the words, but they still didn't make sense.

Meg's husband had been killed. Eighteen months ago. Eighteen *fucking* months ago. And she'd never contacted him. She'd never bothered to let him know.

Nils had to sit down, suddenly feeling every one of the past forty-four hours he'd been awake.

Didn't she think he would care?

Didn't she think he'd want to know?

Christ, he'd spent the past five minutes working to convince Sam and WildCard that he and Meg had just been friends. He'd been spinning hard, lying his ass off. Yes, they'd been friends, but they'd been way more than friends, too. What he shared with Meg Moore had transcended mere friendship.

Or so Nils had believed.

But Meg hadn't called him when Daniel died.

Maybe he and Meg weren't friends. And maybe what he'd said to Sam and WildCard had been wrong—for an entirely different reason. Maybe Meg was the one who didn't consider him her friend. Maybe he was just some officer in the

Navy she'd wasted some time with briefly back in the summer of 1998.

Maybe she didn't think of him at all—at least not until she found herself in the Kazbekistani men's room, holding three men at gunpoint.

Nils still couldn't believe it. Meg Moore holding three men at gunpoint.

He went to work, reading every word of every fax. They had three hours before the transport touched down in DC, four before they arrived at the K-stani embassy.

He willed the plane to move faster, dying to get there and find out why the hell Meg was doing this. Dying to find out why, after all this time, she'd asked for him by name.

Still dying to see her again.

Four

$\backsim \hspace{-0.3em} \frown$

It HAD BEEN Meg's first encounter with U.S. Navy SEAL Team Sixteen's Troubleshooters.

She and Daniel were both officers in the U.S. Foreign Service, working and living inside the protective walls of the American embassy in Kazabek, Kazbekistan.

It had been the day after Christmas 1997. The day after Meg had found out about Daniel's second affair.

At least she thought it was his second, although, knowing Daniel, he could well have had many others between number one and number two. To rephrase, it was the second affair that she had found out about.

She'd been numb with anger and hurt, and when a team of three Navy SEALs burst through the hallowed gates of the American embassy in possession of the man the K-stani government claimed was their public enemy number one, she'd welcomed the intrusion.

She'd been the only staff member who had.

There'd been such an uproar, she'd gone into the lobby to see if she could help and had found the three SEALs—one of them injured—and their "guest," a man known only as Abdelaziz. They were tending to their wounded man right there, on the cold marble floor.

All four men were dressed in the ragged garb that most lower-class K-stani civilians wore. It was part Western—jeans and faded T-shirts that read "Just Do It" or "Hard Rock Cafe"—and part traditional—greatcoats and woolen hats that kept out the winter's chill.

Their faces were smudged with dirt and blood, and the man who'd been injured was shivering from the cold.

"What on earth are you doing still in the hall?" Meg

asked. It wasn't hard to tell which one of them was in charge—it was the tall one with the light brown eyes. Had to be. She read "leader" in his face, in the set of his shoulders, in his every move. She looked around at the small crowd that had gathered. "These men need medical assistance and you're standing here . . . ?"

She spotted Laney by the stairway, her mouth hanging open, file clutched to her ample chest. "Get a doctor," Meg ordered her assistant, then turned back to the brown-eyed man.

"It would be appreciated if we could be moved—perhaps upstairs, to an inner room with no windows like these?" He spoke with a lilting Kazbekistani accent as he gestured toward the tall windows that faced the street. "I realize it's understood that this embassy is a sanctuary, but I'm a target right now. It wouldn't take much more than a high-powered rifle and a little lack of either respect or understanding to take me out."

The brown-eyed man wasn't in charge. He was Abdelaziz—the man behind this uproar.

"Where's the ambassador?" she asked the wide-eyed junior staffers. "Where's the administrative officer?"

"Out at the front entrance," Chris Chenko volunteered, "telling the Kazbekistani Army officers just how big a mistake it would be for them to roll through the gates with their tanks and storm the embassy."

Oh, dear God. "How about the PAO or IO?" she asked, hoping for somebody, *any*body, even though she already knew the answer.

"Everyone's out front, Mrs. Moore," she was told.

Abdelaziz was watching her, and she gave him what she hoped was a reassuring smile. "Okay, let's get you upstairs. We can use my office temporarily." She looked back at the wounded man. "Do you need help carrying him?"

One of the SEALs—a young man with a nasty scrape on his cheek that had bled down into the collar of his shirt—shook his head. "No, ma'am, we've got him." He had a drawl reminiscent of James Garner's Maverick, and eyes the color of a Texas sky.

Meg swiftly led the way up the stairs, Abdelaziz on her heels.

"Thank you," he said, and meant it.

She glanced back at him. "I can't believe they just left you in the lobby."

"There's a somewhat . . . tense situation out there. And the government's not the only one who's after me."

"The way I've heard it is the government thinks you're a terrorist, and the terrorists think you're working for the government." Meg opened the door to her office and stepped back to let him in. "Which is it, Mr. Abdelaziz?"

"The truth is never as clear as we'd like it to be," he said cryptically, flashing her a smile.

He had beautiful teeth, an incredible smile. In combination with his too-warm eyes, the effect was impressive. Abdelaziz was an outrageously handsome man.

An outrageously handsome *young* man. Probably about the same age as her little sister, Bonnie—about twenty-three or four.

Much younger than Meg.

Although, ever since discovering Daniel's infidelity, purely by accident, from a fax she wasn't supposed to see—it wasn't as if Daniel had wrapped up the truth and left it as a gift for her under their straggly little Christmas tree—Meg had felt about a million years old.

Her great-uncle Andrew who was pushing ninety-seven looked younger than she felt today.

The doctor arrived, and Meg locked her file cabinets and stepped back, out of her office, to give the men their privacy.

To her surprise, Abdelaziz followed, closing the door behind him.

"The SEALs trust you to wander about on your own?" she asked.

"I'm not wandering—I just stepped outside to thank you again."

"Please stay with them," Meg said, "until we know for sure how this situation is going to be handled. And please don't take this personally, but I'm going to put a guard outside the door. Some people seem convinced you're a terrorist. There are children in this compound, and—"

"You don't have to explain or apologize."

"I'll call the kitchen for food and get you something hot to eat," she told him briskly. "I'll send for some towels and clean clothes, too—you could all use a shower. There's a bathroom in the basement, next to the workout room. When you're ready, I'll have a guard escort you downstairs."

He moved back, away from her. "I'm sorry. We must smell terrible. The past few days have been filled with . . . challenges—some more malodorous than others."

"I can't imagine where you've been or what you must've been doing." She paused. "Or who you really are."

He was even more attractive when he laughed. She wished her sister Bonnie were here to meet this man, and then, in flash, she realized she wished nothing of the sort. She wished *she* were Bonnie. Fresh out of college and just starting out. Free to allow herself to be charmed, even for just a moment, even by a dangerous man.

"It's best if you don't try to imagine anything." He gestured to the closed office door. "I should go back and . . ."

"Good idea," she said. "I'll get that food." But first the guards. "Let me know if you need anything else."

"You've already been more than kind, Mrs. Moore." If he'd been clean, he would've bowed and kissed her hand— Meg had no doubt of that. As it was, he just gazed at her with those disconcertingly luminous light brown eyes. "The safe haven of your office is sincerely appreciated. As is your kind offer of food and a shower. I am most grateful."

Such Kazbekistani dignity and formality coming from this ragged and bloody young man made Meg smile. "It's my pleasure."

"The pleasure is mine, *fy siwgwr aur.*" He'd slipped into another language but it wasn't Russian or even one of the lesser known K-stani dialects, either.

Fy siwgwr aur was . . . Welsh? Yes, it was a term of endearment that translated clumsily into "my golden sugar." For a moment, Meg was convinced she was losing it—that the stress of the past few days was getting to her. But he continued on, still speaking in Welsh, of all odd things. "Yours is the most beautiful smile I've seen in all my life. It makes me forget I haven't slept in four days."

Meg couldn't believe it. She couldn't believe this ragged Kazbekistani was speaking Welsh, couldn't believe he actually meant those honeyed words. *Beautiful smile. My golden sugar.* Good grief.

Unless maybe he was the kind of man who had a good nose for sniffing out lonely, pathetic women. Maybe her current unhappiness was etched on her face. Or perhaps he was one of two or three million Kazbekistanis who knew about Daniel's affair with Leilee. Why not? It wouldn't surprise Meg one bit to find out she'd been the last person in all of K-stan to know what a total, lying bastard she'd married.

"You don't see it at all when you look into a mirror, do you?" he asked her softly, still in near perfect, lyrical Welsh. "You don't have any idea what you look like, of the power of your smile. Would you smile for me, I wonder, if I . . ."

The words were ones she didn't know, but their meaning was more than clear. Shockingly clear.

This was ridiculous. What could he possible be thinking? He was barely out of diapers and she was an ancient and jaded thirty-one. And that was completely ignoring the fact that she was married. Although she suspected Abdelaziz wouldn't want anything longer than a single night of passion.

And maybe, like Daniel, he just didn't find marriage to be that big a deterrent to casual sex.

"I want to see you smile when I—"

"Oh, please," Meg interrupted him, unable to listen to another ridiculous word. "Just go back in with the SEALs, *sugar.*"

He stared at her.

"I'll cut you some slack for the lack of sleep. And you're young, so maybe four days without sex has done something weird to your brain as well, but believe me, I *do* know what I look like, thank you very much."

She looked like *exactly* what she was—the still somewhat pretty mother of a seven-year-old. And maybe that was part of her problem with Daniel. Maybe when *he* looked at her beside him in *his* mirror, *he* didn't like what he saw anymore.

Or maybe he was just a lying, cheating son of a bitch for whom fidelity wasn't part of his working vocabulary.

"You speak Welsh?" Abdelaziz choked out, startled back into English. Apparently she'd shocked the hell out of him.

"Yes," she answered in that language. "That seems like a little detail you might want to check in advance next time you start waxing poetic, Romeo."

"No one speaks Welsh. At least no one in *Kazbekistan* does."

"I do. And so do you, apparently." She had to laugh at the improbability of that. "How on earth did *you*—"

"My mother was Welsh." He had the good grace to be embarrassed, his too-handsome face actually flushing beneath all that mud and grime as he realized all that he'd said to her. "I'm really sorry, ma'am. It wasn't my intention to offend you. I never would have said any of that if I knew you could understand."

"Oh, so it's okay to say such things to a woman if she *can't* understand?"

He was so young. And so terribly embarrassed. Still, he had guts. He didn't run away, escaping back into the sanctuary of her office. He stood firmly in front of her, forcing himself to look her directly in the eye. "I apologize. And I beg you not to let my despicable behavior reflect upon your treatment of my men—the other men."

"Why don't you go inside," she said gently, "and let the doctor check you out? I'll get some food and some clean clothes—and I'll also find some rooms with beds so you and your friends can get some sleep. And tomorrow we can all start over."

He bowed, and wisely, he went into her office without uttering another word.

In the end, it was her files that were moved out of her office rather than the refugee and three SEALs.

When it was clear they were determined to stay put, Meg made arrangements for cots to be moved in. And when she stopped by in the morning to transfer some files from her computer's hard drive onto a disk, Abdelaziz was fast asleep, spread-eagle on the floor.

He lay there as if completely boneless, in complete abandon.

It was the way a child might sleep.

Or a man who hadn't slept for four days straight.

Still, he stirred before she finished with the computer, lifting his head and pushing himself wearily up onto his hands and knees, off the floor. "Report," he said.

Sam, the SEAL with the Texas drawl, was awake, sitting up with his weapon held loosely in his arms. "The team commander is still asleep. I gave Mrs. Moore permission to get some information she needed from her computer."

Abdelaziz lifted his head and looked directly at her. It was obvious that he'd been unaware that she was in the room until Sam had given him warning. He leapt to his feet—she'd never seen a man move that fast before—raking his fingers back through his sleep-mussed hair and straightening his clothes.

"As far as I know," Sam continued, "there's been no change in the political wind. Unless Mrs. Moore has some news she wants to share. Of course, she may not be feeling too kindly toward us, since she's going on day two without her office."

"The only rooms available were on the top floor, which is a far more vulnerable position than here on the second floor." Abdelaziz's smile was rueful. "Here I go, about to apologize to you. Again. I'm sorry for any inconvenience we've caused you, but I needed to sleep and I wouldn't have slept up there."

"As long as you don't mind me coming in to use the computer, it's not that big an inconvenience," she lied.

His smile said he knew better. And he was still embarrassed about yesterday, as well. As he should be. "Have you heard anything from the front line?" he asked.

Meg hesitated, not sure what to tell him. The K-stani government had threatened to kick all the Americans—ambassador, staff, and civilians—out of their country if Abdelaziz wasn't surrendered to them within the next twenty-four hours. The American oil companies couldn't afford to be kicked out, so they'd added their voices to the ongoing shouting match.

The general feeling of the embassy staff—including her husband Daniel—was to placate the Kazbekistani government and secure their shaky position in this oil-rich paradise by giving up Abdelaziz.

Which would be virtually the same as putting a gun to the man's head and pulling the trigger. If they gave him up, he would be executed.

But probably tortured horribly first.

Abdelaziz read her silence correctly. "The news is that good, is it?"

"The ambassador doesn't have much to go on," she told him, "since you've refused to answer his questions. How can he vouch for your innocence when the government accuses you of all these terrible crimes?"

"What happened to innocent until proven guilty?" he murmured.

"That might be true in America, but we're not in America."

As she watched, he crossed the room and looked down at the wounded man, the leader of the SEALs, Ensign John Nilsson.

"Is he all right?" she asked quietly. There was a sheen of sweat on Nilsson's forehead and his eyes were closed. He was sleeping, but only fitfully.

"He should be in a hospital," Sam said tightly.

Abdelaziz nodded in agreement. "We're going to do whatever we have to, to medevac him out of here."

"Anything short of turning yourself over to the Kazbekistani government," she corrected him.

"Yes, that probably wouldn't be a very good idea."

Sam snorted. "Probably?"

Abdelaziz turned and gave Sam a long, measured look.

Meg remembered that look later that day, when she received word that the ambassador had arranged for a chopper to fly the Navy SEALs to an aircraft carrier in the Mediterranean. She was in the middle of translating some desperately needed document, vital for the ongoing negotiations, when she was told of their departure.

"Navy *SEALs*?" she asked Laney. "Plural? Are you sure? Aren't they just flying out the one SEAL—the injured man?"

"No." Laney was smug about having received the information first. "All three of them left. I saw them as they headed to the heliport an hour ago. They're already gone."

The three SEALs had left the American embassy. Had they really just walked away—and left Abdelaziz behind to face his fate alone?

An hour ago, Abdelaziz had been in the middle of a meeting with the U.S. ambassador and several key members of his staff. Meg knew that the meeting had been dragging on for hours, as the ambassador tried to convince Abdelaziz that they would do everything in their power to see that he received fair treatment and a fair trial upon his surrender to the Kazbekistani government.

Meg had heard that at one point, Abdelaziz had requested several K-stani officials be brought into the dialogue—which soon turned into a shouting match that caused the meeting to end and Abdelaziz to be escorted back to her office.

Where his Navy SEAL companions were no longer waiting for him, having left K-stan without him.

Or had they . . . ?

All of a sudden it all made sense. All of a sudden, Meg *knew*.

She stood up, nearly knocking her chair over backward. "Laney, finish this for me."

"But—"

She was out of the room before her assistant could complain. She ran down the hall, down the stairs, toward her office.

Two guards were still posted in the hall. They didn't try to stop her, didn't even blink as she breezed past them and opened the door.

And there he was.

"Abdelaziz, my *ass*," Meg said. "You're really—"

He moved so quickly, she didn't have time to let out more than a very undignified squeak as he grabbed her arm, pulled her inside the room, shut the door behind her, deftly covering her mouth with his hand.

Her computer's CD player was on, she realized, and he pulled her toward it, cranking the speaker volume so that Shania Twain thundered throughout the room. If the office were bugged—and it probably was—whoever was listening wasn't going to hear more than that music.

Meg could hardly breathe, he was holding her so tightly, one arm wrapped around her, pinning both of her hands. When he spoke, his voice was practically inaudible, his lips brushing her ear. "Don't you dare do or say anything that will put my men in danger."

His accent was completely gone.

She'd guessed correctly. The SEALs *hadn't* left Abdelaziz behind. They'd walked him out of the embassy right under the Kazbekistanis' noses, while *this* man had been distracting both the American diplomats and the K-stani government. They'd carried Abdelaziz onto the waiting chopper and flown him out of the country, pretending he was Ensign John Nilsson, injured in the line of duty.

While in truth, she was standing pressed uncomfortably close to the real Ensign John Nilsson, the very solid and healthy Ensign John Nilsson, his hand clamped hard over her mouth.

"The helo won't be safely on board the carrier for another twenty minutes," he breathed into her ear. "If you give me away, the K-stani Air Guard could try to force it down."

And was his plan to stand here, with his hand over her mouth, for that entire twenty minutes?

Meg made a writing motion with the one of her hands that could still move an inch or two, and somehow he understood. He shifted her over to her desk and gave her a piece of paper and another few inches of mobility to her right hand so she could pick up a pen.

Meg wrote quickly, in clear block letters, "Promise me I'm not helping a terrorist escape to the United States."

She felt more than heard Nilsson laugh over Shania's rich voice. "I promise," he breathed into her ear. "He's not a terrorist, Meg. He's CIA. But if you tell anyone I told you that, I'll deny it."

Meg picked up her pen again. "What are they going to do to *you*?" she wrote.

He laughed again. "What can they do? I'm not the man they're after."

"We better make sure they believe that. Let me go," she wrote.

"If I do, will you scream?"

"About what?" she wrote.

Again, she felt the warm vibration of his laughter. "Well, good," he said into her ear. "Just watch what you say—the room is bugged—we found the mikes."

Meg stepped away from him, turned down the music, turned to face him. "Do you have identification saying that you're . . . who you are," she said to him. In Welsh. Because the two people in Kazbekistan who spoke that language were both here in this room. Nothing they said in Welsh would be understood by anyone listening in. And it would take the K-stani government weeks—if not months—to find a translator.

He grinned at her. "You're brilliant," he said, also in Welsh.

She should have known he was American yesterday, from the first moment he'd smiled. His was definitely an all-American smile.

"No ID," he added. "Not on a covert op like this. We go in completely sanitized."

"How was it possible you pulled this off?" she asked. He'd actually *asked* to meet with the K-stani officials this afternoon. How gutsy was that? "Weren't you afraid someone would know you weren't Abdelaziz?"

"We're about the same height and build," he told her, "and about the same age. Same general description—brown hair and eyes. I took a gamble there were no detailed photos of old Abdel lying around, and won big time."

Meg shook her head. "Still . . ."

"I used an old con," he explained. "We came running in here with the K-stani Army pointing at us and shouting about Abdelaziz, right? The U.S. ambassador comes to see us and everyone points to me when he asks who's Abdelaziz. And why would we lie, right? So when the K-stani officials were invited to join our little discussion this afternoon, I'm officially introduced as Abdelaziz by the U.S. ambassador. Now both sides are convinced I'm their man.

"Believe me, the members of the K-stani government were

the ones who thought they were getting away with some kind of con. By shipping out all three of the SEALs who'd been sent to protect me while I was in that meeting . . . ?" He laughed. "They're probably still congratulating themselves on their deviousness."

He was amazing. But if the K-stani government believed him to be Abdelaziz . . . Forget about the fact that they were wrong. He was in danger.

For starters, they had to change his appearance. Right now, with the exception of his perfect smile, he looked like someone named Abdelaziz. For his own safety, he had to transform back into Ens. John Nilsson as quickly as possible.

"We'll give you a haircut," she decided. "A buzz cut. Something really GI Joe. And I'll see if I can find a uniform."

His smile faded. "I don't want you to get into trouble for helping me."

"I won't." She moved toward the door. "Do you trust me enough to let me start looking for something a little more military for you to wear?"

He held out his hands, palms up, in a gesture that might have been interpreted as surrender. But combined with his words and that warmth in his eyes, it became part of the nicest compliment she'd ever received. "I trust you completely, Meg."

Meg managed to scare up a Marine uniform. That and the haircut she gave him made him look far more like an American.

The next few days were crazy. Kazbekistan nearly declared war when they found out that Abdelaziz had been spirited out of the country. And the foreign service staff at the embassy was furious, too. It took a solid week of frantic explanations and apologies to convince the K-stani government that they had been duped as well. And even then the ambassador and his staff were left looking and feeling extremely foolish.

Meanwhile John Nilsson was kept locked in Meg's office, under guard.

It was entirely possible that if Meg hadn't kept bringing

him food, he wouldn't have been fed. She brought him
books and newspapers and often stayed to keep him company. She brought Amy to visit with him, too, mostly to remind him—and herself—that she was married and much
older than he was. Anything other than friendship would be
completely inappropriate.

It was one evening that he was sitting beside her daughter,
coloring in her Anastasia coloring book while Meg pulled
more files off her computer, that he looked over Amy's head
and spoke to Meg in French.

He was a languages specialist, and out of all the languages
they'd found they both spoke with proficiency, French
was the one for which they shared a similar high level of
understanding.

"I had a meeting today with the ambassador."

Meg looked up at him, waiting for him to continue.

He set down the blue crayon he'd used to color in Anastasia's ballgown. "Your husband was there."

Meg glanced at Amy. They'd lived in Paris for several
years. "Was he?" she replied—in German.

"Ja." He smiled his understanding. "I don't mean to pry,"
he said in German, too, "and at first I thought I shouldn't say
anything, that this is probably none of my business, but I
have to tell you that I overheard something another man asked
him, something about, well, his estrangement from his wife.
His estrangement from you."

"You're right," she said, focusing her attention back on
the computer screen. "That's not your business."

"Are you sure, Meg?" he said quietly. "Because if my being here has caused a problem—if your helping me has
made him that angry with you . . . I mean, it's obvious he's
still really pissed at me. He actually suggested turning me
over to the Kazbekistanis in place of Abdelaziz."

Meg looked up at him then. "They can't seriously be
considering—"

He smiled fleetingly at her concern. "No. It's just . . ." He
sighed and started over. "Your husband's taking this personally, and as much I enjoy your visits, if it's making things
bad for you at home . . ." He shook his head. "I'm never go-

ing to be able to thank you for everything you've done. The thought that I'm causing you problems is making me crazy."

"On Christmas, I found out that Daniel had an affair." There it was. The truth. She hadn't told anyone, hadn't even said the words aloud before now. Meg's eyes filled with tears that she desperately tried to blink back. She stood up. "It's almost Amy's bedtime."

John stood up, too. "Are you and Daniel . . . separating?"

"I don't know," she admitted, still speaking in German so that Amy couldn't understand. "I kicked him out on Christmas. I give him another day or two before he comes to negotiate his return.

"And will I take him back?" she added, anticipating his next question. "I don't know." Yes, she did, and yes, she probably would. For Amy's sake. "The affair happened a while ago—he says he hasn't even spoken to this woman in over a year and a half. But . . . it's not the first time he's cheated on me."

Why was she telling him this?

They were friends, she realized. She trusted John Nilsson as much as he trusted her.

"He doesn't deserve you," he said quietly.

Meg managed a smile as she gently tugged on one of her daughter's ponytails. "Come on, Ames," she said in English. "Time to go."

Later that night, long after Amy was in bed, there was a knock on the door to her apartment.

Meg opened the door expecting Daniel.

But it was John.

He was flanked by guards and wearing the greatcoat and clothing he'd had on the day they'd first met.

"I'm going home," he told her.

Meg had suspected the SEAL was going to be allowed to leave soon, but . . . "Tonight?"

He nodded, looking past her to the small living room, taking in the fact that she was alone. "May I come in for a minute?"

She stepped back and he came inside, closing the door behind him, leaving the guards outside.

Before she could speak, before she could even think, he

pulled her into his arms and held her close. "Christ, Meg, I'm going to miss you."

She resisted for all of a half a second, and then held him just as tightly. She was going to miss him, too. God, when was the last time she'd had a friendship like this one? When had she *ever* had a friendship like this, with someone she could confide in completely, without fear of her darkest secrets becoming public knowledge?

And yes, the man was pleasant to be around for other reasons, too. He was attractive. It was hard not to think about how incredibly gorgeous John was, particularly when she was wrapped in his arms. He had a great body and a smile to die for. He was smart and funny and extremely sweet in a twenty-five-year-old kind of way.

He was the little brother she'd always wanted.

Wasn't he?

It didn't help that his embrace wasn't at all brotherly. It didn't help that he ran his hands through her hair and down her back, fitting her exquisitely, perfectly, intimately against him.

And it didn't help at all when he pulled back to look at her, and she saw something in his eyes that she hadn't seen in a good long time when Daniel looked at her.

He pressed a piece of paper into her hand. "That's my phone number," he told her. God, his eyes were hypnotizing. "Both home and work." He smiled fleetingly. "Of course, I'm away a lot. But if you're ever back in the States, call me, and I'll get leave."

Meg nodded, unable to speak. Who was he kidding? She wasn't going to call him. She was married. Her husband hated his guts. They both knew damn well that unless it was by accident, they were never going to meet again. She felt her eyes fill with tears, but still she couldn't look away.

"Ah, shit," John Nilsson swore. "I promised myself I wasn't going to do this. . . ."

He kissed her.

It wasn't a brotherly kiss.

It wasn't even close.

He tasted twenty-five years old. His mouth was hot and sweet and impossibly delicious. His lips were both soft and unyielding, and he swept his tongue into her mouth as if it belonged there. And oh, God, for the next few heartbeats, it did.

Maybe it was the knowledge that she wouldn't call him, wouldn't see him again, that made Meg kiss him back with such complete abandon. Maybe it was the way he'd looked at her just moments before, with such genuine desire in his eyes.

Maybe it was a lesson in the powers of temptation, a sign from above that she should ease off a little on the holier-than-thou self-righteousness when confronting Daniel about his past transgressions.

But the truth was, the entire world faded into gray when this man kissed her. Nothing else existed. There was only his mouth on her mouth, his tongue against hers, his hands in her hair, on her back, pressing her against him as if the way she was clinging wasn't close enough to satisfy him.

The doorbell rang, startlingly loud in the stillness, and they both pulled back, both breathing hard.

Oh, God, what was she doing? What had she just done?

He must've seen the shock in her eyes. "I'm sorry." His voice was hoarse.

"No, I'm sorry." This was her fault. It had to be. She was older and more experienced. She was *married.*

"I have to go." He reached for the door, but then stopped, turning back to her. "Call me, Meg. Jettison that deadweight of a husband and come back to the States. Call me when you get there."

As she gazed into his eyes, she was as tempted as she'd ever been in all of her life.

But then he was gone, the door closing tightly behind him, and sanity returned. Meg knew the difference between reality and fantasy. And this man was pure fantasy.

That kiss was no more real than if it had happened in a dream.

Call me.

She knew that she never would.

Call me.

Meg sat in the men's room of the Kazbekistani embassy,

aware that despite her attempts to keep her distance, she'd finally done just that.

She'd finally called John Nilsson.

Five

"**W**HAT THE FUCK are *you* doing here?"

Sam knew the moment the words left his mouth that this was not the kind of greeting that would win him any points.

In fact, Alyssa Locke's cold gaze got pretty damn arctic. "Ensign Starrett. Just my luck."

His bad luck, too. He'd never have expected to run into Alyssa Locke in the Kazbekistani embassy lobby during a hostage crisis, never in a million years.

Yet here she was. She was out of uniform, either on leave or . . . "I heard rumors you quit."

Her chin went up. Jesus, she had the world's most perfect chin. "I resigned my commission as an officer in the Navy because I received a better offer from the Bureau."

"You're FBI?"

He couldn't keep the horror from his voice, and she smiled tightly. "Special counterterrorist unit."

Which meant that there was a good chance they'd be working together with some frequency, since the FBI often called in the SEALs for military assistance.

They'd be working together in the field, out where bullets could fly and shit could hit the fan and splatter. Alyssa had always wanted to get her hands dirty. She'd wanted to operate out in the real world. Frankly, she'd wanted to be a SEAL, and she'd finagled herself into a place where— amazingly, if she kept with it—she'd someday be authorized to order SEALs around, out in the field.

Sam held out his hand, forced a smile. "Well, shit. Congratulations."

Out of all the things he might have said and done, she

hadn't expected that. Not that he really meant it, but the effort surely counted for something.

She chose to pretend he was sincere, hesitating only slightly before taking his hand. Her fingers were cool and slender—as perfect as the rest of her, and a perfect fit in his hand as well. "Thanks."

This was the first time he'd ever touched her. The first time she'd let him. She pulled her hand free way too soon, just a little too fast, as if she'd noticed that perfect fit, too, and gotten just as freaked out by it.

And then they were standing in the middle of the main entrance to the K-stani embassy, just staring at each other. At least Sam was staring at Alyssa. She jerked her gaze away and was looking anywhere but at him.

The room was filled with chaotic activity, but at least the press—thank God—had been kept outside on the sidewalk.

"Is Tom here?" she asked. "And Jazz?"

Sam pointed across the room to where his CO and XO had found both the agent in charge and several top Kazbekistani officials. They were standing there, with Nils, deep in conversation. Nils was nodding. He kept glancing at the closed-off staircase that led to the second floor, as if he wished he could skip the briefing and take the stairs two at a time up to the men's room where Meg Moore was holding the hostages.

"I never got a chance to thank you back in Massachusetts," Sam told Alyssa, suddenly uncertain as to where to put his hand now that he wasn't holding hers. He finally settled on folding his arms across his chest, keeping his armpits closed.

He stank to high heaven. They all did—coming straight in the way they had from last night's training op. He could see Nils across the room, most of his greasepaint sweated off, leaving his face looking slightly muddy and battleworn. Sam knew he looked the same.

"You know," he added, "for saving the lieutenant's life when he was up on that roof."

Alyssa Locke had been in a sniper position in a nearby church tower while Lt. Tom Paoletti had been up against two tangos—one of whom had a gun aimed at the lieutenant's teenage niece—on the roof of the nearby Baldwin's Bridge Hotel. From her perch, Alyssa had had an opportunity to take out the gunman with a single shot, and she'd done it unflinchingly, her aim straight and true. She'd saved the niece, an event that had ultimately saved Tom.

She'd saved the niece, but she'd also taken her first human life.

She nodded curtly now, as if she didn't want to spend a lot of time thinking about it.

Sam changed the subject. "So how come you didn't come visit me in the hospital?"

He'd been shot in that same run-in with a believed-to-be-dead terrorist. A bullet had lodged in his shoulder, another had grazed his head. He'd spent most of the ensuing action unconscious, wouldn't it figure? Way to impress his commanding officer. But after it was over, he hadn't remained in the hospital's ICU for very long.

He'd enjoyed hero status at the hospital, with a steady stream of visitors coming to see him. But none of them had been Alyssa Locke.

She laughed at his question now. "You hate me," she told him flatly.

"Whoa," he said. "Wait a minute—"

"We can't talk for more than two minutes without arguing, Roger." Locke had the annoying habit of calling him by his given name. His own mother didn't call him *Roger* anymore, for Christ's sake. "I didn't think pissing you off would help your recovery."

"I don't hate you," he insisted. "You're the one who . . . well, you hate *me*."

"Ah," she said, with a tight little smile that was really no kind of smile at all. "That's right. Rednecks give me a rash. *That's* what it was."

God *damn* it— Sam took a deep breath. Forced himself to stay cool. "Regardless of our personal differences in the past," he managed to say, albeit a little bit tightly, "I just wanted you to know I was damn glad you were in that church tower that day."

Her smug little smile faltered.

Sam nodded curtly. "I'm sure I'll see you around. . . ."

Ma'am.

That's all it would have taken. Just one little word, just a punctuation of respect, and the beginnings of a truce may well have been declared.

But when he opened his mouth, something else entirely came drawling out. ". . . sweet thing."

And instead of a truce, Sam saw World War Three declared in this woman's eyes.

He beat a quick retreat, the devil in him laughing, which, naturally, only made it all the more worse.

Meg's cell phone rang, interrupting her singing.

She was singing to pass the time, singing to keep herself awake. She'd gone through all of the American, Russian, and French folk songs she knew, and had just started in on the English, Irish, and Welsh. "Johnny Has Gone for a Soldier." "Llwyn Onn." "Buttermilk Hill" or "Shule Aroon." "Here I sit on Buttermilk Hill. Who could blame me cry my fill . . . ?" Most of the songs were about pain and despair—an appropriate soundtrack for this terrible, awful day.

Osman Razeen still sat watching her, seemingly unblinkingly, as she answered the phone.

It hadn't yet been six hours—it had barely been five. Maybe Max Bhagat was calling to tell her that there was going to be a further delay. Oh, God, she didn't think she could handle that. She wanted John here now.

She didn't say anything into the phone, she just waited.

"Meg?"

It wasn't Max's voice. It had been years, but it sounded like . . .

"It's John Nilsson," he continued.

Relief ripped into her so intensely she nearly dropped the phone. Breathe. Keep breathing. Keep holding the gun on Osman Razeen. He was watching her, waiting for her to make a mistake.

"What are you doing in there?" John asked.

Waiting for you.

"Well," she said, when she could finally speak without sounding like Mary Richards imploring Mr. Grant to help her, "I've gotten myself into something of a situation here."

He laughed. God, had it really been *years* since she'd heard his warm, rich laughter? It seemed like just yesterday.

"Yeah, I couldn't help but notice," he told her. "How about you put the gun down, let those guys go, and I come in and we talk?"

"That's not how it would happen, and you know it." If she put down the gun, a SWAT team or maybe John's SEAL team would burst through the door. She'd be on her stomach, face pressed against the tile floor, with her hands roughly cuffed behind her back in a matter of seconds.

He was silent for a moment. Then she heard him sigh. "What can I do to help you, Meg? Can I come in? I'm right outside the door."

"No weapons," she told him. "Nothing under your jacket or shirt, Ensign."

"It's Lieutenant now. Junior grade."

Lieutenant. Of course. He'd been promoted. It had been years since he'd been an ensign. "Congratulations."

"Yeah, we've got some catching up to do." He paused. "I just heard about Daniel. I—" Another pause as if he'd suddenly changed his mind about what he'd been going to say. "I'm sorry for your loss. Look, I'll come in in my T-shirt, hands high. No weapons, nothing hidden, no threat."

She could do this over the phone. She *should* do this over the phone. But she wanted to see him. She wanted to look into John Nilsson's eyes and see reassurance that he was going to help her, that he *could* help her. "Just . . . promise you won't try to shoot me or take my gun."

"You got it."

"Say it."

"I promise."

"Make sure you open the door only wide enough to slip in," she ordered him. "No one comes with you. No sudden moves. I'm serious, John. I'll shoot these people if I have to."

"Give me a sec," he said, "to get my jacket off."

The connection was cut. Meg put down the phone, held her gun with both hands, humming a bit more of that folk song to steady her nerves.

Yes, indeed, she and John Nilsson had some catching up

to do. It was entirely likely that he was married by now, and if not married, then certainly attached.

But whether or not he was married had nothing to do with saving Amy. She and John Nilsson had once been friends. She was counting on him to remember that.

He knocked on the door. "Meg? It's me. I'm coming in."

The door opened. Just a little. And he slipped inside the room.

Meg wasn't sure what she'd been expecting. Possibly for him to be wearing his dress whites. Or at least some other kind of naval uniform. Instead he was completely dressed down in dirty BDUs, dusty boots, and a T-shirt that was stained with sweat. Black greasepaint smudged his face and he had a heavy stubble of beard covering his chin. His eyes were rimmed with red and lined with fatigue. Just like the first time they'd met, it had been a while since he'd last slept.

He was bigger, broader, taller than she'd remembered, particularly with his arms up, fingers laced and resting on his head. With his arms in that position, his biceps were flexed and they strained against the sleeves of his T-shirt. His face had filled out some, too, making him look more like a man and less like a twenty-something kid.

But his smile was pure twelve-year-old despite the concern in his eyes. "Hi."

Tears welled. *Save me. Save Amy.* She wanted to throw herself into his arms and beg him to help her. But this room was bugged. Everyone and their Kazbekistani brother and FBI sister were listening in. And Amy's and Eve's lives depended on her doing this right.

"May I sit down?" he asked.

"No," she managed to say.

Surprise flickered across his face, but he quickly hid it. "Okay. Your rules. I'll stand." He moved slightly, leaning against the wall, so that she could easily see both him and her hostages.

"You won't be in here for long," she explained.

"Oh, yeah?" he said. "Because I was kind of hoping we'd take a little time to talk. You know, so you could tell me what this is all about and—"

"Remember that folk song?" she interrupted, "that we always used to sing? You, me, and Amy?"

They'd never sung anything together, not even once. Not in Kazbekistan. And Amy hadn't even been home—she'd been visiting Eve in England—those two weeks John had spent in Washington in the summer of 1998.

John blinked. Just once. But other than that, he'd managed to keep his face impassive.

"Which one?" he asked evenly. "We sang so many."

Thank you. He was as smart as he was handsome. And obviously willing to let her do this her way.

"It was called 'Achub Fi.' " *Save Me.* "Do you remember that one? The chorus goes, *Save me, Save me, Save me,*" she sang to him in Welsh to the tune of a Welsh folk song. *"Amy and my grandmother have been kidnapped by Extremists from the Pit."* Her words didn't quite line up with the notes, but she forced them to fit. *"The Extremists have a spy so tell this to no one in this building, or they'll be killed. Save me, Save me . . ."*

"Save me." He joined in, singing along with her. He had a terrible voice. "I remember you always loved that song. But we need to talk about what you're doing, what you want—"

"I want a million dollars," she told him in English, for the microphones. "In small, unmarked bills. I want a helicopter, up on the roof, large enough for me and all three of my . . . guests. I realize it may take some time to make arrangements for those things, so in the meantime I want six pairs of handcuffs and a dead-bolt lock I can easily attach to this side of the door. Go."

John hesitated. "Meg, who put you up to this? I know you wouldn't do something like this on your own."

Meg knew he had to ask despite what she'd just revealed to him in Welsh. His job as negotiator was to come in here and find out as much about this situation—and her motives for being here—as possible. He was playing out the scene for the cameras and the mikes.

"Get me those cuffs. Then maybe we'll talk."

He still didn't move. "How about if one of these men— only one—walks back out of here with me. As a show of good faith—"

"No." She knew he'd had to ask that, too, to make this look as real as possible for all the people listening in.

John nodded. And as he looked at her, he sent her a silent message with his eyes. *I can help you.*

She couldn't keep tears from blurring her eyes and she held her breath, knowing she would be unable to do anything but sob if she tried to speak.

"I'll be back soon," he promised.

"No way can we give her those handcuffs," said the FBI negotiator, a man named Max Bhagat who was calling the shots for this operation. "Obviously she wants to cuff each of the hostage's hands to a different pipe underneath the sink. Look at the way the room is set up. Six sinks, three hostages. And what was that song she was singing? Does anyone know what language that was?"

Lieutenant Paoletti looked at Nils.

Shit. "She's really into world music." He tried to sound casual. "She knows the most obscure folk songs."

Now what? Pretend he didn't know this song was in Welsh, and risk having Bhagat—who seemed to be an incredibly thorough son of a bitch—call in another languages specialist who just might be able to translate the Welsh words Meg had sung? Or tell a half-truth? He made up his mind.

"This one's in Welsh. It's one of those story songs," he improvised on the fly, "about a woman who found out her husband was cheating on her. It's got a lot of verses, and at the end she drowns her competition in a well. Really cheery little number."

Bhagat leaned forward. "Is it one of those suicide folk songs, where the narrator kills herself at the end?"

"No, no," Nils said hastily. Christ, don't let him start thinking that Meg was going to blow away all of her hostages and then put a bullet into her own brain. If Bhagat thought that, he'd kick down the door in thirty seconds. "It was just a song, sir. She always liked that melody. I'm not even sure if she understood the words. I mean, I translated them for her a few years ago, but . . ."

Nils felt a bead of sweat trickle down his back. Lieutenant

Paoletti was watching him steadily. Nils had never asked, but he'd always thought his CO could tell when he was lying.

And brother, was he lying now.

To the FBI and the Kazbekistani officials.

It wasn't by choice. Nils was more than willing to tell Bhagat the truth—but not with the K-stanis listening in.

"What exactly was your relationship with Margaret Moore?" Bhagat asked.

Shit again. Okay, start with the truth.

"I haven't seen her since July 1998. We met in Kazbekistan, at the American embassy there, in December of '97. We became friends. I was here in DC about six months later, heard she'd separated from her husband and moved back to town, so I, you know, looked her up. She's a nice looking woman and . . . Well, we got together a few times . . ." Yeah, like a few times a day for two solid weeks. " . . . but it was strictly platonic, sir.

"To be honest—" He looked Bhagat in the eye, knowing that he did honest and sincere particularly well. "—if she'd said the word, I would've made the relationship more, um, intimate, but she was still married and intending to reconcile with her husband." Her lying, cheating, sack of shit, completely unworthy of her husband.

"I don't know why she asked for me now." And that was another bald-faced lie. He knew *exactly* why she'd asked for him. Because he spoke Welsh. Because she was desperate. Because her daughter's life was at stake. "I mean, other than the fact that she feels she can trust me."

Bhagat was silent, gazing down at the notes he'd made on the legal pad in front of him.

"I think we should give her the cuffs she's asked for," Nils said for what seemed like the four thousandth time. "She's on edge, she's got that handgun aimed toward the ambassador and the other men at all times. Frankly, we should do everything we can to make her feel as comfortable as possible, and then just wait her out. She may have a small amount of food in her bag, but she doesn't have a lot. If we wait long enough, she might get so hungry, she'll let us bring food in. And then we can spike her chicken salad sandwich."

"She wants the cuffs and the dead bolt because she's afraid of falling asleep," Lieutenant Paoletti commented. "She's exhausted."

"No dead bolt for the door. No way," Bhagat said flatly. "That's a no-brainer."

"I think our next step should be to wait, sir," Nils recommended. "Let her wonder what's going on. Let me go shower and get changed before I go in to talk to her again. If I go back in there still looking like I was yanked out of a training op, like I've dropped everything to be here, *she's* running the show. But if it's clear that I've taken the time to shower and shave and maybe eat a nice meal, then the emotional ball's in our court."

Bhagat was nodding. But Nils had to drive the point home. "No SWAT teams storming down the door, right, sir? Because if you call out that order, you should also order two body bags in advance. Because she'll shoot. She'll only get off a single shot before the team can take her out, but she *will* take one of the hostages with her."

"As opposed to her reaching her limit and taking out all three before we can even get up there?" Bhagat pointed out.

Shit. "She's not going to do that, sir. I *know* her." Nils looked beseechingly at Lieutenant Paoletti.

"I recommend taking Lieutenant Nilsson's advice," Paoletti said in that easygoing, you-may-be-the-agent-in-charge-but-we-all-know-I'm-really-the-one-in-command attitude of his. He turned to Nils. "Grab a shower and some food and get back here."

Now Nils had to figure out a way to get the lieutenant to come out of the embassy with him.

"There's a Marriott right across the street," Paoletti added. "We're billeted there—I figured we'd want the proximity. Wolchonok's already gotten you a room."

Senior Chief Wolchonok. The senior chief was how Nils was going to get Paoletti out of the embassy. All he'd have to do was make a phone call. Wolchonok would say, "L.T., hate to bother you, but we need you at the Marriott, ASAP."

"What's this about, Senior?" the lieutenant would ask.

"Can't tell you over an unsecured line, sir," and Paoletti

would be on his way. Grumbling, no doubt. But if Wolchonok asked, he'd come.

Getting the FBI over there was going to be a little bit harder.

Nils stood up. "Excuse me, gentlemen."

At Paoletti's nod, he left the conference room and went out into the lobby, trying his damnedest not to run.

Save me. Christ, the look in Meg's eyes as she'd sung to him had nearly killed him. Nils was no stranger to desperation, but this was unlike any he'd ever seen. Maybe because that desperation was in Meg's eyes, on Meg's face.

K-stani Extremists had her kid. What were the chances that Amy was still alive? Minuscule. But until he knew otherwise, he had to play this as if the kid *were* still alive.

Tell no one inside this building. He wouldn't. But he had to figure out a way to get the FBI over to the Marriott. He supposed he could always call the Bureau, bring someone over who wasn't already attached to this situation and—

"Whoa," he said, stopping short. "Lieutenant Locke. What are you doing here?"

"Lieutenant Nilsson," Alyssa Locke greeted him coolly. "I'm part of the team that set up the surveillance mikes and cameras giving us a look and listen into that men's room upstairs. And it's not Lieutenant anymore."

"You're FBI," he realized. Thank you, Jesus. He threw his arms around her, pulling her close in a hug. "Play along," he breathed into her ear. "Pretend we're best friends." He released her. "Great to see you again. Hey, as long as we're all in wait mode, why don't you come on over across the street with me? I'm going to shower, then we can grab some lunch."

Locke looked at her watch. "I guess I could—"

"Great." He grabbed her arm and pulled her with him past the checkpoint—manned now by U.S. Marines—and out the side door.

They skirted the mob of reporters and cameras and crossed the street at close to a dead run.

"What's going on, Nilsson?" Locke asked.

"I need your help."

Save me. Wolchonok was in the hotel, in a conference room right off the lobby, thank God, waiting for him. He raised an eyebrow a fraction of an inch as he glanced from Locke to Nils.

Yeah, right, Senior. Yes, Locke was a babe, but not even Nils with his current scumbag rep was either stupid or horny enough to bring a woman back to his hotel room for a little midafternoon messing around right smack in the middle of a hostage situation. Assuming that Nils went for walking ice cubes like Locke in the first place.

Wolchonok greeted Alyssa with a nod. "Lieutenant Locke. How are you?"

"Confused. Nilsson, what—"

"Senior Chief, do you have a room for me?" Nils asked.

"Yes, sir. L.T. said you were on your way over." The senior chief held out a key card. "You're in room 1712. It's a suite—lucky you, they're short on rooms." Another glance at Locke. "You're doubled up with Sam Starrett."

"You poor thing," Locke murmured. "That almost makes me feel sorry enough to forgive you for dragging my ass over here. What the hell is going on, Lieutenant?"

Nils pulled them close, lowered his voice, and told them.

Maram wanted to kill the prisoners now.

Umar didn't want to deal with disposing of the bodies. He was tired after making the drive all the way from Washington. Even if they took them into the swamp and shot them— eliminating the need to clean the blood off the walls and floors afterward—they'd still need to dig a pit to bury them. And even then it would be just their luck, he told Maram, if animals dug up the bodies, leaving various bits and pieces to be stumbled upon by the authorities. Where would that leave *them*?

The old woman and the little girl didn't speak the language, but they clearly understood that it was their imminent fate that was being argued about.

The man known only as the Bear sat silently, watching them.

The little one was still groggy from the sleeping drug, and she nestled closer to the ancient lady. Man, she was old. She looked as if she'd lived at least a century already. But she still had her wits about her, and her dignity. She'd even managed to smile at him a few times. She was afraid, but she kept her fear in check.

It didn't seem right to treat her with such disrespect, to make her rest those old bones on the floor. If they were going to kill them, they should do it now, forget the inconvenience. But even though Maram had been his sister-in-law, back a long time ago, before his brother Yusef had been taken to prison and tortured to death, she didn't always listen to him.

"Nana, tell me again about Dunkirk," the little one whispered. Amy was her name. It was a good name for her—it fit her long, curly hair and her heart-shaped face. She was a pretty little thing.

"Even though I was an American," the old lady whispered back, "I was living in England in 1940, when Hitler's army attacked France."

Hitler. The Bear knew all about Hitler and his Nazis. His Yugoslavian grandfather, gone from this world for ten years now, had spoken of Hitler often, always spitting after saying his name. Hitler had been the devil on earth.

"Months earlier, England had sent her army, the British Expeditionary Force, to help defend France from a German invasion. But when Germany finally attacked, it was like nothing the French or English soldiers had ever seen before. It was called *Blitzkrieg*. Lightning war. The German panzers—their tanks—moved at impossible speeds, covering dozens of miles of battleground in a single day. At the time, this was quite remarkable. It was terrifying for those of us listening to the radio reports, hearing of town after town that had fallen in what seemed like the blink of an eye."

This was clearly a story the old woman had told little Amy countless times.

"The German air force," she continued, "was called the Luftwaffe, and those planes rained bombs and bullets down on the British and French soldiers, most of whom were horribly unprepared to deal with *any* kind of battle, let alone this blitz of destruction. The French army was believed to be the best fighting force in all of the world, but they quickly crumbled. And they and the BEF were pushed back, all the way to the north of France, to the beaches of a little French town called—"

"Dunkirk," the little girl finished for her. But then she lowered her voice, leaning closer to the old lady. "Mommy's probably really worried about us, isn't she?"

The old lady just held her tightly. She didn't try to lie to her. "Yes, I'm sure she is."

Amy glanced across the room at Maram and Umar, fear in her eyes, then whispered even more softly. "Is she going to come for us and save us?"

"I know she would if she could. But I don't know if she can." The old lady looked directly at him, obviously aware that he was listening to everything they were saying. "Do you want me to tell more of the story?"

Amy nodded, her head tucked close to her great-grandmother's skinny breast.

"So there they were," the old lady continued, a little bit louder now. He didn't have to strain quite so much to hear her. "Over a quarter of a million British soldiers. Stranded in Dunkirk, France. Separated from their homeland by the English Channel."

A quarter of a million . . . He translated the expression into his own language and . . . A quarter of a million was a *lot* of men.

"Now, the British navy was in something of a bind," she said, "because no one had anticipated France would fall to the Germans so quickly. There weren't enough ships to move all those men back to safety across that channel of water. *And* it didn't take long for the Luftwaffe to completely bomb all of the piers in Dunkirk's harbor. The water was shallow there, and the few large naval ships that *were* available couldn't get close enough to fetch the men. So the navy began appropriating all sorts of small boats. Ferries and fishing vessels. Navy officials came knocking on doors all up and down the coast of England, informing people that their boats were now a part of the British navy.

"Once the word got out, all across England anyone who owned a small boat—pleasure yachts, dinghies, rowboats, truly anything that could float—gathered in Ramsgate Harbor to help save our boys in the BEF from certain death. That harbor was right down the lane from where I lived. So I went, too. I was only sixteen, and I was a girl to boot, but I took my stepmother's yacht—she was called the *Daisy Chain* and she could fit twenty-five people comfortably, fifty squeezed in tight and low in the water. I took the *Daisy Chain* into Ramsgate with all the others.

"It was remarkable, Amy. I'd never seen so many boats— the *little ships*, they called us—in one place before. We were an amazing motley armada. But we were determined to bring our boys home.

"I'd really only meant to bring the *Daisy Chain* into Ramsgate and turn her over to the navy, but there were no extra men to take her across to France, so . . ."

"You tucked your hair up under your hat." Amy gazed up into her great-grandmother's eyes.

Maram must have lost the fight to lazy Umar because she stomped up the stairs. He could hear her slam a door shut.

Amy and her Nana would live at least until tomorrow.

Amy's Nana heard the door slam, too, but she only glanced briefly at him before returning her attention to the little girl. "Good thing I didn't have hair like yours." She tugged gently on one of Amy's curls.

"Your hair was blond and so beautiful. Mommy says you used to look like a movie star."

The old lady batted her eyelashes. "Don't I still?"

"Yes." He hadn't meant to say it aloud, but there it was. Now she knew for sure he was listening.

She didn't seem to mind. Instead she gave him another one of those dignified smiles. "Thank you, sir."

Sir. He could count the number of times anyone had ever called him *sir* on the fingers of one hand.

"I'm Eve," she told him, as if they were meeting at a party. "And this is Amy, my great-granddaughter."

He glanced over, but Umar, Khatib, and Gulzar had gone into the kitchen and turned on the TV.

It was starting to drive him mad, the incessant yapping of the commercials and talk shows. "Turn it down," he bellowed.

Umar shouted back, telling him to attempt the anatomically impossible. But the volume went down a little—no doubt thanks to Khatib.

"What's your name?" the old lady, Eve, asked him.

He looked toward the kitchen, but he was definitely alone in the room. He knew he shouldn't be talking to them. He should keep them silent. But with the TV on, Umar, Khatib, and Gulzar would never hear.

He'd always loved the stories his grandfather had told—of fighting the Nazis with Tito in the mountains of Yugoslavia, and he wanted to hear how this story ended. It wasn't possible that a quarter of a million men had been taken across the English Channel by an armada of small boats. They might've saved a few thousand, sure, but . . .

"I'm called the Bear," he told them, hoping he wouldn't get onto Maram's blacklist for admitting that.

"I'm afraid I can't say pleased to meet you, Mr. Bear—for obvious reasons," Eve told him. She looked down at Amy. "Where were we?"

"You tucked your hair up under your hat."

"That's right." She gave the Bear another smile. "This is her very favorite part. I'd learned to navigate the *Daisy Chain* the summer before, so I gave her full throttle and made the crossing myself. Now, I've made that channel crossing many times, but—and I'm awfully glad to say it—I've never made a crossing quite like that, before or since then.

"There were mines in the channel—too deep to do any damage to the *Daisy Chain*, but that didn't stop the larger ships from being blown to kingdom come. German U-boats—submarines—were out in force, as well. Again, they didn't target us small potatoes. But the Luftwaffe—they were a different story. They bombed and strafed—shot at—the men waiting on the beaches, and us, as well, as we approached. But not one of the little ships around me turned back. Not a *one*.

"As we approached, we could see the smoke from the battle. Dunkirk was burning, and it looked as if all of France were on fire."

He could picture her behind the wheel of a boat, chin held high as she sailed into a smoky storm of bullets and bombs.

"We worked for days. I ferried men from the beaches to the larger ships, until those ships were filled. And then I took on as many soldiers as I could and headed back toward Ramsgate. I can't even tell you how many trips I took across the channel. The evacuation went on until the fourth of June—it's all rather a noisy blur."

"How many men were saved?" Bear couldn't keep himself from asking.

The little girl spoke up. "Nana helped save at least five hundred of them herself."

"*Possibly* as many as five hundred," the old lady corrected her gently. "Do you remember the total number of Allied troops evacuated?"

"Three hundred and thirty-eight thousand," Amy announced, "two hundred and twenty . . . seven?"

He snorted his disbelief. "No way."

"Two twenty-*six*," Eve said. "It's true." She sighed. "But what I wouldn't have given for that number to have been higher." She glanced at him before she looked down into Amy's eyes. "True confession time. I didn't really cross that channel because I wanted to save all those stranded British soldiers. At least not at first. I first crossed the channel because I wanted to save one soldier in particular. I never told you this before, Amy, but even though I was only sixteen, I was married—and I had been for a year. The man I wanted so desperately to save was the man I loved. He was my husband."

Amy sat up, her eyes losing some of her fear. "You were married when you were sixteen?"

"Fifteen, actually," Eve admitted.

"But . . . I've seen your wedding pictures. You told me you got married right after the war."

"Well, I did," Eve said calmly. "I was married—for the *second* time—right after the war, when I was twenty-one. My first marriage wasn't exactly legal because I was so young at the time. And of course it was never consummated."

"What's consummated?"

He was unfamiliar with that English word, too, but he could guess what it meant from the context. He studied his boot, wondering how the old lady was going to handle the question.

"Do you know where babies come from?" she asked the girl. Good start.

"Of course I do," she scoffed. "Girls can get pregnant if

they have unprotected sex with boys. Mommy talks to me about it all the time because some of the sixth grade girls in my school tease the fifth grade girls about still being virgins."

"Dear God," Eve said. She swiftly collected herself. "Well, in that case you know, then, that when two people get married, part of their relationship as man and wife is a sexual one, right?"

Amy nodded.

"That's what consummated means. It's when two people who love each other enough to get married make love for the first time. In the olden days, it sealed the marriage, made it even more binding. When I was fifteen, I thought I was old enough to marry this man because I loved him so much. But when our wedding night came, well, some people might think I chickened out, but I like to look at it as being brave enough to admit I'd made a rather large mistake. Of course, when my new husband found out how old I truly was, that I'd basically tricked him into marrying me, he was furious and . . ." Eve laughed softly. "If I'm going to tell this story properly, I should start at the beginning, shouldn't I?"

"But did you save him?" Amy asked. "Your first husband? At Dunkirk?"

The old woman sighed and shook her head. "No," she said quietly. "I didn't."

Six

ENSIGN STARRETT WORE only a pair of shorts.

Alyssa Locke tried to focus on the video monitor, but the well-muscled, too-damned-handsome-for-his-own-good SEAL had positioned himself directly beyond it, right smack in her line of sight.

Of course the shorts were a big improvement over the barely there towel he'd had wrapped around his waist when he'd first come out of the bathroom.

If he'd been surprised to step out of the shower to find that the hotel suite he was supposed to be sharing with Lt. John Nilsson had become command central for this op within an op, he hadn't let on. In fact, upon hearing the news that Meg Moore's daughter and grandmother had been kidnapped by K-stani Extremists and that they had to keep all information about this from becoming public knowledge for their protection, Starrett had merely nodded and drawled, "Thought it had to be something like that."

Locke was glad Nils had brought her over here. She was pleased to be part of this top secret operation, glad to be already in position when Max Bhagat was brought into the room and brought up to speed, glad to be working in a small team with Lt. Tom Paoletti again.

But she wasn't glad that Sam Starrett was part of the team, with his bimboy body, his redneck prejudices, and his smart mouth.

Sweet thing.

As if she'd ever, in a million years, fall prey to his questionable charms. *Sweet thing,* pah. She wasn't *sweet* and she was no man's *thing.*

WildCard Karmody looked up from where he was figuring out how to create the equivalent of a digital tape loop with his computer.

"The Welsh singing thing was very smart," he said, taking a moment to stretch and run his fingers through his already messed, mad-scientist hair. "Meg's using her brain. And it makes sense for her not to want to just stand there and have a whole conversation in Welsh with Nils. Anyone listening in would know right away that there was an exchange of information going down. But this folk song thing was brilliant. Have I mentioned that I think I'm in love with this woman?"

"Yes." The answer came in unison from Starrett, Wolchonok, and another SEAL Locke had just met, a shiny young ensign with a pretty face named Mike Muldoon.

Without yet having had the chance to talk with her further, Nils's theory was that Meg had created this entire hostage situation as a way to get the FBI's attention. This way, she could get their help without putting Amy at risk.

And as unlikely as some people might think it would be for the Extremists to have infiltrated the K-stani embassy in Washington, Nils seemed convinced that such a thing was possible. Locke suspected he was being overly cautious, but she was willing to give him the benefit of the doubt. After all, he'd spent a considerable amount of time in the Pit.

Surveillance of the men's room would continue across the street at the makeshift FBI headquarters in the K-stani embassy. To the K-stani officials and anyone else there that might be listening in, it would appear as if the FBI and SEALs were continuing with their plan to sit and wait. To try to starve Meg out.

Meanwhile, over here at Troubleshooter Central, this new, secret team of SEALs and FBI agents were hard at work, devising a method of getting Nils into that men's room undetected so he could talk to Meg.

The plan was for Nils to deliver the handcuffs Meg had demanded, and somehow communicate to her that he would be coming back again, very soon, but not through the bathroom door this time.

The plan was then to jam the surveillance coming into the FBI's HQ over at the embassy—to replace the actual video and audio from the bathroom with a digital version of a tape loop.

The K-stani officials at the embassy would continue to see Meg and her hostages sitting in silence—the footage from the tape. They wouldn't have a clue that in reality, Lieutenant Paoletti's Troubleshooter squad would be covertly gaining access to that embassy men's room from the room directly above it. They'd be dropping in, so to speak, on Meg Moore and her captives. And Nils would be able to talk to her and get the complete, nonspeculative version of her story. He'd find out who exactly had taken Amy, and what were their demands.

Somewhere in the room a pager went off, and everyone checked their belts.

Locke herself nearly jumped out of her seat. On her recommendation, Jules Cassidy had been called in to assist, and she could feel his eyes on her now, from his seat in front of the other video monitor, across the room.

She glanced at him and shook her head, no. It wasn't her pager. She'd heard nothing from her sister all day. Which was just as good. If she got a page now, telling her to come to the hospital, she wasn't in a position to get up and go. Not without kissing her career good-bye.

"It's mine," Senior Chief Wolchonok called out. "It's a heads up code from Lieutenant Paoletti. Johnny's getting ready to go in."

As Locke watched on the video screen—surveillance footage pirated from the same signal being watched by the FBI and K-stani officials across the street—Meg lifted her head and glanced toward the door. She refreshed her grip on her handgun, aiming it at her hostages.

"Come in slowly." Her voice was remarkably natural-sounding over the speakers. This was one expensive setup that Paoletti had managed to conjure at such short notice.

"Lieutenant Nilsson is coming into the room," Locke announced.

Starrett pushed himself up off the couch and came around to look over her shoulder.

Locke kept her eyes on the screen. "Would you mind putting on a shirt?"

"Actually, I would," he said in that infuriating Texas drawl. "This is my room and I'm still taking a break."

"I don't have any trouble with it," Jules commented blandly.

Locke had to work to keep a smile from slipping out as Starrett turned abruptly and went into the other room to get a shirt. *Thanks,* she mouthed to Jules, who blew her a kiss.

On the video monitor, Nils was cuffing Meg's hostages to the sinks. This was good. After he left, they'd get about fifteen minutes of footage of all of them sitting there. Wild-Card would make that digital loop from that video, and then they'd be on to phase two.

"They've been asking me a lot of questions." Nils's voice came over the speakers as she sensed Starrett's overwhelmingly large presence behind her again. At least now he was dressed. "About us. I mean, no one can quite believe we didn't have some kind of hot affair three years ago."

"Oh, God." Meg shook her head. "I'm so sorry if I've gotten you into trouble."

"You haven't."

On the surface, they were having a simple conversation, but Locke—because she knew what to look for—could see that Meg and Nils were having an entirely different conversation with their eyes.

But were the hidden messages they were sending about this current situation? Or did it have more to do with the real truth about what went down between them three years ago? Locke smiled. She was one of the people who didn't quite believe Nils and Meg Moore had been "just friends."

Look at the way he looked at her.

Of course, maybe that *was* just friendship she could see in his eyes, and she, Locke, was the twisted one. Maybe she'd lived so long with men calling her *sweet thing*, she could no longer recognize genuine friendship between a man and a woman.

She glanced across the room at Jules. Unless, of course, the man was blatantly gay.

"I always hoped I'd see you again," Nils said, "but this wasn't exactly what I had in mind. I was thinking of something more along the lines of a phone call. Like, 'How are you, John, how about we get together for dinner?' " He looked directly into Meg's eyes. "And then I'd say, 'Great, I'll see you at eighteen hundred hours—at six o'clock sharp. We'll go out for drinks first and you can tell me all about how Amy's doing in school.' "

Understand what I'm telling you, Meg. You're going to see me at six o'clock.

She was wearing a watch, and as he gazed at her, she glanced at it. He knew it was just past 1640. She wasn't going to have to wait too long.

She was trying to hide her relief, and he also knew she'd received his message.

Christ, she looked exhausted.

"Are you sure you can't tell me what this is all about?" Nils asked again because the K-stani officials watching would have expected him to ask again.

She shook her head.

"I know you're upset because I didn't bring a dead bolt with the handcuffs," he said, feeding her the excuse she needed.

"Yeah, I told you to bring a dead bolt, but you didn't, so . . . I'm not going to talk to you." *Thank you,* Meg told him with her eyes.

You're welcome. "Would you believe me if I told you we haven't been able to locate a Home Depot store?"

John Nilsson wasn't a religious man, but right now he was praying that this would work out. God, what were the chances that Amy Moore was even still alive? Slim to none, if it really were the Extremists who'd taken her.

"No." Meg was looking at him hungrily, as if he were her lifeline. "No dead bolt, no explanation. In fact, I think you better go. Find out what's keeping my helicopter."

She didn't want him to leave. In fact, her lip actually trembled.

Nils went out the door before he did something really stupid—like promise her everything was going to be okay.

"In 1938, I lived in Hollywood, California," Eve told Amy and the Bear. Unlike her story of the part she'd played in the evacuation at Dunkirk, this was a tale she'd never told anyone before. Not her own daughter, Elizabeth, not her granddaughters, Meg, Bonnie, or Kiley, either.

Oh, she'd told them the vague facts, sure, but never the details. Even now, she held some of it back.

Her childhood hadn't been a particularly happy one. Her mother, a screen actress, had gotten a divorce from her father, a well-known film director, when her little brother Nick was only three years old. Eve had been eight at the time. Eight going on thirty. Good thing, because from that moment on, she was Nick's . . . what did they call it today?

Primary caregiver.

Her beautiful mother was irresponsible. The fan magazines called her *wild* and said that she had a childlike quality—a description that always made Eve roll her eyes.

Not that Eve and Nick didn't love her. Because they did. They adored her. And she adored them—whenever she happened to stumble across them.

In 1938, when Eve had just turned fifteen and Nick was ten, things went even further downhill, fast.

Both her mother and father were killed in a plane crash. Their divorce had been a friendly one, and they were working together on a movie when tragedy struck.

Eve and Nick went to live with Emily, their father's second wife and now widow, who gave them plenty of room to grieve as she went on about her life.

Which, in February of 1939, included getting remarried to James Hertford, a well-known and extremely wealthy English playwright.

Eve and Nick were dragged along and tossed onto James's seaside estate in Ramsgate, in southeast England, while Em and James dashed about Europe on their honeymoon.

When they returned, they enrolled both Eve and Nick in the best English boarding schools James's money could buy.

It was hell. The worst of it was being separated from her little brother. He hated his school—because it was there that something Eve had helped him hide for years was finally revealed.

Nick couldn't read.

Once it was known, everyone assumed his inability to decipher words came from neglect, but Eve knew better. She'd tried and tried for years to teach him to read, but to no avail.

He was miserable at the school. He was made to feel stupid, called lazy and careless—while none of those things were true. He ran away more times than Eve could count, and she knew she had to get him out of there before he disappeared for good.

She finagled her own escape from her school—no big deal, she simply slipped out the window and called the headmistress from the phone in the bookshop in town. She pretended to be her own American stepmother, asking the school to put Eve on the next train to London.

Which, of course, they did.

She'd been hoarding the spending money that James and Emily sent in extremely generous wads, and made a quick detour in London's fashion district. In a blink of an eye—and the lightening of her purse by quite a few English pounds—gone was the schoolgirl. In her place was a beautiful young sophisticate.

Thanks to a very mature figure, a great deal of poise and acting ability—all gifts from her late mother—and some carefully applied makeup, Eve could easily look much older than she was. In fact, during her brief stay at Ramsgate, Eve had told the estates' caretakers that she was twenty—and the middle-aged couple had swallowed it whole.

Dressed to the nines, Eve breezed into the headmaster's office at her brother's school and withdrew him.

They, of course, were only too glad to see him go.

Free at last, and reading in the paper that James and his new bride were in London for the opening of his newest play, Eve and Nick returned to the estate in Ramsgate to regroup.

They didn't have enough funds to buy passage on an oceanliner back to the United States. Nick wanted to steal the silver, but Eve flatly refused. They may have been orphans and down on their luck, but they weren't thieves. And it might take a while, but she'd get a job. She looked twenty. She could earn the money they needed. How hard could it be?

Her master plan was foiled when Emily and James came rushing back to Ramsgate. Who knew they'd actually bother to visit Eve and Nicky at school?

And instead of sending them back, James—a decent guy for an Englishman—put them under the supervision of his Ramsgate caretakers for the rest of the spring and the coming summer. However, Nick had to spend at least part of the time studying with a special tutor James was hiring.

Eve agreed to the deal, despite the fact that she dreaded the arrival of the tutor. He'd be dreary and old, with bad skin and teeth, big bushy eyebrows, and a long skinny face. He'd talk in that stupid accent with long, slow, drawn out vowels, taking so endlessly long to make his point that Eve would long to grab him by his pencil neck and shake him. He'd smell like mothballs and lye and the passed gas of the kidney pie he'd had for dinner last night and the night before.

And, Eve vowed, the first time he called Nick stupid would be the last.

By then, she'd have gotten a job in town and earned the money she needed to get them back to California. Please, heavenly Father . . .

But there were no jobs in town. There were no jobs, period. England was in the throes of a depression as bad as—or worse than—the one going on back in the States.

One day, when Eve had been unable to get a job, when she was driving back from Ramsgate—James kept three different cars in the garage of his estate and she saw no reason not to use them at her leisure despite her lack of driver's license—as she was pulling up to the main house, she first encountered her brother's new tutor.

He had just ridden up on his bicycle and had accepted a drink from Mr. Johnson, the caretaker.

At first she'd thought he was a traveler passing through, a young man on break from college, biking his way across the English countryside, stopping for a drink, or—even more likely—to ask if he could camp for the night in the nearby woods.

"You can sleep up by the orchard if you promise not to light a fire," Eve said to him as she slid out from the car's expensive leather seats.

The young man laughed—his grin was infectious and his eyes actually twinkled—and she realized he was older than she'd first thought by about five years. "Do you always greet strangers with non sequiturs?"

She looked at his bicycle—old but well-kept; his clothes— that of a traveler, jacket off and sleeves rolled up to beat the heat, one pant leg tucked into his sock to keep it from getting caught on the bike's chain; his face—damp with perspiration but still strikingly attractive, framed above his very English and somewhat patrician forehead and long elegant nose by thick, dark, wavy hair; his eyes—hazel, with long, dark lashes, and still dancing with amusement.

"Of course, you're pretty enough to get away with just about anything, aren't you?" he added.

"Aren't *you* looking for a place to spend the night?" she asked.

Something shifted in those hazel eyes as they skimmed her from the hat that went perfectly with her eggshell-colored suit, all the way down her silk-stocking-clad legs to her matching pumps. She'd seen that look in a man's eyes plenty of times before and knew what it meant.

If she were her mother, she'd pull her shoulders back a little bit, throwing out her breasts, showing off her female attributes. But Eve was tired and her feet hurt. It had been a long, disappointing day and the last thing she needed was some stupid college boy drooling on her, no matter how pretty his eyes were.

She reached up to pull her hat pins free. She couldn't wait to get back to her room so she could change into her blue jeans, her cowboy boots, and one of her father's old shirts. She'd find Nicky and they'd take a walk over to the beach and . . .

"Actually, no," the young man said. Despite the heat, he rolled down his sleeves and slipped his arms into his jacket, the perfect gentleman. "I'm here to see young Nicolas Linden. I'm his new tutor, Ralph Grayson." He wiped his hand on his pants before holding it out to her. "I was told he had an older sister, but I'm afraid they didn't mention your name."

This was Nick's tutor.

His name was spelled Ralph, but he pronounced it the crazy English way—*Rafe*.

He had a poet's or maybe a piano player's hands, with long, graceful fingers. They should have been cool and otherworldly, but they weren't. He was hot to the touch.

"I'm Eve," she told him.

"Eve," he murmured, still holding onto her, his eyes at least as hot as his hand. "Delightful."

And Eve knew in a flash that she held the ultimate power. Ralph Grayson had no clue he was casting lustful looks at a fifteen-year-old girl. All she needed was for him to say or do something completely inappropriate—one kiss was all it would take—and she'd control him. Then if he upset Nicky—which he would invariably do—she'd whisper the truth about how old she really was into his ear and tell him she'd keep their little nasty secret, provided he resign immediately.

And then, poof, like magic, he'd be gone.

She pulled back her shoulders and gave him her mother's million dollar smile. "The pleasure's completely mine, Ralph. May I call you Ralph?"

"Absolutely. I have to confess, I was looking forward to working with your brother and to spending the summer near the seaside, but now I'm completely ecstatic."

Cripes, he shoveled it on pretty thick. Eve pulled her hand free. "Why don't we go inside? I'll get Nick and a pitcher of lemonade."

"*Excellent* idea."

Or maybe he was just stupidly enthusiastic about everything.

"This house is *gorgeous*," he proclaimed as they went inside. "Do you know its history?"

She shook her head, and he regaled her with the duke of this and the lord of that all the way to the sitting room.

"Nicky likes plays," she interrupted him midsentence as he was saying something about visits to this estate a million years earlier from someone named Prinny. "Our mother was an actress."

The tutor nodded, suddenly serious. "Thank you," he said, as if she'd presented him with the royal jewels. "Anything else I should know that might help?"

"He hates tutors."

The smile was back. "I assumed as much."

"I'll send him right in," she said, and hurried out of the room. Why had she told him even that much, instead of leaving him to face Nick's evil eye on his own?

She found her brother in the kitchen, telling one of his ridiculous tall tales to a giggling Mrs. Johnson. They were waiting for a chocolate cake to finish baking.

"Your tutor's arrived," she told him, hating the surly, almost hunted-animal look that came into his eyes at the news. "He's not old and smelly like we thought, Nick. He's young and he seems nice." She gave him a hug, whispering into his ear, "And if you don't like him, I'll make him leave, I promise."

Hope bloomed, banishing the desperate animal, and Nicky nodded. There wasn't much in this world that he could count on, but Eve had never broken a promise to him yet. Unlike their mother, she'd never made him a promise she couldn't keep.

"He's in the sitting room," she told him now. "Go and meet him. I'll be there in a sec with lemonade."

Mrs. Johnson helped her find a tray, and Eve carried the pitcher and three glasses carefully back down the long hallway.

"Ralph," she heard the tutor say as she went into the room. "Like Ralph Rackstraw in *HMS Pinafore*."

Nothing. Nick didn't even blink. And James had given them tickets to see *Pinafore* when they'd first arrived in England. Nick had loved it—he'd laughed his butt off.

Eve poured them each a tall glass of lemonade as Ralph, undaunted, tried again.

"Do you know I'm in line to be the king of England?" he asked. He was so focused on Nick, he barely even glanced up to thank her as she handed him a glass.

"You don't really expect me to believe that, do you?" Nick scoffed. Bingo. Ralph had gotten him to speak.

"It's true." Ralph set his glass down on the end table nearest him. "We're distant cousins of the queen's. In fact, my eldest brother's an earl. And if he and all seventeen hundred and fifty-eight other members of the royal family die, I'll be crowned the next king. But you don't have to call me *Your Highness*. Ralph will do."

Nick was stunned. "You want me to call you by your first name?"

"I thought that might be a good idea," Ralph replied. "You don't mind, do you? You Americans prefer informality, right? Just do me a favor and don't pronounce my name the American way. Ralph," he said, heavy on the *L*, then shuddered. "Sounds kind of like the noise your dog makes when he loses his dinner, doesn't it?"

Nick laughed but caught himself and stopped. "I don't want a tutor," he said flatly. "I don't want to learn to read. I've gotten along just fine without it—at least everywhere but at that stupid school."

"Ah." Ralph nodded in understanding. "Well, then." He thought about that. "If you don't want to learn to read, I can't very well force you, can I?"

Nick was completely unprepared for such a reasonable response. He didn't know what to say and his evil eye faltered.

"Tell me then," Ralph continued. "What *do* you want to learn how to do?"

Eve felt invisible. It was really pretty amazing. She was used to being the center of attention but neither Ralph nor Nick seemed to know she was even in the room. She crossed her legs with a whisper of silk, but Ralph didn't so much as glance in her direction. Every fiber of his being was focused on Nicky.

Who had crossed his arms and was back to glaring at Ralph, chin held at a decidedly aggressive angle. "I want to learn to box."

The Englishman didn't hesitate. He didn't even blink. "Excellent. My brother and I both boxed at school. Between us we had two pairs of gloves. I can ask my mother to send them—"

"There are gloves out in the garage," Nicky informed him. "Hanging on the wall."

"Better and better," Ralph declared. "However, since it's been some years, and since I've never actually tried to teach anyone to box before, we'll need to make a quick trip to the town lending library to get a book on rules and technique. What say we go now?"

"Now?" Nick's voice cracked in surprise. "Well, sure."

"I wonder if your sister would drive us in that car of hers." Was it possible he'd forgotten she was in the room? Eve cleared her throat and he looked over at her, his eyes dancing. He was enjoying himself. He'd gone up against her brother's evil eye and had actually come out of it sparkling. "Oh, hello, Lady Eve. Unless this old place has its own library . . . ? "

"It does." Even more amazing—Nick was actually excited and letting his excitement show. "There are shelves and *shelves* of books," he said in his regular voice, not that angry and dripping-with-scorn voice, nor even that dead, flat tone he used when he was forced to be at least partially polite to teachers and tutors. "More than you could count if you spent an entire *week* at it. And there're ladders on wheels to get up to the top shelves."

"Well, then lead on, Nick old pal. Isn't that what you Americans call each other?"

They went down the hall at Nick-speed, and Eve had to run to keep up. She finally stopped and kicked off her high-heeled shoes, but by then she'd lost them. When she reached the library, they were already inside.

Ralph was on one of the ladders, showing Nick how—if he pushed just so—gently though, not with a great deal of force—he could glide all the way from one side of the room to the other.

"Any chance these books are in any kind of order?" the tutor wondered aloud as he climbed down to give Nick a turn.

"They're arranged by subject, fiction's by author," Eve informed him. James Hertford loved his books.

Nick was riding the ladder back and forth now. "You're the first tutor who's ever taught me anything useful," he proclaimed.

"Then we're off to a fabulous start. Tell me, if this were your library," Ralph called up to him as he quickly scanned the shelves, "would you file Boxing under Boxing or Sports?"

"If this was my library," Nick pronounced, "I'd toss all the stupid books out in the yard and use this room for a theater. Or maybe a zoo."

"See now, I like it just as it is—as a library. Because even though I'm rusty when it comes to boxing, as long as I know how to read, I can find a book, read it, and relearn everything I might've forgotten and— Aha!" Ralph said, triumphantly pulling a book from the shelves. "*A Gentleman's Guide to Boxing.* Just the thing! Come quick, Gentleman Nick, and show me those gloves and— No! I've a meeting in town with my new landlord. And I must pick up my trunk—it's coming in via train. I really just stopped in to say hello. Classes don't officially begin until tomorrow. Which is good actually. It gives me time to read this book."

"But aren't you staying here?" Nick asked. "With us? This place has forty bedrooms at least and—"

He cut himself off, the funniest look on his face. It was the first time in his entire life that he'd ever implored a teacher to stay.

Lord, Ralph Grayson was good. Nick was completely enthralled and totally unaware that the lesson he'd just been given had little to do with mastering the library ladders and everything to do with the mighty power of books.

"Why don't you go dust off those boxing gloves," Ralph told the boy. "I'll be back in the morning, first thing. I promise."

In a flash Nick was gone.

Leaving Eve alone with Ralph.

"I'm sure you're probably wondering whether I've gone completely mad." He was gazing down at the book he still held, but now he glanced up at her, amusement in his eyes.

"No," she said quietly, "I'm not."

He smiled at her. Now that Nick was gone, *she* was the focus of all that energy and intensity. It made her heart feel as if it had lodged in her throat.

"Good," he said. "I hope I'll see you tomorrow, too. I don't suppose you also harbor a secret yearning to learn to box?"

Eve laughed, suddenly giddy with hope that this would work out, that this man truly was the answer to all of her and Nicky's prayers. "No, but I don't suppose you'd teach me how to sail? James bought Emily a yacht for a wedding gift, only she gets seasick, so they're probably going to sell it. I'd love to go out in it at least once before they do and . . ." She was babbling. She sounded like a ten-year-old. If she didn't shut up, he'd guess that she wasn't twenty after all, and then she wouldn't have the power to . . .

Make him leave.

She didn't want him to leave.

But she would. Sooner or later, he'd get down to the business of trying to teach Nick how to read. And then even *he'd* get frustrated and end up calling Nicky stupid.

It was senseless to hope that he'd be any different. Because hope only hurt. It lifted you up, sure, but then, when dashed, it dragged you lower than you were when you started.

Hope stank.

"Would you like me to drive you back into town?" she asked as she walked Ralph toward the door, hoping he wouldn't notice the sudden rush of tears to her eyes. Maybe in the close confines of the car, if she gazed at him from underneath her eyelashes, he would try to kiss her.

And then she'd have all the ammunition she'd need to use against him.

"No, thanks," he said. "I have to get used to the bike ride, and anyway, it's not that far."

As if he'd just read her mind, his gaze dropped to her mouth for just a second. But then he looked back into her eyes and his always-ready smile faded. "Are you all right?" he asked softly. "I know this can't be easy for you, with your parents' death still so recent."

He'd said *death*. He'd actually said the word, instead of trying to soften it up and make its horror and ugliness into something polite by using some asinine euphemism like "passing."

Eve liked Ralph Grayson so much, it hurt. "Thank you," she managed. "I'm . . . all right."

They'd reached the front hall and he paused, turning to face her. "I understand now why Mr. Hertford made arrangements for me to have lodgings in town. You're almost unbearably lovely."

He didn't say the words as if he were only teasing. He

spoke them almost reverently, as if they were the gospel truth, and for a moment Eve was thrown.

She'd never received such a forward compliment before.

What would her mother do?

She'd play it as if it were a flirtation. She'd throw out her chest, look at him from underneath her eyelashes, and flirt shamelessly back. "By any chance, are you asking me to have dinner with you?" Eve said the words, but it was her mother's voice she heard.

And Ralph laughed—the way men had laughed with her mother. Deep and rich and intoxicatingly warm, his laughter seemed to wind its way around her. And for the first time, Eve understood why her mother had enjoyed making her collection of men laugh.

"Yes, actually," Ralph said, "I suppose I am. Are all American women always so direct?"

"Not all," she countered. "Just . . . the interesting ones." That was a line stolen from one of her mother's movies, right down to the little hesitation after the word *just*.

"So will you?" he asked, his eyes all but throwing sparks. "Have dinner with me, Eve?"

Oh, dear Lord. Was that enough? The fact that he'd asked her out? Or would she actually have to go out with him, too, to hold it against him later?

She wanted to go and yet she didn't.

Eve opened the front door, hoping he wouldn't notice that her cheeks were flushed. "I'm making you late for your appointment."

"Hmmm. Suddenly *not* so direct . . ."

"Maybe you should ask me again sometime, when it doesn't seem so much as if it were my idea." Another of her mother's saucy lines—this one not from a movie, but from real life. Eve had heard her mother say it to more than one handsome man. She'd practiced saying it herself, into the bathroom mirror. This was the first time she'd ever made it all the way through without laughing and rolling her eyes.

"Fair enough." Instead of going out the door, Ralph stopped right next to her, close enough for her to feel his body heat. He didn't speak for several seconds, until she looked up at him. "I don't suppose it's been long enough yet to qualify as *again sometime* . . . ?"

Up close, his eyes were a remarkable swirl of green and brown. And while he'd clearly shaved this morning, she could already see the shadow of stubble on his chin and cheeks. This was not some mere boy she was dallying with. This was a grown man.

Wordlessly, quite terrified, she shook her head no.

"It hasn't been that long since you've been out of school, has it?" he asked.

Again Eve shook her head. If only he knew . . .

"Me, neither," he told her. "And, you know, I really miss it. I would've liked to have been a student forever, just always keep learning. But you don't have to be in school to do that, do you?"

She found her voice, afraid he'd think her some kind of an idiot if she just kept shaking her head. "I guess not."

"This summer, I'd planned to learn the history behind the caves here on Thanet," he said, still in that hypnotizingly gentle voice, "maybe explore some of the Roman ruins on the island. I was looking forward to that. But suddenly I seem to have developed an intense fascination with the New World."

He was going to kiss her. She'd seen men looking at her mother the way Ralph was looking at her right now. He leaned closer and . . .

"Well," she said loudly, stepping back, away from him, giving him her most blinding smile as her heart pounded. "See you tomorrow, then."

Ralph blinked. And stepped back.

She knew she'd confused the heck out of him.

Well, tough, because he'd confused her, too.

"Right," he said. "Until tomorrow."

Eve watched him ride away, down the long, picture-perfect drive toward town. She sat heavily on the steps, her knees still trembling, as she both dreaded and anticipated the coming day.

Seven

❦ ❧

SIX O'CLOCK.

It started as the smallest of sounds, over in the far corner of the room, up by the ceiling.

It was a buzzing. Just the faintest hint of a noise.

Then it got louder and it was accompanied by a small amount of plaster, just a dusting, falling from the ceiling into one of the bathroom stalls.

Osman Razeen glanced up, but then quickly looked away.

He thought it was a rescue team—coming to blast them free and to blow Meg away.

Meg would have thought so, too, except that it was six o'clock, and John had done everything but flat out tell her he'd be back at six. Sharp.

"Meg."

It was John Nilsson's voice.

"Yes." Somehow he'd figured out a way to drill a hole into the ceiling so they could talk without anyone overhearing or seeing. Maybe he'd scrambled or altered the signal being sent via all the cameras and mikes the FBI had put into place. It didn't matter how he'd done it. It only mattered that no one knew.

"I'm going to cut a bigger hole in the ceiling and come down," he told her. "Don't shoot me, all right?"

"Promise me the people in this embassy don't know this is happening," she said, dizzy and sick from the knowledge that if John were lying and she believed him, Amy amd Eve would die. But, God, she wanted to believe him. "Promise me they can't see or hear this."

"I promise."

Her hostages looked startled. They looked at each other, looked up at the ceiling, looked at her.

"Then I won't shoot you," she promised John.

Whether or not she shot Osman Razeen was a different story. Meg aimed her gun at Razeen's heart as the buzzing sound started up again, louder this time. Her own heart was pounding.

This was it. The moment of truth.

She sat looking into her hostage's eyes, picturing herself being charged with first degree murder, thinking about the terrible gamble she was taking with *Amy's* life by not simply killing this man right here and right now.

It wasn't as if he were Mother Teresa. He was a terrorist.

All she had to do was squeeze the trigger and he wouldn't be a terrorist anymore.

He wouldn't *be* anymore.

But once John dropped down through that hole in the ceiling, once he was in this room with her, she'd be past the point of no return.

Her hands started to shake, and she set the gun down on the floor. She was *already* past the point of no return. What happened to her didn't matter anymore. But she knew one thing for sure—if she were going to shoot Razeen, it wasn't going to be by mistake.

Meg hugged her knees into her chest, watching bits of plaster fall from the ceiling like snow now. But the main chunk of the ceiling was somehow pulled up and out, leaving behind a dark space that was soon filled by John's face and shoulders.

"May I come down?"

He'd nearly always been so polite and well-mannered. Even when he was kissing her.

She nodded, unable to speak. She knew he saw her gun on the floor. He saw everything. He always had.

"What's going on?" the ambassador finally dared to ask as John pulled back and then lowered his legs and then the rest of him from the hole in the ceiling. He swung himself over the metal frame of the stall and dropped lightly, athletically, onto the tile floor.

He started toward her, and Meg couldn't stop herself.

She started to cry.

And John was there, down on the floor next to her, pulling her into his arms, onto his lap, holding her close.

"They took Amy," she sobbed.

"I'm sorry," he said. "Christ, Meg, I'm so sorry."

"What's going on?" the ambassador said again, louder this time.

Nils let Lieutenant Paoletti handle it as the CO, his senior chief, and Sam Starrett also lowered themselves down into the K-stani embassy men's room. Max Bhagat and several of the FBI agents weren't far behind.

He didn't try to do more than hold on to Meg, all but ignoring the murmur of voices as Paoletti and Bhagat explained the situation to the three former hostages. Young daughter kidnapped . . . Meg under duress . . . only way to get the FBI's attention . . . no one knows they're in here . . . going to take them out through the ceiling, leave a tape loop running while they pretend to wait out the situation.

He sensed more than saw Sam claim possession of Meg's handgun. Sensed Sam reach out to touch Meg briefly on the back in a vain attempt to offer a little more comfort.

Nils wanted to tell her it was going to be all right, but Jesus, he had no way of knowing that her daughter and her grandmother weren't already dead.

"I'm here," he said instead, painfully aware of how little that might mean to her. He tried again. "You're not alone in this anymore, Meg."

She clung to him, and he held her just as tightly, stroking her hair, kissing the top of her head, wishing . . . Christ, he didn't know what he wished.

Maybe he wished that she could've been in his arms any place else in the world and at any other time but here and now.

She wasn't alone—to hell with that, too. A lot of good it would do her, to know she wouldn't be alone as she buried her daughter.

God *damn* it. Nils felt his own eyes burn, felt sick to his stomach, felt the awful injustice of a dead ten-year-old lodge tightly in his chest and make it hard to breathe.

He could feel Lieutenant Paoletti standing off to the side, giving both of them some space. But they didn't have much time. The Kazbekistanis wouldn't believe that Meg could hold her hostages and sit in the men's room under siege without food or sleep forever.

"I need you to be tough for just a little bit longer," he told her. "Can you do that for me, Meg? We've got a lot of questions that only you can answer."

She was shaking, trembling, but she somehow managed to nod yes. She released her death grip on his neck and pulled back to look at him, wiping her eyes with one shaky hand.

"They kidnapped Amy and my grandmother," she said. "They said they were Kazbekistani Extremists, and that if I didn't come here and abduct or kill the new ambassador—they didn't really care which—they'd kill them. I'm so sorry, John, I didn't know what else to do. They told me if I told anyone, if I asked for help, they'd know it and Amy and Eve would die."

Her eyes welled with tears again, but she wiped them fiercely away. "I didn't know what to do," she told him again. "But then I thought of you. I thought if anyone could get me out of this . . ."

"You did the right thing," he reassured her. "Calling me—asking for me—was the right thing."

She looked over to where Wolchonok was unlocking the hostages' handcuffs, her voice suddenly sharp with fear. "What is he doing? He's not just going to let them go, is he? If the Extremists don't think that I'm still locked in here with them . . ."

"It's all right." Lieutenant Paoletti approached. "We've got a tape loop running. On the surveillance monitors, both you and the hostages will look as if you're sitting here, waiting. In truth, we're going to be taking all of you out of here and over to a safe location. No one's going to see you leave, no one's going to know."

"The hostages have agreed to remain in isolation in one of our safe hotels until we can find more information as to the whereabouts of your daughter and grandmother," Max Bhagat added.

The two men sat down right there on the floor to talk to

Meg. As they introduced themselves, Meg shifted away from Nils, out of his arms.

That was typical of her—even at a time when no one would fault her for leaning on a friend. With her initial outburst over, she now had to stand alone.

"Why don't you tell us what happened, Meg," Paoletti said, in that soft-spoken, easygoing manner he had of making everyone around him feel as comfortable as possible. "Start from the beginning and take your time."

Meg nodded. She held her hands in her lap, gripping her own fingers tightly—but even that wasn't enough to hide the fact that she was still trembling.

Maybe she stood alone because that was what she'd always done. Maybe it was the only thing she knew how to do.

"I had to pick up some files for a translating project I'd been hired to do," she started, "and Amy, my daughter, wanted to take Eve, my grandmother who's visiting us from England, to the Smithsonian for her birthday."

Her voice trembled and she had to stop to clear her throat.

Nils could understand what it was like to want to appear strong, so he wouldn't take her hand unless she gave him some kind of sign that she wanted him to do that.

But there was strength in numbers, too, and he didn't want her to forget that from now on, she *didn't* have to go through this alone.

So he shifted closer to her, there as they sat on the tile of the Kazbekistani men's room floor. Just a little bit. Just enough so that his knee touched her leg.

And she didn't shift away.

It wasn't much, but it was a start.

Sam was gathering up his gear, getting ready to move to another suite in the hotel that had just become available, when Alyssa Locke came in.

Her partner, Jules Cassidy—the short, too-pretty guy with the bleached blond hair—was there with two other FBI agents, monitoring the tape loop WildCard had set up, making sure that any Kazbekistani officials could pop into the FBI surveillance room at the embassy at any time and see continuous images of Meg and her three hostages, still sitting in the men's room.

Even though they were all long gone.

"What are you still doing here?" Alyssa greeted her partner with a warm smile.

Sam didn't even rate a cold nod.

"I was just about to head home," the little fucker said, "but my incredible ability to prognosticate told me you were about to arrive, so I decided to wait."

"Someone called and said I was on my way over," Alyssa interpreted, giving him another kickass smile.

No fucking fair.

And talk about a complete waste. Teaming Alyssa Locke up with a guy who was gay? And Sam was flat-out sorry, but even if the FBI had a "don't ask, don't tell" policy similar to the U.S. military, when it came to Cassidy, there was no need to ask anything. There was absolutely no question as to which way *his* wind blew.

Of course, maybe that was why he'd been teamed up with Alyssa Locke. No male agent would be comfortable letting Cassidy guard his ass—because they wouldn't want the little fruit anywhere *near* their ass.

Alyssa, however, seemed genuinely to like the man.

"What news cometh from the front lines, oh goddess of information?" Cassidy asked.

She flopped down next to him on the couch and Sam almost did a double take. Locke didn't *flop*. And yet . . . She was sitting there, slouched back, as if she were as exhausted as he was. As if she, too, hadn't slept since before she could remember.

As if she were human.

After the SEALs had pulled all three of the former hostages and Meg out of the K-stani men's room, Locke had been part of the team that had spirited them out of the embassy and away to another location—a safe and very swanky hotel—across town.

He moved closer so he could hear her conversation with Cassidy.

"Meg Moore was questioned for hours, and her story held up," Alyssa reported. "Oh, and you'll like this, Jules. There was a security camera in the parking garage where she said the Extremist first contacted her. Everything happened exactly the way she described it, *and* we've got the guy on videotape. We've IDed him as a suspected K-stani terrorist. Nobody has a clue how he got into the U.S. He's wanted for a number of violent crimes—including planting a bomb in a Kazabek school bus."

She rolled her head on the cushiony back of the couch to look at Cassidy as she continued. "Which was probably not something Meg Moore needed to hear. The man who's connected with the kidnapping of her daughter is a wanted child killer."

"Shit," Cassidy said.

"Yeah." She sighed. "She kind of lost it. Fortunately a doctor was on hand. He gave her something to help her sleep. As for our other guests—the ambassador and the other two Kazbekistanis are being very gracious about this. They're cooperating fully."

"By letting the FBI house them in a hotel with room service provided by DC's best French gourmet restaurant and all the pay-per-view they can watch?" Cassidy snorted. "After thinking I was going to die like a dog gunned down near the urinals in a men's room, I'd be pretty happy with option B as well."

"They didn't *have* to cooperate," Alyssa told her partner.

"How many times have you worked with Max Bhagat?" Cassidy asked.

"This is the first. I mean, I knew who he was and—"

"Ah."

"What does *ah* mean?" she asked.

"It means, 'Ah, you've never worked with Max before.' "

She gave him a far friendlier version of her cold stare than Sam had ever received. "Which means . . . ?"

"He's a really good negotiator," Cassidy said, "to the point that he's completely able to manipulate nearly any situation to his favor. I'm betting after five minutes with Max, neither the ambassador nor the other two hostages would have considered *not* cooperating. Because Max probably leaned heavily but oh-so-subtly on the concept that not cooperating would make them look as if they *were* connected to the Extremists who kidnapped sweet little Amy Moore. So there they go, whisked off to a *safe* hotel room where they can't make any phone calls or communicate with anyone, where they're locked in and placed under twenty-four-hour guard. But because Max is Max, they're happy to be there and even though it's probably going to take four days longer than anyone anticipated, they're going to leave thanking *him*. Why don't you sit down and take a load off?"

It took Sam several seconds to realize Cassidy had aimed that last question at him.

Alyssa turned her head to look up at him, but then looked quickly away.

"Sorry," Sam said. "I was just . . . you know . . ."

"Eavesdropping?" Cassidy asked cheerfully. "It might've worked better if you'd actually tried to hide behind the couch."

Alyssa was still leaning back against the sofa cushions, but somehow she was no longer relaxed.

"I wanted to know how Meg was doing," Sam admitted.

"She was extremely upset when the news came down about that terrorist's prior with a school bus, but she's sleeping now," Alyssa reported, still not looking at him.

Wasn't this nice? They were able to have a civilized conversation, an exchange of information, without someone getting pissed off and needing to leave the room.

"Where was Nils during this?" Sam asked.

"He was in a meeting with Lieutenant Paoletti," Alyssa told him. "I don't know what about."

Sam did. "He was probably requesting leave, arguing that his relationship with Meg was making it impossible for him to concentrate on the things he's supposed to be concentrating on. He's such a Boy Scout."

Alyssa dared to glance up at him. "I thought you two were friends."

"We are," Sam said. He smiled. "And he's only a Boy Scout some of the time. The rest of the time, he's the most devious son of a bitch I've ever met."

"Which, naturally, you see as a plus."

If he'd wanted to, he could've let that comment sting. Instead he rolled it off his back. He was too tired to fight. "Absolutely."

"Are you sure you don't want to sit down?"

If it had been Alyssa asking that instead of Cassidy, Sam would've stuck his butt in a chair. But she wasn't joining in, asking him to stay. In fact, she had her eyes closed now.

"Nah, I'm on my way out of here. Wolchonok got me reassigned to a room that's a little more private than Grand Central Station, and I'm planning to be unconscious in about five minutes, so . . ."

He picked up his bag, glanced again at Alyssa. "See ya," Sam said.

"Later," Cassidy replied.

Alyssa didn't say a word, didn't give him even a dim smile, didn't open her eyes.

She wasn't asleep, she was just waiting for him to leave.

Frustration rose in a wave around him and Sam forgot about being too tired to fight. "Would it kill you," he growled, "to *pretend* to be polite?"

She opened one eye. "To a jerk like you? It might."

Every single retort that sprang to his lips was unprintable. He might've said something unspeakably rude anyway—she pissed him off that much—if the realization hadn't suddenly hit him.

She really hated him.

She wasn't kidding, it wasn't even partially in fun.

Alyssa Locke *despised* him.

"I'm sorry," he said quietly, because he was. Sorry that she felt that way about him, sorry that he'd been unable to resist pushing her buttons every single time they met, sorry for himself because unless hell froze, she wasn't ever going to smile at him the way she smiled at Jules Cassidy.

She opened both eyes and even sat up, but he didn't wait around for her to fire another verbal missile at him. He took his bag and left.

Eight

IT WAS 0422.

Normally Nils wouldn't have found the fact that it was 0422 to be a problem. It wasn't the first time he'd been up and out before dawn. But normally when he was up and functioning coherently at 0422, that usually meant he'd gone to sleep a little earlier than 0100.

Yes, he'd gone to bed much too late after being awake for too many days in a row, *and* the call had come in to the hotel suite much too early, at 0405, waking both Nils and Sam Starrett from a deep sleep.

It had not been a wrong number, as much as Nils had wished it to be.

The FBI wanted to talk to him, pronto. In fact, they were sending a car.

That car—a dark sedan, conspicuous for its lack of conspicuousness—had just dropped him across town at the safe hotel he'd helped bring Meg to just hours earlier.

As Nils was escorted upstairs and into a conference room that held both FBI Team Leader Max Bhagat and Lieutenant Paoletti, he wished he'd taken the time between 0405 and 0407 to shave.

The hotel suite was hopping for the early morning hour. Something was up. Or maybe—and the hair on the back of his neck stood up—something had gone very wrong.

"What's going on? Where's Meg?" He looked to Lieutenant Paoletti for answers, but the CO just shook his head.

"Where's Meg is a very good question." A bleary-eyed Bhagat motioned for Nils to sit down on the opposite side of the table. "We were hoping you'd be able to help us answer that."

Christ, the Extremists had grabbed her.

Nils *knew* he shouldn't have left her and gone back to his own hotel to sleep. He should have pushed his way into her room despite being told that she'd been given sleeping pills and was fast asleep. After what she'd been through, he should have insisted upon seeing her, insisted upon standing guard beside her bed.

But as angry as he was at himself and at the FBI for letting this happen, he forced his voice to sound calm as he faced Bhagat. "No, sir, I'm afraid I can't answer any questions. When did Meg's abduction take place?"

Bhagat exchanged a look with Lieutenant Paoletti.

The lieutenant turned to Nils. "I told them you didn't have anything to do with this."

Confusion mixed with frustration and just enough nausea from fear for Meg's safety and lack of sleep to make him want to grab Paoletti—one of the nicest guys in the world—by the collar of his shirt and shake him hard.

"With what?" he asked instead, his teeth only slightly clenched. "L.T., what the hell's going on?"

He had a million questions. What time was Meg reported missing? Were there signs of a struggle? Signs of bloodshed or—please, God, no—foul play? Were the FBI tracking her right now?

"You're right about there having been an abduction." Bhagat rubbed his eyes. "But Meg wasn't the abductee, Lieutenant Nilsson. She was the abductor."

Nils heard the words, but they didn't make sense. And then they made too much sense.

Paoletti was nodding. "She had a second side arm."

"Was there a reason you didn't search her in the men's room, Lieutenant?" Bhagat asked.

She had a second side arm? Nils couldn't believe it. But God, he *hadn't* searched her in the men's room.

"No, sir," he answered Bhagat. "She'd surrendered her weapon and . . ." And she'd been in his arms, crying her heart out. It had never even occurred to him that he might want to pat her down. He looked at Paoletti. "Are you sure about this, sir, because . . ."

"According to the FBI guard, she held him at gunpoint, took his cuffs, his side arm, too, and locked him in a utility closet. Then she went in and took—"

"The ambassador?" Even as he said the words, Nils didn't believe it. And yet . . . He could still see that desperation in Meg's eyes. "After the doctor gave her something to sleep? No way."

"The doctor gave her sleeping pills." The look in Paoletti's eyes told Nils what his CO thought of that doctor. "He left her with a full prescription. It's now assumed she didn't actually take any."

"And it wasn't the ambassador," Bhagat informed Nils. "Meg Moore left the premises with another of her hostages— a diplomatic aide named Janko Tuzak. Does that name ring any bells, Lieutenant?"

The FBI team leader still wasn't convinced Nils didn't know *some*thing. And at this point, with both Bhagat and Lieutenant Paoletti telling him that Meg had conned them all—particularly *Nils* . . .

The thought that Meg had baldly lied to him, that she'd had a second handgun—probably hidden in her boot—was one Nils couldn't quite wrap his brain around. He didn't know *some*thing—Christ, he didn't know *any*thing. Including which way was up.

But Bhagat had asked him a question.

"Janko Tuzak." Nils shook his head. "No, I don't know him, sir, don't know the name."

"Maybe you'll know him by his *real* name—Osman Razeen."

Oh, *fuck*. "Are you telling me that Meg left here with a weapon and a hostage, and that hostage is *Osman Razeen*?" Nils looked at Lieutenant Paoletti and saw the truth echoed in his grim expression.

Bhagat nodded. "I guess that name's more familiar to you, huh?"

Nils felt the earth listing a little bit more to the side. "Osman Razeen, the GIK terrorist leader . . . ?" It was a stupid question. What kind of answer did he expect? *No, Osman Razeen the K-stani ice cream man.*

"The one and only," Bhagat informed him, apparently used

to dealing with idiots. "Wanted by the U.S., the Kazbekistani government, *and*, it seems now, the Extremists. Everyone wants a piece of him."

"Does Meg know who he is?" Nils asked, but as soon as the words left his mouth, he realized how stupid they were, too. He was batting a thousand here. Of course she knew.

He couldn't believe this. This was like some awful nightmare that just kept on getting worse and worse. "She told me the Extremists were targeting the new ambassador," he informed Bhagat and Paoletti. She'd looked him in the eye, and *told* him. "She didn't say anything about Tuzak or Razeen or . . ."

Fuck. Meg had *lied* to him. She'd used him as much as she'd used that second handgun in her boot to get herself and Razeen out of the K-stani embassy.

"How well do you really know Meg Moore, Lieutenant?" Paoletti asked gently. "Is it possible that she has ties to the Extremists? Or maybe to Razeen? Is it possible she was in on this from the start?"

Nils couldn't answer. How well *did* he know Meg? Not well enough, apparently. She'd *lied* to him. She'd used him.

For Amy's sake.

He closed his eyes and he could see Meg's face as she sat in that men's room. He could see her desperation and smell her fear.

He could feel her arms around his neck as she sobbed into his shoulder, see her brown eyes filled with tears as she told him the Extremists had ordered her to kidnap . . . the freaking *ambassador*.

She'd looked him in the eye and she hadn't even blinked as she'd lied.

To him.

"I don't know anything anymore, sir," Nils admitted to Paoletti, working hard to keep his voice from shaking and his hurt and anger from showing. "I thought I knew her pretty damn well. Ten minutes ago, I would have sworn on my mother's grave that there was no way in hell Meg would voluntarily get involved with any kind of terrorists. But I also would have insisted that she was incapable of lying to me, too. Obviously, I was wrong about that."

He looked from Paoletti to Bhagat. "If you're looking for answers, sirs, you're not going to find them from me. I'm as clueless as you are. She conned me completely, because even as I hear myself say all that, there's a part of me that's thinking I don't believe *any* of this. There's a part of me that's dead positive there's been a mistake, that despite the fact that she lied, *she's* still the victim here—that whatever she's done is because she thinks it's going to help save her daughter."

Nils stood up, pushing back his chair. "That's a pretty thorough con job." He had to get out of here, or he'd start asking Bhagat to make sure his agents didn't use excessive or—God help him—deadly force when they tracked Meg down. He had to leave before he started trying to convince the FBI that there was no way Meg would ever fire that weapon she had—the one that made her "armed and dangerous" on the APBs that were surely going out. But maybe he'd be wrong about her again, and this time his mistake would cost some of those FBI agents their lives.

He looked at Paoletti. "Sir."

His CO nodded. "You can go."

"But don't go far," Bhagat added.

The sky was getting lighter in the east, and Meg knew that back in Washington her disappearing act had surely been discovered by now.

She headed steadily south through Virginia on Route 95, still unable to believe she'd actually gotten this far.

The FBI would be looking for her. She was going to have to keep moving. She'd stop for coffee only at fast-food drive throughs, answer the call of nature at the side of a deserted road.

Osman Razeen was snoring in the backseat of the car, proof that the doctor's sleeping pills worked—particularly when triple dosed.

They'd be looking for her car. It was pure luck that it had still been parked on the street, three blocks away from the Kazbekistani embassy.

She'd racked up $150 in parking tickets, but it hadn't been towed. And the spare key was still where she'd always left it—in the little hidden box inside the left front wheel well. Her father had attached it there the first time she and Amy had visited, after they'd returned from overseas. She'd rolled her eyes at the time, but she hadn't argued with him. He'd attached a similar box to the very first car she'd owned, back when she was nineteen and still in college. She was grateful for it now.

Still, it wouldn't take the FBI long to figure out that her car wasn't in the parking garage beneath her condo building, and it would take about a second longer for them to get her plate number and put out an APB.

Yes, they'd be looking for her, but her car's color, make, and model—a three-year-old white Ford Taurus—was a popular one.

And she'd already switched license plates with a similar-looking car that was parked around the back of a cheap motel outside of Fredericksburg.

With any luck, the owners of *that* car wouldn't notice the different plates—her old plates—until long after she'd arrived in Orlando.

And exchanged Osman Razeen for Amy and her grandmother.

Meg didn't want to imagine what would happen to Razeen—or herself—after she made the exchange. In fact, there were a lot of things she didn't want to imagine.

Including the look on John's face when he realized she'd lied to him.

Meg looked at the clock on the dashboard. Four thirty. He was probably being told she'd escaped right now.

Despair and fatigue flowed through her in a dizzying wave, and she took another slug of her long-cold coffee.

So what? She made herself sit up taller and rolled her head slightly, trying to release some of the tension from her neck. She'd lied.

It wasn't as if she'd never lied to John Nilsson before.

Truth was, she'd lied to him pretty much endlessly, starting back in late June, nearly three years ago, starting with the words she uttered after seeing him for the first time in six months.

"John? Oh, my God, I didn't recognize you!"

Yeah, that had been pure baloney.

Meg had recognized him instantly, even before he called out to her, even just from the flash she'd seen of him out of the corner of her eye.

She'd recognized him from the way he was standing, from the smooth line of his jaw, from the glint of the late afternoon sun on the bit of his dark brown hair that escaped from beneath his hat.

And from his eyes.

U.S. Navy Ens. John Nilsson had average brown eyes. Unremarkable light brown eyes. Meg had spent the past six months convincing herself that several billion other people on this planet had eyes just like his.

But gazing into them again, she knew she'd been wrong.

He laughed at her words, and the Washington, DC, sidewalk seemed to shift beneath her feet. "Yeah, it's the dress whites. Bet you didn't think I'd clean up so well, huh?" he teased. "Try not to faint, all right?"

The stupid thing was, she *was* feeling lightheaded. Dear God, as good-looking as John had been dressed as a K-stani terrorist, he was perfection in his Navy dress uniform, rows of ribbons on his chest along with the gold trident that identified him as a SEAL.

The uniform made him look older—yeah, right. It made him look all of twenty-six.

"What are you doing here?" she asked, trying not to think of the way his tongue had felt in her mouth, trying not to blush at that sudden sharp memory.

"I'm in DC to make an appearance before an inquiry board," he told her. "They're conducting an investigation into that, um, incident in K-stan six months ago."

She forgot about being embarrassed. "You're not in trouble, are you?"

He made a face. "Nah. It's nothing. Some high-powered feathers got ruffled, and as the SEAL team leader, I've got to waste a few days explaining why I made the choices I did without going into any of the specifics about the op—the operation."

Meg wasn't quite sure whether to believe him. If it really

were nothing, he would be in California with the rest of his team, wouldn't he?

"I was there, too," she reminded him. "If there's anything I can say or do or add to your testimony that'll help . . ."

He smiled a warm, broad, relaxed smile that made his eyes even prettier. "Thanks, but . . ." He shook his head. "There's no testimony. Honest. It's really not that big a deal.

"So how are you?" he continued. "I heard you've been in DC for a while. Nearly six months, right?"

Call me. Meg couldn't hold his gaze. She'd thought about calling him, but only at two A.M., during her wildest dreams. "Amy and I left the Pit a few weeks after you did."

"Just you and Amy?"

She could feel him watching her. He was still smiling, but it was no longer so relaxed. "Yeah. Daniel and I are separated."

"I'm sorry," he said.

She glanced at him—she couldn't help it—and he snorted and rolled his eyes. "No, I'm not. I'm thrilled. He's an asshole. Congratulations, Meg. Let's have dinner tonight to celebrate."

Meg shook her head. "I can't."

"Sure, you can. Bring Amy, too. I'd love to see her. How is she? Probably three inches taller."

"No, it's not that." Meg took a deep breath. "Actually, Amy's spending the next two weeks visiting my grandmother in England." As she said the words, she felt another flare of anger at Daniel. "I'm just . . . I'm . . . really busy."

Another lie.

She had no plans for tonight because Daniel wasn't due back in town until some time next week.

Daniel's timing was—like nearly everything else he did—completely self-centered and oblivious to anyone else's wants and needs. Meg had told him Amy's schedule for the summer dozens of times. And he *still* couldn't manage to schedule his visit to Washington for one of the *other* six weeks that his only daughter would also be in town.

John was right. Her husband was an asshole.

And yet Meg had agreed to meet Daniel. To discuss reconciliation. He'd spent the past six months in therapy, dealing—allegedly—with his fidelity issues. He claimed that he'd changed. That he'd grown.

He'd been sending her and Amy gifts—surprise packages, flowers, wine. And child support checks that were four times the amount Meg had requested.

He sent her email nearly every day. He wanted his family back. But apparently only on his schedule.

"Even busy people have to eat," John told her. "Come on, I know this really great little Italian place that's completely off the tourist route. We can get something quick—a pizza if you want . . ."

Meg wasn't sure what she wanted, but as tempting as John's dinner invitation was, she knew that the last thing she *needed* was to have dinner in a quiet little Italian restaurant with a twenty-five-year-old man who kissed like a dream.

"I'm having dinner with Daniel next week," she told him. "We're going to be talking about getting back together, so . . ."

John didn't miss a beat. "Then you really need to have dinner tonight with a friend."

Meg just looked at him.

"Yeah, I'm disappointed," he admitted. "But that's the last you'll hear of it. If you don't want me to, I won't hit on you, Meg. I won't even bring the subject up again. I can do friends. We can play it that way. We did it before, right?"

"Did we?" she had to ask.

He put on a pair of sunglasses, hiding his eyes. "Yeah," he said. "Right up until the end, we were great as friends. And as far as me kissing you . . ." He shook his head as he smiled tightly. "I've spent about six months trying to figure out the best way to apologize, but I'm damned if I know how to do it. To be honest, I've had a real bitch of a week, I got into DC late last night, got up too early, and got ready for an oh-seven-hundred meeting that was postponed four times and finally—fifteen minutes ago—pushed off until the day after tomorrow. Besides you, I don't know a soul in DC, so if you turn me down, I'll end up having room service while I watch TV in my hotel room. Please, *please,* have dinner with me and let me try to apologize. I've missed you, Meg—I want us to be friends again."

Meg had agreed to have dinner with him. She knew all about being lonely. She was a sucker for sincerity, too, and his had seemed off the chart.

"I've missed you, too," she'd told him, and lied again. But that time her lie hadn't been to him. Her lie had been in telling herself that she could handle friendship with this man, in convincing herself that up until that last night in Kazbekistan her feelings for him *had* been that of a sister. She'd let herself pretend that they could easily slip back into that safe, well-defined relationship.

She should have known better than to believe herself.

As Osman Razeen continued to snore softly from the back of the car, Meg gripped the steering wheel more tightly and headed south as swiftly as she dared.

Once again leaving John Nilsson behind.

"Nana, I'm so hungry." Amy was trying desperately not to cry.

They'd awakened a half hour ago to the scent of eggs frying and some kind of corn bread being toasted.

The ropes that had been tied around Eve's ankles and wrists dug into her skin. Her stomach growled and there wasn't a single muscle in her body that didn't ache.

Last night—with their hands tied—they'd eaten the last of the lunch they'd prepared for their picnic by the Smithsonian. The man named the Bear had brought Eve's bag in from the van. Tossed it to them after rifling through it. The sandwiches had been smashed, but Amy hadn't complained. Now all that was left was a pack of butterscotch candies.

The Bear came into the room with a plate of food, but then sat down in the only chair, and proceeded to eat it himself.

"Please," Eve started to ask for something for Amy to eat, but he sharply shook his head, holding his fingers to his lips, glancing almost furtively back toward the kitchen.

The others were back there—the three men and that awful woman.

As the three other male kidnappers started talking again, arguing about God knows what, speaking in that unintelligible language over the incessantly blaring TV, the Bear leaned toward Eve, his own voice low. "We're running low on supplies. Don't ask for food, there's none to spare. If you stay silent and make no demands, then killing you is far more difficult a prospect than simply letting you sit. If you start asking for food, that all changes. Don't give us a reason to take you out into the swamp."

He scowled then as if he regretted his words, his semikindness. He had one of those faces that was almost entirely covered with beard. The rest seemed to be all big bushy eyebrows and darkly tanned skin.

When he scowled it was not at all ineffective.

The Bear focused his glower at his plate as the woman with the dead eyes, still carrying her enormous gun, came through the dining room and stopped in the doorway to look in at them. She was silent, and the Bear didn't even glance up at her. He just kept on eating, methodically cleaning his plate.

Eve tried not to look at her, tried to shield Amy from her soulless gaze. She tried to pretend they both were invisible, tried to look as if they weren't even using up very much oxygen.

Finally the woman went away.

The Bear kept on eating, finishing up the last of his eggs as Amy tried not to cry.

"Nana, my hands hurt."

"Shhh."

Eve could hear the woman clumping up the stairs, heard her door slam shut. From the kitchen came the sound of the TV. They wouldn't be seeing much more of the other three men until Howard Stern was over.

Abruptly the Bear stood up.

He put his empty plate down on his chair. As he came toward them, Eve tensed. But although he grabbed them roughly, he only cut their wrists free. He was still scowling as he snapped his jackknife shut and returned to his seat.

It was possible that this young man still had a bit of a soul, a morsel of conscience.

Eve rubbed Amy's wrists as she leaned back against the wall, holding the little girl close.

"Do you want to hear more of my story?" she pretended to ask Amy, when in fact, she was asking the Bear.

But he didn't move. He just kept on glaring at the floor.

Amy nodded yes. But then, with a glance in the Bear's direction, she whispered, "Mommy must be worried about us."

Eve could only imagine the panic Meg had to be feeling right now. Still, getting Amy upset about that wasn't going to help. "I think she'd be very proud of how brave you're being."

Another glance at the Bear, and Amy leaned closer, lowered her voice even more. And spoke in French, God bless the child for her cleverness. "What are we going to do?"

Eve's own French had never been particularly good. She didn't have Meg's or Amy's natural gift for languages. She remembered the year that Meg was twelve, she'd invited the girl to visit her in England for the entire summer. Two weeks after she'd arrived, Eve had discovered her granddaughter carrying on a conversation in Welsh with the woman who came in daily to clean the house. Two *weeks* and she'd already learned enough to chat. By the end of the summer, she was speaking like a native.

However, after more than fifty years and many trips across the Channel to France, Eve's French could be described as shaky at best.

But she knew enough to be able to communicate with Amy. "We wait," she told Amy now, in her patchwork French. "If I tell you to do something, if I tell you to run, you don't ask, you just do it, do you understand? You run and you don't stop running. You go get help and let the police come back for me."

Amy nodded, her small face so serious, her mouth a tight little line.

Children were growing up much too quickly these days. Eve thought of the sixth grade girls in Amy's school, taunting the fifth graders because they were *virgins*. How the world had changed since she was a child.

"You must try very hard not to cry," Eve continued in English. It didn't matter that the Bear overheard this part. Besides, she'd used up most of her broken French. "Especially if that woman is around. We must be very quiet then."

Amy nodded again. "I won't cry." Her lip trembled.

Please, God, help me keep this child alive. Eve glanced at the Bear. He was glowering at them again, and had been ever since Amy had first spoken in French.

"Where was I in the story?" Eve asked calmly.

"Ralph spent about a week teaching your brother to box," Amy remembered, "while you hid from him."

"That's right," Eve said. "And then it happened. The awful day I'd been dreading. Ralph finally sat down with Nick and a reading primer."

She settled Amy more comfortably against her. "I was going into the library, thinking Ralph and Nick would be safely ensconced in the garage practicing their jabs and hooks. My plan was to take a book and lose myself up in the orchard until Ralph had gone safely back to town. But they weren't in the garage, Nick and Ralph. They were there in the library. And as I went in, Nicky bolted out of there so fast, he knocked me over. Literally. I went flying. Arse over teakettle right there in the corridor."

Amy only managed a wan smile at Eve's use of the A-word.

"He didn't stop to see if I was dead or alive," Eve continued. "He just shouted, 'Make him go away,' and bolted, the little beast. But Ralph had been right on Nick's heels, and although he managed not to step on me—which I honestly appreciated—he had to do what I'm positive was the world's very first triple lutz. It was beautiful—or it would have been if he hadn't skidded on a throw rug and landed hard on *his* butt."

Thank God she'd been wearing her blue jeans. It would have been horrendously embarrassing if she'd been lying there with her skirt up over her head.

"Are you all right?" Ralph scrambled to his feet, sliding a little more on the throw rug as if he were part of some slapstick vaudeville act, before he managed to regain an upright position.

Eve had smacked the back of her head on the floor. It was throbbing and she felt a little queasy, but she wasn't about to tell *him* that.

"Nick!" she called in the direction her brother had vanished. "Get back here, you little creep!"

"No, let him go," Ralph said. "I mean, well, he's already gone, and it was . . . it was entirely my fault for . . . for . . ."

As he helped her to her feet, she knew without a doubt that he'd never seen a woman in blue jeans before. He looked stunned.

"Did you call him stupid?" She glared at him. "I may be a girl, but I swear, if you called my brother *stupid*, I'll throw you off this property with my bare hands and then I'll get a gun and *shoot* you if you try to come back!"

"Didn't you just call him names yourself? Something like . . . little creep, it was, I believe."

"Please leave." Eve could do haughty quite well. It had been one of her mother's specialties, too, used on those rare occasions when things weren't happily going her way.

"I didn't call him stupid," Ralph told her calmly. "I'd never say such a thing to a child. He was the one who used the word. And I informed him he was wrong, that I happen to think he's uncommonly bright. He then proceeded to call *me* stupid and ran from the room. I'm going to go track him down and give him the rest of the day off—tell him to go find young Rupert Harrison from down the lane and spend the afternoon fishing. What *are* you wearing? It's lovely but I think you might've misplaced your six guns and cowboy hat somewhere west of the old Chisholm trail."

"Women wear trousers like this in California all the time," Eve told him defiantly. That wasn't exactly true—movie actresses like her mother had worn blue jeans at times, because they created such a stir. Eve wore them because they were comfortable. And they reminded her of home.

"I see." Ralph nodded. "My mistake." He cleared his throat. "Tell me, have I done something to offend you? You've managed to avoid me quite admirably this past week—one would think you'd trained for years with Scotland Yard. However, if there's something I should apologize for . . . ?"

Eve felt herself blush. "I just thought it might be easier for you to do your job if I weren't around. I was . . . trying to help."

"That's very kind," he said. "But unnecessary. In fact, I

think Nick was a little disappointed that you didn't come to watch him box."

"But I did watch," she told him. "Nicky knows. I told him I . . ." She'd told him she didn't want to get too close to his tutor. That her plan to get rid of him depended on her remaining something of a mystery.

Ralph smiled at her. "Well, then," he said. "One of us was definitely disappointed. If it wasn't Nick, it must've been me. Look, if you're still keen on helping, I could use some today—some real help, that is. I need a ride into town—if you're not in the middle of something else. Like a roundup of the herd of longhorns on the back forty."

She narrowed her eyes at him.

"I have to confess to an addiction to American dime novels," he admitted with a smile. "If you give me a ride, I promise I'll make no more cowboy jokes."

He wanted a ride. "Well," she said. "Sure, I can drive you to town. What for?"

He didn't seem at all put off by her less than gracious inquiry.

"It's a long story; I'll explain in the car." He was already halfway down the hall. "Let me set things straight with Nick, and I'll meet you by the garage in ten minutes. Is that long enough for you to change?"

Eve crossed her arms and lifted her chin. "Why would I change?"

He turned back to face her. "You should, of course, wear whatever you like. Of course."

"But . . . ?" The word was there, dangling unspoken, so Eve said it for him.

Ralph cleared his throat delicately. "You will, however, cause minor traffic accidents in your, ahem, current outfit— as well as make it difficult for fifty percent of the population to concentrate on the task at hand—myself included. And no doubt the other fifty percent will spend some not small amount of time giving you thoroughly disapproving looks."

"I'm American," she said. "I get thoroughly disapproving looks from Englishwomen as soon as I open my mouth and speak."

"I apologize for that." He took several steps back toward

her. "Of course, I must add that I doubt your generalized statement is *entirely* accurate—surely there are one or two Englishwomen out there who don't automatically disapprove of beautiful young Americans, but nevertheless, I do apologize."

"The way I figure it, if *most* of you English are going to disapprove of me—and it's not just the women, it's the men, too—I might as well wear whatever I damn well want, right?"

"Now, *there's* a good American attitude. Your ancestors must've been those fellows who threw all the tea into Boston Harbor," he told her. "And by the way, have I mentioned how completely, utterly, *entirely* I approve of both what you're wearing and the fact that you're an American? If you like, I'll even sing a few bars of your 'Star Spangled Banner' while I salute you."

Eve laughed. She couldn't help it.

"Don't you dare change your clothes," he ordered her. "Drive me into town just like that—I'll be the envy of every man within a hundred mile radius. And we'll stick our tongues out and recite your Pledge of Allegiance to anyone who disapproves. How's that?"

He was serious.

Well, *half* serious, anyway.

And Eve knew she'd been right in keeping her distance from Ralph Grayson. She liked him. Much too much. She liked the idea of him here for the entire summer. But he'd already started trying to teach Nick to read, and even though he hadn't called her brother stupid, Ralph's lesson had made him *feel* stupid.

It wasn't going to work.

Make him go away.

Eve still had the power to do just that.

She'd let them be seen in public together. She'd hang on his arm and flirt with him mercilessly. She'd lean close and gaze into his eyes so that anyone who saw them would assume they were romantically involved.

And then she'd tell him how old she really was.

"I'll meet you by the garage in a few minutes," she told Ralph.

His smile was warm and immediate.

And Eve felt like a snake.

"It wasn't until we were in the car," she told Amy and the Bear, who was definitely listening, "and I was about to make the turn to go into Ramsgate, that he told me to take a different road entirely. And I realized then that when he'd said he'd wanted a ride into town, he'd meant Town with a capital T. He wanted to go to London. Of course, I was terrified—I'd never driven into the city before.

"I pulled over to the side of the road, ready to cop to the truth, about to have a panic attack. I was about to confess that I didn't have a driver's license, sure that he would realize I wasn't really twenty years old, but he didn't even blink when I told him he was going to have to drive. He thought I was nervous about driving in the city—didn't give my reasons a second thought. We just switched seats, and he took over the wheel.

"And while I was catching my breath," Eve told them, "he told me that we were going to London to do some research at one of the larger libraries there."

She could see him as clearly as if it were yesterday. The window was open and he rested his arm on the door. The wind tousled his hair as he turned to her and smiled and said, "Have you ever heard of something called *word blindness*?"

Mystified, she'd shaken her head no.

"Ralph believed that Nick was dyslexic," she told Amy and the Bear. "But this was back in 1939, remember, and it wasn't called dyslexia at the time. And it was pure luck— no, I take that back. It was conscientiousness and a desire to be informed about everything under the sun that made Ralph read an article about the innovative work several doctors were doing with people who couldn't read. People for whom their inability to read seemed due to physical limitations rather than lack of intelligence. Apparently they'd discovered some new techniques that helped these people. But Ralph had read only one small article, and we were going into London to find out as much about this as we possibly could.

"He told me that he hadn't mentioned anything at all about this to Nick—he didn't want to get his hopes up.

Ralph wasn't sure how this new teaching method worked, if it even would work with Nick, or if Nick truly was afflicted with this word blindness."

"The only thing I know for certain," he'd told her in the car that afternoon, with the wind blowing through his hair, looking like the poster boy for all of England, "is that your brother is *not* stupid."

They talked about Nick, nonstop, all the way to London. Ralph had been impressed, just from talking to the boy, at how well-read he was for someone who couldn't get through a baby's primer. Nick had told him that Eve read to him. At least an hour, sometimes more, usually two, every day. But in the weeks since he returned from that awful boarding school, he'd avoided their nightly sessions. It seemed to make him angry—as if having his sister read to him was proof that he was stupid.

Eve admitted to Ralph that she had also written for Nicky in the past. He had a vivid imagination and he would dictate long, complicated, fascinating stories while Eve wrote it all down, longhand, as fast as she possibly could.

"Maybe he's not merely not stupid," Ralph speculated. "Maybe he's some kind of genius."

And if *that* weren't enough to win her heart forever, when they were on their way back home, after many exhausting hours finding far too little information, Ralph broke the silence in the car by turning to Eve again.

The sun had long gone down, and she knew he must've been tired, but he didn't look it in the darkness.

"I've been thinking and it seems to me that the first thing we need to do is restore Nick's self-confidence," he told her. "We need to figure out a way to renew his spark, to make him *want* to learn again—to learn about everything—not just to read. Even if he never does read, Eve, he has to realize that doesn't make him stupid. And there *are* other ways for him to gain the knowledge he needs to be a well-rounded man. We'll just have to be a little creative—and make him understand that there's nothing wrong with listening while someone reads aloud. I'd be in heaven," he admitted with a smile, "to have you following me around, reading to me all day."

"He pulled up the drive," Eve remembered, "and stopped the car outside of the garage. We both got out of the car, and he started getting ready to ride his bike back into town. It was very late—the Johnsons had already gone to bed and we were alone, and I was unable to stop myself. I thanked Ralph for all he was doing, all he'd already done, and I found myself sort of launching through the air, toward him. It was strange. I knew it was the last thing I should do, but there I went. Right into his arms. And I hugged him, and thanked him again, and even cried a little bit—I was so overwhelmed at the thought that he might actually be able to help Nicky, that we might have found someone who was on our side.

"He was surprised, I think mostly because I was suddenly so emotional. It's one thing to have a girl in your arms when you're standing out under the moon, but it's another thing entirely when she's all weepy. But he was very kind, and he held me close—although he was still very much the gentleman.

"I told him that I had been trying to think of ways to make him leave, but now I hoped he'd stay forever."

Ralph had laughed at that, but when he'd pulled back to look at her, his eyes were very serious. "Forever's a long time," he whispered.

His arms were still around her, and he was holding her so tightly she could feel the taut muscles in his shoulders and chest. He wasn't much taller than she was, but he was solid.

On the passenger ship from New York, a boy named Horace Wilkins had asked her to dance. He was seventeen and skinny and he'd held her much too close. She'd been afraid if she leaned too hard on Horace, he'd snap in half.

That wasn't so with Ralph. Ralph made her feel almost small and delicate.

And instead of smelling like the gin Horace had guzzled—showing off, no doubt—Ralph smelled like the butterscotch candy he'd bought for her in London and they'd shared in the car on the way home.

Would he taste sweet as well, she wondered wildly, if he kissed her?

His eyes were dreamy as he gazed down at her, and she

realized he was touching her, running his fingers through her hair.

"I want to kiss you," he murmured. "All day long, I've been dying to kiss you."

Eve's heart was already hammering in her chest, and now it got so loud, it seemed impossible he didn't hear it, too.

She stood there, frozen, just staring up at him.

And yet he didn't move either. He just looked at her. "I think I'm waiting for permission," he finally said breathlessly.

How could she give him permission to do something that would get him into such trouble?

Eve shifted back slightly, and he released her instantly. She put even more space between them, determined not to repay his kindness this way. "I . . . have to go inside."

He was uncertain and embarrassed. He tried to hide it behind a smile, but she could see it in his eyes, clearly illuminated by the full moon.

"I'm sorry," he started to say. "That was stupid of me. I'm a complete idiot and . . ."

He thought she didn't like him.

With her hand on the knob of the door leading into the house, Eve knew she should tell him the truth—that she was only fifteen—but she also knew that if she did, he'd never tell her that he wanted to kiss her again. Instead, she blurted out a different truth.

"I want to kiss you, too," she told him, needing him to understand, wanting his uncertainty to be banished.

The fire that leapt in his eyes was immediately hot. "Then why are you over there when I'm over here?" He started toward her.

She opened the door, about to bolt inside and slam it behind her. "Because you scare me."

As she watched, wary, Ralph forced himself to stop, to take a step back, away from her. "I do? I'm sorry, I didn't mean to—"

"Not *that* way," she tried to explain, but she was just making this worse. "It's not your fault. It's nothing you do. It's me. It's . . . this way you make me feel. As if when I'm with you nothing is bad, nothing could go wrong."

"But, Eve, that's *wonderful*."

"No, it's not," she told him, wanting to stamp her foot and cry. Wanting to throw herself into his arms and tell him the truth, wanting him to kiss her anyway to reassure her that it didn't matter, nothing mattered except for the fact that he'd fallen madly in love with her, too. "It's complicated and . . . and . . . You don't understand. There's no way it could work between us."

That was one of her mother's lines. *There's no way it could work between us.* She'd usually said it to appease some ardent young man who was convinced their week of passion should be immortalized by marriage—or at least another week of passion.

When her mother said it, she always added a tragic sounding sigh and an expression of desperate resignation.

Eve had to add nothing. The quaver in her voice was completely real. So was the sudden rush of tears to her eyes.

"Good night," she said with as much dignity as she could muster, going inside and shutting the door on both Ralph and the moonlight.

Nine

⤬

Nᴵᴸˢ ˢᴬᵀ ɪɴ the hotel room that had been Meg's for just a few hours before she left the premises with side arm in hand and a notorious Kazbekistani terrorist in tow.

He'd been turning this over and over in his head, and he couldn't believe that Meg was motivated by anything but fear for her daughter.

Someone had kidnapped Amy.

That much had to be true.

They were probably K-stani Extremists, just as Meg had said. She *had* been contacted by a man who was IDed as having ties to the Extremists. The videotape from her condo's parking garage confirmed at least that.

Yet she'd definitely lied when she'd told Nils that the Extremists had targeted the new ambassador for death.

In retrospect, it hadn't made much sense—why should they want to get rid of the ambassador? But Nils hadn't thought twice about it at the time. K-stani Extremists' motives didn't necessarily follow any rules of order or logic. Still, he should have wondered.

But targeting Osman Razeen . . .

Now *that* made sense.

Razeen was a longtime leader of the Islamic Kazbekistani Guard—called the GIK—a former political party outlawed by the K-stani government a decade ago. A few years back, Razeen had attempted to unite the GIK with the more radical Extremists.

Needless to say, he hadn't succeeded.

In the Extremists' somewhat volatile opinion, Osman Razeen had betrayed them, betrayed Islam, and therefore needed to die.

The Extremists and the GIK were all terrorists in the eyes of the K-stani government, and in the eyes of the U.S. as well—particularly after the GIK claimed responsibility for a bomb that killed over two hundred U.S. military personnel.

So while Meg had lied about the Extremists wanting the ambassador, it was probable that she'd merely substituted the ambassador for Osman Razeen, that the rest of what she'd told him was the truth. And it was possible that that substitution was her only lie—that and her lie by omission when she'd failed to mention the second gun hidden in her boot.

Of course, who knows what else she'd failed to tell him. If all along her plan had been to take Razeen out of the embassy, she probably had some way to contact the Extremists. She hadn't mentioned anything about that to anyone.

Still, lying by omission was the easiest way to lie. Nils had told her that himself. "If you're going to lie, stick as close to the real truth as possible. Don't give yourself too many things to remember. If you do, there's too many potential screwups waiting to happen."

He'd said those very words to Meg in DC nearly three years ago.

Nils closed his eyes. It was the day after he'd followed her over to the foreign service offices. The day after he'd managed to bump into her again "by accident."

They'd had dinner the night before—just two old friends, reconnecting after months apart.

For the most part, they'd managed to keep the conversation light. And the few times Meg had mentioned her dumb shit of a husband, Nils had kept his jaw tightly clamped shut.

He hadn't said any of the things he'd been dying to say. That she shouldn't be wasting her time with that loser. That anyone who'd cheat on her didn't deserve a second chance.

Nils also didn't mention that Daniel Moore was the main reason he was in DC for this pain-in-the-ass inquiry. Moore wanted heads to roll—Nils's in particular—for publicly embarrassing the staff at the American embassy in K-stan six months ago. He was pushing hard to bring charges up against Nils and his team of SEALs.

That wasn't going to happen—Nils had been reassured by both Team Sixteen's CO *and* Adm. Chip Crowley himself. In fact, the admiral had shaken his hand and thanked him for getting Abdelaziz out of K-stan—for a job well done.

But Daniel Moore was high enough on the food chain in the foreign service office to demand this inquiry—this complete and utter waste of Nils's far-too-precious time.

Nils was going to have to go in there, answer a bunch of tough questions without revealing any details of what had been a highly covert op, and—worst of all—he was going to have to apologize.

He could do it. He could give the most poetic, most sincere sounding apology and not mean a single word. And he *would* do it, because Admiral Crowley had asked him to.

He'd stand there and look Daniel Moore in the eye and apologize for something he'd not only done right, but he'd also done well.

But wouldn't it be sweet if, as he stood there making that apology, he was remembering—in detail—how he'd nailed Moore's wife?

Moore's extremely *hot* wife. Whom the bastard not only neglected and cheated on, but whom he'd let move half a world away, in a separation that had lasted nearly six months.

Nils couldn't believe Meg wanted to get back together with the prick.

And now he was going to have to make that apology looking into the prick's eyes with the knowledge that after the inquiry was over, Moore was probably going to go home to her and . . .

God, Nils wanted her.

He sat there at dinner, tied in knots, convinced that this woman wasn't going to sleep with him—not tonight, probably not in this lifetime. Yet despite knowing that, he was *still* happier than he'd been in months. Simply because she was smiling at him again.

Meg had mentioned—really just in passing—that while Amy was gone, she was hoping to find the time to paint the girl's bedroom.

That was how Nils had found himself, at 1015 the next

morning, on the twelfth floor of a modest DC apartment building, elbow-deep in pale pink paint.

And *that* was how he found himself walking down Pennsylvania Avenue at 1145—after Meg "convinced" him that they should escape the paint fumes in the apartment while the first coat dried, and go out to eat.

Yeah, he'd taken a lot of convincing.

"So where are you taking me for lunch—the White House?"

Meg turned to give him one of those smiles that melted his guts. "Would you believe me if I told you I have a personal connection to the Oval Office and I'm welcome there any time for lunch?"

"Yes."

She laughed. "For a Navy SEAL, you're pretty gullible, Nilsson."

"No, it's just . . . some people can't lie, and, sorry, Meg, but you're one of 'em."

"What, do I have a guilty twitch that gives me away?"

Nils laughed and put his hands in the pockets of his shorts. He had to. He'd been about to reach for her. To take her hand or put his arm around her shoulders. What was he doing here? This was an exercise in total frustration.

"I don't know," he said. "Tell me a lie, and I'll watch for one."

She laughed as he took advantage of the opportunity and let himself really look at her. She had laughter lines around her eyes, and a wide, generous mouth that was almost always curving up into a smile. He knew she was older than he was, but he couldn't even guess by how much. Not that it mattered to him. Her attitude was pure eight-year-old. She loved life completely and it showed it her eyes. It made her ageless and so beautiful, it hurt.

"I don't even know where to start," she admitted. "I don't know any lies."

"See?" he said.

"No," she said. "Wait. Help me out here. Give me a clue—what do people lie about?"

"Relationships. They lie when they cheat on a lover. Although those are mostly lies of omission. I mean, it's not as if when you come home, your wife says, 'So how was your

day, dear? Have any adulterous affairs with anyone I know?'
so that then you can lie and say, 'No.' "

"That's not funny."

"Sorry." He *was* sorry. But what he really wanted to say
was that her getting back together with her cheater husband
was *also* extremely unfunny. He opened his mouth, but she
stopped him with a touch on his arm.

"Let's not go there," she said. "Please?"

For several heartbeats, Nils just gazed into her eyes. *Please.*
How could he do anything but acquiesce?

They walked for a minute in silence, heading west on
Constitution Avenue now, with Nils wishing she was still
touching him, wishing he'd had the nerve to tell her that he
wanted to talk to her about Daniel. As her friend, he wanted
to make sure she'd thought this reconciliation thing through.

As her friend—yeah, right.

Meanwhile, he'd completely killed their conversation.
What had they been talking about anyway? Lying? Great.

"People lie about their past," he told her. He knew all
about that. "So why don't you tell me a lie about when you
were a kid. I know—tell me about when you were sixteen
and you ran off to join the circus."

Meg looked at him, eyes wide. "But I *did* run off to
join the circus when I was sixteen. Well, it wasn't really a
circus—it was one of those traveling carnivals."

For a half second, Nils actually believed her. But then she
went on.

"Life at home was so miserable, I figured *any*thing was
better—"

"Nah," he said. "Nope. You lose. Your delivery was really
good—that big eyes thing was a great touch, but you need to
remember who you're lying to. I know you pretty well. You've
already told me you had a storybook childhood. Parents
who backed you no matter what you did, two adoring younger
sisters, right? Bonnie and . . . Kelly?"

"Kiley." She looked at him with admiration. "I can't believe you remember that."

"Yeah, well, I didn't remember it."

"Close enough."

"No," he said. "No such thing as close enough. Not if

you're trying to get away with a lie. You have to be exact, every time. No slipups. See, what you did wrong was you took what was already a big lie—running away to join a carnival—and you made it more complicated than it had to be by lying about the way it was at home, too. If you'd told me you'd run off to join the carnival because *even though things were great at home*—the truth, right?—your mother once got you so mad that you wanted to scare her. And then you think of a time when your mother got you really pissed—something that really happened, and you plug that little truth into your big lie and . . ."

Meg was laughing.

"What?" he asked. Her laughter was so contagious, he found himself smiling back at her.

"I can't believe you're teaching me how to lie."

"I'm not," he said. "Teaching you. Because you're never going to use any of this. I mean, when are *you* going to lie? Never. Maybe when you rob Fort Knox, right?" He snorted. "Like that's going to happen."

"I don't have a lot of opportunity in my job to practice lying," she agreed. "Unlike you." She gazed at him, all teasing gone from her face. "If I hadn't guessed that you weren't Abdelaziz, would you have told me, John? You know, after the real Abdelaziz was safely on board that U.S. aircraft carrier?"

He didn't answer right away, and she smiled. "I know you, too, you know, and right now, you're deciding whether to tell me the truth or to lie. I won't be able to tell the difference. But I would appreciate the truth."

The truth.

"No, I wouldn't have told you," he admitted.

Just as he'd expected, she didn't like the truth, and he tried to explain. "I didn't want you to get into trouble, and if I'd told you—"

"Didn't it occur to you that I might want to help you? That I would be *able* to help you? Come on, John, we were already friends and—"

This time he cut her off. "But we weren't," he said. "Not really. You were friends with Abdelaziz."

Christ, why had he said that? Talk about writing all your insecurities on your ass and then mooning the world.

Meg, of course, didn't miss it. "How often do you do that kind of role-playing thing—you know, take on different personas?"

All the time. In fact, every minute he was awake.

Nils could do a convincing version of slightly bored and very relaxed even when facing enemy fire. But for the life of him, he couldn't seem to pull it off right now. Or maybe it would have been convincing to most people, but not to Meg. He was certain that despite her protests otherwise, this woman could see right through him.

"Not often," he told her. "Most of our missions are covert— we go in and out without anyone knowing we've even been there."

She was watching him as they walked, and he could've sworn that she could see everything that he *wasn't* saying, streaming out behind him in a long, tangled, messy trail.

But she didn't call him on it. She nodded. "I can't even imagine what it is that you do."

"Mostly I do what you do. I'm a languages specialist. I translate . . . stuff."

Meg laughed. "Yeah, except you probably don't do your translating the way I do—in an office, on a desk, with plenty of good light and a definite shortage of people shooting at me."

"People don't shoot at me."

That was the truth—at least most of the time. But Nils knew she didn't quite believe him.

They walked for a moment in silence, until Meg turned to him and said, "Where did you grow up?"

"Long Island."

"What's with the accent?"

"What accent?"

"My point exactly," she said. "Now, I'd figure you were lying about Long Island, except that you're smarter than that. You *know* I'd wonder about the accent, so you must *really* be from Long Island. Unless you figured *I'd* figure you *had* to be telling the truth because you had no New York accent—"

"Amagansett," he said. "Out by Montauk and East Hampton. You know, silver spoon country. Old money. We don't do accents." He did his best slightly bored aristocrat for her. "How droll of you to think otherwise."

It got the laugh he was hoping for.

"So why'd you join the Navy?" Meg asked.

"You mean, instead of the family business?" Nils smiled. Everything he was telling her was the truth. It was entirely up to her as to how to interpret it. "You would have had to meet my father to understand. He died two years ago, had a stroke about five years before that. He couldn't speak and was in a wheelchair, but he was still capable of driving the nurses crazy at the retirement home."

"Your mother . . . ?" she asked.

He shook his head. "She's been . . . gone a little bit longer." That one wasn't quite a full lie, but it was close. His mother had been dead for so long he almost couldn't remember what it was like back when she was alive.

Almost.

"I'm sorry," Meg said. Most people didn't mean it when they said they were sorry, but Meg did.

"Your folks are both still around, right? Still living in . . ." Nils made a face. "Don't tell me . . . I'll get it . . . Massachusetts . . . western Boston suburb . . . Ah, hell, help me out here."

"Nope," she said. "This time we're talking about you. I'm still trying to figure out which part of that story you just told me was the lie."

"Why would I lie to you?" he asked.

"I don't know," she mused. "I haven't figured that out yet either."

Sam found John Nilsson sitting on the floor in what had been Meg Moore's hotel room.

"I should have searched her," Nils said, shaking his head in disgust, as Sam hunkered down next to him.

"You were at a disadvantage," Sam told his friend, "considering that you've wanted to get with her for three years now. She was crying on your shoulder, man—you were distracted." He laughed. "And you know, I still don't know if there should be an *again* added to that first sentence. You are one secretive bastard, Johnny."

"She's going to die. The FBI are going to track her down, and they're going to use deadly force and . . . Ah, *Christ.*"

Sam stared out at the blandly decorated hotel room, pretending not to see the tears in Nils's eyes. "We could find her first."

"Yeah, right." Nils laughed, but there was no humor in it. He used the heels of his hands to brusquely wipe his face. "Like I have any kind of a clue where she went when she left DC."

"Well." Sam cleared his throat. "That's the interesting part. Remember that long-distance tracking device Wild-Card's been working on?"

Nils looked up sharply, meeting Sam's gaze for the first time. His eyes were redrimmed; it was obvious the man hadn't slept more than a few hours in too many days to count.

"She's moving south on Route 95," Sam told his friend. "I'm on duty in about five minutes, so unless you want to wait for my shift to end—"

"Hell, no. Sorry, but—"

"I figured. That's why WildCard's in the lobby with his laptop. If the two of you leave now, with a little luck, you can find her and be back by dinnertime."

"For the next few weeks," Eve told Amy and the Bear, "Ralph and I worked with Nicky. We were determined to erase his fear of learning, of being labeled *stupid*. We focused on having fun. I remember, Ralph made us dress up as smugglers from the days of the Napoleonic Wars and took us exploring the network of caves that ran all along that part of the coast.

"And we did our own archeological dig—uncovered mostly mud and a few suspiciously familiar looking spoons I'm sure Ralph seeded in the site. We went fishing and studied the local marine life, flew kites and learned about weather and wind, and had picnics by the sea. And as we sat on our blanket, Ralph would beg me to read aloud to him—to *him*, not to Nick, mind you. Of course, Nick couldn't help but overhear.

"And slowly but surely Nicky came to life again. We started to read not just from books, but from plays as well—with both Ralph and me playing a role. And one day Nick cleared his throat and asked if he could take a part, too. Ralph was so low-key about it. I was about to faint, I was so thrilled, but Ralph just matter-of-factly figured out a method for feeding Nick his lines. It was the most wonderful day."

She smiled ruefully at Amy. "At least until we returned to the estate for dinner. Ralph had been watching me during our walk home—I could feel his eyes on me. And I knew I'd done a poor job that day of pretending to be indifferent to him. Ever since that night in the moonlight, I'd been careful not to be alone with Ralph, and I tried not to let him see just how much I adored him. But that wasn't easy to do. Of course he never spoke of it when Nick was around, but he didn't understand why I always ran away from him.

"And that evening, just as I suspected, he asked for a private word with me. Nick went inside, and . . . there we were."

The early evening sun was still hot against her face. Her clothes were dirty and damp from perspiration and the sea spray. Tendrils of hair had long escaped her twist and they hung lankly around her sunburned face.

And yet Ralph looked at her as if he saw none of her imperfections.

"Why won't it work?" he asked, completely dissolving the past few weeks, bringing them right back to where they'd left off that night they'd come back from London. The ever-present glint of humor was gone from his eyes. He was utterly serious.

Eve had to tell him the truth. But she couldn't squeeze the words out past her heart, which was lodged firmly in her throat. She just shook her head and started for the door.

He caught her hand. "I have to know. Is it because . . . are you promised to someone else? Someone back in California?"

"No," she said before she could think straight, before she

realized that lying and saying yes would make Ralph—always such a gentleman—back away for good.

"Then there's hope," he said. "I dream of you at night, Eve."

She turned and ran—as fast and as far as she could.

"I stayed up for hours that night," Eve told Amy and the Bear, "writing Ralph a note, explaining that I was much younger than he thought. I wanted to be honest with him—to do the right thing. But my good intentions were completely blown to Hades the next day."

Nick had woken her up, pulling back the heavy curtains in her room to reveal brilliant sunshine and a near perfect morning. Mrs. Johnson was packing them a picnic basket, he announced. They were going out for a jaunt in the *Daisy Chain*.

Ralph knew her weaknesses well. And although she'd planned to excuse herself from the day's adventures, to drop her note into his hands and vanish from sight for a few million years, she found herself—a short hour later—floating on the almost ridiculously calm surface of the usually far more turbulent English Channel. The note she'd written was in the pocket of the dress she'd thrown on over her bathing suit.

"Today we shall read a play," Ralph announced grandly, after they'd eaten their fill of Mrs. J.'s delicious cold chicken, "by Master William Shakespeare." He took out his familiar tin of butterscotch candies. Butterscotch, he always said, went famously with the Bard.

Nicky was tempting fate, risking an unplanned dip in the ocean by dangling himself off the bow, but he turned eagerly, coming back to join them on the deck. He caught the piece of candy that Ralph tossed to him. "I'm Puck!"

"Excellent," Ralph enthused. He held out the tin for Eve, far too much of a gentleman to throw candy in her direction. "Except for the fact that Puck doesn't play a part in *Romeo and Juliet*."

"Oh, yuck, a love story?" Nick leaned over the rope railing and pretended to throw up over the side.

Ralph grabbed him by the waistband and hauled him

back. "It's actually about murder and revenge, about two families who have been bitter enemies for years."

Eve saw that he had two worn copies of the play, yet he didn't open either of them once as he told Nick the opening of the story. He talked them right up to the scene where Romeo and Juliet first meet.

And then he gave one of the copies of the play to Eve.

"I don't suppose you'd want to be Romeo?" he asked Nick. "Or possibly Juliet? Remember, in Shakespeare's day, women weren't allowed on stage and boys played all the female parts."

"You wouldn't get me into a dress," Nick swore. "Not if you paid me a *thousand* dollars. I'll be the audience today," he decided. "Although I'd rather be fishing."

"I'm sure old Will had one or two folks in his audience who'd rather have been fishing," Ralph countered. "When we're done here, let me know if you think this story could've distracted them sufficiently, too."

"It's not gonna work," Nick muttered.

"If I were a betting man, I'd be tempted to place a wager on that."

Eve stood up, gesturing to the top of the cabin. "This can be Juliet's balcony," she told Ralph. "I can climb up there and—"

"And you will," Ralph countered, scrambling up to stand right there. "I always thought no red-blooded Romeo in his right mind would stay on the ground below after hearing Juliet say, 'O Romeo, Romeo, wherefore art thou, Romeo?' "

He spoke in a high voice, struck a pose, and Nick collapsed in a fit of giggles.

"Although rather long in tooth, *I* will be fair Juliet." He fluttered his eyelashes and Nick was with the program, although still a little grudgingly. "And Eve shall be my Romeo."

He jumped down off the cabin roof with a completely unladylike thud.

"You won't need this." Eve wound her hair up and put Ralph's hat on her own head. She began unfastening her buttons. "And *I* won't need my dress."

Ralph turned quickly away, the way he always did when

she stepped out of her clothes on the beach. It was silly—she was wearing a bathing suit underneath. What was the big deal?

All he succeeded in doing was to make her completely self-conscious. Which was dumb, since her blue and green flowered bathing suit covered her far more than the skimpy suits her mother had worn, lounging by their Hollywood pool.

"You better give Eve your pants," Nick ordered his tutor. "She doesn't look like much of a man in that. Better give her your shirt, too."

That would be a coup. Ralph never took off his shirt, even when they went swimming. But he did it now, pulling it over his head. And sure enough, there was a flush of pink on his cheeks as he handed it to her. He couldn't quite manage to meet her gaze, because—horrors—he was standing shirtless in front of her.

And the really dumb part was that he was built like a movie star. His skin was pale, though—but that was to be expected since he never took off his shirt.

"Every time I see an English baby, I'm amazed." Oh, cripes, she hadn't meant to say that *aloud*.

Ralph looked questioningly up at her, and, of course, she *had* to be gazing directly into his eyes as he figured out what she'd meant—that her amazement came from seeing the proof that an English man and woman had actually managed to quit having tea and apologizing to each other long enough to procreate.

They'd had this argument about Englishmen versus Californians—completely in fun—before. She thought that the English were too bloody polite. But now it took on a whole new edge.

"You'd prefer it if I weren't polite?" he murmured as he handed her his pants, too.

With his clothes on and his eyes twinkling, Eve could forget that he wasn't sixteen or seventeen. But dressed only in his bathing suit, it was obvious Ralph Grayson was a full-grown man. The muscles in his shoulders and arms were well defined and—it was hard not to stare—he had hair on his chest.

Thick and dark, it looked as if it would be soft to touch.

Eve jerked her gaze away, feeling her own cheeks flame, felt them heat even more as she realized the note she'd written to him last night was still in the pocket of her dress. Which he was now rather grimly stepping into.

"You'd make a fortune in Hollywood," she told him in her mother's voice—light and breezy—as she pulled on his trousers. They were still warm from his body heat, and his shirt was slightly damp from perspiration. It smelled of his soap and the distinctive brand of cologne he wore. It smelled of Ralph. She breathed in deeply as she pulled it over her head.

His pants were much too big for her, and she pulled his belt as tight as it would go.

"I'm not that good an actor, I'm afraid," he replied.

"I didn't mean as an actor," her mother's voice countered. "I meant as a gigolo." With his British accent, pretty eyes, and gentleman's manners . . . yeah, he'd make a bundle.

"Is that supposed to be some kind of California style compliment?" His voice was light but his eyes held danger.

Why was she doing this? She was playing with fire.

Nick was laughing at them both, unaware of the undercurrent of tension. "Eve, you look like a boy with your hair up like that, but Mr. Grayson is the funniest looking girl I've ever seen."

Ralph hadn't been able to button the top few buttons of her dress, and dark hair poked through the gapping neckline, in direct contrast with the tiny blue flowered print. It *would* have been funny, if she hadn't completely ruined things with her stupid comments.

"Act one, scene five," Ralph told Eve, flipping through the pages of his playbook.

"I'm sorry," she blurted. "I don't know why I'm so rude sometimes."

"I do, and it's all right," he said quietly. "I've got you figured out—so you can't offend me." He glanced up at her, and the smile he gave her was so sweet, Eve felt her eyes start to fill with tears.

"The line is yours," Ralph told her. " 'What lady's that which doth enrich the hand of yonder knight?' " He looked at Nick. "Romeo spots me while I'm dancing," he added, doing something that might be called dancing if you were from Mars, "and it's love at first sight."

The picture Ralph made, dressed as he was, hopping from one foot to another, swishing the skirt of her dress around, was unbearably funny.

Nick laughed so hard, he nearly fell off the boat.

Ralph would have won his bet. It wasn't long, as they read through the few scenes that were actually between Romeo and Juliet, and talked through the rest of the story, that the boy was completely absorbed by the play.

And by the time Juliet awakened from her feigned death to find Romeo dead by his own hand from poison, Nick was holding his breath.

" 'What's here? A cup closed in my true love's hand?' " Ralph wasn't reading anymore. He knew these words by heart. Eve kept her eyes tightly shut as she felt him gather her into his arms. He radiated such heat, she felt nearly on fire. After he gave it back, her dress would smell like Ralph. She would never wash it again.

She prayed he wouldn't feel the way her heart was pounding.

" 'Poison I see has been his timeless end.' " His voice broke. " 'O churl, drunk all; and left no friendly drop to help me after? I will kiss thy lips; haply some poison yet doth hang on them, to make me die with a restorative.' "

And then it happened.

Ralph kissed her.

It was the softest kiss, just the sweetest, gentlest pressing of his lips to hers.

Eve opened her eyes.

They were nose to nose, and she was in his arms, half lying across his lap.

She expected him to be shocked. She thought he would be appalled at what he'd done, but instead she couldn't begin to read the odd expression in his eyes. Was it a glimmer of . . . satisfaction? Had he planned this from the start?

"But wait, methinks I best try that again," he said. "Perhaps a deeper kiss will do this thing."

The lines weren't in the script, but he spoke in perfect, poetic iambic pentameter.

And he was going to kiss her again.

Eve knew she should move. She should tear herself out of his arms. She should leap up and away before he got himself into even more trouble.

" 'Go breath, go soul . . .' " Ralph's gaze was locked on hers, she couldn't have looked away, let alone moved out of his arms if her life had depended upon it. " '. . . with thou who holds my heart.' "

"That's you, sweet Eve," he whispered, and kissed her again. Not as Juliet kissing Romeo, but as Ralph kissing Eve.

And oh, it was wonderful. His lips were so soft against hers, his mouth was sweet. He tasted of butterscotch and sunshine.

She knew all about kissing from the movies, and she'd always been afraid of laughing the first time someone tried to put his tongue into her mouth.

But suddenly, there she was, kissing Ralph, and it wasn't funny or strange or even the slightest bit disgusting. Instead, it was perfect.

His mouth was warm and he tasted delicious. Dizzy and giddy and melting inside, she clung to him, wanting . . . what? She wasn't sure, but it definitely involved kissing him like this forever.

"Can we skip the kissing part?" Nick demanded plaintively.

Ralph pulled back, and Eve knew from the sudden flare of chagrin and embarrassment in his eyes that he was about to apologize for what had to be the best thirty seconds of her entire life and—God help her—transform back into a proper, too-polite Englishman.

She wasn't ready for that. Not yet. Maybe not ever.

"No," she told her little brother, grabbed Ralph by the front of her dress, and kissed him again.

She could taste his surprise, feel his laughter.

This time, when he kissed her back, he wasn't quite so gentle. This time her mouth—no, her entire body—felt on fire.

It was terrifying. And wonderful.

And over far too soon.

Ralph was breathing hard when he pulled away from her. She was, too—and her heart was pounding. And if it hadn't been, the heat in his eyes would've kicked it into double time.

"You *will* have dinner with me tonight," he told her.

Eve nodded. Yes.

He smiled then, and she knew she had no choice.

She reached around him, into the pocket of her dress, and took out the note she'd written just last night.

She scrambled to her feet and flung it over the side of the boat.

Ralph came to stand beside her as she watched it float for a moment, the ink slowly running and turning the paper blue, before it started to sink beneath the surface.

"What was that?" he asked.

"Nothing." She wouldn't tell him—she *couldn't* tell him. Not now. If he found out the truth now, after kissing her that way, he'd leave. She knew he would. And she'd be unable to bear that.

Instead she'd somehow manage to bear deceiving him.

She gave him a bright smile. "Shall we finish the play? Where were we? Romeo's dead and poor Juliet just found his body."

"No more kissing," Nick said.

As Ralph handed Eve her copy of the play, he smiled, and she knew. There'd be plenty more kissing.

Just not in front of Nick.

Ten

$\sim\!\!\sim\!\!\sim$

NILS HADN'T LIED to Lieutenant Paoletti. Not really.

The SEALs had been assigned to continue to be on standby at the K-stani embassy. Even though there was no longer any threat, even though Meg had escaped with Razeen, the FBI wanted them to remain.

The tape loop was going to be kept running, to avoid the embarrassment of having to explain the current situation not just to the Kazbekistanis but to all the CNN and other news cameras positioned outside. The SEALs' presence would help with the charade, at least until Meg Moore and Osman Razeen were apprehended.

Tom Paoletti had looked hard at Nils when he'd asked for the next thirty-six hours off. "Do you have a guess where Meg Moore is?"

"No, sir," Nils had said, looking Paoletti straight in the eye. And it wasn't a lie. Nils wasn't guessing. He *knew* where Meg was. "I need a whole lot of uninterrupted sleep." That wasn't a lie either. He needed the sleep—he simply wasn't going to get it.

Paoletti nodded. "Go and crash."

"Thank you, sir."

"John."

Nils turned back.

Lieutenant Paoletti looked tired, the lines in his tanned face more pronounced than usual. "This probably isn't going to have a happy ending. You know that, right? Meg's either way over her head with Razeen—in which case he may well have already overpowered her and . . ."

And killed her. Nils nodded. He knew that. There was a

chance he wouldn't be tracking Meg with WildCard's system, but rather Meg's body.

"Or she's working *with* Razeen," Paoletti continued, "in which case she's not who you thought she was. In which case she *never* was."

"I'm aware of that, L.T."

"Good." Paoletti didn't try to force a smile, the way some people might have. This sucked, and they both knew it. He didn't try to pretend that it didn't. It was one of the many things that made him a great CO. "I'm sorry, Johnny. Go get some sleep."

"Yes, sir." Nils turned and went, feeling like shit on a stick for being unable to come clean with the man.

He and WildCard had nearly made it out of the lobby when Senior Chief Wolchonok flagged them down. Wild-Card was needed back at the other hotel. There was some kind of technical glitch with the backup tape loop that only the boy genius could handle.

WildCard told the senior he was on his way, handed Nils his laptop, and gave him a crash course in his tracking system. Nils would need to use a cell phone hooked into the computer, and he could run the laptop with an extension cord that plugged into any car's cigarette lighter. Easy as pie.

WildCard went in one direction, Nils in another. He rented a car, picked up some coffee, and within thirty minutes was heading south on Route 95.

Nils knew Sam would be pissed that he'd gone after Meg by himself, but every minute that he delayed, she was getting farther away. And while he wasn't exactly UA—guilty of an unauthorized absence—there were elements of potential goatfuck written all over this.

Yes, if he managed to find Meg and bring both her and Razeen back alive, everything would be cool. But if something went wrong, the FBI was going to start shouting about aiding and abetting and obstruction of justice and God knows what else. It was bad enough that Sam and WildCard were involved. Nils couldn't bring any of his other teammates into this mess.

The sound of the tires against the road was much too soothing and Nils turned on the radio to keep himself awake. He didn't have time to be exhausted, but his body was struggling to stay alert. The fatigue came in waves—he had to fight harder when it hit. Country music blared, and over it, Lieutenant Paoletti's voice seemed to echo, tinny and distant, like some disconnected DJ who didn't realize the mike was still on.

If she's involved with Razeen, she's not who you thought she was.

This wasn't a good sign. When Nils started hearing voices in his head, echoes of conversations past, he was well on his way to falling asleep.

And at 80 mph, that could be messy.

He opened the hot top on his coffee and took a sip even though it was still close to the temperature of molten lava. It burned all the way down.

Pain was good. Pain meant he was awake. He took another even bigger slug, making his eyes tear. Christ, even his stomach felt scalded.

Paoletti's words still echoed, but he was over the hump. He was awake, and by the time he finished the large cup of coffee, the caffeine would have kicked in.

If she's involved with Razeen, she's not who you thought she was.

That was for damn sure.

Best case scenario had Nils catching up to Meg when she stopped to get some sleep at a roadside motel. He could get through the cheap lock on the door in a heartbeat and once inside . . .

Worst case scenario had Nils walking in to find Meg and Razeen together, in bed.

Yeah, that would be just about as bad as it could get.

Well, maybe not. It might be a little bit worse if Meg then told him she and Razeen had hidden a nuclear device back in DC, and it was set to go off in thirty seconds.

"I don't know anything about you."

Meg's voice rang so clearly, Nils glanced in the rearview mirror to make sure the backseat of this rental car was still empty. No, her voice had definitely only been in his head.

He took another slug of coffee. Come on, caffeine . . .

Come on, brain, stay alert.

It had been—what?—nearly three years since she'd said those words to him? Yeah, it was that summer, six months after they'd first met in K-stan. They were having a picnic down by the Lincoln Memorial. Nils had been in DC for over ten days by then—his inquiry having been postponed for the sixth goddamned time.

He'd figured it out. The foreign service office was waiting for Daniel Moore to arrive back in the States. Apparently he was involved in some diplomatic mission that took precedence over the inquiry, something important enough to put a Navy SEAL ensign on hold for nearly two weeks.

Not that Nils had particularly minded.

After he'd finished helping Meg paint Amy's bedroom, he'd found other excuses, other reasons to show up at her apartment.

And she'd welcomed him.

Probably because he was playing things completely cool, restraining himself from throwing her over his shoulder and carrying her into her bedroom, tossing her onto her bed and . . .

He always greeted her with a smile instead of a soul kiss. He always tried to stay at least three feet away from her, and he never, ever grabbed her in the elevator and nailed her to the wall.

Even though he wanted to more than just about anything.

He played nice, and his reward was that they had lunch and dinner together every day.

And he comforted himself when he was alone in his hotel room at night by telling himself that lunch and dinner were far more than Daniel Moore was currently getting from her.

"I don't know anything about you."

She'd said it while eating a grape Popsicle. He'd never been so jealous of a piece of ice before in his life.

"What, are you kidding?" he'd asked. "I've done nothing *but* talk about myself for the past week. I feel like I've been interviewed by Barbara Walters. What don't you know? I was born on Long Island, when my mother died I lived with my father and my uncle and his wife. We covered this. I attended Milfield Academy—the best private school in the state—went to Yale, joined the Navy—"

"You talk about it as if it's someone else's life," she said. "As if you're listing facts you've memorized or—"

He looked at her. "What is that supposed to mean?"

She instantly apologized. "I'm sorry, I didn't mean to make it sound as if I don't believe you."

"But you *don't* believe me."

"I do. John, I just . . ." She leaned toward him. "I want to know the rest. I want to hear all the parts you're leaving out."

Nils was silent. What could he say to that?

She touched him then. She put her hand on his knee.

"How come you never want to walk past the Vietnam Memorial?" she asked quietly.

He looked down at her hand, knowing that if he were flip, she'd probably take it away. Still . . . "I'm not sure I know what you're talking about," he said.

"We've been down here on the Mall three different times this week, and each time you've gone way out of your way to avoid it."

Nils glanced in the direction of the Wall now. He knew he could probably satisfy her with some bullshit response. He could tell her the Vietnam Wall wasn't something he wanted to spend much time looking at. He could admit he found it too intense, without really telling her why. He could say that it wasn't something he could just walk casually past. Being career military and all . . .

And she would probably be satisfied. He took her hand, lacing their fingers together.

"My father and my uncle Al were both there," he said instead. "They both served in 'Nam."

Meg was surprised, and he watched her try to fit that information in with everything else he'd told her about his family. He'd told her about the family business—without going into detail as to exactly what type of business it was. Food industry, he'd told her, and although it was the truth, it was a very stretched truth. His father and uncle had owned a fishing boat. And after they'd lost that, his dad had had a job as a short order cook at the local diner for about a month or two.

Food industry. Right.

"Al lost his leg," he told her now.

"I'm so sorry." Somehow she'd moved closer, so that her thigh was now pressing against his, so that she could reach up to brush a lock of hair back from his forehead.

Please, God, don't let this woman ever stop touching him. Nils kept talking, wanting her to stay close, wanting her to know.

"Neither of them came home in body bags, but at the same time, neither of them ever really came home." He'd never said this to anyone before. He'd hardly even let himself *think* it. "Whenever I look at it—the Wall—and I see that list of names, all I can think is, why aren't their names up there, too, you know? They should both be listed among the casualties. You didn't have to die in 'Nam to lose your life there."

Meg's eyes were wide. "I don't get it," she said. "How does the son of a Vietnam vet become a professional warrior?"

"SEALs aren't warriors, Meg. We're peacekeepers. What we do is *prevent* wars. And if they start before we can get there, we do whatever we have to do to end 'em, fast." Nils shut his mouth, embarrassed. What was wrong with him? John Nilsson didn't rant like that. He rarely raised his voice.

"Thank you," Meg said.

He looked up at her. She was so close. All he had to do was lean forward a few inches and . . .

Meg released his hand and moved back, away from him, as if she'd just realized she'd been nearly sitting on his lap. "May I ask you another personal question?"

Nils laughed. "Suddenly you feel the need to ask permission?"

She hugged her knees in to her chest, looking up at the hazy clouds. There was the slightest breeze that ruffled her dark hair and kept the afternoon from being too oppressively warm. "This one's *really* personal."

He lay down next to her on the picnic blanket, dying to take her into his arms, but careful, as always, not to get too close. "Shoot."

"Do you have a girlfriend back in California?" she asked.

He laughed as he propped his head up on one elbow. That was an easy question. "No, I don't."

She turned to look at him. "Then, what do you do for sex?"

Nils choked and had to sit up, fast. "I can't believe you just asked me—"

She rearranged her legs so that she was sitting tailor style as she laughed at him. "I *told* you it was kind of personal."

He looked at her over the tops of his sunglasses. "*Kind* of . . . ?"

She actually blushed even though she was still laughing. "Okay, so it was a really rude and intrusive question. It's none of my business, but I like you and—"

"If there really is a God, you'll finish that sentence by saying that you want to have sex with me."

She laughed even harder, pushing at him slightly. "*No, that's not* what I was going to say. Don't be ridiculous. I just . . . You're such a nice guy, John, and you probably don't get a lot of time off, and it just—I don't know—seems a shame that you aren't taking advantage of this week. There are probably a million single women in this city who would *love* to have dinner with you. With hardly any effort you could—"

"Get laid?"

"Maybe find someone special, and yes," she said, rolling her eyes, "get laid, too. In a good way."

"Is there a bad way to get laid? Gee, I wasn't aware."

"You know what I mean. I'm not talking about a cheap one-night stand. That's dangerous these days, anyway. I'm talking about a meaningful relationship with someone—"

"Special. Right. Well, maybe I've already found someone special." Nils didn't know what demon made him say that, but it instantly took all the teasing and fun out of the conversation.

Meg wouldn't look at him. She began gathering up their garbage from lunch—sandwich wrappers and the paper that had been around her Popsicle. "I have a friend named Joelle. She's single, she's really sweet—pretty, too. She's about your age and she's—"

"Horny?"

She looked up at him, recrimination in her eyes. Not funny. "She's special." She went back to organizing the garbage. "I was thinking about that embassy function tomorrow night. I don't think it's a good idea for you to go as my escort. I'm afraid—"

"You're afraid that you like me too much," Nils realized. Holy Christ. *That's* what this was about.

"These past few weeks have been great," she said quietly, and he tried to focus, to listen, "but it's not real, John. I can't give you what you need, and all you're giving me is . . ." What? He was dying to know, but she broke off, shaking her head. "Look, it would be a lot easier to be friends with you if you were dating someone, *any*one. If not Joelle—"

"How do you know what I need?" he asked.

The look she gave him would have been comical if he'd felt like laughing, if his heart hadn't been lodged somewhere between his Adam's apple and his bronchial tubes. "I'm sorry, you are *so* not the priest type. I know what you need, Nilsson."

"Well . . . maybe getting laid's just not a priority for me right now."

She gave him another look. "Now why don't I believe that?"

"Not all men are like Daniel," he told her. "We don't all think with our dicks. Excuse my crudeness."

"That's such bullshit," she said, surprising him even more. He didn't know she knew that word. "The entire world revolves around sex, and you know it."

"I disagree."

"Prove it."

He laughed. "Yeah, right. How?"

She moved fast then, faster than he'd thought her capable of moving, and straddled his lap, pushing his shoulders back, down onto the blanket.

He was completely unprepared, completely caught off guard.

She'd nearly knocked the air out of him, and there was no way he could catch his breath, not with her lying on top of him, her breasts against his chest, her hands holding his wrists above his head, her mouth a fraction of an inch from his, the warmth between her legs ground intimately against him . . .

Sweet Christ.

"What are you thinking now?" she breathed.

Nils kissed her. How could he not kiss her with her mouth so close, with her body so soft against his?

And oh, God, her mouth was as sweet as he remembered. He kissed her hungrily, frantically, unable to stop himself even though he knew this wasn't real. Even though he knew he was failing her test.

Prove it. He was proving something here, but he wasn't sure exactly what.

And then she was gone. Just like that, she'd rolled off of him.

Leaving him gasping for air, with an instant hard-on that was embarrassingly obvious through his flimsy cotton shorts.

"If getting laid weren't a priority," she told him, her voice shaking, "if, like most men, you weren't thinking with your *dick*, you would have laughed and gently pulled me off you. You might've been embarrassed—probably more for me than for you. You might've apologized. What you *wouldn't* have done was try to stick your tongue down my throat."

"Are you *completely* insane?" Nils said as soon as he could speak. "Do you do this all the time, Meg? Because there are men who might not understand your little lesson— men who might not like being teased like that. You do this to them, and you just might find yourself with a lot more than you bargained for."

"I can't see you anymore," she said.

Oh, Jesus, now she was trying not to cry. How the fuck did this get so crazily out of hand?

"Look, give me Joelle's number. If you want me to, I'll call her, I'll—" He reached for her, but she jerked away.

"Don't touch me!"

"I'm sorry."

She was up and heading for a garbage can. He followed. "Meg, you've got to cut me some slack here. This friendship thing is all uncharted territory for me. You've got to give me credit for trying. I mean, how many days have we spent together? About ten, right? Ten days, and I only try to . . . to stick my tongue down your throat once—and when enticed, might I add? That's pretty damn good in my book."

"I'm having trouble keeping my hands off of you."

She spoke so softly, still facing the garbage can, it took Nils a moment to realize what she'd said. And then he couldn't speak. He was using all of his energy, all of his focus, on *not* reaching for her, on *not* taking her into his arms.

"Maybe that's not such a bad thing," he finally said.

"It is," she said. "It's a terrible thing. I'm married. I took vows. And I know what you're thinking. That Daniel took vows, too, and he didn't manage to keep his, but . . . I need to go. I have work to do this afternoon."

He followed her back to the blanket. "Do you want me to bring over a pizza—"

"No."

"—later? We could talk. I think we need to talk."

She gathered up the blanket and jammed it into her bag. "I think you need to go back to California."

"Meg, you're my best friend—"

"That's ridiculous. We hardly know each other."

He followed as she headed toward the street. "I disagree." He'd told her more about himself than he'd ever told anyone. They might have been friends who desperately wanted to become lovers, but they were, first and foremost, *friends*.

"I have a deadline. I'll be working until late tonight. I'm really sorry, John." The tears were back in her eyes. "This is completely my fault. I thought I could ignore my attraction to you."

She waved to hail a cab, and a taxi skidded to a stop in front of her. "I'm sorry," she said again, climbing in and shutting the door.

"Drive," he heard her order through the open window, and the taxi pulled away, leaving Nils standing in the street.

"Call me," he shouted after her. "Meg, please? *Call me!*"

There was no way Starrett could have spotted her.

But he was moving more quickly now and Alyssa Locke had to work to follow him. He disappeared for a moment in a crowd of lunchtime shoppers but then reappeared—his bright blue baseball cap standing out in the crowd.

Lt. John Nilsson had gone missing.

It wasn't official. He'd been given thirty-six hours of free time by his CO, and there were still quite a few hours to go before he was AWOL.

But he wasn't in his hotel room. It was possible he had a girlfriend in the area that no one knew about, but it was even more likely that he was off the map.

Meg Moore was gone, and Nilsson had followed. Locke was sure of it.

And although Ensign Starrett had been questioned and claimed to know nothing of Nilsson's whereabouts, she knew better. Roger Starrett and John Nilsson were tight. Starrett knew exactly where Nils was—and it was just a matter of time before Nils contacted him.

Locke had taken it upon herself to be Starrett's shadow during all her off-duty hours. She'd talked Jules into helping her out, and between the two of them, they had Starrett covered.

Who needed sleep anyway? Locke sure as hell wasn't getting any. Not with her sister Tyra on the verge of going into the hospital. Trailing Starrett helped keep her mind off that— at least it should have. But today she was so damn distracted, she barely could have followed her*self*.

She trailed Starrett now down a crowded city sidewalk. He was pretty far in front of her, but then he took a hard right—into a McDonald's.

Figures he liked fast food.

It took her close to a minute to reach the door, but once there, she could see his cap through the front window as he stood in line to get his daily dose of high cholesterol.

So she waited outside, pretending to windowshop at a jewelry store while keeping her eye on that blue cap, wishing she had the money to buy one of those expensive watches for Tyra.

Starrett finally made his way to the head of the line, ordered his Double Heart-Attack to go, paid, and turned to leave.

"No!" Locke couldn't believe it.

The man in the blue cap wasn't Sam Starrett or Roger

Starrett or Houston or Bob or whatever dumbass redneck nickname the SEAL was going by today. In fact, the man in the blue cap wasn't even a man. He was a woman who was about as tall as Starrett, but that's where the similarities ended.

She'd been screwed.

Locke wasn't aware she'd even spoken aloud until a honeyed voice behind her drawled, "Just name the time and place, sugar—I'll be there with bells on."

Starrett.

She spun around to find him grinning at her. His cap was gone, and she took grim satisfaction in seeing that without it, he had hat hair. There was a big, unattractive, sweat matted, indented ring around his head where heat and the cap had given his hair that special, unmistakable style.

"Your big mistake was focusing on following a piece of clothing rather than an entire person," he told her. "It's nothing to be ashamed of—that's a pretty typical beginner's error."

"What did you do?" she asked. "Pay that woman to wear your hat?"

"Twenty bucks if she'd keep it on for ten minutes." Starrett's teeth were much too white and straight. Redneck assholes were supposed to be missing at least a few.

"So you knew I was following you?" Duh, obviously. She rolled her eyes, disgusted with herself. "Stupid question."

"I spotted you back by the Starbucks."

"*That* soon?" She couldn't hide her dismay.

To her surprise, he didn't make fun of her. "You're really pretty good," he said. "Actually, you're exceptionally good. But remember, I'm a SEAL, Alyssa. When you trail someone who's had that kind of training, you've got to be better than exceptional. You got to figure I don't go anywhere without constantly checking my six—turning around and seeing who and what's behind me. It's automatic—I just do it. And another thing. You might want to work a little bit more on blending, you know, into the crowd?"

Locke looked down at her dark pants and suit jacket. "I blend."

"Yeah—provided the crowd's all FBI agents. You want

to trail someone on the street—especially if you're a hot-looking babe—dress down, skeeve up a little. Jeans and T-shirt. Sneakers. No makeup. And how the hell did you expect to keep up in *those* shoes?"

"I was doing fine." That was a lie. She wasn't doing anything close to fine. She was hot and exhausted and distracted and thinking of Tyra—waiting for her pager to go off or her cell phone to ring.

"Feet hurt?"

She hesitated only slightly as she looked into Starrett's neon blue eyes. "Yes."

He smiled, and for once it wasn't one of those Boy Howdy cowboy grins. It was a real smile. He gestured with his chin just down the street. "You want me to wait while you run into the drugstore and pick up some Band Aids?"

She blinked at him. "Wait?"

"You're following me because you think I know where John Nilsson is, right?"

She didn't answer. No way was she telling him that.

"Naturally you can't admit it, but we both know I'm right. Which means that even when we shake hands and say, 'So long, have a nice day,' you're going to keep on following me. FYI, I'm walking all the way to that fancy toy store—it's probably still about four blocks down. My niece's birthday is next week and since I'm not going to be able to visit, I'm so screwed." He laughed. "I'm going to have to send her the entire damn store. After maxing out my credit card, I'm heading all the way back to the hotel, stopping at as many bars as possible along the way. Your feet'll be bleeding by then if you don't get Band Aids."

"*You* have a niece?" She couldn't help asking—she couldn't imagine it.

"Briana. She's going to be four. She's my older sister's kid. Lives up in Boston." He knew what she was thinking and he gave her another of those real smiles. "Imagine that. I have relatives who don't live in a trailer park. I was thinking of getting her a collection of toy guns so she could shoot all those awful Teletubbies."

Locke had to work not to smile, too. What was wrong with her? Or maybe she should ask what was wrong with

Starrett? What was he up to, anyway? Aside from that initial rude comment about naming the time and place, calling her *sugar*, he was actually being . . . friendly . . . ?

"I don't suppose it would help if I stated again—for the record—that I do not know where John Nilsson is," he said.

She just looked at him.

"Right." He laughed. "Come on. Go grab those Band Aids, and we'll try this again. You know what they say— practice makes perfect."

Starrett sat down on a bus stop bench, and as Locke went toward the drugstore, she glanced back at him. He made a "go on" motion with his hands.

So Locke went inside. It took about ninety seconds to find the Band Aids and pay for them. She went back outside and . . .

Starrett was gone. The bench was empty.

"*Damn* it!"

Her cell phone rang. She flipped it open. "Locke."

"Mistake number two, angel face. Don't let the suspect out of your sight." It was Starrett.

She should have known. She should have suspected that his being so freaking nice was just the setup for this particular assinine punch line. She could hear him laughing at her. "You're such an asshole."

"I couldn't resist," he said. "I'm sorry. I was sitting there, and . . ."

"Where are you?"

He laughed even harder. "Nice try."

She flagged down a cab. He'd said he was going to that toy store. She'd simply get there first.

"I don't supposed you'd want . . . Nah, forget it," he said. "If I asked you to have lunch with me, I'd be having lunch, but you'd just be having some up close and personal surveillance. That would kind of ruin it for me, you know what I mean?"

"I don't need to meet you for lunch to find you," she said. She covered the mouthpiece and leaned forward to speak to the taxi driver through the slit in the clear plastic shield. "There's a toy store a few blocks down . . . ?"

"You only *found* me after I disappeared in the Micky D's

because I let you find me," Starrett countered. "If I don't want to be found, you're not going to find me. Let's get that straight. The first thing you need to do, lesson number one, dear heart, is to learn your place."

Locke laughed in disbelief. "Which, according to you and some of the other Neanderthals you work with, is on my back with my legs spread, am I right?"

Starrett was silent. "Shit," he finally said. "I'm momentarily stunned by the picture that brought to mind. Don't do that to me, Locke, I have a vivid imagination. My brain's likely to explode. Among other body parts."

"Fuck you." She heard herself say it and wished she could take it back. What was it about this man that always brought her down to his degradingly foul level?

"Why, thank you," he said. "Fuck you, too, babe. The sooner the better—you're way too uptight. Hey, I bet that cabdriver would do you if you threw in an extra twenty bucks."

Shit. *Shit!* Locke turned around to look out the back window. Wherever Starrett was, he'd been watching her get into the cab.

"Of course, we both know you're saving yourself for me," he continued, laughing again.

"Yeah, in your dreams."

"What I meant by you learning your place was that you've got to lose this James Bond mentality. Humility, Alyssa! You haven't earned your license to kill—not yet. You want to be a great FBI agent? Sign up to train with the SEALs. You could probably even get into some kind of modified BUD/S program—modified because you're FBI, not because you're a woman. Don't start making those insulted noises at me. Jesus, you *do* need to learn to relax. What do you say tonight, my hotel suite? Hmmm? You and me—we could do a little stress management exercise that I *highly* recommend. We'd have the place to ourselves, because, you know, John Nilsson seems to have disappeared."

Locke made a strangled sound.

"No? Too bad." Starrett said. He sighed. "In that case, so long, sweet thing. Have a *real* nice day."

Eleven

❧ ❧

THE CLOCK ALARM went off a few minutes after six.

The heavy curtains kept out the light of the late afternoon—what little light there was. The day had turned gloomy and overcast, the clouds threatening rain.

Meg had checked into this rundown motel a little after noon. She'd reached her limit and had to sleep. She'd tried pulling off the road and sleeping in the car, but it was too bright, she was too worried about someone seeing Razeen in the backseat. And she desperately wanted to use a real bathroom.

Osman Razeen was still asleep on the other motel bed, his arms stretched uncomfortably over his head. Meg had had to position him that way, using the handcuffs to lock him to the wooden headboard.

She was going to have to dissolve another handful of sleeping pills into a glass of water and pour it down Razeen's throat, praying that she didn't give him too many, knowing that she couldn't afford to give him too few. She had to keep him completely out of it. And then she had to get him back in the car.

Meg stretched, wishing she had enough time to take a shower and—

Oh, God! She sat up, fumbling for her gun. The shadowy figure of a man had just stepped out of the bathroom.

"Freeze!" she said. "Don't move! Who are you? What are you doing in here?"

Maybe it was one of the Extremists. Maybe they'd somehow followed her here. Maybe Amy and Eve were out in the parking lot right now.

She reached over and turned on the light.

"Oh, my God," she whispered.

It was John Nilsson.

He glanced once at Razeen, then turned his attention back to Meg, taking in her messed hair and long-smudged makeup, her rumpled clothes, her gun.

Held with a shaking hand.

Meg used her other hand to support it, aiming directly for John's chest. Please, God, don't let her shoot him by accident.

He looked as bad as she did—no, he looked worse. His eyes were rimmed with red, his chin covered with stubble.

"God damn it," he said. "What were you thinking? I was so goddamn sure I was going to find you *dead*. Give me the gun."

He took a step toward her.

"Don't come closer!"

He stopped. Glanced again at Razeen. "Do you know who this is?" He was really angry. She'd never seen him angry before, she realized. Not like this. "This is Osman Razeen, a Kazbekistani terrorist leader. You don't get to be a terrorist leader, Meg, by playing nice. If you give him even half a chance, he'll slit your throat."

"I know who he is." She couldn't keep her voice from shaking. "I'm trading him to the Extremists for my daughter and grandmother."

"So you *did* lie to me. You fucking looked me in the eye and *lied*. The Extremists want the ambassador dead. Help me save Amy. I can't do this on my own. *Achub fi.*" *Save me.* He shook his head, his voice getting even louder. "Jesus! I went out on a limb for you, Meg. On my good name and honor, I convinced both my CO and the FBI that you were telling the truth, that you were in trouble and wanted and needed our help."

"I'm sorry."

"Fuck sorry!" he shouted. He was actually shouting at her. He was livid. "Sorry doesn't cut it when the bullshit you've been shoveling is way up past your head. You were just *using* us. You were using *me*. You know, Meg, when it comes to getting fucked by you, I would have preferred finishing what we started three years ago."

Meg flinched at the harshness of his words, but she knew she deserved that. She deserved everything he was saying, and all of his anger, too.

He was breathing hard, and he drew in a deep breath, letting it out in a rush of air. He looked as exhausted as she'd felt when she'd stopped to sleep, six hours ago. "God damn you."

"God doesn't have to," Meg whispered.

Some of his anger melted from his face, leaving behind . . . sorrow? "Come back with me, Meg. *Please*. Let the FBI find Amy."

"I can't." He was inching closer. She couldn't actually see him move, but somehow he was getting closer. "Stop it, John! Stay back."

There was a sudden sharp crack, and Meg turned to see Razeen launch himself off the bed, directly at her.

He was awake.

It was a rather inane thought since of course he was awake—the man was in motion, in midair.

As the world went into slo-mo, the details were suddenly crisp and clear, but her ability to react was nonexistent. She was frozen in place.

The splintered wood from the bedframe exploded out. Razeen's eyes were open and focused intently on her gun, his lips back in a snarl. He hit her hard, his shoulder against her right arm, and the gun went flying in a burst of pain.

He smelled like perspiration and urine and the garlic chicken he'd had for dinner, courtesy of the FBI safe hotel. His body was heavy against hers, pushing her back against the bed. He scrambled off of her, wrists still cuffed together, going after the gun.

She could see it, gleaming faintly, under the cheap motel desk that was attached to the wall. If Razeen got there first . . . "John!"

He was already there, already grabbing Razeen by the jacket, flinging him back to the other side of the room. But Razeen had grabbed the desk chair, taking it with him, turning and brandishing it now as a weapon.

Shrieking, Meg dove for the gun as Razeen swung—not at John, but at *her*. As her fingers closed around the cool metal of the handle, she braced herself. This was going to hurt.

She heard the sound of breaking wood, and turned to see that John had stepped directly between Meg and the chair. He'd caught the brunt of the blow on his shoulder and back, his arm held up to protect his head. It could have killed him. Couldn't it have? A blow like that to the head?

She was screaming again, trying to get the gun up and aimed at Razeen, praying that John wasn't hurt. Please God, please God . . .

But Razeen was left defenseless, holding a useless bit of wood, and, as Meg watched, John lit into him. Two quick punches and one hard elbow to the back of the man's head, and Razeen dropped to the floor.

John turned back to Meg, breathing hard. "Are you all right?"

He was bleeding. A piece of the chair had cut him—he had a gash on his right arm, by his wrist. He glanced once at it, then ignored it.

"Oh, my God, the last thing I wanted was to put *you* in danger, too!" She couldn't catch her breath. Perfect—now she was hyperventilating. She scrambled out from under the desk, gun in one hand, the other over her mouth and nose. "Stay back! I'm not kidding, John! I think you better just leave."

"Meg. Jesus. I'm not going to *leave*. Not without you." There were splinters of wood in his hair. "What if I hadn't been here? What if I hadn't found you? You'd probably be dead right now."

How *had* John found her . . . ? Realization dawned and was joined by a rush of panic. "Oh my God, the FBI's got this motel surrounded, don't they?"

He rubbed the back of his neck, rolled both his shoulder and his eyes. "Don't be ridiculous. If they were out there, I'd be talking to you through a bullhorn. They'd never let me come in here like this."

Meg moved to the window, peeked out through the curtain. The parking lot was nearly as deserted as it had been when she'd pulled in at noon. There was one other car out there—one with Maryland plates. It had to be John's. Was it possible the FBI was there, but completely hidden?

She looked at John. "How *did* you find me?"

"That's not important."

"Yes, it is. If it wasn't through the FBI—"

"I just . . . found you, Meg. I can find you. I'm good at finding you, all right? *Too* good, sometimes. Shit."

Why wouldn't he tell her? He had to have used the FBI to track her. That had to be it. She was going to walk out that motel room door—either with or without John Nilsson, and within seconds she'd be down on her face in the gravel parking lot. Her guns would be gone, and Osman Razeen would be taken into custody.

And Amy and Eve would die.

Meg aimed her gun at Razeen's head. "I think the FBI's out there. So now I have no choice. Thanks a lot, John. Now I've *got* to kill him." Her voice shook, her hand shook, her very soul was shaken. But if it were a choice between Razeen and Amy . . .

She looked at Razeen's dark hair, imagined it matted with blood. All it would take was for her to tighten her finger on this trigger.

And this man's life would be gone. Oh, God . . .

"Wait," John said. "Wait. Meg. Okay."

She hadn't managed to convince herself that she could actually do this, but apparently she'd convinced John.

"WildCard—Kenny Karmody, remember him?" he continued, talking low and fast, as if he were afraid if he spoke too loudly, she'd be startled and pull that trigger. "He just developed this new tracking system, and Sam Starrett was helping him beta test. You remember them, right?"

She nodded. Starrett and Karmody. They'd been with John in K-stan, with Abdelaziz.

"It was purely by chance, but Sam dropped one of the test tracking devices into your jacket pocket. I'm the only one who followed you here. I swear to you, Meg. The FBI doesn't even know about WildCard's system."

She lowered the gun. "I'm supposed to believe you came all this way all by yourself?"

He looked at the gun, looked at her, and she knew he was

going to try to take it away from her. She aimed at Razeen again.

"Sit down," she ordered John. "Right there on the floor. Right now."

He sat. "Your turn, now. Lower the gun."

She did.

"Thank you," he said. "Jesus." He took a deep breath, let it all out. "WildCard was supposed to come with me, but he couldn't get away. Sam was on duty. I didn't want to wait for either of them. Meg, you've got to believe me about this. The FBI's not out there. I'm the only one who knows where you are. You're not in danger, there's no reason for you to kill Razeen. Let's get that established here, okay?"

Meg looked at her jacket. It was where she'd left it this morning, on the foot of the bed she'd slept in. She reached for it now, reached into the pocket and . . .

Found a curious, round piece of metal, about the size of a watch battery. It was slightly warm to the touch.

"That's it," John said. "That's the tracking device. It worked really well. I think WildCard's about to make a fortune with this thing. Wouldn't *that* be a kick? WildCard a millionaire?"

She dropped it onto the desk, picked up one of her boots from the floor, and crushed it.

Meg could see from John's eyes that he knew what that meant. She wasn't going back with him. And he wasn't going to be able to follow her any farther.

"Meg, please," he said. "If you don't come back with me, you're probably going to die."

"How can you ask me to quit?" she said, just as quietly. "I've come this far. . . ."

"I don't want you to die."

"I don't want my daughter to die."

"Meg," John said gently, "you've got to know that she's probably already—"

"Don't say it!"

"Dead."

No. She wouldn't believe it. She'd pretend he didn't say it. She had to get back on the road. And even though Razeen was still unconscious, she had to force-feed him more sleeping pills and make sure he stayed unconscious, this time all the way to Orlando.

But first she had to figure out what to do with John. She peeked out the window again. His car was a midsized model. It would be a little uncomfortable, but it would have to do. "Give me the keys to your car."

He took them from his pocket. "Meg . . ."

She let him talk, but she didn't listen. Instead she thought of Amy. Amy who wasn't dead. Who couldn't be dead. Whom she wouldn't allow to be dead, god damn it.

She thought of Amy as she made John empty three sleeping pills into a glass of water, as he carefully poured the mixture down Razeen's throat.

It occurred to her as he did that that she probably shouldn't let John touch Razeen—in case he had more of those tracking devices. She didn't want him planting one on either of them.

So instead of having John load Razeen into the back of her car, she left the unconscious terrorist on the floor of the room. Still focusing on Amy, she led John at gunpoint across the deserted parking lot. It was starting to rain, a cold, relentless drizzle that mirrored her emotions perfectly. She thought of Amy as she used John's keys to open the trunk of his car. She thought of Amy as she ordered him inside that trunk.

"I'm sorry," she said as she locked him in, then threw his keys way out into the woods.

It started to pour, and she hurried back into the motel room. A quick trip to the bathroom, and then she'd wrestle Razeen into the car and be back on the road.

Eve had to go to the bathroom.

It had come down to a toss-up between what would upset their captors more—asking to use the facilities, or wetting their pants.

She'd considered simply asking to be allowed to go outside to relieve themselves, but she was afraid once outside, it would be easier simply to take them into the swamp and kill them, rather than bringing them back inside.

She'd had ten more butterscotch candies left.

She'd offered one to the Bear, even though that would be one less candy she could give to Amy. "We need to use a bathroom."

He'd looked at the candy, looked at her, then had silently turned and gone upstairs.

Eve gave one of the candies to Amy and put the last ones back in her pocket as she listened to the sudden sharp voices from upstairs. The Bear had gone to talk to the woman.

She'd held tightly to Amy. Please God, if you're real, if you're up there, now would be the perfect time for that helicopter of SEALs to appear over the house. They'd be sliding down on ropes and . . .

The upstairs door opened, and the Bear came back down the stairs. He was a big man with big feet, and she'd come to recognize the sound of his footsteps.

He came into the room, cut the ropes around their ankles, and gestured for them to follow. His face was grim, and for a moment, Eve didn't know if they were going to the bathroom or out into the swamp. This man liked them, she was almost positive that he did. Wouldn't it be the ultimate irony, a double tragedy, if he'd been the one ordered to kill them? And he would do it, too. He'd have to, or the others would kill him.

But they went to the stairs instead of out into the swamp.

He wouldn't take them upstairs if he was going to kill them.

Thank God, they were going to live another day.

Amy went quickly up, but Eve took her time despite her need to reach the loo immediately. She slowly pulled herself up by the banister, taking one step at a time, well aware that the man who'd nearly pushed her up the stairs to the house had pulled himself away from the TV in the kitchen to watch.

"I'm sorry," she said. "I'm going as fast as I can."

"Not that one," Bear said sharply as Amy started for a bathroom that was near the top of the stairs. "Your using that would make it unclean. There's another here, in the back."

That's why they'd come all the way upstairs. There was a small lavatory off the kitchen that the men all used. One for the men, one for the woman, and one for the infidels. Good thing there were three bathrooms in the house, or she and Amy probably *would* have been taken into the swamp and killed.

The thought was chilling.

Eve shuffled down the hall after Amy and the Bear. Amy had stopped short in the doorway to a room.

It was crusted with dirt, the formerly white tile dingy and gray—brown in some places. But it had a toilet, disgusting as it was.

And a window. There was a window on the far side of the tub.

"Thank you," Eve told the Bear. She took Amy's hand and pulled the girl inside, shutting the door behind them.

Amy was eyeing the toilet. There was no seat, no paper.

But they'd both been camping. It was hardly worse than some of the latrines they'd used. Eve went first, and after she washed up, she left the water running in the sink. Holding her finger to her lips, she looked at Amy, then stepped into the bathtub to take a closer look at the window.

It was old, with a wooden frame and a torn screen. It had been painted shut, but that paint was blistered and peeling, the wood rotting from the humidity.

Eve pushed at it gently, to see if it would open.

It gave, but just a little. With Amy's help, she could surely haul it open, but it would make an enormous amount of noise.

And once it was opened, then what? They were on the second floor. Sprout wings and fly to the ground?

Eve wet her fingers again in the sink and rubbed at the grime in one corner of the window so she could peek outside.

The very back of the house—the kitchen—was a single-story addition to the original structure. It extended out beyond this bathroom, its roof providing a place to stand after exiting through the window. Still, that roof was pretty steep. Although there was some kind of back porch down at the end. If they could make it that far, they could use the railing to climb down and . . .

If they could make it that far.

She couldn't even figure out a way to get the window open without everyone in the house knowing about it.

Eve climbed out of the tub, checking to make sure she'd left no footprints behind. There was a torn plastic shower curtain half hanging from a bar, and she pulled it mostly closed. That would hide the window from the Bear's view when they opened the door.

The trip downstairs was as slow and labored as it had been going up. But finally they were back in their room. As Eve lowered herself carefully back onto the floor, the Bear didn't bother to tie their ankles together again. No doubt he was thinking that her bad hip kept them tethered. Good.

Amy curled up, her head in Eve's lap. She was learning to escape her hunger through sleep.

Still, just the same, Eve put her hand on the child's forehead, checking to be sure she wasn't running a fever.

Amy's head was cool.

She smelled faintly of butterscotch.

Of Ralph.

Eve closed her eyes.

"We have to go back to the house. Nick's surely waiting for us by now." But instead of helping her to her feet, Ralph kissed her again.

They'd spread a blanket on the grass, alongside a stream, not far from the estate. They'd shared a picnic lunch, during which time Ralph had been uncommonly silent. He'd barely eaten half of his meat pie.

And when she'd asked him what was wrong, he'd pulled her into his arms and kissed her as if there were no tomorrow.

It wasn't as if he'd never kissed her before, because over the past few weeks, he had. He kissed her good night almost every evening. He'd kissed her a time or two on the beach, when no one had been around.

But he'd never kissed her like this, never with them both lying back on a blanket, with the weight of his body partly covering hers.

Eve knew all about sex. Her mother had explained the mechanics to her when she was barely even eight. It was the day after "Uncle" Sergei had come into Eve's bedroom, drunk and completely naked. Eve had laughed at how funny he'd looked, but her mother had been furious. It was one of the few times her anger hadn't been an act.

Sergei had been kicked out of the house, never to return, and Eve had lost a bit of her childhood as she'd learned for the first time about the power that women—even an eight-year-old girl—had over men.

It had taken her until now to learn that there were some men who had a similar power over women—and that Ralph was one of them.

She knew Ralph had a great deal of experience when it came to sex. With a face and eyes like his, he'd been—as her mother was fond of saying—not just around the block, but circling it for a while. His good looks would have probably been enough, but combined with that glib tongue . . . Ralph could talk his way into just about anything, including, as her mother also would have said, a girl's panties.

Eve had been expecting him to try something like this weeks ago. She'd even had a speech prepared.

Except he didn't seem to be trying much of anything. He rolled away from her, onto his back, one arm up over his eyes.

"I'm such a coward."

Eve sat up, not sure at first just what he was talking about.

"I planned this so carefully," he continued, "so that we'd have this time without Nick around, and then . . ."

And then she knew. He'd brought her out here, to this deserted spot to . . . Taking a deep breath, she launched into her speech. "Ralph." A good start. "I've got to tell you that you, well, you may have gotten the wrong impression about me from the way I sometimes dress and talk." She sounded breathy and childish, and she tried to lower the pitch of her voice in an attempt to sound more sophisticated. But she couldn't do it. This was too important. She may have rehearsed this speech, but its content was something she believed completely. "The truth is, I believe with all my heart that a man and woman should be married before they . . . before . . ."

He looked up at her, his eyes wide. "Dear Lord, you didn't think—" He sat up and started to laugh. "You *did*. You thought I was planning to try to . . ."

Eve felt her face turn bright red.

He reached for her and grabbed her before she could stand up and walk away, walk anywhere, walk to the stream. Walk *into* the stream.

"Not that I haven't thought about it or wanted to—badly, I might add and . . . It was definitely my fault for kissing you that way. I mean, I was practically on top of you, so it makes sense that you'd think I was trying to . . . Heavenly God, save me, I'm just making this even more embarrassing, aren't I?"

But he wasn't. Like everything else he touched, he was making it bearable. As she glanced into his eyes, Eve felt her heart beating, so huge and heavy in her chest. And she suspected that if he truly tried to take advantage of her, she'd be unable to refuse him, as frightened as she'd be.

She loved him.

This wasn't just some silly attraction, like the crushes her mother used to get on the young men who came to lounge around their swimming pool.

"Please know that I respect you far too much to even suggest you compromise yourself and your beliefs with me in any way," he told her. "But I know myself well enough to be aware that what I *should* do often gets knocked aside in the heat of the moment. If such were the case, I'd take responsibility for my—our—actions. At least I would under normal circumstances. However." He cleared his throat. All laughter was gone from his face. He was suddenly so serious. "My circumstances have suddenly rather drastically changed and you deserve far more than—"

"Ralph, is there any chance you could explain what you mean in *American*?" What was he telling her? Eve felt a stab of fear. Circumstances?

He laughed, but it sounded forced. "Am I being too English?"

"Quite, old man. Pretend you're John Wayne."

He laughed again. "I'm not sure I can. You see, I'm trying rather hard not to cry—I can't imagine Mr. Wayne's ever had that particular problem."

Eve looked at him. Sure enough, there were tears in his eyes.

With one arm still around her, he got out his tin of butter-scotch. He opened it with his thumb and held it out. "Better take one. It might sweeten the news I have to share."

Bad news. He had bad news about his *circumstances*. Heart pounding, Eve took a candy, slipped it onto her tongue. She could barely taste the familiar sweet flavor.

Ralph drew in a deep breath, looked her in the eye, and forced a smile. "Eve, I've received a letter from my father. I've been called up to serve in the BEF—the British army. I've been assigned to an antitank division that's bound for France. There's no way around it. I have to report for duty in just over two weeks."

He was leaving.

There was nothing he could have said—short of telling her that Nicky'd been killed—that would have devastated her more.

"I'll have to go to my parents' house about a day before that," he continued. "To pick up my gear."

Eve was frozen. She couldn't move, couldn't speak, couldn't breathe. Inside she was screaming. Inside, she'd thrown herself on the ground and was kicking her feet and sobbing, the way she'd done when she was four or five. *Don't leave me. Mommy, don't leave me!*

For the first time since she could remember, she'd felt safe. With Ralph around, she'd felt protected, taken care of. She'd started living again, instead of just surviving.

And now he was going to leave.

He was watching her, as if he expected her to say some-thing. What could she possibly say?

"Well, that's that, then." She called up all of her mother's acting talent to make her voice sound matter-of-fact, to make the expression and smile on her face look natural, instead of as if she were being eaten alive inside with grief and anger.

Ralph looked away, out at the water.

"Yes," he said. "I guess that is that." He nodded. "That's that. Right." He took a deep breath. "I'll, um, I'll spend the next few weeks—at night, of course—working out lesson plans for Nick, using those doctors' methods. That way you can carry on with him. Keep up the progress we've been making. It's just . . . my room in the boarding house is rather warm at night. I've found it's nearly impossible to write—I perspire and the ink runs. If you don't mind, I'd like to work in your library . . . ?"

"That's fine." Eve stood up. "Of course you may." Suddenly they'd gone back to being strangers. How could he talk so calmly of the next few weeks when her heart was shattered?

They packed up their picnic and returned to the house.

As they walked back, he didn't even try to hold her hand.

It might've ended there—and there were countless times when Eve wished that it had.

She spent the next three days numb. Ralph was there at the estate, teaching Nick, tying up all the loose ends. But other than that, he was already gone. He was polite to her again, nothing more. There were no more kisses on the beach, no kisses in the hallway as he pulled her into some shadowy alcove for a giddy, breathless, and far-too-brief moment of stolen passion.

He still stayed for dinner each evening—a gloomy affair despite his attempts to entertain Nick—but he retired to the library right after. No more walks on the beach or in the garden. No more stargazing from one of the balconies. No more late night talks of books and plays and dreams.

For several mornings in a row, Eve had found Ralph still in the library, slumped over his notes, fast asleep.

And then it happened.

Nick woke her up in the middle of the night—just past 1:30. He'd just gotten sick all over the bathroom. His head was pounding and he felt miserable.

His cheeks were bright red and he was frighteningly hot to the touch.

Eve got him cleaned up and put him back into bed, and went running for the library.

Ralph was still there. His eyes widened at the sight of her and she realized she hadn't taken the time even to put on a robe over her cotton nightgown.

But she didn't have to do more than utter the words *scarlet fever* before Ralph was running back down the corridor with her, to Nick's room.

One look at the boy, one touch of his head, and Ralph was

heading for the telephone. Eve didn't know what he said or who he called, but a doctor pulled into the drive within twenty minutes.

Ralph woke the Johnsons, and together they worked to bring Nicky's fever down. It was dawn before he was sleeping, although only fitfully.

Eve was getting a blanket and pillow from her room, preparing to curl up in a chair beside Nick's bed, when Ralph stopped her in the hallway.

The Johnsons had gone back to bed, and the doctor had departed as well, promising to return in the early afternoon.

"He'll get through this, Eve," Ralph told her. "Nick is going to be all right. He's strong. He's a fighter."

She nodded, but she knew his words were just that—words. Back home in California, Jilly Renquist had had scarlet fever. She was strong, too. A sturdy little girl of eleven. But she'd died.

"You should probably go," Eve said. "It's been a long night."

"No," he said, "The damage is already done, so I'm going to stay here. Mrs. Johnson made up a room for me."

Damage, what damage? He didn't make any sense, but then again none of this did. Scarlet fever was contagious. Why was it that Nick had gotten it, but not Eve or Ralph?

"I know you want to be with him now, but I'll come in and sit with Nick in a few hours so you can get a chance to sleep," he continued.

She shook her head. "I'm not going to leave him."

"Of course not. We'll bring a cot into the room for you. You can sleep right there while I watch over Nick."

She was too tired and too frightened to argue. She just nodded and turned toward her little brother's room.

But Ralph stepped in front of her. "Eve, there's something else you should know."

Whatever it was, it wasn't good. He was having trouble looking her in the eye.

"I realize this is probably not the best time for this, but it wouldn't be fair for me to withhold this from you—you've always been honest with me, so . . ."

Yeah, sure, she'd been honest with him. He had no idea.

"American, Ralph," Eve said. "Think John Wayne."

"Yes, well, I'm not sure old John would particularly give a damn, but . . ." He took a deep breath. "Both Dr. Samuels and Mrs. Johnson pulled me aside tonight to caution me and tell me . . . well . . . Doc Samuels actually gave me some *condoms*. Do you know what those are?"

He had her attention now. She nodded as she blushed. Yes. "Why would he . . . ?"

"Apparently the fact that lately my bicycle's been parked out front when the milk delivery comes in the morning is the subject of a great deal of gossip in town. Mrs. J. mentioned it to me, too. She told me to pull my bike around into the garage if I'm planning to, ahem, spend the night. She then told me with huge disapproval that what you and I do is, of course, no one's business but our own."

"Mrs. Johnson and Dr. Samuels think that you've . . . that we . . . ?" She giggled, her hand up over her mouth. Oh, *dear*.

"Not just them—the entire town," Ralph told her grimly. He didn't find it funny at all. "I denied it, but . . . Eve, your reputation is in shreds, and it's completely my fault."

"Well, they're all wrong." She laughed again, a burst of disparaging air. "They're all fools."

"Yes, well, I'm afraid we have no choice, now," Ralph said. "You'll have to marry me."

Eve laughed harder. But then she stopped. Holy Christmas. He was *serious*.

"I'll get a special license, we can have a small ceremony before I leave for the army." He looked about as thrilled as if he were discussing his impending execution.

Eve stared at him. The really stupid thing was that she *wanted* to marry him. More than anything—in two or three years, when she was old enough—she would have been the happiest woman on the planet if he asked her to marry him.

Asked her. Not ordered her. Because *he* wanted to, not because they *had* to.

She'd been a burden to other people all her life, and she was *not* going to live that way with Ralph. No matter how tempting an idea it was.

She wanted to weep. Instead, she glared at him.

"I don't give a damn about my reputation," she told him. "I don't care what people think. So forget it. I'm not marrying you."

"Eve. Think about it."

"This is 1939," she shouted at him, suddenly horribly angry—at him, at herself, at Nick for getting sick and worrying her so, at the *entire* world. "I'm a modern woman! I don't *have* to get married. I don't have to do anything unless I want to, and, trust me, the *dead* last thing I want to do is marry someone who doesn't love me! Anyone who thinks otherwise can just go to hell. Do you hear me? *You* can just go to H-E-double-L!"

She stormed away, but he ruined the effect by following her. "That kind of thinking might've worked in California, but I assure you—"

"So I'll go back to California. I want to, anyway. I *hate* it here. I hate everything about stupid England." I hate *you*. She didn't say the words, but he recoiled from them as if he'd heard them, loud and clear.

He stopped following her.

"Just leave now, Ralph," she whispered. "Go join the army early. This waiting for you to go is killing me."

She made it into Nick's room and closed the door behind her before bursting into tears.

Twelve

~ ~

MEG BACKED OUT of the parking spot in front of the motel room, glad that she'd refilled the gas tank earlier that day, before she'd stopped to sleep.

The rain was still coming down like a giant faucet had been opened overhead. It was thick against the windshield, sloshing and splashing as she set the wipers onto high speed in an attempt to see just a little bit. It was noisy, roaring onto the roof of the car.

It was crazy to get onto the highway with the rain coming down this hard, but Meg had to get moving. Even crawling along at twenty miles an hour would be better than standing still.

She looked in her rearview mirror at John's car one last time.

She hated locking him in the trunk. But she had no choice. She was his enemy now. His job was to stop her.

Resolutely she put the car into first gear and moved forward, peering through the pouring rain, searching for the parking lot exit and the road that led to the highway.

"Oh, my God!" Meg stepped on the brakes, hard, to avoid hitting a man who'd suddenly appeared, from out of the rain and mist, directly in front of her car.

He was soaking wet.

He was John Nilsson.

He moved closer, and as she stared at him through the swishing windshields, she could see his mouth move. *Meg.*

Somehow he'd gotten out of his trunk.

Somehow? Of course he'd gotten free. He was a Navy SEAL. What was she doing, thinking she could lock him anywhere? No wonder he'd gone in so willingly—he'd probably been laughing at her the whole time.

Meg threw the car into reverse. She'd pull out the other way—the motel's driveway went all the way around the building. If she couldn't lock him up, well, she was going to have to outrun him. He might've been able to get out of the trunk in a snap, but it was going to take him some time to find his car keys in the woods, in the dark.

It should have been easy to do—after all, she was in a car and he was on foot. But as she hit the gas, he leapt forward, right onto the front hood.

She went faster and faster in reverse, and the car started to whine, but she wasn't outrunning him. She was taking him with her.

He was clinging to the hood with the tips of his fingers.

Meg hit the brakes, turned the steering wheel hard, but he didn't slip off.

She slammed the gears back into first, but all she could think was, God, what if he *did* slip off, and she ran him over?

She didn't want to kill him.

The car came to a shuddering halt, and she sat there, staring at him through the windshield.

He looked back at her unblinkingly, completely motionless except for his fingers. He took the opportunity to get a better grip on the edge of the hood, right up by the windshield.

His hair was completely soaked as if he'd been standing under a shower, and water was streaming down his face.

"Please get down," she said.

He read her lips. "No." He shook his head.

He couldn't hear her and she couldn't hear him through the glass and over the roar of the rain, but she didn't need to hear to know they'd hit a standoff.

And Meg couldn't help it. She started to cry.

John just watched her, his face expressionless, his eyes hard. And then he said something, something about the hotel, something that was too long and complicated for her to be able to lip-read, particularly with tears blurring her vision.

She rolled down her window a half an inch.

"Cut the tears," he said. "That may have worked to manipulate the guard back at the safe hotel, but I'm smarter than that. I'm going with you, Meg. Get used to the idea. You're not leaving here without me—even if I have to ride like this all the way. Of course, if you try to drive on the interstate with me up here, the police will probably pull you over."

Meg couldn't stop crying. She should have locked him in the trunk and driven immediately away. Of course, he probably wouldn't have gotten into the trunk if he hadn't known it would take her some time to drag Razeen out to her car.

Damn it. Damn *him*.

Okay. Okay. She could handle this. After all, she was the one in the car. All she needed was for him to get down off the hood, and she'd drive away as fast as she possibly could. John was fast, but there was no way he could keep up with a car. She had the definite advantage here.

Meg wiped her eyes and got ready to hit the gas. She nodded at him through the windshield. "Okay," she said. "You win. You can come with me." She hit the unlock button, but kept her finger right there, on it, ready in case he started to move. "Get down off the hood."

As soon as he got off the hood, she'd floor it.

But he didn't move. Not an inch.

Rain was coming in through the open crack of the window, getting her even more wet than she already was.

John just looked at her, and she knew that *he* knew she had no intention of letting him get into her car.

"Open the passenger side window," he countered, "and I'll climb in from up here."

She wiped her eyes again. God, she couldn't stop crying.

Could she risk flooring it and try to shake him while he was climbing in? Or would the open window give him an even better handhold on the car? Even if she started raising the window the moment he began to move—which would be hard to do since she'd have to reach across and crank the window up—he'd still get his hands around the frame. And with a well-placed kick, he could easily break the half-opened window.

"Come on, Meg," he said. "I'll just climb in and we'll talk while you drive. That's all I want. Just to talk to you."

Yeah, right. Like he wouldn't go for her gun while she was driving? How was she supposed to drive and keep her gun on him at the same time?

No, this was why in the movies the criminals always made the kidnapped or carjacked person drive. That way they could sit in the passenger seat and hold the gun.

God, this was crazy. How had her life suddenly become a bad movie?

"I'll shoot him," she said. "Razeen." Threatening that had worked before.

John's mouth tightened. "If you do that, Meg, I can't help you. So please don't. Open the window and let me climb in. I need you to trust me. Right now. Please. *Trust* me."

"What?" Her voice shook. "Trust you to take my gun and haul me back to DC? Because you know what's best for me? Gee, where have I heard *that* before? That worked out so well the last time, didn't it? Get off my car!"

A muscle jumped in the side of his jaw. And with the rain running down his face, he almost looked as if he were crying, too.

"I did what I thought you wanted," he said. "That night. You had too much to drink and I didn't want it to happen that way, Meg. Not like that. You want to talk about it? Great—it's about time. I wanted to talk about it when I got back from the Middle East, but you're the one who never returned my calls. Let me in. We'll talk about it now."

Oh, God, that long-ago night was the *last* thing Meg wanted to talk about—not now, not ever.

She could still feel the heat of his body, pressing her against the wall in the hallway just outside her bedroom door. She could taste his kisses, hot and sweet, feel his hands on the bare skin of her back as he peeled her dress from her shoulders and—

No. This wasn't helping. Every minute they wasted here was a minute she wasn't getting closer to finding Amy.

"You want me to drive?" John pressed. "Let me in the driver's side. That way you can hang on to your gun. Come on, Meg. I just want a chance to talk to you. You drive away from here without me, you're going to end up dead, and I'm going to end up hating myself for the rest of my life for letting you get away. Don't do that to me."

He was silent for a moment, just watching her through the windshield.

"I've let you get away too many times before," he said quietly. She could barely hear him over the rain. "I'm not letting you go this time. Not willingly. Not when you need me—and dammit, you *do* need me."

Meg shook her head. "No, I—"

"Yes," he said. "You called me. You asked for help, and god damn it, I'm going to help you whether you like it or not."

"You already did—"

"What are you afraid of?" he bulldozed on. "You think I've got another of WildCard's tracking devices on me? Well, I don't. Besides, if I did, it's electronic and I'm soaked. It would've been ruined by the rain."

"I'm supposed to believe that a Navy *SEAL* would develop a tracking device that couldn't be used underwater?" Meg shook her head.

"This was a prototype," he told her. "Sure, the next step is to waterproof it, but WildCard didn't get that far—and you don't believe me, okay, fine. I'll . . . I'll take off my clothes. That way you'll see there's nothing hidden on me."

That way she'd also have a naked man on the hood of her car. All she'd need was one car to pull into the parking lot and . . .

Talk about drawing unwanted attention.

"Don't," she said sharply, understanding that that was his plan. He was trying to make it so that she had no choice—so that she *had* to let him into the car. "John! Stop!"

But he was doing it. He was taking off his clothes, one hand at a time—careful always to have a tight grip on the hood of her car.

He threw his jacket down onto the driveway, and then his T-shirt. Kicked off his sneakers and socks.

Unfastened his jeans.

Meg hit the horn, rapped her gun against the windshield. *"Stop!"*

Somehow he looked even bigger without his shirt on. "Let me in the car."

"No." She started driving. Slowly. So that if he did slip off, she wouldn't run him over.

It wasn't easy for him to get out of his wet jeans, but somehow he did it while holding on to the hood. Oh, dear God, he had even more muscles now than he had three years ago.

And he still wore plain white briefs.

His right arm tightened as he let go with his left and reached for that waistband.

Meg hit the brake. "Okay! Okay! It's kind of obvious you've got nothing hidden on you! You've made your point!"

"So let me in."

"I *can't.*"

The rain was starting to let up, just a little, and Meg could see car headlights approaching on the road. With luck, whoever it was would just drive past. With luck, they wouldn't pull into the parking lot. With luck . . .

The car pulled into the motel lot. It was moving slowly in the rain, but it was heading straight for them.

John saw it, too, and took off his briefs.

And there he was. Completely, gloriously naked and gleamingly soaking wet, clinging to the front of her car, like some surreal hood ornament.

The approaching car looked as if it had lights mounted up on the roof, as if it might be a police car.

Meg looked at John, looked at her gun. If she didn't let him into the car, if that *was* a cop and he came over to find out what the hell the *naked man* was doing on the hood of her car, she'd have to kill Razeen. Right now. In the next few minutes. Seconds, maybe.

She couldn't breathe.

And John knew what she was thinking. "Don't do it, Meg," he said. "Don't go past the point of no return. Let me in."

Meg opened the driver's side window, cursing the entire time. She said words she didn't even know she knew how to pronounce as she scrambled over the parking brake and into the passenger seat. As John Nilsson, dripping wet, slipped into car, as naked as the day he was born.

"Drive," she ordered him. "South on 95. I swear to God, John, you pull any tricks—like driving to the police station or heading back toward DC—I'll kill Razeen."

He put the stick shift in gear and pulled out, past the oncoming car.

It was a roof rack, some kind of ski rack, not a cop car's lights.

John handed Meg something and it wasn't until she took it from him that she realized it was his briefs. They were soaking wet and he'd wadded them up in an attempt to wring them out.

"Check them," he said. "I want you to be sure I haven't attached one of those tracking hoo-ha's to the elastic band."

She sat there, completely numb, holding tightly to his underpants and her gun as he pulled onto Route 95 heading south.

This was absurd. She was in a car with the one man who'd played a part in nearly every one of her fantasies for the past three years, he was buck naked—and she couldn't bring herself even to take a peek.

"The faster you do it," he said, squeegeeing the water from his face and hair, "the faster I can put 'em back on."

He turned on the defroster, turned the fan up high. The rain plus his body heat was steaming up the windows. The cool air felt good against her flushed face.

How had this happened? How had this gotten so completely out of control?

"You're in an awful big hurry to get these back," Meg said. "It would be just like WildCard to hide some kind of homing signal in a pair of underpants."

John laughed. "Yeah, it would be. I'll have to suggest it to him. He'll like the idea."

"Maybe I should just throw them out the window."

"Be my guest. I brought 'em in here for you. You're the one who won't even look at me."

"I'm not looking at you because I'm mad at you," Meg countered. "I'm furious. I'm . . ." Her voice broke. "Terrified," she whispered. And then she said the unthinkable. "If Amy's dead . . ." She felt bile rising in her throat, felt her stomach churn, her blood turn to ice.

"Life goes on," John said quietly. "Believe it or not, Meg, life does go on. It takes a while. Sometimes years. Sometimes longer."

But it didn't. It wouldn't. Not for Meg.

"I won't let her be dead." Meg fought the urge to vomit, cursing herself for being weak. She had to stay focused. She had to believe that she could save her daughter. She had to be strong. "I won't. I won't *think* it, I won't *believe* it."

"I was only seven when my mother died," John told her.

She turned to look at him in surprise, then turned quickly away.

Oh, my God.

She'd made the mistake of looking at him. It was dark in the car, thank goodness, and he was mostly in shadow, but, oh, my *God*.

"I know I kind of led you to believe I was older than that when it happened," he continued, "but I wasn't. So, see, I know what it feels like to lose someone irreplaceable, to lose someone you need as much as you need air to breathe. If you want me to be completely honest, I'd have to tell you that I'm *still* not over her death. I'll never be *over* it. But I learned to live with it. And that's what you'll do, too—if you have to."

"No," she said. He was wrong. If Amy were dead, yes, she'd have a chance to go on living, but she wouldn't want to. And if Amy weren't dead . . . Please God, let Amy still be alive.

She looked down at the wet wad of fabric she held in her hand. "I can't take the chance that you're lying to me about this."

"Fair enough." He reached over and took the briefs and threw them out the window.

He could have just as easily done the same thing with her gun. She tightened her grip on it as she turned slightly to face him. She had to watch him, and oh, Lord, in the greenish light from the dashboard, all his muscles seemed to glow, like some exotic living anatomy textbook. "Keep both your hands on the steering wheel," she ordered him.

"You're the boss."

Was she? It didn't feel that way. Meg kept her eyes carefully on his face. Only his face. Now what?

It wouldn't be long until the sun came up, until truckers going past could look down, into her car and see—her gaze drifted—*that*.

Oh, my God.

She was going to have to find him something to wear. Some of the truck stops sold T-shirts and running shorts. But how was she going to get them? Leave John and Razeen in the car while she went inside? No way. Even if she took the keys, John would probably be able to hot-wire the car in the time she was inside the store. She'd come out, and he'd be gone. With Razeen.

But she certainly couldn't send John in, naked. Not that he'd ever willingly get out of the car.

Unless he took the car keys . . .

She was going to have to figure *some*thing out. And soon.

Meg took off her jeans jacket using the method she'd seen John use to take off *his* jacket while out on the hood. One arm at a time, the other hand firmly holding on—in this case to her gun—while she finally shook the jacket free.

She held it out. "Take this."

He glanced at her, and wisely didn't make any kind of comment about the fact that she'd told him to keep both hands on the wheel. He took her jacket and covered himself.

It didn't help.

Five miles wasn't enough.

Sam had run hard, pushing the pace until Jenk and Wild-Card started to whine. They'd both been up too late the night before, WildCard surfing the Internet, and Jenk with some woman he'd met at the hotel, in town on a business trip— lucky little son of a bitch.

Sam had slept badly, too, but he didn't have as good an excuse.

He hadn't seen Alyssa Locke once since he'd left the hotel for PT with a small group of the other SEALs early this morning. Yet ever since he'd stepped out the door, he'd had this little jangly sixth sense buzz that made him believe she was out there, watching him.

Somewhere.

As Wolchonok led Jenk and WildCard back toward the hotel, Sam picked up his pace and headed out toward the Lincoln Memorial. On a hot, restless morning like this, with the humidity starting to build and the weather threatening to storm by the late afternoon, he was good for at least five more miles.

If he tried to go back to the hotel now, without running any farther, he'd jump out of his skin.

He ran faster and faster, with that little jangle still making the hair on the back of his neck twitch, before he realized what it was exactly that he was trying to do.

He was trying to shake Locke.

Not so that he could lose her, but just so that he could see her.

He was dying to see her.

No, he was dying to do more than that.

Yeah, like *that* was ever going to happen.

Still, a man could dream. He could talk to her, watch her face, look into her incredible eyes, and carry that memory with him when he went back to the hotel to take a shower.

But Sam lost her before he got close enough to see Lincoln looming over him. He didn't know how he knew it, but he knew that she was gone.

He circled back, retraced his steps.

And there she was.

Sitting on a bench, bent over, head way down between her legs, like she was going to faint or barf or both.

Sam sprinted the last few hundred yards. "You okay?"

Her eyes were tightly shut, and she didn't open them. "Go away."

She was soaked with sweat. That was no big surprise, he was drenched, too. But she was wearing sweatpants and a T-shirt, while he wore only a pair of running shorts.

He touched her neck, checking her pulse. She was much too hot and her heart rate was too high. She was on the verge of overheating.

"What the hell are you doing wearing all these clothes?" He pulled her T-shirt up. She was wearing a colorful running bra underneath it, so he yanked the shirt over her head.

"Hey!"

A reaction. Thank God. It wasn't time to call the ambulances. Yet.

He pulled at the waistband of her sweats and—Jesus—she had shorts on under there.

"What is wrong with you?" he asked, as he half lifted her up, peeling the sweats down her legs. Damn, she had gorgeous legs, with mocha-colored skin that was smooth as silk. He tried not to touch her, aware of how uncool it would be to take advantage of her that way, yet wanting to just the same.

"Get away from me!" She kicked him feebly in the leg.

"Then do it yourself."

She struggled to get her sweatpants over her feet, and Sam impatiently grabbed her running shoes and pulled them off.

And there she was. Alyssa Locke. Dressed only in a barely there pair of running shorts and a yellow sports bra.

"I don't need your help."

At least she'd had the good sense to sit on a bench that was in the shade.

"Don't move," he ordered her, and sprinted back to where he'd run past a hot dog cart. Four plastic bottles of water cost the entire ten dollar bill he carried in his shoe. Damn. He could practically guarantee that when this was over, she wasn't even going to say thank you.

He opened one of the bottles, took a slug himself as he dashed back to Alyssa.

He shoved that bottle into her hands as he opened another and poured it on her.

"Hey," she sputtered, "don't get my cell phone wet!"

He took it from her, stuck it in her sneaker, then kept going. He used the third bottle to drench her T-shirt and wrap it around her head.

Then he sat next to her, opened the last bottle of water, and took a drink.

"Just answer one question," he said. "Just one. You live in DC. You know how hot it can get. It had to be in the high seventies before we even left the hotel. Why the hell did you even *think* you'd need sweatpants on a day like today?"

She looked at him. And she leaned one arm along the back of the bench, stretching her legs out in front of her. Even with her T-shirt tied around her head, she was amazing to look at, with those five-mile-long legs and all that bare skin showing. She wasn't stacked, not by any definition of the word, but in his book, huge breasts were way overrated.

Alyssa Locke managed to be both athletic looking *and* delicate.

Sam had a real thing for *delicate*.

She was all woman, and even though he knew she was going to smack him any minute, Sam couldn't keep himself from looking at her. Somehow he managed to keep from drooling. But just barely.

"That's why," she said.

It took him a minute to realize what the hell she was talking about, but then he understood. She'd worn sweatpants even though it was promising to be a million degrees today because she didn't want to stand out in the crowd.

Jesus. That was one hell of a problem to have.

"You should wear light colors," he said, thinking aloud. "Shorts that are longer than those—the dorkier looking the better. And I've seen these lightweight T-shirts—they're kind of like a really fine mesh. Air goes right through them."

"I have that stuff," she told him. "I just haven't had time to do the laundry in about three weeks." She reached down and picked up her cell phone, checking to see that the power was still on.

She was waiting for a phone call.

Sam looked at her closely. She looked exhausted, and not just from the heat. She had circles beneath her eyes, as if she hadn't slept well in a long time.

He watched as she put her shoes back on, as she stared at her phone again.

He would have expected her to be talking up a storm, in self-defense. Explaining that she'd never let the heat get the best of her before, trying to turn this into no big deal, deflating the situation so that he'd have no story to tell when he got back to the hotel.

Instead, she was a million miles away.

Someone wasn't calling her. Someone was keeping her

from sleeping at night. It had to be a man. Some complete jerkoff who needed his head examined.

"So, what's up?" he asked. "Something's going on with you. What is it?"

She turned to look at him, and for a fraction of second, he thought she might just tell him. But then—as if she suddenly realized who she was talking to, a shuttered expression came into her eyes. She shook her head.

It was just as good. He wasn't sure he was feeling up to hearing about Wayne or Alfonse or Joey or whoever the hell was messing with Alyssa Locke. In more ways than one.

"Want to share a cab back to the hotel?" he asked.

She got defensive. "I can walk."

Screw *that*. "I'm taking a cab—or at least I would if I hadn't spent all my money buying water to pour on your head. I know saying thank you is outside your abilities, but the least you could do is pay for the freaking taxi."

"I'll pay you back for the water, of course."

Oh, Jesus. "I don't want you to pay me back for the water. I want you to pay for the cab. And then I want you to sit with me. In it. Okay?"

Somehow she nodded. Somehow they made it to the street where they flagged down a taxi.

They rode to the hotel in silence, and Locke paid the fare.

"Thank you," he said to her in the lobby. "Look, I'm going to be over at the K-stani embassy until probably around thirteen hundred. That's when my watch ends. We're doing only four hours on—Paoletti's trying to make this kind of like a vacation for us, so . . . Anyway, you can relax for those four hours. Maybe even get some sleep?"

She checked her phone again.

Or . . . maybe not.

"I wasn't going to faint," she said. "Out there. You know. I was fine. I didn't need your help."

Jeez, she was worse than some of the men he knew. "Okay," he said easily, exactly the way he spoke to the guys when they hit some kind of physical limit and wanted to pretend that the entire world didn't already know about it. "Glad to hear it. My mistake. See you later."

Sam turned to go.

"Thanks, Starrett," he thought he heard her say.

But then again, maybe it was just wishful thinking.

Nils drove in silence.

Meg was sitting as far from him as she possibly could, while still being in the front seat of the car.

Why didn't you call me when Daniel died? Nils kept his teeth tightly clenched over the words. Now was probably not the best time to ask her that, although, god damn it, he really wanted to know.

She wouldn't look at him.

Taking off his clothes had worked to get him into the car, but now that he was here, she wouldn't even look at him.

And it was drafty.

He had to get something to wear.

He knew he should be talking. He should be sending out a continuous stream of words, trying to talk her into seeing the logic of letting the FBI do their job, of turning herself and Razeen in.

But he was exhausted. Just sitting here in a car with Meg beside him was harder than hell. He'd made so many mistakes in the past, he needed to do this right.

And he didn't know how or where to begin.

In the past, he'd made the mistake of thinking that being with her would be enough—that things would work out if only they could share the same air in the same room for long enough to have a conversation.

He'd thought if he could simply convince her to let him escort her to that embassy party, he'd have a chance. A chance for what, he wasn't sure. To set their friendship back on track? To sleep with her? To frigging *marry* her? No. Yes. Maybe. Christ, he didn't know. And maybe that had been a part of the problem.

And thinking that simply getting together with her would fix everything had been about as wrong a thought as he'd ever had.

Instead of clarity, things had gotten even more muddy and confused.

The party at the embassy had started at 2000 hours.

It was a postdinner birthday celebration for the K-stani

ambassador. It was more than politically correct for Meg to put in an appearance since most of her freelance translating work came out of the birthday boy's office. It was a necessity for her to show.

Nils had planned to go with her. It was the closest thing to a real date that they'd made—even though it wasn't real and it wasn't a date. It was work. She was working and he was simply her escort. His job was to wear his dress uniform and look good. And to make sure that the K-stanis wouldn't be affronted or offended by the concept of a woman showing up at an official function all alone.

She'd left an apology on his voice mail at the hotel, canceling their plans, and he'd called her back. Going to this thing scandalously alone would be nearly as potentially damaging to her career as the implied insult of not going at all.

Surely she could trust him to behave himself at a formal function, in a crowd of hundreds of people?

She'd finally relented—after he'd told her that the inquiry was set for the morning. And that tomorrow, after that inquiry—whether it was postponed for the five millionth time or not—he was going wheels up. He was going to meet the rest of SEAL Team Sixteen on the other side of the world. He couldn't tell her specifics, couldn't say for how long he'd be gone.

But he was leaving. And Meg had agreed to see him that one last time.

He'd picked her up at 19:45, and they'd taken a taxi to the embassy.

She looked beautiful, dressed in a formal black gown and a modest jacket that kept her shoulders and arms covered. She wore her hair up and more makeup than he'd ever seen her wear before. She looked elegant and sophisticated. Remote and untouchable.

She looked like Mrs. Daniel Moore.

She hadn't looked at Nils once, not *once* that entire endless taxi ride.

But he offered her his arm as she got out of the cab, and she finally met his gaze. There were tears in her eyes but she blinked them back. And she smiled, although tremulously.

"Did you have to look so good tonight?" she whispered.

"Did you?"

"This can't happen," she told him.

They were out on the sidewalk in front of the Kazbekistani embassy. He hadn't yet shut the cab's door. They could still get back in, blow off this party, go back to Meg's apartment and . . .

"It *can't*, John," she said as if she'd been able to read his mind.

Nils nodded. Closed the taxi's door. "I know."

"I'm sorry for what I did yesterday."

"Don't be." They started up the stairs. Meg still held his arm, and he put his fingers over hers. They were both wearing gloves, but that didn't matter. He was touching her.

"I'm sorry for a lot of things," she said as they went past the checkpoint, as Meg handed the K-stani guard her invitation and Nils took off his hat and gloves. They went through the metal detectors and into the embassy lobby.

"Maybe after this party ends we can go someplace and talk. I think we should talk, Meg."

"About what? About the fact that Daniel will be back in town tomorrow?"

A waiter went past with a tray of champagne flutes, and Meg grabbed two. She handed one to Nils. "Here's to doing the right thing. Or maybe doing the stupid thing. It's a little less clear tonight, isn't it?"

Nils clinked his glass with hers, catching and holding her gaze. "Here's to two of the very best weeks of my life."

"Well, there's a toast designed to chill a husband's blood."

Meg nearly dropped her glass and Nils knew without even turning around that Daniel Moore was standing behind him.

He stepped around Nils, taking Meg's hand and bringing it to his lips. "Darling. Obviously you weren't expecting me until tomorrow. I'm sorry I didn't give you appropriate warning, but I was able to catch an earlier flight."

"Daniel, this is my *friend*, Ens. John Nilsson. He's with the U.S. Navy—"

"SEALs," he finished, smiling tightly at Nils. "I know

who your *friend* is. I've spent the past six months trying to get him court-martialed."

"What?" Meg looked from Daniel to Nils, her eyes wide.

"Congratulations, Ensign—brilliant move to get back at me by seducing my wife. Bravo."

"You said it was just an inquiry," Meg said, still gazing at Nils.

"It is," he told her. Christ, this was awkward. He looked at Daniel Moore, trying to judge how upset the older man was. Had he been drinking? Nils didn't think so. Still . . . "Maybe we should take this conversation outside."

"First an inquiry and then a hearing," Daniel said. "And then, if I'm lucky, a court-martial. Maybe, Ensign, *we* should do nothing. Maybe *you* should go home and let me talk to my wife."

Nils didn't move. "What Meg is going to tell you, sir, is that despite what you thought you overheard, our friendship has not overstepped any bounds—"

Meg stopped him with a hand on his arm. "John, will you excuse me for a minute?"

He looked into her eyes. "Do you want me to leave?"

"Yes," Daniel said.

She ignored her husband, shook her head. "No. *I* want to leave." Her voice shook. "I want to go home. Would you mind flagging down a cab? I'll be out in a minute."

He nodded, holding her gaze for a moment longer. *I'm sorry,* he told her silently.

Somehow she managed to smile. "It's okay."

"You've got him well trained," he heard Daniel say as he walked away. "I suppose that's one of the benefits of having an affair with a teenager."

Nils waved down a cab, then waited for Meg to appear. He was determined not to make things more miserable for her—this was definitely bad enough. He'd put her in the cab, pay the driver, and send her home.

And then he'd go back to his hotel, get packed. As badly as he wanted to, he wouldn't go back inside the embassy and have a man-to-man talk with Daniel Moore, set the fucker straight. No, instead he'd go to the inquiry in the morning, and then he'd leave town.

He'd call Meg one more time—when he returned to the States in a month or so. And maybe, just maybe, she'd tell him that she was leaving that bastard for good.

Teenager. Jesus. Yeah, maybe Nils looked like a teenager to a senior citizen like Moore. What was he? Fifty years old? Christ. Why had she married him?

Because he was handsome, wealthy, and powerful. Because he was high class, an aristocrat. He was the real thing, while Nils was just a cheap knockoff.

What had he been thinking? That Meg would trade in Moore for someone like *him*? And even if she were willing, was *he*? He wasn't looking for a lifetime commitment here, was he?

Finally, *finally,* Meg came out of the embassy.

"I'm so sorry about that," she said.

She was trying not to cry and the sight of her standing there, chin held high despite the fact that she'd been completely trashed by whatever that asshole had said to her, broke his heart.

He opened his mouth and uttered some of the most difficult words he'd ever said. "Are you sure you want to leave? If you really want to get back together with him, Meg, maybe you should bring him home with you. You know, to talk."

"He has an important meeting in an hour—something that can't wait until tomorrow." She laughed as she climbed into the cab, but it sounded brittle and thin. "He wants me to go home with you tonight. He actually thinks I should sleep with you."

Nils stared at her through the open door, certain he'd misheard.

"Get in the cab, John," she said. "It's your lucky night." And then she burst into tears.

Thirteen

~~~~~~

Eᴠᴇ sᴛʀᴏᴋᴇᴅ Aᴍʏ's hair. "Ralph didn't leave for the army early," she told the little girl. "He stayed and helped me nurse Nick. He was there around the clock for a full week, no complaints, always willing to do the nastiest jobs. He was always there, covering me with a blanket if I drifted off to sleep, forcing Nick to keep drinking, helping him fight that terrible fever.

"He was there when the fever broke, too." Eve shook her head, remembering. "That was a day, I'll tell you." She smiled at the Bear, wishing he would stop scowling so. "I cried more *that* day than I did the entire week that Nick was so sick. And Ralph was there. Somehow he knew just to hold me, to let it all come out. And then he tucked me into my bed and made me sleep.

"He was still there, sitting beside *my* bed this time, when I woke up."

It was extremely improper, Ralph alone with her in her bedroom. But the Johnsons and Doc Samuels all thought she and Ralph were lovers. They thought she and Ralph had . . .

She sat up. "Where's Nick?"

"He's fine. Mrs. J. is with him. He's sleeping now, but . . . He had two whole bowls of her chicken soup, Eve. I give him two days before he's out of bed and running around again, good as new."

She sank back against her pillows, suddenly shy, hearing the echo of her own voice, shrill and ugly, telling him to go to hell. "Thank you so much for everything you've done," she said. "I don't think I could've made it through this without you."

Without you.

If this had happened two weeks from now, she would have had to. He was leaving.

Tears flooded her eyes again. How could that be? Surely she'd cried herself as dry as Death Valley last night.

"Hey," he said, sitting beside her on the bed, taking her hands in his. His hands were so warm. "Everything's okay now."

"But it's not," she said, and no matter how hard she tried to call forth the spirit of her mother, this time she couldn't do it. This time the tears spilled down her cheeks, and her lip trembled. This time the words escaped. "Don't leave me! Please, *please*, don't leave me!"

And she was sobbing, again. This time not for Nicky, but for herself.

"Oh, Eve," Ralph whispered, holding her tightly. "I don't want to—you have to know that the last thing on earth I want is to leave you!"

She knew nothing of the sort. She only knew that he'd been so cool again after telling her he was leaving. She only knew he'd asked her to marry him a week ago as if it were an impending jail term, a life sentence.

"Marry me," he said again now. "Not because we have to, but because we want to—because *I* want to. God, Eve, I do want to. I love you."

He pulled back to look at her and there were tears in his eyes, too. "I did it all wrong when I asked you before. I thought you didn't want me, I thought . . . That day by the river when I told you about the letter from my father—I wanted to ask you to wait for me to come back, but I couldn't. You're so young and so beautiful—it just wasn't fair. So I sat there, hoping, *praying,* that you'd offer to wait for me, that you'd promise to wait until I came back home. I couldn't ask it of you, Eve, but see, if you *offered* . . . But you didn't, and I thought—"

"I will wait for you," she said. "Ralph, I'd wait for you *forever.*"

He laughed at that, laughed and kissed her. His mouth was warm and he tasted of butterscotch. "There'll be no waiting. Not now. I'm not leaving you with the entire town talking about you and . . . You're marrying me— I mean . . ." He took a breath. "Please, Eve, I love you, will you do me the honor of becoming my wife? I've already filed for a special license. All you have to do is say yes, and we can be married tomorrow."

Eve looked down at Amy and over at the Bear. "How could I say no," she asked, "when the one thing I wanted more than anything in the world was to say yes?"

John was almost completely silent as he drove—except for one finger that tapped out a Latin sounding beat on the steering wheel.

Meg knew that he loved salsa music even more than he loved country—although he'd never admit to liking either, not in a million years, not even to her. He pretended to listen to classical music, and had actually done his homework. He could tell Mozart from Haydn and could name pieces and movements and opuses. But classical music never lit his eyes on fire the way a fifteen-piece salsa band could.

Meg wanted to ask him what he was thinking, but she didn't dare. She was afraid of what he might say.

Of course, maybe she was flattering herself. Maybe, unlike her, he didn't spend hours of his life thinking about that night. That awful, terrible, wonderful night.

Daniel had been at the embassy party. She'd been surprised to see him. Surprised, and yet not surprised, too. It was completely like him not to call from the plane. It was his MO to assume that whenever he appeared, other people would simply change their schedules and rearrange their lives to accommodate him.

Daniel had taken one look at her there at the party with John, and he'd jumped to rather obvious conclusions.

Meg couldn't afford for this to get ugly, not careerwise, nor emotionally. So she'd asked John to get her a cab. He didn't like leaving her there, alone with Daniel, but he'd gone out front to do as she'd requested.

"So how long have you been sleeping with him?" Daniel asked tightly once they were alone. "You do know he's just using you to get back at me."

"I'm not sleeping with him," she'd told her husband evenly.

"That's something *you* might've done—sleep with a friend. Not me. Not even if I wanted to."

And she had wanted to. Daniel was good at reading between the lines, and she knew he hadn't missed that implication.

Tears came into his eyes. But were they real tears? She honestly didn't know.

"You're right," he said quietly. "Forgive me. I'm . . . jet-lagged and jealous of everyone who's even had the chance just to talk to you these past few months."

She wanted to believe that he meant it. But it had the same tone of his usual bullshit. Just once, she wanted the truth from him.

"God, I've missed you." He reached for her, and she stepped back. "Okay," he said. "We're still there, huh? Not over the anger yet, apparently."

"We have a lot of talking to do," she told him. "You didn't think you could write me a few emails, send a few presents, and then just move back in, did you?"

But he had thought that. "I've already apologized more times than I can count," he said. "I'm not sure what else I can say. I can't take back what I've done."

He wasn't being flip. He seriously didn't understand why she didn't just welcome him back into her arms. After all, he'd said he was sorry.

Sorry.

God.

She'd let him in one evening, back while they were still in Kazbekistan. Amy had been asleep, and Meg had let him weave his apologetic words around her. She'd let him back into her bedroom, and the entire time they'd made love, she'd pictured him with Leilee.

And wasn't *that* fun?

Damn straight she wasn't over the anger yet.

"Here's what we should do," Daniel told her now. "You should go home. I'll convey your regrets to the ambassador and—"

"I'm not sure tonight is the best time for us to talk," she interrupted.

He looked at his watch. "No, I can't tonight. I've got a

meeting in about an hour. I think tonight you should go home with your SEAL friend."

She stared at him. "Excuse me?"

"Yes," he said. "You heard. That's what I think you should do. Go home with him. You want him? He's a good-looking kid, and I'm sure he's been very nice to you. So do it. Have a revenge affair, Meg. Get back at me by screwing Junior's brains out."

She couldn't believe what he was saying. Her mouth was hanging open.

But Daniel was serious. "Get it out of your system—all the anger you're carrying around. Just . . . do it. Get back at me, and then we can both just let it go."

"You actually want me to . . . ?"

"I don't *want* you to," he said. "Of course I'm going to be jealous." He had to blink hard to keep from crying. She'd never seen him like this—certainly not in public. Dear Lord, it was possible he was finally being completely truthful. But, God, what a truth. "I don't know what else to do. I love you and I want you back. And I know you love me. Maybe if you do this, you'll feel better and you'll get over some of the anger. And then we can move forward with our lives."

He kissed her hand again, and walked away. Meg drained the glass of champagne she was still clutching, grabbed another from a passing tray. God, she needed a real drink.

Somehow, she made it out to the front of the embassy, and there was John, looking majestic in his formal dress uniform, with his hat and gloves. He had such concern on his face, such worry in his eyes, she almost didn't make it into the cab before she started to cry.

She was so inappropriate—the things she said to him. But he got into the cab anyway, and just held her while she cried on his shoulder.

She couldn't tell him all of what Daniel had said—not in the cab. She couldn't bear for the driver to overhear.

It wasn't until they were back upstairs, in the privacy of her apartment, that she told him.

Meg had one bottle of alcohol in her kitchen. A bottle of rum she'd bought to make daiquiries last spring, when Nancy, her college roommate, was coming to visit. Only Nancy the

party girl had come bearing stories of rehab and sobriety—
thank God—and they'd had virgin daiquiries. And Meg had
hid the rum in the back of her cabinet.

She found it now and took it into the living room with two
glasses.

"I think I'm going to pass on that," John said as she held
one of the glasses out to him. "I have this sneaking suspi-
cion it's not going to help."

But he'd gone ahead and poured himself a stiff drink
when she'd told him what Daniel had said to her in the
embassy.

"I know that he wants me to sleep with you only to cancel
out his own guilt," she told him, trying not to cry. "But how
could he even suggest this?"

"He shouldn't have," John told her. "He was completely
out of line. If you want my opinion, you should ditch him
for good."

The rum burned a numb path all the way to her stomach
and she poured another glass. She wanted to feel that numb-
ness all over.

"Tell me the truth," she said. "Did we run into each other
by accident two weeks ago?"

John sighed and shook his head. "No. I knew you were
going to be there at the foreign service office."

"And was I, um, was I supposed to be like . . . some kind
of means for you to get back at Daniel for the trouble he's
caused you?"

He was silent, looking down at the drink he held in his
hands, and Meg felt the world start to slip even more side-
ways beneath her feet. "Oh, God . . ."

"It might've started that way," he said, looking up and
straight into her eyes. "It *did* start that way. And I am so, so
sorry about that. I hadn't been able to stop thinking about
you, about that kiss, and Moore's been relentless about this
pain-in-the-ass inquiry, and I think I probably thought . . .
But it changed so fast—it changed the second I saw you
again, Meg. When you smiled at me, I knew everything else
was bullshit. I just wanted to be with you. That's all that
counted, all that mattered. There was no motive to it after
that point, I swear to God."

Meg wanted to believe him. But how could she?

"Think about it, Meg," he implored her. "If I really only wanted to seduce you to get back at your husband, I wouldn't have spent two weeks saying good night to you at your door." He managed a weak grin. "That tongue down your throat thing would've happened a whole hell of a lot sooner."

That had to be the truth, didn't it? God, she was so sick of having to guess.

"How much trouble are you really in?" she asked, wanting to know what else he'd lied about.

He shook his head. "None," he said. "Not really. It *is* just an inquiry, and no matter what Moore says, it's not going any further. I'm going in there and I'm going to apologize for the methods my team and I used to get Abdelaziz out of K-stan. But I'm not going to apologize for the fact that we got him out. Considering what we were up against, we executed our mission successfully, and in private, I've been thanked and rewarded for getting the job done. In public, I'm taking the blame, and I'm being chastised to appease all the assholes. I'm going to be denied promotion for a year. That should make Moore happy. Don't tell him, but to me, it's no big deal. In return, behind closed doors, I'm getting some extra perks that more than make up for it."

She believed him. She *chose* to believe him. "So. My husband wants me to have sex with you."

John knocked back some more of his rum. "Yeah, I'm still feeling a little weird about that."

"This has the potential to be devastatingly painful." Meg poured herself another glass. "I mean, even if I wanted to, how could I be so cruel to you? To just *use* you, like some kind of toy . . . ?"

"There are, well, there're worse things you could do," he said. "I mean, being used—in that way, as a sexual plaything—it's not really that awful an idea considering that I'm dying for you to use me any way you want."

She stared at him.

"Kidding." He smiled weakly. "I'm kidding. That was my Woody Allen impression. How'd I do?"

Meg started to cry.

He moved next to her on the couch. "Oh, come on, it wasn't *that* bad."

"Doesn't he know me?" she asked. "How could he think I'd sleep with someone else, even with his permission? God, that's so sick! Doesn't he know that those vows I made are *sacred*? Hasn't he heard anything I've said to him all those years we were married? If he thinks I could just . . . God, maybe he never bothered to get to know me at all!"

He gently took the glass from her hands, pushed the bottle out of her reach. "Maybe he knows you too well," he countered. "Maybe by telling you to have an affair, he gets to relieve some of his own guilt. Yet at the same time, it's a double win for him because he knows you'll never do it. Permission slip or not, he *knows* you're not going to sleep with me tonight."

God, John was probably right.

She turned to look at him, and realized that he was sitting right next to her. *Right* next to her. Up this close, his eyes were more than light brown. They were filled with flecks of green and gold and darker brown. They were filled with . . . desire.

He looked away, embarrassed, as if he were aware of what she'd seen in his eyes. "I should go."

Meg knew exactly what she should do if she wanted to shake up Daniel, if she didn't want him to get away with playing those kinds of head games with her.

She should make love to John.

Not sleep with him or screw him or however crudely Daniel had put it. She should make love. She should *love* him.

She put her hand on his knee. "Don't go."

He looked at her hand, looked back into her eyes. "Hmmm. Yeah. I'm thinking, um, that I should, you know . . . definitely leave. And now would probably be a good time."

Meg snatched her hand away, closed her eyes, horrified and embarrassed. "I'm sorry. Oh, my God, I've become Mrs. Robinson!"

"What?" John laughed. "Wait, are you nuts? How old are you? Thirty? You're only five years older than me. That's nothing."

"I'm thirty-one."

"Six years. Big deal. If you weren't married, babe, I would've been all over you a long time ago. And thanking the Lord that a woman as beautiful and intelligent and wonderful as you would want anything to do with me."

Meg opened her eyes. "Then don't go." She touched his face. "Please?"

She could see everything he was thinking as it flashed across his face and in his eyes. He wanted to do the right thing, but he wanted her.

He wanted her.

As desperately as she wanted him.

She leaned forward and gently brushed her lips across his in the merest promise of a kiss.

"Oh, God," he said, and he kissed her—*really* kissed her.

It was an explosion of passion, an eruption of need. He swept his tongue into her mouth possessively, as if he were reclaiming lost ground, as if he were reminding her that in truth she'd belonged to him since he'd kissed her back in Kazbekistan all those months ago.

His arms were hard around her as he crushed her to him, as he kissed her longer, deeper, as he pulled her onto his lap and . . .

Meg sat up as John put on the signal blinker. He was taking the exit, pulling off the highway.

"What?" she said. "What are you doing?"

He looked at her and she felt herself blush. That was stupid. Why was she blushing? There was no way he could know that she'd just been thinking about kissing him. Thinking about that night. Except now that she'd blushed, he could probably figure it out.

"I need some clothes," he said. "The sun's going to come up soon. There was a sign for a gas station—it said it had a twenty-four-hour minimart attached. I figured there was a chance that they'd at least have a T-shirt for sale. And while you're at it, I could use a serious cup of caffeine. I'm starting to hear voices."

Meg stared at him. "I'm not leaving you in this car with Razeen."

Nils pulled into the lot across the street from the Shell

station and turned off the headlights. The attached store was open, gas pumps lit up, but aside from the lone store clerk inside, it was completely deserted.

There was a repair garage on the other side of the convenience store, and the two big bays were dark. One was shut, but the other was open, as if it were being aired out.

The rain had let up to a soft drizzle, making the pavement shine.

Nils looked more closely at the open bay door. Was that . . . ? His vision was excellent, but it was too dark and they were too far away for him to see clearly.

"I don't know how we're going to do this," Meg said tightly. "Because I'm *not* leaving you in the car."

"Right, and as soon as *I* go in, you take off without me," he said. "Unless I take the car keys—except the clerk might notice I don't have any pockets to put them in."

"I'm not going in there without you," she said.

Nils chewed on his lower lip. The clothes were starting to be secondary to his need for coffee. He was lightheaded from lack of sleep. They could probably find a twenty-four-hour McDonald's with a drive through—although he was going to get some looks from the cashier when he approached the pickup window.

Unless . . .

He turned to Meg. "How about we compromise? How about I borrow Razeen's pants, we lock him in the car, and we both go into the store. I get to hold the car keys, you get to hold your gun. In your pocket, of course. We don't want to get the clerk too upset, and the sight of me wearing Razeen's pants may be all he can take."

Meg laughed. It was a good sound.

But just as quickly she stopped laughing, and he knew she was trying not to cry. She was remarkably tough. If their roles were reversed, he wasn't sure he'd have made it even half this far.

"I'm sorry," she said suddenly. "When I asked for you—back in the embassy men's room—my intention wasn't to put you into danger or to get you into trouble. I didn't plan for it to happen this way."

Nils nodded. "But you did plan it, didn't you? When I

came in there, you weren't really asking for help. You were just looking for a way to get Razeen out of the embassy."

He wanted her to tell him it was otherwise—that she hadn't intended to deceive him at all, that she simply seized the chance she was given when she found herself and Razeen in the safe hotel, under relatively lax guard.

"I'm sorry," she whispered. "You have to understand, I'd do anything to get Amy back. Anything." She looked at him, and with the headlights off and the dashboard dark it was hard to see her. She was just a shadow. A gleam of eyes.

"Back at the safe hotel," she told him, "I was ready to sleep with the guard—and I would have if it hadn't been so easy to get his gun from him another way. Someday, when you have children, you'll understand."

Nils shifted in his seat. He didn't want to hear this.

"I *will* kill him," Meg said. "If I have to, I'll kill Razeen. Don't think that I won't."

He knew that she would. He'd seen her eyes back in the motel room. She was capable of pulling that trigger if she thought it would save her daughter. "You don't have to kill him, Meg."

"That's right," she said. "I don't. I can trade him to the Extremists."

"I meant, you can turn him in and let the FBI—"

"No."

"Handing him over to the Extremists is the same thing as killing him. You might as well be pulling the trigger of the gun that executes—"

"I don't care," she said fiercely. "He's a terrorist. He's a terrible person. It's not as if he doesn't deserve whatever bad things happen to him. I'm not going to risk Amy's life to save his. That's a no-brainer, John."

She was talking to him—that was good. He didn't like what she was saying, but at least she was talking.

"There are lots of other options, Meg," he said, "besides turning Razeen over to the Extremists. If we went back to DC, we could release a story to the news media—we could announce that you lost it, that you started shooting in the men's room, and that Tuzak what's-his-name—whoever Razeen was pretending to be—is dead."

Meg was already shaking her head. "I already thought of that. I can't risk it. If the Extremists doubted it at all, they'd kill Amy. There would need to be a body."

"So we'll have a body."

"A *dead* body."

"The FBI can make it look real."

She wasn't buying it. "I'm doing it my way. If I deliver Razeen to them, there's no chance of any mistakes."

"And what makes you think they'll just let you walk out of there?" Nils asked. "Assuming they're even still alive? Do you honestly think the Extremists will just hand Amy and your grandmother to you and let you all walk away?"

She shut down. Just like that. And he knew there was something else she was keeping from him.

"I don't want to do this," she finally said. "I don't know if I trust you to go into that store. What if you signal the clerk somehow? What if—"

"I won't."

"Oh, I'm just supposed to take your word?"

"Yes. Trust me, Meg—"

"Let's just keep driving. We'll deal with your clothes later. God, standing still like this is driving me crazy!"

"Maybe if you're lucky," he said loudly, over her, "they'll kill you first so you don't have to watch Amy die."

Meg flinched as if he'd slapped her.

"Gee, I'm so glad you came along for the ride," she whispered. "Without you I wouldn't have been able to reach my full capacity for misery."

Nils closed his eyes and exhaled, hard. "I'm sorry," he said.

"Yeah, right."

"Dealing with terrorists is one of the things I do for a living." He worked to keep his volume down, his voice calm and gentle. "I know about the GIK and the Extremists, I know the people we're dealing with here, Meg. I'm an expert, okay? I'm part of a team that governments come to when they need expert advice in dealing with terrorist situations like this. Because we're experts, they trust us to come up with expert solutions. They trust us, trust *me*. Why can't you do the same?"

She didn't answer, didn't look at him.

"I thought we were friends," he continued. "What happened? The Meg Moore I knew a few years ago would trust me enough to let me help. The Meg I knew would *never* be able to kill another human being—she'd find another way to save her daughter."

The Meg he thought he knew would've called him when Daniel died. Or maybe she wouldn't have called right after. Maybe she would've waited a year, and then called.

Unless that night that had meant so much to him had meant nothing to her.

"Two weeks," she said. "We were friends for two weeks, John. A little longer if you count the time in Kazbekistan. What makes you think you even scratched the surface of who I am? You don't know me. You never did."

He couldn't believe that. She was the most open, honest person he'd ever met. *He* was the one who'd withheld himself from her.

"Please trust me," he said. "Just a little. Just enough to believe that I won't try to hand signal some night-shift store clerk who's probably got an IQ of forty and wouldn't understand me anyway." He put the car in gear, turned the lights back on. "We'll drive around to the back of the garage where no one will see us. I'll get out of the car—with the keys—and put on Ozzie's pants. Then we'll drive back around to the front, and we'll go inside. Together."

Meg nodded. Just once.

That was all he needed.

Nils pulled across the street, into the Shell station lot. He drove past the garage bays and . . .

He stopped. Backed up.

"What are you doing?"

"Look."

Meg looked, but he knew she didn't see it. She wasn't thinking like a fugitive, but then again, he hadn't expected that of her.

"Hanging right inside the garage," he said. "The easy answer to our prayers."

It was a pair of coveralls.

They were stained with grease and weren't looking too fresh, but they seemed large enough to cover him.

Stopped where they were, on this side of the building, the convenience store clerk couldn't see them. "Why don't you just hop on out and grab them?" Nils said.

She looked at him. "I don't think so."

He turned off the engine, took the keys, and held them out to her. "There's no way I can hot-wire a car in the two and a half seconds it'll take you to—"

"You want 'em, *you* take 'em."

Nils stared at her. "You don't want to steal them," he said. "You'll lie to the FBI and even execute a man without a fair trial, but stealing a forty-dollar pair of coveralls, no sir, no thanks, that's going too far." He started to laugh.

Meg grabbed the keys from his hand, opened the car door and was back inside with the coveralls before he could blink.

"Drive," she said.

He drove.

Locke had lost Starrett.

Again.

She'd been right on him when he'd left the hotel in the early afternoon. She'd dressed in sneakers and jeans and a baggy T-shirt, and she'd felt herself become invisible in the crowd of tourists that swarmed the streets.

He'd gotten a sandwich from a sub shop and had eaten while he walked. Strolled, really.

And then he was gone.

One minute he was casually throwing his sandwich wrapper into a trash can, and the next he was nowhere to be found.

It was completely her fault. She'd been lulled into thinking he was going to stroll the entire afternoon away. She'd let her thoughts stray, she'd been checking her cell phone to make sure Tyra could reach her if she needed her and . . .

Poof.

Gone.

She'd searched the area for hours, expecting Starrett to turn up. Expecting him to call.

What good was losing her if he wasn't going to taunt her afterward?

But it wasn't until much, much later that her cell phone rang. She was in her car, driving the area she'd walked earlier, cursing herself and hoping he'd just magically show up.

She answered breathlessly, her heart racing, thinking it was finally Tyra. "Locke."

There was a moment of silence, then Starrett's voice. "It's only me. Sorry."

Somehow he knew she was waiting on a phone call. "What do you want?"

"No luck finding Nils yet, huh? He still hasn't checked back in?"

She didn't say a word. There was no way she was going to give *him* any information that he didn't already know. For all she knew, he was with John Nilsson and Meg Moore right this very moment.

"I guess not. You on duty?" he asked.

"No." She was off until late tomorrow morning.

"I'm at a pool hall," he said, "bored to tears. You know how to play?"

"No."

"Want to learn?"

"No."

He laughed. "Want to know where I am?" He didn't let her answer. He just rattled off the address.

"This is going to be really funny, right, Roger?" Locke said, flipping through her map book until she'd found the street he'd named. "When I come all the way down to that shitty part of town, and walk into some biker bar, and you're not there. That's going to be some joke when it's just me and five three-hundred-pound white supremacists, huh? As a person of color, I don't appreciate being walked into a potentially dangerous and volatile situation."

"Whoa, wait—I would never do that."

"Then you be there," she said. "You be there when I show up."

She hung up the phone, feeling like a fool for rushing over at Starrett's beck and call. But she didn't have anything else to do, and she was going to feel really stupid when she called Jules and had to tell him that she'd spent the entire afternoon with her thumb up her butt.

Her cell phone rang again and she tensed. "Locke."

"Hey, it's me," her partner said, as if she'd conjured him just by thinking about him. "Lookit, I can't help you out with Cowboy Sam tonight. I'm sorry, I know I promised to set up camp outside his hotel room from midnight to six, but I'm being sent south."

Locke ran a stale yellow light. "Anything I should know?"

"Nilsson's rental car just turned up at a roadside motel. Apparently someone fitting Meg Moore's description checked in earlier. They're both gone now, but the car's still there. I'm going to go check it out, see if the local boys missed any vital clues."

"They're sending you without me?"

"I actually talked Bhagat into letting you stay back here," Jules told her. "It's a nothing assignment and you know it—checking something that's already been checked? The car was broken into. There was nothing inside it. And just a muddy pair of jeans and a T-shirt in the parking lot. An old pair of sneakers and socks. Nilsson must've thrown a change of clothes into the backseat, and when some local thief broke into the car, they grabbed everything. When they realized it was just some clothes, they must've just dropped 'em where they stood. Still, I'm going to go down there, look at the car and go, *hmmmm*. Then fly back to DC and tell the boss everything that the local guys already told me."

"Call me when you get back."

"You bet. Sorry about tonight."

"No problem," Locke said. "I'll cover it. Hey, did you hear I nearly keeled over this morning? It's getting hot out there. I'm telling everyone—we all need to be careful. Summer's here. Push fluids."

"You okay?"

"Yeah, it was nothing. I'm just . . . letting folks know." It was a preemptive strike, to steal Starrett's thunder. If everyone already knew she'd gotten a little overheated this morning, Starrett couldn't make it sound worse than it really was when he told his version of the story. Which she had no doubt he would do.

"Take care of yourself," Jules ordered. "Get some sleep."

"Yeah, maybe I will tonight." But probably not.

Locke hung up the phone as she pulled into a parking space just past a building that bore a sign saying POOL HALL. Well, *there* was an original name. She checked her map again, checked the numbers on the other buildings. This was definitely the address Starrett had given her. She locked her car behind her.

Four motorcycles on the sidewalk. No swastikas painted on any of them—always a good sign.

She straightened her shoulders and took a deep breath, and went in the door.

It was dark inside, with the perpetual dank of a room that never saw sunlight. It smelled like stale beer and mildewing particle board. A long bar lined the wall right by the door, and there was a worn path in the cheap tile leading to it.

There were four pool tables in the back and . . .

Starrett.

He was there.

He was standing off to the side of a game being played by a group of young women—college students from the look of them. As one of them set up her shot, the others hung on Starrett's every word.

From a safe distance, Locke could understand and even appreciate his appeal. He was handsome but not too pretty, with a face that was all masculine angles and edges. He wore his hair much too long for a Navy officer, tied back in a pony tail. She knew that meant he still spent much of his time in extremely hostile, dangerous places where looking like a U.S. Navy officer would have been bad for his health. On one level—a very distant level—she had to admire him for that.

He was taller than most men, and well built, with long legs, narrow hips, broad shoulders, and the kind of muscles that meant he used his arms for picking up more than a pen and paper. He wore a snug black T-shirt tucked into a pair of worn-out blue jeans that were stacked over—what else? Cowboy boots.

And that, Locke realized, was a hint that he probably wasn't going to try to outrun her. Earlier today, when he'd lost her, he'd had his sneakers on.

He *probably* wasn't going to outrun her, she reminded herself. With Starrett, she could assume nothing.

After all, why had he called her here if his goal wasn't to humiliate her again in some way?

Keeping an eye on him, Locke sat at the bar and ordered a soda. It wasn't long before he came and sat down next to her.

"Bored, huh?" she said.

"To tears." He smiled at her as if he were actually glad to see her.

"Right." He smelled good. She didn't want him to smell good and she didn't want him to smile that way. She took a sip of her soda, frowning across the room at the young women who were still glancing in Starrett's direction. Anything to keep from getting swallowed up by the blue of his eyes.

He turned to gaze across the room, too. "They're a little too young for me." He hooked his boots over the rungs of the stool and signaled to the bartender for another draft beer. "I prefer my women to be women, not schoolgirls."

"And you're telling me this because . . . ?"

"Because you seemed, I don't know . . . interested?"

"I'm not."

He toasted her with his beer. "My apologies. I guess it was just wishful thinking on my part."

"Someday," Locke said as he drank a full half of the mug, "I'm going to head an FBI counterterrorist team, and you're going to be assigned to assist me. I'm going to be in command, and you're going to have to do exactly what I order, and you're going to remember all those tired come-ons and innuendos that were designed to intimidate me and—"

"I'm not trying to intimidate you," he scoffed. "If I were *trying*, you'd be intimidated."

She rolled her eyes.

"I'm just . . ." He squinted up at the TV in the corner, where a baseball game was playing in silence, the mute on. "I've always been . . . afraid of you, I guess."

Locke swiftly hid her surprise. Of all the things she'd expected him to say, that was not one of them.

"I was always scared you'd actually talk someone into letting you join the SEAL units," he explained. "Scared they'd meet you and realize you were good enough to make the Teams. And I'm sorry, Alyssa, but the entire dynamics would change drastically if we started letting women in. I guess I was always just afraid you were going to be the one to actually kick down the door. So I treated you like shit."

Never in a million years had she thought he'd admit any of that. Locke laughed—a mix of disbelief and surprise that she couldn't contain. "You *still* treat me like shit."

Starrett shrugged. "I don't treat you any differently than I treat anyone else."

"Yeah, right. You're always trying to get Jenk or Stan Wolchonok to go back to your room and get naked with you."

"I wasn't *really* trying to—" He laughed. "That was just talk."

"Meant to intimidate."

"Meant to be funny," he countered. "Where's your sense of humor? You know, women are always shouting about equality, but then when you get it, you don't like it. Typical. So you want me to teach you how to follow someone without ever getting made?"

She blinked at the sudden change of subject.

He smiled. "That's not a trick question."

"Yes."

Starrett nodded. "Good."

"What's the catch?"

"No catch."

She narrowed her eyes at him.

"Really," he said. "You're already good—just not good enough. I'm bored, we're both here in wait mode with nothing better to do." He gave her another of those whole body cowboy shrugs and an aw shucks grin.

Locke didn't trust him. She didn't like him. And she knew he didn't like her.

There had to be a catch.

Fourteen

❧ ❧

"**I** NEED YOU to talk to me," Nils said. The coveralls he'd put on were comfortably loose and warm despite the slight smell of gasoline that clung to them. They also had his name on them. *John.* Stitched in gold thread above the pocket. He'd laughed when he'd first seen it, but Meg hadn't even cracked a smile.

She shook her head now. "I don't want to talk about this anymore. I'm sorry, John. I don't want to hear it. You're not going to get me to change my mind, so talking isn't—"

"No, we don't have to talk about Razeen or the Extremists. We can talk about anything. Just to keep me awake. Seen any good movies lately?"

"You're kidding."

"Yeah, actually I was." He glanced at her. The hazy sunshine brought out the lines of worry and fatigue on her face. Her eyes were distant, as if she were hundreds of miles away. With Amy.

Meg wouldn't tell him where they were heading—or even if they were getting close to their final destination. All she would say was south. Route 95 south.

Nils cleared his throat. "Actually . . ." Just say it. What was she going to do? Get angry enough to grab a gun and start taking hostages? "I was wondering about Daniel."

Meg kept her eyes glued to the road that stretched out into the distance in front of them, but he knew that he'd gotten her attention.

"Until a few days ago I had no idea he was dead," he admitted. "And the report I read didn't go into detail—not beyond, well, 'Car accident in Paris, dead on arrival at . . . Saint Something Hospital.' "

"St. Luc." She turned and looked at him. "What do you want me to tell you, John? That he was with his new mistress when he was hit by a drunk driver who killed them both? That he was coming back from an illicit weekend in the country while I was home with Amy, who had a stomach virus?"

"No, I—" He broke off. Looked at her. Looked at her again. "Oh, shit, you're serious."

"He tried. He really tried to be—" she started, then shook her head. "What am I doing, defending him?"

"Jesus, I'm sorry," he said. "Why—" He stopped himself, but then plowed forward. This topic was already painful for her, why not throw some of his pain onto the table, too? "Why didn't you call me when he died?"

"I couldn't."

"Why not?" he pressed, knowing that the truth could crush him, but needing to hear it just the same.

She wouldn't look him in the eye. "I just couldn't, all right? It was . . . I was . . . God, John, everyone knew about Ashley—that was her name—and it was like some freak show. It was so public. I had to deal with all this grief and anger and . . . and . . . *shame* while everyone watched. And then there was Amy. The worst was having to explain to Amy what that woman was doing in the car with Daniel." She laughed, but there was no humor in it. "The son of a bitch."

"If you'd called me, I could've helped. Meg, I would've come. My CO's great, he would've let me take the time."

Tears hung in her eyes. "If I'd called you, you would've been someone else for them all to stare at." She slowly shook her head. Looked back out the window at the road. "Besides . . ."

"What?" he asked, wanting to know. Besides, *what*?

She just shook her head again.

"So. Why didn't you call me later?" he asked, trying not to sound as if he were in the process of committing emotional hara-kiri, as if his casual question weren't the equivalent of taking a big knife and cutting himself open, exposing himself, raw and bleeding, for her to kick aside. "After you moved back to DC?"

"I didn't know where you were."

That was bullshit and they both knew it. "You could have found me easily enough—at least got a message to me."

She sighed. "It had been *years*," she said, and he knew she was venturing closer to the truth. "For all I knew . . ."

She looked out the window again.

Nils waited fifteen seconds. Thirty. Forty-five. "What?" he asked, unable to keep his mouth shut a second longer.

She shook her head.

"*What?* Come on, Meg, for all you knew *what?*" Hurt rasped in his voice, but he couldn't stop. "Don't leave something like that dangling, god *damn* it!"

It came out in a burst. "For all I knew, you didn't even remember me!"

Silence.

Meg stared out the window again as Nils hung onto the steering wheel.

He was stunned. He didn't know whether to be aghast at her lack of self-confidence, or insulted by her lack of faith in him.

What had she thought he'd meant that night?

I want you so much. He'd kissed her mouth, her neck—her head thrown back, desire etched on her beautiful face. She'd opened her eyes and tugged him down the hall toward her bedroom, unbuttoning his jacket, sliding her hands up underneath his shirt. He could hardly breathe, hardly think, and he kissed her again, just kissed her and kissed her, pinning her against the wall, there in the hall outside her bedroom door.

He knew they needed to talk more before they made love. *If* they made love. Jesus, she was married. And back then, that had mattered to him. Or maybe just *she* had mattered to him. He knew they should slow down. But what he knew hadn't quite caught up with what he wanted.

Nor with what *she* wanted. He felt her fingers on his belt and . . .

"I'm offended," he said, yanking himself back to the present, shifting slightly in his seat, wishing that none of this mattered anymore, that time had done what time was supposed to do and had taken the edge off of everything he'd felt for her, everything he'd wanted so desperately.

Instead that edge had been honed to a razor sharpness that could slice him to pieces if he let it.

It had been the last time he'd seen her in years. She'd unzipped his pants and . . .

And he'd been all over her, too, pulling off that ridiculous jacket, slipping her dress down past her shoulders, filling his hands with her breasts as he kissed her again and again. *I've never felt anything like this before. God, Meg, I've never wanted anyone as much as I want you. . . .*

"How could you think I wouldn't remember you?" he asked her now. He'd lifted his head, looked into her eyes. *I've been waiting my whole life for you.* "Didn't you think I meant anything that I said?"

She didn't. She hadn't. She shook her head now, unwilling to admit it. "I didn't know what to think."

" 'I want you so much,' " he quoted himself. "I think I must've said it five thousand times. Gee. What could I have meant?"

"I thought it was just . . . you know . . ."

"A line?" he supplied the word for her. "Yeah, I've found that always works really well. Tell a woman that you want her so much that you can't even breathe, and then *don't* sleep with her when she tells you in plain English that she wants you, too. If I hadn't cared about you enough to *remember* you, I wouldn't have walked out of there that night."

Jesus, talk about regrets. He should have taken what she'd offered, gone for the single night, to hell with what she'd feel in the morning.

He'd done plenty of one-nighters since then—usually all with married women. He'd pretended that it was the excitement of breaking the rules, of taking something that didn't belong to him that had attracted him to Meg in the first place.

But he'd proven himself wrong again and again, waking up in some stranger's bed, unsatisfied and disgusted with himself.

And aching for Meg.

"I thought—" She closed her eyes. "I didn't know what to

think. You were so young and everything about that entire situation was so emotional. I thought you were swept up in the moment. I thought . . ." She took a deep breath. "John, I never really felt as if I knew you. I mean, it always seemed to me as if you—the *real* you—were hiding behind this fiction you'd created, this make-believe life. And this, I don't know, this *earnest sincerity* that you could do so well was just part of the charade. It was real for that moment, but I never really believed it was more than a game."

Nils didn't know what to say. It was the biggest sacrifice he'd ever made in his entire life—walking away from Meg that night, knowing that he could have her, make love to her, spend the next few hours in paradise.

And she thought he'd been playing some game.

"I didn't forget you," he told her quietly. "Not for one minute."

He could see in her eyes that she still didn't quite believe him.

And he knew that that was his own damn fault.

Alyssa Locke's cell phone rang.

If Sam hadn't known she'd been waiting for some vital phone call, he wouldn't have guessed there was anything going on.

The expression on her face didn't change one bit, yet without moving a single muscle, her tension level elevated from tightly wound to near breaking. Still, if he hadn't been watching for it, if he wasn't hyperaware of her every move and her every breath, he wouldn't have noticed.

She turned away from him to take the call, as if by presenting him with her back, she'd created some kind of cone of silence that would keep him from overhearing her conversation. "Locke."

Sam drained his beer and pretended not to listen.

"Oh, my God, oh, my *God*!" Alyssa turned back, gripping the bar as if she'd fall out of her chair if she weren't holding on.

Sam stopped pretending not to listen.

"Okay," she said into the phone. "All right. I'll . . ." She looked directly at Sam as if she'd just remembered he was there. "Shit! I can't get over to the hospital right now. Tell her . . ."

She had tears in her eyes. For the briefest split second, Sam was positive he'd actually seen tears in Alyssa Locke's usually arctic eyes. But then she blinked and they were gone.

"Yeah," she said to whoever was on the other end of the connection. "And tell her I'll be there as soon as I can."

"What's up?" Sam asked as she slipped the phone back into her fanny pack. She was still clinging to the bar with one hand. "Are you all right?"

She looked into his eyes. Normally she looked around him, above him or through him, but right now, she actually met and held his gaze.

"That was the phone call you've been waiting for," he said. "Anything I can do to help?"

He'd surprised her, and as he watched, he could almost see her brain work, processing the fact that he'd known she'd been waiting on a call, processing . . .

"Why do you want to help me?" she asked.

"Which hospital is it?" he countered. "I was originally thinking you were waiting on a boyfriend to call, but that wasn't . . ." *Tell her* . . . she'd said. *Her* . . . "Is it your mother? Is she sick?"

"My mother died when I was a teenager."

Oh, hell. "I'm sorry." His own mother hadn't ever been much of a prize, but she loved him. Despite marrying his asshole of a father, she'd never done anything truly awful, like go and die on him.

"It's my sister," Alyssa told him. "Tyra. She just went into labor. She's having a baby. Her first baby. It's been kind of a . . . rocky pregnancy."

Rocky must be putting it lightly. Alyssa was still hanging on to the bar as if she'd fall on her head if she let go. She was terrified.

"Is she local?" Sam asked. "Or is this happening out in California? Don't I remember you telling me something about growing up in California?"

She'd never said anything like that to him—never volunteered anything about herself. Yet this was a way to get her talking. She'd correct him without realizing she was revealing personal information.

"No," she said. "I grew up right here, in Washington."

Jackpot.

"Tyra's over at the Howard University Hospital," she continued.

"You want to go over there?" he asked. "You should. I'll wait here."

"Yeah, where have I heard *that* before?"

"Well, good," he said, "at least you're learning."

Alyssa didn't respond to his smile. She looked at her watch. "I'm going to call the hospital for an update in five minutes."

"Look, why don't you just go over there? We weren't really going to do anything tonight anyway. I can do my Yoda imitation for you tomorrow."

She shook her head. "I shouldn't let you out of my sight."

"Oh, hell. What happened? They found Johnny's car—no Johnny, no Meg," he guessed.

She narrowed her eyes. "Did he call you?"

Crap, he was right. "Where'd they find it?"

"So what you're telling me is that he *did* go after Meg."

Oops. "I didn't say that."

"And I didn't say anyone found anything," she countered.

Sam had to smile. "Well, there we go. Neither of us knows shit."

For a half a second, he thought that she was maybe going to smile back. But instead she looked at her watch again.

"Come on," he said, sliding down from the bar stool. "You're going to the hospital. Do you have a car, or did you take a cab over here?"

She dug in her heels. "If Nilsson's going to contact you, it's going to be soon. I'm not going anywhere without you. Not until he turns up."

"Well, guess what?" Sam said. "*I'm* going to visit your sister in the hospital. You can either follow me over there, or drive me in your car, save me cab fare. Your choice."

She still didn't move. "Why would you do this?" she asked. "You're actually willing to spend the evening in a hospital . . . ?"

"I have a sister, too," he reminded her quietly.

For a moment, she just stared at him, as if he were a talking dog or an alien from another planet. Her eyes were luminous and the expression on her face was one he'd never seen before. He knew that for some reason she was walking an emotional tightrope, and his kindness wasn't helping. It was confusing her, making her teeter on the edge of some kind of meltdown.

"Besides," he told her, with a grin and a waggle of his eyebrows, "it's part of my devious plan to get you into bed."

Now, a comment like that she could handle. It made sense in her world, gave her a point of reference. She snorted and headed for the door. "In your dreams."

Sam followed her out the door. Absolutely, in his dreams. Every single night, probably for the rest of his cursed life.

"You're finally glad that I'm here," John said as he loaded Razeen back into the car. "Admit it."

"I am," Meg said. She shut her eyes. "But I'm not."

They'd pulled off the highway and onto a deserted country road in Somewhere, Georgia, to make a pit stop.

Osman Razeen had been only semiconscious and drooling as John had helped him out of the car. A locked gate fenced off what looked like a deserted factory way back from the road. The wildly growing underbrush near the chainlink made a perfect makeshift rest room. They were mostly hidden from view, but John couldn't grab Razeen in a fireman's carry and escape into the woods.

Razeen couldn't stand up by himself, let alone unzip his pants to relieve himself. If John *hadn't* been there . . .

Meg had sat in the grass several dozen yards away from the car and kept an eye on the two men, trying not to watch too closely. While John had Razeen, she had custody of the car keys. No way was she going to risk John loading Razeen into the car, jumping in, and driving away without her.

Still, there was no doubt about it. She was not ready for a full-time career in hostage taking. She was worried about Razeen—about that blow to the head he'd received back in the motel room, about the amount of sleeping pills she'd already given him. It was probably time to give him more, yet he'd seemed so out of it.

John sprawled beside her, reclaiming the car keys and putting them into the front pocket of his coveralls. "Mind if I take a quick combat nap? I just need twenty minutes. . . ." His eyes were shut and his breathing steady almost before he hit the ground.

He was out. Sound asleep. Just like that.

That was impossible. Wasn't it? He couldn't really be asleep. Could he?

Meg sat up and, other than the steady rise and fall of his chest, he didn't move.

She leaned forward, toward him, over him, watching his face for any little sign that he was faking it.

I didn't forget you. Not for one minute.

John's words had made her want to weep. She wasn't sure which was worse—thinking that he wasn't telling the truth, or thinking that he was.

He was asleep on his back, one hand on his chest, the other tucked under his head. He'd already gone into deep REM sleep—she could see his eyes moving beneath his lids. She didn't think there was any way he could've faked that.

The car keys were right there, in his front right pocket.

All she had to do was carefully reach in and take the keys. And drive away without him.

She had to do it. For his sake as well as hers.

But mostly for hers.

She leaned closer. For Amy and Eve's sake, for her own sake, for *John's* sake, she had to get those keys.

Amy was sleeping again.

Even the Bear was dozing. Everyone in the house was taking a siesta in the thick afternoon heat.

Everyone but Eve.

She couldn't sleep. Not after telling Amy about her wedding to Ralph. The memories were too strong.

She'd told the girl only some of it—how nervous she'd been standing there in the church in Ramsgate. How handsome Ralph had looked.

How angry he'd been—later.

But she hadn't told Amy everything. There were some parts she'd never share with another soul.

Such as the look in Ralph's eyes as she met him at the front of the church.

She was wearing the closest thing to a white dress that she had—her off-white suit that was designed to look demure even while it clung to her every curve.

She wasn't sure if this marriage would be legal, if, as a fifteen-year-old, she was even allowed to sign her name on that document without her guardian's permission. Ralph would probably know something like that.

She'd slept badly the night before, tossing and turning, trying to decide whether or not she should tell Ralph the truth. And then the decision was taken from her. She didn't have the opportunity. She hadn't seen him—not until it was too late, with the minister standing nearby, ready to perform the wedding.

It was supposed to be the most casual of ceremonies. They'd do it all over again with his parents and Nick in attendance, in a few months, when Ralph got leave from the army.

Still, he'd dressed in his best suit for the occasion, as had she.

No, she would never forget the way Ralph looked at her, with such hungry love in his eyes.

It was terrifying. And exhilarating. He loved her. She knew that without a doubt.

And she was sure at that moment that she would simply never tell him. She'd smudge her date of birth as she signed the marriage papers. From this moment on, she'd be twenty years old. She *was* twenty years old.

But she still felt only fifteen inside.

"You look so beautiful," he murmured as he took her hand.

"So do you." Shoot. *Go away, mother, I don't need you anymore.* Eve was going to marry Ralph, and he was going to love her for the rest of his life. She would make sure of that. From now on, she didn't need to be a smartass. She wouldn't need to be outrageous, or to flirt with that same edge of desperation that had laced her mother's every word, inaudible to anyone who didn't know her well.

Unlike her mother, Eve *was* going to live happily ever after.

Starting today.

The ceremony passed in a blur.

Ralph slipped a ring on her finger—a beautiful, delicate band of gold that fit as if it had been custom-made. *That's* where he'd been this morning. She wanted to cry. Where had he found the money for this?

"You may kiss the bride."

"I can't believe this is real," Ralph whispered as he drew her into his arms. He gazed at her as if memorizing her face, taking his sweet time before covering her mouth with his own.

It wasn't the kind of kiss she'd been expecting in a church but it didn't take more than a heartbeat for Eve to forget where they were, to forget everything but Ralph.

Still, when he released her, her face heated in a blush. But the minister had turned away, a smile on his lips.

She and Ralph were married now. It was okay for him to kiss her. It was okay for him to . . .

What was she doing? Her hand shook as she signed the documents. There was no need to smudge anything—it was all completely illegible.

Ralph took her to dinner in town. Eve doubted she ate a thing—she could remember none of it. It was all she could do to breathe. Mrs. Ralph Grayson. She was Mrs. Ralph Grayson. As Ralph smiled at her from across the table, her heart felt near to bursting. It was almost enough to cancel out the fear that was coursing through her veins.

Almost, but not quite.

What had she done? She'd lied to the minister, lied to God. And if that weren't bad enough, she'd lied to *Ralph*.

And she was going to have to keep on lying to him, for the rest of their lives.

She wasn't going to live happily ever after, she was going to live untruthfully ever after. Deceitfully ever after. Dishonestly ever after.

"Let's get a room at the hotel," Ralph said, "go right up after dinner." He was gazing at her as if she were a gourmet delicacy the chef had presented. The heat in his eyes was unmistakable and she had to look away as fear flickered, sharper.

Tonight would be their wedding night. And every minute that passed brought it another minute closer.

Thank God for Nicky still being under the weather. She stammered something about wanting to go home and check on him. She hoped Ralph understood.

Something in his eyes told her he understood completely.

So she was spared. Going to a hotel would have been terrifying. Surely this would be easier in the familiarity of her own room. Wouldn't it?

Eve took a deep breath. She was going to do this. She'd married Ralph. She loved him. She *was* old enough for this. After all, Juliet hadn't even been fourteen when she married her Romeo.

Surely all new young brides were frightened.

She was just a little more frightened and a little bit younger than most.

Back at the estate, she went in to check on Nick, but he was already asleep. Mrs. Johnson had been sitting with him. She quickly went back down the stairs to the kitchen and the quarters she shared with Mr. J. with few words and a furtive, disapproving glance in Ralph's direction.

"Didn't you tell her we were getting married?" he asked as, satisfied that Nick was sleeping restfully, his forehead cool, Eve gently closed her brother's bedroom door.

She shook her head. "I didn't tell anyone." Not even Nicky. It hadn't seemed real.

Until now.

And now it seemed *too* real, with Ralph following her into her room as if it were *his* room, too.

He laughed. "So she thinks I've come here to make wild, illicit love to you? Maybe I should go show her the license so she won't think poorly of me all night long."

But instead of chasing after Mrs. J., he shut Eve's bedroom door behind him. And locked it. The click seemed to echo in the sudden silence.

Or maybe she'd just imagined that it had. Because Ralph didn't seem to notice. He was carrying a bottle of wine and two long-stemmed glasses, and he set the glasses down on her bedside table.

"I have a present for you," he said as he opened the bottle. "I brought it up here earlier. It's on your desk."

Eve was pretending to look out the window—anything to keep from staring at Ralph standing there beside her bed. Their bed. They were married, and her bed was their bed now. She was so nervous, she thought she might be sick.

But instead, she turned, obediently, toward her desk. There was a box there—prettily decorated, tied shut with a red ribbon. She hadn't noticed it. Of course, she wouldn't have noticed an elephant standing in the corner of her room right now.

He carried a glass of wine to her. "Go on, open it."

Eve took the glass and set it on the desk to hide the fact that her hand was shaking. She touched the satin of the ribbon, afraid to open it, afraid to look at him. He was standing so close.

"I don't have a gift for you." Her voice shook.

He drew her into his arms. "You've already given me all my heart desires, don't you know that? Just by marrying me." He kissed her and his mouth was so gentle, so sweet. "Please, don't be afraid, Eve. We'll go slowly tonight. I promise." He touched her cheek. "Trust me, all right?"

Trust him. What could she possibly say to that? She hadn't trusted him with her deepest secrets—instead she'd lied to him.

He didn't seem to need a response. He picked up the box, drew her back so she was sitting on the bed with him. "Open it."

He took off his jacket and kicked off his shoes and pulled his feet up onto the bed. He moved so that his back was against the headboard and his legs stretched out, as if he were sitting on Nicky's bed.

As if they were friends, not newly married husband and wife, about to . . . About to . . .

Eve slipped her feet out of her pumps, and tucked them up underneath her, too, careful to stay down at the foot of the bed, glad for the space he was giving her, aware that he'd done it on purpose.

They were going to take this slowly. He wasn't going to jump on her right away, and start taking off her clothes and . . . The relief that flooded through her nearly made her weep.

"It's really nothing that spectacular," Ralph said easily, gesturing toward the box. "So if you've got ideas that the Grayson family diamonds are in there, just banish those thoughts now, all right?"

He sounded no different than he ever had. Nick might have been right beside them, telling them to come on, they were taking too long, he wanted to go for a jaunt in the *Daisy Chain*.

She didn't have to be afraid.

Except she still was. Mother, *help*. "Do the Graysons have family diamonds?" she asked, as if she actually cared.

"One or two here and there," he said. "So you like diamonds, do you?"

She absolutely couldn't care less. But her mother had been wild for them, for anything that glittered. "If someone handed me a box of them, I wouldn't turn it down."

She untied the ribbon and lifted the lid.

The box was filled with . . . letters? Dozens of letters.

"I wanted you to know without a shadow of a doubt that I married you because I want to. I've loved you from nearly the moment we met," Ralph told her now, softly, almost as if he were uncertain. "I wrote those letters to you, Eve. And even though I never dared send them, I meant—and I mean— every word written there. I know it's not much of a gift compared to diamonds . . ."

Eve opened one of the letters, unfolding the paper. "June 2, 1939," was written across the top in Ralph's neat hand. That was weeks ago, soon after he'd first arrived. "My Dearest Eve," she read silently, "I dreamt of you again last night. These days I find myself eager to fall asleep, because you come to me in my dreams. It's the hours spent awake that have become such tribulations. I find myself desperate to see you, to exchange even the briefest of words with you, to be granted the smallest of smiles. Why do you hide from me? What are you afraid of? I am yours, always, until the end of time, Ralph."

What are you afraid of? Oh, Lord. She was going to be sick.

She picked up another, dated several days later. "Dear Eve, I float! You spent the day with Nick and me! Suddenly I'm sixteen again, and would sell my soul for a chance just to hold your hand.

"What is it about you that I love the most? It's not your beauty, although I can't deny you have the power to move me with just a smile. Is it the fact that you've read and adored so many of the books I adore, too? Is it your unembarrassed desire to keep on learning despite the fact you're long out of school? Is it your love of life? That you seem so unself-consciously childlike at times and so wise beyond your years at others? Is it because when you look at me with such admiration in your eyes, I know it's real, not some contrived false emotion designed to flatter or manipulate?

"I've never met a woman so unafraid to speak her mind, so unafraid to laugh out loud, so honest and true."

Oh, God. Tears filled her eyes, but Eve couldn't stop reading.

"I dream of making beautiful love to you, but the truth is, I could sit across the room from you and still be completely satisfied. Just being with you is enough. Please, Heavenly Father, let this summer last forever. I am yours, always, until the end of time, Ralph."

"July 15. Dearest Eve, Tonight I'm dying. I spent the day with you and Nick, while harboring the most dreadful secret.

"I'm leaving Ramsgate. A letter came from my father, and I couldn't bring myself to tell you of its contents—that I've been called into the army—for fear it will change everything between us.

"I kissed you good-bye tonight, knowing that I have less than a fortnight of good-bye kisses left to steal. I want the next few weeks to continue on, untarnished by this grim news.

"But tonight I feel like the blackest of scoundrels. I am a liar, not for telling a mistruth, but for omitting a truth. You are everything that is good and honest and—"

Good and honest.

Eve refolded the letter, put the cover back on the box.

Honest and true.

She *was* going to throw up.

Ralph had poured himself another glass of wine while he watched her read and he took a sip of it now. "Say something, would you? It's rather like cutting my heart out and putting it in a box for you. I should have given you diamonds, shouldn't I have?"

But he *had*. He'd given her a box of perfect diamonds.

"I'm a little embarrassed," he admitted. "A little light-headed, and—"

Eve started to cry.

It wasn't just that the tears she'd been blinking back suddenly overflowed. It was an emotional explosion. They were noisy tears, stormy tears, sobbing, gasping, runny-nosed tears that wouldn't stop no matter how hard she tried.

It was stupid—she who never cried had now burst into tears three different times over the past few weeks. Ralph must've thought she was a complete ninny.

No, he didn't. He thought she was *good* and *honest* and oh, *God*!

She would have run for the door if he hadn't reached her first and pulled her into his arms.

"Oh, Eve, oh, damn, what have I done?" He sounded ready to cry himself. "I didn't mean to upset you—"

It wasn't his fault. He'd done nothing wrong. He'd given her the most romantic, most precious gift anyone had ever given her in her entire life. *She* was the villain here—and what a villain she was. A liar and a fake and a cheat.

"I'm so sorry," Ralph said. "The last thing I wanted to do was to make you cry. God, I should have just bought you a bracelet. What was I thinking? Please, forgive me."

Eve loved the box of letters and she loved him. If there was any forgiving to be done here, it was *him* forgiving *her*. But there was no way she could say any of that, so she kissed him.

He hesitated only the briefest fraction of a second, and then he kissed her, too.

It wasn't enough, and she kissed him harder, deeper, uncertain of what it was she really wanted, but sure that she didn't want his gentle restraint.

She got much more than she bargained for. It was as if she had lit a match and set Ralph on fire. He kissed her hungrily, possessively, demandingly, again and again, deeper, longer, pushing her back onto the bed, his thigh pressed up hard between her legs, his hands . . .

She didn't know when it changed. When her passion turned to fear. Maybe it was when he shifted his weight, pressing his entire body where his one leg had been. Maybe when his chin had rasped roughly against her cheeks and her neck as he kissed her throat. Maybe when she tried to pull away, but found he had her completely pinned.

"Stop," she gasped. "Don't! *Don't!*"

He was off of her in a flash, sitting on the edge of the bed, breathing hard, head in his hands as he began to apologize, again.

"It's not your fault." She pulled down her skirt from where it had ridden up, shockingly, all the way to the tops of her thighs. "It's *my* fault."

"I promised I'd go slowly." He turned and looked at her. "But I lied. I don't think I can, Eve—"

"I'm the liar," she told him. "I should have told you a long time ago. I'm not ready for this. I'm so sorry!"

"I want you *so* badly. I know you're frightened, but—"

"I'm only fifteen!"

Silence.

He stared at her, a flurry of emotions crossing his expressive face. "My God," he breathed. "Please tell me this is a joke?"

Eve shook her head. No joke.

"You're fifteen . . . years *old*?" His voice broke.

She nodded, unable to look into his eyes, where shock was turning into anger.

Ralph started to laugh but it was strained and humorless. "Well, that took care of my . . . overwhelming, uncurbable passion. Nothing like facing charges as a pedophile to douse any romantic urges. Jesus, Eve, you're *fifteen*? How could

you . . . ? Why didn't you . . . ? You knew that I thought . . .
What in God's *name* were you *thinking*?"

She stuck with honesty. "That you would leave if you
knew the truth. I know you thought I was older and—"

"Damn right I would have left! I'm a teacher! I'm supposed to be *teaching* children, not— Oh, my *God*!" He stood
up and started to pace, an explosion of energy, unable to
sit still a moment longer. "I should have known. How the
bloody hell could I not have *known*?"

He turned to stare at her, angry tears in his eyes.

"How could you be fifteen? You don't look fifteen. And
yet . . ." He smacked himself in the head. "Jesu Christe, I
should have *known*."

"I'm so sorry. I know you wanted to . . . But, I need some
time—a few days—to . . ."

"You don't need a few days. You need a few *years*! Oh,
my God, I've ruined you. You're a *child* and I took your trust
and—"

"I'm so sorry. Please . . ." Don't go.

But he was putting on his jacket, his movements jerky.
"I'll call my father's solicitor in the morning, make arrangements for an annulment. Maybe with his help, we can avoid
a scandal. Here I was, thinking I was keeping your reputation from being shredded, while in fact, all along, you were
ruining *me*."

"No." Her tears had started again. "Wait. Ralph, no one
knows how old I really am. My own stepmother thinks I'm
seventeen or eighteen. We just won't tell anyone. And . . .
and . . . You said we could take things slowly tonight." Eve
prayed that this could still have a happy ending, rather than
the train wreck they seemed careening toward. "Why can't
we just take it *really* slowly? And maybe this fall when you
get leave, I'll be ready to . . . We'll be able to . . ."

"You want me to continue this charade?" He was incredu-
lous. "Can't you just hear it? 'Going back to England, eh,
Grayson?' 'Indeed, Major, I'm going home for the weekend
to see if my fifteen-year-old wife's old enough yet to con-
summate my marriage.' God *damn* you." He started for the
door. "The solicitor will send you the paperwork necessary.
There'll be a generous settlement, of course."

"I won't sign it!" she cried. "I don't want your stupid money! I love you! And you love me!" She clung to the box of his letters like a life buoy.

He turned back and his face was hard, his eyes like that of a stranger. "I fell in love with someone honest. Someone who never would have used such deceit and trickery the way you did. The person I fell in love with apparently doesn't exist."

Eve gazed at him, stricken. There was nothing she could say, no argument that could challenge that.

"Sign the papers when they come, Eve," he said quietly. "My solicitor will do his best to keep this entire incident hushed up. For both our sakes. And with the settlement money, you'll be able to get out of town and go back to California."

Incident. Just like that, he'd reduced the months of magic that they'd shared to one cold, impersonal word.

"I will regret meeting you for the rest of my life," he whispered.

As Eve watched, Ralph went out the door without looking back.

Fifteen

$\backsim\!\!\!\!\!\!\!\!\!\sim\!\!\!\!\!\!\!\!\!\sim$

SAM DIDN'T KNOW *what* in hell was going on.

Traffic had been a pain in the ass, and it had taken them just short of forever to find a space in a parking garage near the hospital. Alyssa had lightened her load by tossing her fanny pack into the trunk, and they'd headed for the hospital at a dead run.

They took the information desk by storm—Alyssa more tense than he'd ever seen her before.

And when a quick phone call to the maternity ward revealed that Tyra had given birth to a little girl just thirty minutes earlier, and that both mother and child were doing remarkably well, Alyssa Locke, the coldhearted ice bitch, actually started to cry.

Sam was stunned.

He was completely speechless.

It wasn't as if she'd started sobbing, tears pouring down her cheeks as she gasped for air. No, didn't it figure? Alyssa Locke cried like a man.

She cried the way WildCard Karmody had cried when he'd gotten that Dear John email from Adele Zakashansky. The way Nils had cried when Meg had gone AWOL. Her eyes filled with tears that she couldn't blink back and she turned her head away, as if she hoped Sam wouldn't see.

So, like with WildCard and Nils, he pretended not to see.

And, upstairs, he pretended not to watch and listen as Alyssa hugged her sister and the sister's husband, a tall black man who gave Sam a handshake, a candy cigar, and a tired smile as they came into the private hospital room.

The baby's name was Lanora, and for some reason, that got the tears started again—both from Alyssa and her sister.

227

But it wasn't until they'd left the maternity ward that Alyssa had a total meltdown.

Of course, being Alyssa Locke, she managed to do it quietly, and with dignity.

One second she was walking beside Sam, heading for the elevators. And the next, she just stopped walking.

She sat down on a waiting area sofa, covered her face with her hands, bent over as if she had a stomachache, and silently wept.

Sam wanted to *do* something. With any other woman, he would've been right there, next to her, putting his arms around her, giving her a shoulder to cry on, whispering words of comfort into her ear.

But Alyssa wasn't just any woman.

So instead he sat down across the room, far enough away to give her privacy. Close enough so that she could keep an eye on him.

It was what he would have done if Mike Muldoon or Frank O'Leary had started to cry.

Clearly there was something else going on here besides a sister giving birth to a healthy baby girl.

But chances were that he was never going to find out.

Nils didn't move. He didn't change his breathing, didn't open his eyes, but he was instantly awake.

Someone was touching him—reaching into the front pocket of his pants.

Friend or foe?

His brain was fuzzy from exhaustion, so it took him a few seconds longer than usual to remember where he was, what he was doing there, and who the hell could be touching him.

He was outside—he could feel the sun on his face, smell the recently cut grass. He was lying on his back, on the ground and . . .

Meg Moore. Razeen. Kidnapped daughter. Meg Moore. Hostages in the K-stani men's room. *Meg.*

He was in Georgia, taking a desperately needed break from the hypnotizing drive south on the relentless sameness of Route 95.

And that was Meg's hand inching farther into his pocket.

He could smell her hair, feel the warmth of her body as she leaned over him.

She was going for the car keys.

God *damn* it.

Hadn't anything he'd said to her gotten through?

Apparently not.

Nils kept his eyes shut and his breathing steady as he felt her hesitate. The pockets of the coveralls were deeper than she'd thought.

Maybe she wouldn't do it. Maybe she'd give up because she really didn't want to ditch him here, in backwoods Georgia. Maybe she'd give up because she wanted him with her, *needed* him, even though she couldn't yet admit it to herself.

She reached farther. And froze.

You bet, sweetheart. That's *exactly* what you think it is.

One of the biggest problems with going commando under a pair of loose coveralls was that nothing lined neatly up.

"Oh, God," she breathed.

But she kept going.

Nils managed to keep his eyes closed and to keep breathing. God bless Master Chief Vandegrift for drilling Nils's BUD/S class relentlessly when it came to waking up silently and feigning sleep or lifelessness. Although, as much as he now tried, his body was having a decidedly *non*lifeless reaction to her hand against his inner thigh.

He tried to focus on the fact that she had her hand in his pants for all the wrong reasons. She was going to take the keys. And then she was going to stand up, get in the car, and drive away without him.

Or maybe she wouldn't. Maybe after she got the keys, she wouldn't be able to do it. Nils stayed silent and still, wanting to wait and see what she would do.

He knew he could stop her. At any time. Even after she got the keys and got to her feet.

He knew he could outrun her to the car, even starting from a completely prone position like this. He could overpower her easily, take her little handgun pretty damn easily. But he didn't want to do it that way. He didn't want to *take* her handgun.

He wanted her to give it to him.

If she gave it to him, there would be no mistakes. No one would be at risk for being accidentally shot. If she gave it to him, she'd be voluntarily turning herself in. Any chance that she had of making right all her wrongs depended on that.

Painstakingly slowly, she pulled the keys from his pocket.

Please don't do this, Meg.

"I'm sorry, John," she whispered, almost as if she'd heard him. "I don't have a choice."

It seemed like the right time to open his eyes. "There's always a choice."

Startled, she tried to jerk her hand free, but she was trapped by his pocket. She lost her balance and fell forward, directly on top of him, her arm pinned.

"Ouch, ouch, ouch!" Her wrist was twisted, and he reached between them to free her hand from his pants, deftly removing the keys from her fingers as he did so and stashing them in his left pocket.

"You're awake," she accused him, struggling to sit back up.

But he had both arms around her now, and he wouldn't let her go. "Actually," he said, "I'm not sure about that. For all I know, this could be a dream. One of the better ones I've had lately, if you want to know the truth."

She'd stopped struggling, but she was breathing hard as she gazed down at him. Her face was maybe two inches away from his. Maybe less. "You can't come with me," she said fiercely. "You *can't*."

"Although if this was a dream, you wouldn't snarl at me, you'd kiss me."

Meg closed her eyes in exasperation. "John—"

He supposed he took advantage of the fact that her eyes were closed and her lips were parted. But frankly, he wasn't thinking of much beyond what he wanted. He just covered her mouth with his and kissed her.

He could taste her surprise, mixed with sweet coffee and *Meg*.

After nearly three years, he was finally kissing Meg again.

She made a soft sound in the back of her throat that

might've been despair, but then she kissed him back so hungrily, he was sure he had to be dreaming.

She was fire in his arms, her breasts dizzyingly soft against his chest.

Nils opened his mouth to her, letting her kiss him ferociously, drinking in her passion, straining to pull her closer. He couldn't get enough of her, even at a moment like this, when he wasn't quite sure where he ended and she began. He'd never been able to get enough of her—he doubted he ever would.

Her hands were in his hair, touching his face, his neck, and then his chest as she reached between them and unfastened the top buttons of his coveralls. And then, dear Lord, she was straddling him.

She kissed him again, even more deeply, as she pressed herself against him, as her hands continued to work his buttons free.

No, strike that. As *one* hand continued to work his buttons free. The other was dipping into his left pants pocket.

Shit. Nils opened his eyes to a sky that was a miraculous shade of blue just as she broke away from him, car keys in her right hand, gun in her left. "Don't move!"

"Ah, Christ." Nils let his head bounce back against the ground.

She was scuttling away from him, still on her butt. She put the keys into her pocket and held the gun with both hands. "Just . . . don't move!" Her voice shook.

"I'm not moving," he said. But then he did move. He sat up, fast, to hide the tent pole effect that being completely aroused created with the baggy coveralls. He felt his face heat from embarrassment—when was the last time he'd actually blushed? He didn't know which was worse—being taken in by her again, actually believing that she'd wanted to kiss him that way, or having her witness such an obvious and crude proof of his desire.

"Stop," she ordered. "Don't come any closer!"

"What are you going to do, Meg, shoot me?" He would have preferred her shooting him over running that sexual con game. At least he knew how to deal with the pain from a bullet wound.

"I'm going to get into the car, and I'm going to go find Amy."

She'd do anything to save Amy—she even would have slept with the guard at the hotel if she'd had to. She'd said that herself. The guard, or anyone, including Nils, apparently. *If* she'd had to. God *damn* her.

And god damn himself, too. This was his fault for kissing her. What did he think? She'd willingly take a time-out to neck by the side of the road when every cell in her body was screaming for her to go rescue her daughter?

Nils shouldn't have kissed her, shouldn't have taken advantage of her that way. And he couldn't fully blame her for turning around and taking advantage of *him*. He'd been in her shoes plenty of times—on a dangerous op and in a position where he would have done and said anything to reach his single-minded goal.

"I'm sorry," he told her, his anger snuffed, his voice quiet. "I shouldn't have kissed you, but I wanted to and . . . I'm sorry."

That got through to her far better than shouting would have. As Nils watched, Meg's eyes filled with tears. "I'm sorry, too."

"Not sorry enough to take me with you, though," he said with an attempt at a smile. "I'm afraid I'm not sorry enough either—not enough to let you leave me behind."

"Why are you doing this?" she asked.

If she had to ask that, she didn't have the slightest clue about anything at all. He wanted to cry, too. How could she not know?

But she'd said she didn't know him, couldn't tell when he was being honest and when he was hiding behind some . . . what was it she'd said? Some well-conceived fiction.

Nils looked at her. Even sitting there, weapon clutched in both hands, she looked vulnerable and completely out of her league. A stranger in a strange land. Would she even be able to recognize if he answered her with the bald truth?

"You need me," he said. That was the easy part, so he said it again. "I'm doing this because you need me." The hard part was more difficult to spit out. But he did it. "Almost as much as I need you."

She was surprised. He wasn't sure she believed him, but at least he'd succeeded in surprising her.

"You don't need me." She spoke with such certainty.

"Oh," he said, "right. I don't know how I feel—whereas *you* do."

"No," she said. "Nope. No way. I would never presume to know *anything* about the way you feel." She laughed in exasperation. "Not even when your tongue's in my mouth and your hand's down my pants. Who knows *what* you could be thinking."

"I'm thinking that I need you." He still had to work to say the words, but it wasn't as hard as the first time.

"Why would you just suddenly say that to me now? We don't see each other for nearly three years, and suddenly you need me?"

"It's not sudden," Nils said as evenly as he could. "I wasn't in a position where I could tell you before. You weren't free—"

"Dammit, I'm not free now!"

He just watched her, waiting for her to explain.

"I'm ready to die," she said more quietly. "To save Amy. There's no question, John, if it's her or me, it's me I'll sacrifice. But I can't—I *won't*—let you die, too. And the only way I can be sure that won't happen is for you to stay here, now. Please. Let me leave without you."

Her calm acceptance of her fate made his chest and throat feel tight. So naturally, he made a joke. "If you don't want me to die, threatening to shoot me seems a little counterintuitive."

She didn't laugh.

They might've sat there, staring at each other, at an impasse for much longer, but the sound of a car approaching made Nils lift his head.

Shit. "Police car at four o'clock."

"What?" She didn't understand him.

"Back and to your right," he quickly explained. "We've got a visitor and it's a cop."

Once Meg understood, she made the handgun disappear, fast, turning to peer worriedly up the street at the approaching police vehicle.

The cop was local, male, and riding alone.

Come on, keep driving, Billy Bob. Everything's fine here. Just a man and woman stopped to take a little rest, maybe have a picnic and a little roll in the grass by the side of the road.

Nils watched the cop's eyes, saw what the man saw. That the car was nice, a white sedan in good condition. The woman looked nice, too, but the man—Nils—wasn't so fresh. He needed a shave. Looked like he needed a shower, too.

The cop looked at him harder and Nils knew what he was thinking. That Nils had either just gotten off from work, or he was an escaped convict who'd stolen some coveralls from some garage a few miles up the road—maybe after killing everyone in the service station.

The cop looked at Meg again, his eyes narrowing. On second glance, she definitely looked frightened—as if she might've been taken hostage by an escaped murderer.

"Smile," Nils hissed to Meg, but it was too late.

The cop was young and full of himself, probably itching to throw his weight around. He wasn't in any kind of hurry to get to the donut shop—if they even had a donut shop in Nowhere, Georgia. As Nils watched, he stopped his car and got out.

Ah, shit.

Meg's car was between them and the cop. He would surely look inside as he went past—and see Osman Razeen, handcuffed and tied up in the backseat.

No, Officer, that's just my wife's crazy cousin—went on a bender and beat the crap out of Aunt Doreen. He's nasty when he gets this way. We had to restrain him so we could take him back to the rehab center in Florida. Although he'll probably just escape again.

"Everything okay here?" the cop called out in his Georgia drawl. It was much thicker and gooier than Starrett's Texas twang.

"Everything's fine, Officer." Nils stood up, and Meg was right beside him.

But the cop wasn't talking to them. He'd stopped alongside the car where he'd leaned down to speak to . . .

Razeen. Who was sitting up in the backseat. Wide awake.

While Nils and Meg had been arguing, he'd managed to roll down the window. The car was childproof—he couldn't unlock the backdoor—but the bastard had been about to escape out the window.

Shit.

Nils felt Meg touch his arm. "What are we going to do?" she breathed.

We. Now it was *we*. Thank God. Nils suddenly loved this cop. He loved his meandering gait, his tough-guy squint, his cheap mirrored sunglasses. This cop had turned them back into a *we*.

"Give me the handgun," he breathed back.

She shook her head. "No." She had that look in her eyes again. That on-the-verge look that made him think it wouldn't take much for her to find the motivation to unload her weapon into Razeen's head.

"Meg, stay cool," Nils said just loudly enough for her to hear.

But she didn't move, didn't blink, didn't even seem to know he was there anymore. Just like that, *we* didn't mean Meg and John. *We* meant Meg and her little handgun.

"You all right in there, sir?" the cop asked Razeen.

Nils felt Meg tense as she reached into her pocket for her weapon.

Shit. This was going to be really bad.

"I love you," he whispered, throwing the last of his cards faceup onto the table. "Meg, please don't do this."

It was only late afternoon, but the neon in the window was bright and beckoning. Sam took Alyssa's arm and pulled her into the bar.

"You need a drink," he told her.

"A drink is the *last* thing I need."

The fact that she didn't physically resist, that she didn't immediately yank her arm free from his grip convinced him that she *did* need something stiff that would burn all the way down, despite her listless protest.

It was a working class establishment. Dim with no frills. But it was clean and it had padded stools at the bar.

Sam pulled one out for her. It wasn't meant to be chivalrous. He would have done the same for Nils or WildCard if they were walking around like some kind of zombie, exhausted and embarrassed for giving too much away in public.

But *she* didn't know that. He sat before she did, trying to cancel out the implied respect of pulling out the stool.

"A bottle of my favorite Uncle and couple of shot glasses," he told the bartender, setting a pile of money on the bar.

Alyssa sat down. "You don't fool around, do you?"

"Hell, no." Sam poured them both a shot of the Jack Daniel's. He didn't wait for her. He just tossed back the shot, letting it roar down his throat.

Glory be to God.

Alyssa picked up the glass and sipped it before emptying her glass. She probably got her toes wet before jumping into a lake, too. She didn't make a face as Jack elbowed his way down her throat and into her stomach. She didn't flinch, didn't react, didn't so much as blink. Which meant that she had a reaction. She was working too hard to hide it.

"Good, huh?" He refilled their glasses. "I know *I* feel better already."

She didn't say a word, she just poured back the second shot, drinking right in sync with him.

He reached for the bottle, but this time she stopped him from refilling her glass.

"Mind if I get a real glass with ice?" she asked. "I'd like to return to the illusion that I'm civilized."

"Bartender, two glasses with ice."

"Thanks, Starrett," she said, as Sam poured them both another drink.

He glanced at her only briefly, aware that her gratitude had nothing to do with the whiskey he was pouring into her glass. "It's no big deal."

"It's actually a very big deal," she told him. "And . . . I owe you an explanation."

He pushed her glass toward her, took a sip of his own drink, staring into the amber liquid so that he wouldn't look at her.

She had tears in her eyes again. It was hard work—this pretending not to notice.

"You owe me nothing," he said.

"My mother died when I was thirteen," Alyssa told him, her voice low. "I was the oldest, and I fought hard to keep my sisters and me together. I'd promised my mother I'd take care of them, and I made damn sure that I did."

Sisters. Plural. Hell. Sam knew what was coming. He swallowed a shot's worth of whiskey from his glass and braced himself for it.

"But . . ."

Here it came.

"Two years ago, my littlest sister, Lanora, died while giving birth."

Lanora. It all made sense now. God *damn* it . . .

"It seems almost absurd, doesn't it?" she asked in that same low, controlled voice, her face expressionless. "I mean, here it is, the twenty-first century. With all this technology—" She broke off, shaking her head. "There were complications. She had an aneurism during premature labor, and neither she nor the baby survived."

"I'm sorry," Sam said. Crap, it sounded so inadequate.

But she met his eyes, and whatever she saw there made her nod. "Thanks." She gave him a smile.

It was just a little smile, and it faded almost instantly, but oh, sweet Jesus, Alyssa Locke had actually *smiled* at him.

"Burying Lanora was the hardest thing I've ever done," she said even more quietly than before. "I felt as if I buried my heart with her."

Sam looked at Alyssa Locke, sitting there, staring down into her glass, and he wanted to cry. For years, he'd thought of her as heartless and cold. He'd had no idea what she'd been living through.

"My cousin Jerry died of AIDS five years ago. He was my best friend back in grade school," Sam told her, gazing down at the ice cubes in his own glass. "My sister Elaine and I were the only cousins who went to the funeral. Lainey came to the base and forced me to go back to Texas with her. She wouldn't let me be a coward and hide from it—from the

AIDS and what it meant—like all our other cousins. I've always been thankful to her for that. I don't know what I'd do if *she* died. I know how I felt when Jerry was gone, and we hadn't been close for years." He looked up at her and put it all out on the line. "I can't even imagine the depth of your loss, Alyssa."

She held his gaze a long time before looking away. "I was just starting to come back to life last year, when Tyra got pregnant . . ." Alyssa took a sip of her drink.

Dear God. "So you've been in hell for the past nine months."

She met his eyes again and nodded. "Yeah. It's stupid, I know. All the doctors told me that what happened to Lanora was some kind of freak thing. It wasn't genetic. Tyra wasn't in danger. Intellectually, I knew this. Emotionally . . ." She shook her head. "Emotionally, I've been a wreck."

Her tears back in the hospital had been from relief. After nine months of fear and anxiety, the relief had been too much to handle.

Sam knew from his own experience that positive emotions were harder to control than the negative ones. Grief, anger, pain, and frustration. You got used to stuffing those feelings back down inside. But relief, when it hit, had a knockout punch. It could smack you flat on your ass, make grown men cry like babies.

Like Alyssa Locke had cried.

Sam toasted her with his glass. "Tonight, the waiting is over. Tyra is fine. Her baby is perfect, with a perfect name, too, I think. Tonight, s—" He stopped himself from calling her *sweet thing*, but just barely.

She looked at him sharply, right in the eye, and he knew that *she* knew exactly what he'd been about to say. He cleared his throat. "Tonight, *Ms. Locke,* you can relax."

Alyssa Locke laughed. She was looking straight at him, and she actually laughed and then gave him a smile that nearly rivaled the wattage of the smiles he'd seen her shoot her strange little partner.

"Well, praise the Lord," she said, lifting her glass in a salute. "It's a bonafide two-miracle night."

* * *

"Mighty hot today, to be sitting inside a vehicle like that, with the window only half down," the small-town Georgia policeman said to the dangerous Kazbekistani terrorist tied up in the backseat of Meg's car.

"I am used to the heat," Razeen said in his heavily accented English. He'd gotten awfully lucid awfully fast. He must've been playing at being out of it when they'd first gotten out of the car, Meg realized. "Everything is fine. My young friends were having a lover's quarrel. We all thought it best not to continue it while on the highway. We'll be back on the road in no time, of this I am sure."

Meg looked at John. What the hell was going on? Why didn't the cop see Razeen's handcuffs? And why wasn't Razeen screaming his head off that he was being kidnapped?

She met John's eyes. *I love you.* If he'd been looking for a diversion, *that* had worked. She'd been ready to pull out her gun, but his words—as untruthful as they were—had made her hesitate just a moment. Just long enough for Razeen to start talking.

Why wasn't he giving them up?

"He figures he'll have a better chance getting away from us," John said, low enough so the cop couldn't overhear him. "If he sounds an alarm, he'll be taken into custody. And then he's *really* screwed."

"Where you folks from?" the cop asked Razeen in his thick drawl. "What's that accent you got there? French?"

"French, yes. *Oui,*" Razeen lied. "I am from France. My friends, of course, are American."

"Heading down to Florida?" Apparently, to this cop, a foreigner was a foreigner was a foreigner. "This time of year, we get a lot of tourist traffic just passing on through."

"*Tourists,* that is right," Razeen replied. "My friends are taking me to see your fabulous Disney World. I have heard it is not to be missed."

The cop seemed satisfied that they wouldn't be staying in his jurisdiction for long. "You be sure to enjoy Mickey Mouse, you hear?"

"I will, of that I am most certain."

The cop straightened up and looked at Meg carefully. She knew her eyes were red and her hair looked like hell. He looked from her to John Nilsson and back. He may not have known a Frenchman when he saw one, but he knew the signs of domestic trouble. "Everything all right, ma'am?"

Heart in her throat, she nodded. "Yes, thank you."

He gestured with his head back behind them, toward the fence. "That old factory back there's private property. You best get going as soon as possible. The owner don't like folks hanging about out here."

"I think we're ready to hit the road." John headed around, past the cop, to the driver's side of the car. "Honey, you got the keys?"

He knew damn well that she had the keys. As Meg watched, unable to stop him, he climbed in behind the wheel.

With the cop standing there, there was nothing she could do but get into the car and hand John those keys.

His eyes were apologetic—no doubt because her own were shooting fire. "I'm going to do whatever I have to, to stick close to you," he told her quietly. In Welsh.

I love you. No doubt he'd been doing "what he'd had to" when he'd said that to her. It was no more real than her kissing him to get the car keys had been. She knew that. She'd known it the moment the words had left his lips.

It was stupid the way her heart had leapt so crazily when he'd said it.

As Meg clenched her teeth, John started the car. He did a three-point turn under the cop's watchful eye and headed back toward the interstate.

I love you.

Right. She wanted to cry.

This was just another game they were playing—a life and death game this time. And Meg had just lost this round.

In every way imaginable.

Sixteen

$\sim\!\!\sim\!\!\sim$

LOCKE WAS WELL on her way to being skunked.

She couldn't remember the last time she'd had this much to drink.

She couldn't remember the last time she'd had *a* drink, singular.

She couldn't remember why she'd ever had such an aversion to Ens. Sam Starrett. Ens. *Roger* Starrett. That was the man's real name. Roger not Sam.

Roger-not-Sam was one unbelievably gorgeous man.

Provided, of course, that a woman went for tall, big-muscled, macho cowboy rednecks with long legs, perfect, *perfect* asses, sky blue eyes, and solid senses of humor.

Funny how she'd never particularly noticed his sense of humor before. Right now, she couldn't stop laughing at damn near everything he said.

"Roger." Locke laughed, and he laughed with her. He was nearly as skunked as she was.

"You know, it really used to piss me off when you called me that," he said in his good old boy drawl that used to piss *her* off, but now flowed past her like warm honey, "but right now I don't mind it at all. What'dya know?"

"If your name's Roger," she asked, propping her chin up in her hand on the bar, "why does everyone call you Sam? Or sometimes Bob. I've heard Stan Wolchonok call you Bob. Sam, Bob, anything but Roger."

He laughed, and she made herself frown at him. She was serious. She really wanted to know.

"Bob is from some book," he told her. "I don't remember—you'll have to ask the senior chief. He's always reading something or another, and I think there was some

241

book he read with some guy named Bob Starrett." He poured her another drink. "Sam comes from Houston. You know, Sam Houston, famous Texan? The guys started calling me Houston, and the next thing I knew, I was Sam."

Locke tried to get it straight. "They called you Houston because you came from Houston?"

"No, because my name was Roger, and I was from Texas, and you know, *Roger, Houston*? You know, like NASA?"

"Got it." *Roger, Houston* was what the astronauts said over the radio when they spoke to the NASA base in Houston from outer space. The fact that his first name was Roger had given him the nickname Houston. And once everyone started calling him Houston, the nickname Sam came out of that.

It made sense in a too-skunked sort of way.

Locke sighed and took a sip of her whiskey. It no longer had much of a taste. "Nobody ever gave me a nickname."

"Not true."

She looked at him, sitting there smiling at her, like some kind of cowgirl's fantasy. "*Sweet thing* isn't a nickname, Rog. It's an insult. It's objectifying. You know, all those generic so-called terms of endearment do nothing more than take away a woman's individuality. You call me *sweet thing* and I'm one of two thousand nameless, faceless women you've encountered in your life. You call me *Locke*, I know without a doubt that you know who I am."

"Fair enough. Although two thousand might be a *little* high."

"What if I called you Cute Ass?" she said. "How would that make *you* feel?"

Sam threw his head back and laughed. "Pretty damn good, actually."

"No, it would not."

"Hell, yes, it would. It would mean that maybe you spent some time checking me out. Because I know for a fact that I *do* have a particularly cute ass." He topped off her drink again.

"Trust me, it might be amusing for a while, but eventually it would make you feel as if you had no real value as a human being, and—" Locke stopped. Looked at her full glass. Looked at the bottle of whiskey that was nearly empty. Looked at his glass. Tried to remember when the last time was he'd picked it up and taken a drink. Couldn't.

As an experiment, she picked up her glass, took a healthy swallow, and set it back down on the bar.

"How about if I call you Alyssa and you call me Sam?" he said. "No sweet thing, no cute ass, no Roger. That sound fair?"

"But your *name* is Roger."

"I could argue that you are one very sweet thing," Starrett replied. He laughed at the look on her face. "But I wouldn't dare."

He picked up the bottle of whiskey and refilled her glass to the brim, and she remembered why she'd always had such an aversion to him.

"You are!" she exclaimed. "You're trying to get me drunk, aren't you? You *son* of a—"

"Whoa." He put the bottle down. "I am not. I mean, yes, I am helping you forget your troubles, and frankly," he said with a laugh, "I think I've already done a damn fine job of it, but I promise, my motives here are completely pure. No ulterior motives. Really. I'm not doing anything I didn't do when WildCard had his meltdown a few months ago. I'm just . . . I'm trying to make sure you relax tonight."

He was protesting just a little too much. Locke narrowed her eyes at him. "I think you're trying to get me drunk because you've got a meeting planned later with John Nilsson, and you want to make sure I can't follow you."

He snorted. "That's ridiculous."

But that was exactly what he would do and say if she *were* right and he was trying to throw her off course.

"No, it's not. And, guess what? I can still follow you."

She stood up, just to prove her point. The world wobbled, but she wouldn't let herself teeter. She lifted her chin defiantly at Starrett. See?

He laughed again. "Yeah, right. Siddown, Locke, before you fall on your face."

"I can. Go ahead." She motioned toward the door. "Leave. I'll follow you."

He was sitting on the bar stool, one elbow on the bar, the

other on the back of his seat, just looking at her, something dangerous in his eyes.

"Well, now," he finally said. "As lovely as that sounds, you don't need to follow me. My big plans for tonight include going back to the hotel and scoring some dinner, maybe watching a movie on pay-per-view while I try to rehydrate just a touch, then sleeping this off for about twelve hours straight."

Locke was searching her jeans pockets for her car keys. She had a pair of handcuffs in her back pocket—useful if she ran into public enemy number one, maybe on her way to the ladies' room—but no keys. "I *can* follow you, and I *will.*"

"Come on, I thought we were friends now. And I'm telling you, friend to friend, that I'm not going anywhere tonight—"

"We're not friends, Starrett, we're nemeses who just had a few too many drinks together. Friendship is built on trust. And I trust you about as far as I can throw up." She looked up from her search for her keys. That hadn't come out right. "Throw *you.*"

He was laughing again. "I like the first one better."

She refused to be distracted by his sparkly eyes, white teeth, and that dimple that appeared alongside his mouth. He had a nice mouth, a great smile and— No, no!

She focused on his forehead. "I'm being very, very serious here. I don't trust you, Starrett. I'm not *going* to trust you and—"

"Okay, fine," he said, giving up. "You don't have to trust me. You can come back to the hotel with me and watch me like a hawk all night long. Be my guest."

Locke finally found the key to her car stuck inside several folded five-dollar bills in the front pocket of her jeans. She'd forgotten—she wasn't carrying her usual twenty pound key ring. She'd taken her car key from the ring and tossed the rest of them into her fanny pack, in the trunk of her car. She just had this one little key with her right now.

Starrett swiftly scooped it from her hands.

"Hey!" She glared at him.

"Nemeses don't let nemeses drive drunk."

She had to laugh at that one. "I'm not drunk." She corrected herself. "Okay, I'm a little drunk. I shouldn't drive, I *won't* drive, but neither should you."

"This is exactly why God invented taxicabs." He stood up and pocketed her key. "Look, I really was just planning to get room service and kick back tonight—I mean, that's what I planned before getting sidetracked by Uncle Jack. Years of heavy drinking's taught me to go home after getting a buzz on instead of walking the streets and looking to pick a fight. So I'm not going to fight with you, Ms. Nemesis. I'm going home—or at least to the nearest semblance of home that I've got right now, which happens to be an enormous two room suite in the Marriott. If you want to baby-sit me, I'm fine with that. You can come on up. You can even sleep on the couch if you want. That way you'll know where I've been all night, and I won't have to worry about you, shit-faced and alone—"

"I am *not* shit-faced, thank you very much—"

"And pretending that you're not shit-faced when you damn well *are*, lurking in the hall outside my hotel room, attracting God only knows what kind of attention from whatever lowlifes wander those unprotected halls."

"You mean Karmody and O'Leary?" she asked.

He grinned. "I love it that you just made a joke about two of my best friends. If someone had told me four hours ago that I'd be in a bar laughing at a joke Alyssa Locke made after helping me polish off nearly an entire bottle of Jack Daniel's, I'd've laughed in their face."

"I wasn't joking."

"Let's find us a cab." He headed for the door, looking back to ask, "You following me?"

As Locke went out into the still warm night, it occurred to her that going back to Starrett's hotel room with him was probably a really bad idea.

But the idea of dinner sounded good, and the thought of lurking in the hall outside of Starrett's room all night when she was already exhausted and at least partially inebriated— yes, it was true—sounded even worse.

Besides, she certainly had a better shot at keeping an eye on Starrett if she were right there in his room, didn't she?

It wasn't as if she were going to do something *really* stupid, like sleep with the man.

No, she was just a little drunk, she wasn't stupid.

Locke followed Sam Starrett's perfect ass right into a cab.

"Meg's got her weapon pointed right at you," John said to Razeen as they headed toward the highway. "She'll shoot you right through the back of the seat if you so much as move a muscle."

He gave her a look, and Meg quickly took out her gun, angling slightly in her seat so that she could see Razeen.

He'd pulled the blanket over himself—that's why the cop hadn't seen that he was cuffed and tied.

"How much longer until we get to Disney World, Mom?" Razeen looked her dead in the eye.

Meg tried not to react. That was the second time he'd mentioned Disney World. Did he somehow know that her drop off point was in Orlando?

Maybe the Kazbekistani Extremists had some kind of home base there and Razeen knew about it. But if Razeen knew it, wasn't it likely that the FBI knew, too? God, if she was going to come all this way only to walk straight into the FBI's waiting arms . . .

She couldn't think about that right now. "How long have you been awake?" she asked Razeen.

"A few hours," he told her. "I would greatly appreciate something to drink."

"Don't get close to him," John warned her sharply. "Don't hold a soda for him, don't reach over the back of that seat—don't even *think* about it, Meg."

She looked at him in exasperation. "He's thirsty. What am I supposed to do? Ignore him? I hope that wherever Amy and my grandma are, someone's kind enough to give them water if they're thirsty."

John glanced up from the road, and although he didn't say anything, she knew he didn't think her daughter needed water anymore.

He thought Amy and Eve were dead.

God *damn* him.

Fighting tears, Meg gathered up all the straws, both used

and unused, that they'd gotten from their fast-food drive through excursions. There had been nowhere to ditch their garbage, so she had six of them all together. She set to work attaching them, one inside the very edge of the other—no easy task while she still held the gun.

"You need not worry. I am no longer trying to escape," Razeen volunteered.

"I'm sure you'll understand if I don't just take your word for that," John countered.

"My reaction in the motel was . . . what is the expression? Knee jerk." Razeen looked earnestly into the rearview mirror at John. "I have been thinking, and I believe there are worse things than becoming a martyr for my cause by dying at the hands of the Extremists."

He met Meg's eyes. "Better yet even would be death by an American. Such an event might even make the news on CNN, bringing the world's attention to the story of my people's struggle with a government that works methodically to wipe us out. Although CNN will probably carry it just for one day." He smiled—that same funny, crooked smile that she'd noticed in the photo the Extremist had shown her. "So, you see, your threats that you will shoot me through the back of the seat do little to alarm me."

Osman Razeen wanted to die. For his people, for his cause.

Somehow, when the time came to shoot him—or to turn him over to the Extremists, which, as John had pointed out, was almost the same thing as shooting him—that wasn't going to make it any easier to do.

Aware that John was watching her, Meg jammed one end of the straw—now close to three feet long—into the lid of a paper cup of watery, probably lukewarm soda. She put the other end of the straw over the back of the seat, moving it like a probe, until she got it close enough to Razeen for him to catch it with his mouth.

He sucked, and the liquid rushed through the straw.

John shook his head as he glanced at her again. "You care enough to give him a drink. So why don't you do what you wish Amy's captors would do for her—and turn Razeen over to the FBI?" he said softly in Welsh.

His eyes were too compassionate, too sad, too knowing, and she couldn't look at him.

"That's different," Meg said. "I know the Extremists aren't going to do that." She knew that the Extremists weren't going out of their way to make Amy and Eve more comfortable, too. If Amy and her grandmother were still alive.

The straw gurgled as Razeen sucked the last of the soda from the cup. "I thank you," he said to Meg.

John took the cupful of soda he'd nearly finished drinking from the cup holder and swished it around. "Do you want more?" he asked, looking at Razeen in the rearview mirror.

"I am still thirsty, yes, thank you."

John looked at Meg. "Do you have more of those sleeping pills?" He spoke in Welsh, and he had to get creative with the translation. But it didn't take more than a second for her to understand what he meant.

She did have more pills. In the glove compartment. She got them out without Razeen seeing what she was doing, opened several capsules, and dumped their contents in the last inch of liquid in John's cup.

She repeated the trick with the straw, and Razeen was soon sucking air from John's cup.

"Thank you," Razeen said again. "And . . . good night, am I right?"

Meg turned to look at him, and he was smiling. She hated the fact that he had such a gentle smile.

"That is to say, if I were you, *I* would have given me another dose of that sleeping medication. I know that I am exceptionally clever, but you have been quite clever as well, so . . ." He settled back, making himself comfortable. "Good night. Although, if a condemned man is entitled to one last wish, mine would be that I not be executed while I sleep. I should like to be awake, so I am able to pray."

Oh, *God.*

Meg felt John glance at her, and she knew what he was thinking, knew what he was going to say before he said it.

"It's not too late, Meg."

Meaning to turn herself and Osman Razeen in. Meaning to put Amy's life completely into the hands of people for whom saving Amy's life might not be the highest priority.

One of those people being John Nilsson.

"Achub fi," John whispered, in Welsh. *Save me.* "Save me by letting me help."

She closed her eyes. "Just . . . drive."

This was surreal. Sam was standing outside his hotel room with Alyssa Locke, using his key card to unlock the door. Knowing that she was about to go in there with him.

Into his room.

Into his hotel room.

Sam didn't think of himself as particularly religious, but he never did anything as ridiculous as waste a good prayer on something as insignificant as sex. He was either going to get some or he wasn't. And he was usually capable of being charming enough to get some completely on his own, so he'd always left God out of it.

Until now.

He concluded his prayer for divine guidance in not messing this up with a fervent promise of a lifetime of devotion as Alyssa walked past him into the room.

She smelled impossibly good.

She wasn't, however, walking really straight.

And instead of sitting on the couch, she half lay down, pressing her cheek against the cushions. "I don't think I want any dinner," she said distantly. "I'm so tired."

Sam went into the little kitchen area and got a couple of glasses and some ice. He poured them both another drink from the bottle he'd stuck under his shirt and taken out of the bar. After all, he'd paid for it.

"You need to keep drinking," he advised her, setting the glass down on the coffee table. "Don't stop until you're ready to crash."

"I think I'm ready to crash."

She looked exhausted. There were shadows under her eyes, giving her a slightly bruised appearance. As if life had kicked the crap out of her, and the only way for her to fight back now was to get some sleep.

As Sam looked at her, he could hear a distant flushing sound. It was the sound of his hopes for a passion-filled night going down the drain.

If she was too drunk to sit up, it would be ungentlemanly to take advantage of her, wouldn't it?

Even if she threw herself at him.

He looked at her, half lying there with her feet still on the floor, his eyes following the curve of her denim-clad rear end. Her T-shirt was riding slightly up, and he could see an inch or so of her bare skin just above the waistband of her jeans.

Touching her would be like touching silk. She had the most gorgeous skin he'd ever seen—smooth and flawless and the delicious color of café au lait.

She rolled slightly onto her back to look up at him, and the picture she made lying there—that pretty face with those ocean green eyes, breasts filling out that T-shirt, belly button peeking out—brought the truth slamming home like a kick to the balls.

Drunk or not, if this woman threw herself at him, all that shit about being an officer and a gentleman was going right out the window. *Right* out the window.

If she threw herself at him, he was catching her with both hands and he wasn't letting go.

But she was in no position to move, let alone do any throwing.

"Kick off your shoes and get comfortable," he told her, starting for the other room. "I'll get you a blanket. The couch pulls out to a bed if you—"

"Wait." She struggled to sit up and took a healthy slug of whiskey, as if that would help.

Actually, that was his fault. He'd implied that another drink would help keep her awake.

"No way am I falling asleep," she told him. "As soon as I do, you'll disappear."

"I'm not going anywhere," he said again. Was she nuts? Did she actually think that he would fulfill his lifelong dream of sharing a hotel room with Alyssa Locke only to sneak out on her?

It was true, at this point he was talking about her spending the night on the couch. But maybe come dawn she'd wake up, not too badly hungover, and she'd realize . . . something. He wasn't sure what, but whatever revelation she had would magically make her see how foolish she was to resist him, and how perfect they'd be together. As they made love in the early morning light, she'd breathe his name and . . .

Yeah. What was it she always said to him? *Dream on.*

"Look," Sam said, "if you want, we can push the couch right in front of the door. That way, if I try to leave—"

"Right, and while I'm over there guarding the door, you'd be going out through the sliders to the balcony."

The idea of him exiting via the balcony was completely absurd. But laughing at her when she was glaring at him like this wasn't going to help. He may have a buzz on, but he wasn't so fried he could no longer recognize *that* truth.

"There's a king-sized bed in the other room," Sam said, and the moment the words left his mouth, he realized how ridiculous a suggestion this was. There was no way in hell Alyssa Locke would even *think* about sharing a bed with him, no matter how big it was. But he'd come this far. He might as well finish the thought. "It's big enough to push up against both the door *and* the slider to that balcony."

She stood up.

Alyssa actually pushed herself up off the couch and, taking her drink with her, went into the bedroom to take a look.

She came out almost immediately, holding . . .

The light caught and gleamed and . . .

It was a pair of handcuffs.

"Will you let me cuff you to the bed?" she asked.

Dear, sweet Jesus.

Of course she didn't mean it *that* way, still, Sam didn't hesitate. "Absolutely."

"Just so you know, I'm UA," John said. "I'm guilty of unauthorized absense. If I don't go back with you in tow, I'm completely cooked."

Meg stared at him. "What?"

He glanced at her and nodded. "Yeah, I'm looking at a court-martial and a dishonorable discharge for dereliction of duty and lying to my CO. I'll probably even get jail time."

She let herself get angry. "You're trying to guilt me out. Well, forget it. It's not going to work."

"Unfortunately, I won't be able to write to you from prison," he continued, "because you'll be locked up, too, and prisoners aren't allowed to correspond with other prisoners."

"I never asked you to do this," she said heatedly. "I didn't ask to you to—"

"That's right," he said. "You didn't ask. I volunteered. I knew all about the trouble I could get into, and yet I came after you anyway. Don't you get it, Meg?"

She glanced into the back. Razeen was asleep, and even if he wasn't, he wasn't going anywhere. Last pit stop they'd made John had tied him up, tethering his handcuffs to the metal frame of the front seat so that Razeen couldn't attack them. Or try to escape through the back window.

"You need me," she said tightly to John. "Right. I got that. Loud and clear, thanks. But I'm sorry. I don't need you."

Please, John, don't go. I need you. She heard an echo of her own voice from that night so long ago.

"Not anymore," she whispered.

"Sorry, I just don't buy it."

"Oh," she said, "of course. You know better. You know the real truth is that I haven't slept a single night without dreaming about you since we almost . . . since we . . ." She faltered, because the look he shot her was so penetrating, his eyes so knowing, as if he could see into her head, see all those nights she'd ached for him.

"I should have stayed," he said. "I regret leaving the way I did that night. Of all the things I regret in my life—and believe me, Meg, there's a list—I regret that the most."

"It wouldn't have made a difference."

"I'm not so sure anymore. Maybe if I'd stayed . . ."

I can't do this. He'd pulled away from her suddenly, breathing hard.

Meg still remembered, as clear as if it were yesterday.

"You're going to wake up tomorrow and hate yourself," he'd said. "Even worse, you're going to hate me."

She'd stood there, leaning back against the wall because her legs wouldn't have been able to hold her up by themselves, just watching as he refastened his belt, tucked in his shirt, buttoned his jacket.

"You're serious," she'd said. "You're just . . . leaving? Just like that?"

"I have to go before we do something you'll regret. You've had too much to drink, and—"

"No, I haven't."

"Okay, you haven't," he agreed. "But you're upset and your judgment is skewed. You've got to trust me here, Meg. Look, I'll probably be Stateside again in a few weeks. I'll call you then."

She *was* upset. And he was probably right. Nothing good would come out of this. But she wanted him. God, she *needed* him. "Please, John, don't go." To her horror, her voice broke.

He swore sharply, but then he was back, warm and solid as he pulled her into his arms. "God *damn* it, I don't *want* to go."

"Then stay. Please stay—Daniel's all but written us a permission slip."

He laughed, but it sounded harsh, painful. "I don't want his permission! Christ! I want . . ."

"I *need* you." She kissed him, and he resisted for all of two seconds.

It was exhilarating. Terrifying. He kissed her ferociously, as if he were moments from sweeping her into his arms and carrying her to her bed. But then, again, he pulled back.

"Do you love me, Meg? I know we're friends, and I know—God, I know—there's this attraction between us, but if this is just sex, then you've got to think again. Because tomorrow you'll wake up, and everything we've done tonight will be irreversible. It'll be a part of you—forever. And if you're not going to leave Daniel, it'll be this poisonous lump of guilt that you'll carry with you. I don't want you to remember me that way. With pain and . . . and . . . I don't know, *hatred*. Jesus, I don't want that."

Did she *love* him? No, she couldn't answer that. She wouldn't even consider it. Because if she *wasn't* going to leave Daniel . . .

John was watching her intently, the muscle in his jaw jumping as he waited for her to respond.

It wasn't fair. She couldn't imagine Daniel having suffered so when he'd slept with Leilee. He'd probably slid into her bed and between her legs without a thought of love or friendship or whom he might be hurting.

He certainly hadn't thought about Meg.

Or Amy.

Amy, who, more than anything, wanted her father in her life. Amy, who so desperately wanted her family back.

Meg didn't say a word, but John nodded, as if he knew the direction her thoughts had turned.

"I'll call you when I get back," he said. "In case, you know . . . you change your mind." Somehow he managed to smile. To touch her cheek. "Wish I'd met you first."

She tried to smile, too. Failed because her lip was trembling. John had been sixteen when she'd married Daniel. What *was* she doing here with him? This was crazy. Completely crazy.

"You can always call me," he told her. "If you need me for anything. Any time. Just . . . call me and I'll come."

Meg nodded, knowing that this was really it. After tonight, she truly wouldn't see John Nilsson ever again. After tonight, if they met—even by chance—she wouldn't stop to talk. She'd smile, sure, even say hello, but she'd walk swiftly away. She'd never call him. Never again.

He kissed her once more. Sweetly this time.

It was a kiss to remember.

A kiss good-bye.

He stopped and looked back at her, his hand on the doorknob, as if he wished she would stop him.

But then he turned and went out the door.

And she let him go.

This wasn't going to work.

Locke sat on the floor next to Sam's bed.

The bedframe was put together with nuts and bolts. She could handcuff Sam to it, but it would take him about twenty minutes—tops—to get himself free.

He came out of the bathroom, wearing—oh, God—only a pair of shorts and a smile. "Okay, warden, I'm ready. Lock me up."

"This isn't going to work."

"Hey, it's no big deal. I've got food for if and when I want it . . ." He lifted the lid on the room service platter that had arrived minutes earlier and now sat on the bedside table. He'd ordered three different kinds of sandwiches, all wrapped in plastic, a two-liter bottle of Coke, and a bucket of ice. He'd ordered ice cream, too, but he'd put it in the freezer section of the little fridge that sat out in the suite's kitchenette. "I've got food and the remote control. What more could a man want?"

He reached down and took the handcuffs from her and cheerfully snapped one end onto his left wrist.

Locke shook her head. "Look at the bedframe, Starrett."

He crouched next to her and saw the problem instantly. "Oh, crap." Standing again, he looked around the room.

"Don't bother," she told him, resting her head against the bed. "There's nothing in here that would hold you."

"Well . . ." He cleared his throat. "Actually, there is."

Locke felt the mattress give under his weight. He'd sat down on the bed, next to her, and as she looked up at him from the floor, he reached down and lifted her right arm, pointed to her wrist. "That'll do it."

His hands felt cool against her skin. He had big, work-roughened hands, with almost ridiculously large fingers. One of his nails was bruised, as if he'd recently smashed a finger, but other than that, they were neatly trimmed and clean.

His skin was tan from working outside—he was almost as dark as she was.

She had to laugh. He was actually suggesting she hand-cuff herself to him. Was he completely out of his mind?

Starrett laughed, too. He had a blinding smile, and when he laughed, his eyes sparkled. They were mesmerizingly blue.

"You're kidding, right?" She pushed herself up, to her feet, pulling her hand away from him. God, she was dizzy. Whoever invented alcohol was a total idiot. "*People* are idiots," she told Starrett. "Alcohol, cigarettes, drugs—the more poisonous it is, the more we want it. It's insane. I'm *never* going to drink again."

"That's too bad," he drawled, leaning back on both el-bows, moving into a pose that was almost unbearably sexy, "because you loosen up when you drink. You know, I don't think I've ever heard you laugh before tonight."

"I laugh all the time," she said defensively, wishing he would sit up so that she'd stop wanting to skim her hands across the planes and angles of his muscular chest and arms. And those abs and legs and . . . "Just . . . not when you're around."

God, she needed to sit down—as far from Mr. Sexy as possible. This was going to be one hell of a long night.

Starrett was watching her closely. "It's your call about this handcuff thing. It seems crazy not to do it—I mean, if I'm cuffed to you, I'm not going anywhere without you knowing about it, right?"

She shook her head.

"Course if you're afraid you won't be able to keep your hands offa me . . ."

Locke stared at him. Did he know? Could he tell what she was thinking? God, she wasn't doing something like *drool-ing*, was she? She forced herself to react, to sputter, as if in outrage. "I'm not afraid. Don't think you're so—"

"I can understand the potential embarrassment," he con-tinued. "You've had too much to drink, and who knows what you might do in your sleep. I mean, it's a big bed, but . . ." He shrugged expansively.

Locke reached over and snapped the cuffs onto her right wrist.

Seventeen

~⊙ ⊙~

THUNDER CRASHED. THE storm was directly overhead, and the thunder was the kind that shook the house to its very foundation.

It woke Eve from the restless doze she'd drifted into, and for a moment, she was confused.

What was she doing outside of the bomb shelter during an air raid?

But then she remembered. The war was long over. She wasn't a teenager anymore. She was old and tired. The victim of a kidnapping.

Thunder roared again.

But she wasn't too tired or too old—or too much of a victim—to fight back. She nudged Amy awake. "Play along with me," she breathed to the little girl, who nodded, her brown eyes instantly alert and ready for anything. God bless her.

The electrical storm was putting their captors on edge. How recently had they experienced a rain of bombs in their war torn country? Eve could sympathize with their discomfort. She herself had sat out bad storms in the bomb shelter until well into the 1960s.

She knew the wisest course of action would be to sit tight. To not make waves. To not give the Bear and the others any additional problems.

But Eve knew they were running out of time. She saw the way the woman looked at them.

She had to take this chance.

She caught the Bear's eye. "Amy has a terrible stomach-ache," she told him, having to raise her voice over the sound of the rain pounding down onto the roof. "Please take us to the bathroom before she has an accident."

Amy gave a very convincing sounding groan—just the smallest sound.

The Bear didn't look happy, but he moved toward the other men, talking and gesturing back at them in a low voice.

Eve knew they were deciding whether or not to go to the woman with her request, or to simply take them upstairs on their own.

Amy made another small sound, a gagging sound this time, and the decision was made. Take them up to the bathroom now. Quickly.

The Bear led the way, and Eve moved as fast as she could on the stairs—which wasn't fast enough for the young man, who actually picked her up and carried her the last ten feet. Thunder roared again, and he nearly dropped her. Poor boy. She wasn't completely up on her recent history, but he had to have been just a child when the worst of the last civil war had rocked his country. He'd probably been ten when the bombs started falling, and they hadn't stopped for close to four years.

She squeezed his arm reassuringly, but he scowled. "Be fast."

She knew that this poor boy was probably going to kill them. All he needed was the order, and he would end their lives without a great deal of thought.

But she wanted him to think. She wanted him to struggle. "Thank you, young man," she told him with dignity, granting him dignity, too. "For your kindness and compassion."

"Be *fast*," he said again.

She limped after Amy, down the hall and into the bathroom, shutting the door tightly behind them.

Amy was smiling.

Eve put her finger to her mouth, cautioning silence.

"Help me," she whispered, motioning for Amy to join her in the tub.

The window was unlocked, and she pushed against it, testing it, finding the places that had the most give.

"Put your hands here and here," she whispered to the little girl. "When I say *now*, push up. Not out. Up."

Amy nodded her understanding, and Eve positioned her own hands on the window, waiting . . .

Lightning flashed, right outside the window, and Amy pulled back, startled.

"Now," Eve said, aware that Amy was no longer there. But the thunder had already started to roll, drowning out all other sounds, and she pushed with all her might.

The window groaned, and then Amy was back, pushing with her. It gave with an enormous *creak* that—please, God—was masked by the thunder.

As wind blew the rain into the open window, Eve looked at the door, bracing herself. But the Bear didn't come bursting inside, demanding to know what they were up to.

Eve looked out the window, tempted to leave right then and there. The rain was relentless, making the roof slippery and wet. But that same rain would mask the sounds of their footsteps.

"Amy, quick," Eve said, ready to do it.

But the Bear thumped on the door. "Time's up!"

"Just another minute," Eve called. They wouldn't get far if he came into the bathroom after them and found them gone. In fact, they'd be like ducks in a shooting gallery. He could pick them off at his leisure from the open window. It wasn't as if he'd have to guess which way they'd gone.

Eve left the window open, praying that no one would see it from the ground, praying that they'd have another chance to get up here and make their escape.

She pulled the curtain across the tub, but it moved in the wind.

Taking Amy's hand, she opened the bathroom door only the smallest possible amount and slipped out, closing the door tightly behind them.

The Bear frowned, and Eve pinched her nose shut, shaking her head.

Yes, it smelled in there.

It smelled like fresh air and freedom.

Obediently, meekly, she limped back down the stairs after Amy.

* * *

Sam was floored.

There was no doubt about it. Alyssa was *far* more drunk than he'd thought. He'd tossed that ridiculous challenge out as a joke. A clever six-year-old would've seen that he was baiting her. But instead of laughing in his face, she fell for it.

He looked down at the handcuffs that locked them together. Oh, shit. Now what?

Now he was supposed to spend the night cuffed to a woman he craved more than oxygen.

She was looking a little uncertain now, too. As if she'd just realized what she'd done. As if she weren't comfortable with their arms and hands so close together. As if the reality of the warmth of her forearm brushing against his was more daunting—and dangerous—than she'd imagined it would be.

He didn't look at her, couldn't look at her, praying that she'd back down, that she'd get the keys and unlock the cuffs. It still wasn't too late for her to admit that this was a ridiculous, dumbass idea—that neither of them were going to get a lick of sleep tonight.

"Move over," she ordered, and he shifted obediently to the right side of the bed, realizing with growing dread that she was going to play this out. Right to the end.

An end that would no doubt see him dead—either from frustration, or because she would kill him when *he* finally fell asleep and forgot where he was and who he was with, and why he shouldn't touch her.

"Look, Alyssa," he started. "It's occurred to me—"

"This isn't a problem," she told him with the earnestness of the extremely inebriated.

Yeah, she was drunk. And if she came onto him and he *didn't* gently push her away, he would be a total asshole. He'd be scum, dirt, excrement. He'd be worse than excrement. He'd be toxic waste.

I think this might be a problem for me. The words were on the tip of his tongue, but as he watched, she kicked off her sneakers and snuggled back against the pillows, her shirt stretched tightly across her breasts. His hand was two inches from her thigh. Maybe less. His mouth went dry, and all his warnings and cautions stuck in his throat.

This was going to be torture, but sick bastard that he was, he couldn't bring himself to make it stop.

Sam turned off the light so at least he wouldn't have to watch her lying there.

She sighed, just a small sound, but it was nearly enough to shoot him through the roof.

He prayed for God to send a little more self-control in his direction. And don't—please, Lord Jesus—let him start thinking about sex. Don't let him think about Alyssa's incredible body naked beneath him, straining to receive him, hot and sleek and gorgeous. Don't let him . . .

Too late.

Shit. *Shit.*

"Oh, God," she said, sitting up, tugging his hand with her, panic in her voice. The metal cuffs bit into his wrist, but he welcomed the pain. "Why is the room spinning?"

Uh-oh. "Haven't you ever had the bed spins before?" he asked.

"No. *Bed* spins . . . ?"

Man, she really was new at this. A complete innocent.

"It's normal," he told her. She'd just had another whole glass of whiskey not more than fifteen minutes ago. Maybe when it kicked in, it would knock her out and she would sleep. And maybe in the morning, when she woke up in his bed, she'd accept the magnetic attraction that raged between them and . . . "Just . . . try to ignore it."

Her voice shook. "I can't."

"Sometimes it helps if you leave the light on." Except, if he turned on the light now, she'd have a hard time not noticing the fact that in the past ninety seconds he'd managed to become completely aroused.

And that would go over really well.

"Turn it on," she said. "Please?"

Oh, hell. Worst case scenario, she'd be offended. She'd remove the cuffs and never speak to him again. Best case scenario, she'd look down at him and smile—the way she'd smiled in his dreams and . . . No, no, no, don't think about that! That was only going to make it worse.

Sam reached and turned the light back on, shifting so that he was on his side, facing her, one leg slightly up. Another version of the best case scenario—maybe she'd be too drunk to notice the giant hard-on he was trying to hide.

Except now he was stuck lying here, facing her. Watching her.

He laughed aloud.

Alyssa frowned. "What's so funny?"

"Just . . . everything. It's funny. We're handcuffed together. That's funny. I'm completely . . . Well, trust me, it's funny."

"Having these bed spins isn't funny." She sank back against the pillows, turning slightly to face him, her eyes anxious. "I don't like it."

He didn't either. He didn't—and he did. Part of him liked this *way* too much. She was looking to him for answers, for help, for expertise. When had *that* ever happened—outside of his wildest dreams?

He shifted slightly so that he was holding her hand, lacing their fingers together. "Sometimes it helps if you've got someone to hold on to."

She hesitated, but it was only for a second before she clung to him tightly. For someone with such slender fingers, she was impossibly strong. "Thanks."

She just lay there then, as time ticked painstakingly slowly past, gazing at him with her big green eyes.

"You, uh, want to talk?" he finally asked. "Sometimes it helps if you just kind of talk yourself out." Sex also helped, but he wasn't going to tell her that. "If you lie there, trying to sleep, that's when the room really spins. But if you don't try to sleep, if you talk and just let sleep kind of sneak up on you, it's not so bad."

Somehow he managed to smile at her. He hoped it looked reassuring.

"My mother used to hold my hand at night if I had a bad dream," Alyssa said. "She used to sit on the edge of the bed, and just *be* there, you know?" Her voice turned wistful. "She came in every night and kissed us on the forehead. God, it would make me feel so *safe*."

"My sister, Lainey, did that for me," Sam admitted. "Probably the same way you did for your little sisters."

Her eyes filled with tears. Oh, hell. Bad mistake, mentioning her little sisters. She was drunk, and here he was giving her a reason to turn into a crying drunk.

Sam changed the subject, fast. "Hey, have you met the new guy yet? Mike Muldoon?"

Alyssa nodded, also obviously eager to take their conversation in a different direction. She spoke carefully, enunciating extra well to compensate for the alcohol raging through her system. "Yeah. Well, yes, but not really. I mean, Senior Chief Wolchonok—" She took some extra time with the difficult name. "—introduced me, but I didn't get a chance to do more than say hi before Muldaur ran away."

"Muldoon. And yeah, he's shy."

"Muldoon. Right. Muldoon. Is he for real? Or is that shy thing just part of an act?"

"Oh, he's real. He actually says *gosh*."

"Really?" She smiled, thank God, her almost-tears forgotten.

Sam didn't think he could bear it if she started to cry. He wouldn't be able to keep from pulling her into his arms, and then he'd be in *big* trouble.

"Honest to God," he told her. "He's got the vocabulary of an altar boy. 'Gee whiz, senior chief,' " he imitated Muldoon's voice.

She laughed—victory. "Now I know you're making that up."

"Swear to God. He's from upstate Vermont or Minnesota or maybe Idaho? I forget."

"Vermont's *slightly* different from Idaho or Minnesota, Starrett," she pointed out.

"Not really. See, there's Texas, and then there's the other forty-nine states, all interchangeable. Muldoon comes from small town America—*real* small town. Someplace caught in a time warp. With a population of less than a thousand. Where children address their elders as sir or ma'am, and the F-word isn't uttered even in back alleys—let alone in mixed company. Where women stay home and clean and bake apple pies and—"

"Yeah, thanks. I liked it right until you got to that part."

"And men's jobs are to provide for their families and keep their wives barefoot and pregnant and in those kitchens, baking apple—"

"Yeah, yeah, yeah," she said. "Are you in therapy? Because clearly you have some kind of fixation."

She was teasing him, smiling at him.

"I'm not saying I approve of it," he countered. "I'm just giving you a report on Muldoon. You're the one who wanted to know. Personally, I think it's unnatural. You know, I find myself watching my language around him, wanting to protect his innocent little ears. I swear, it's like having George Bailey—you know, from *It's a Wonderful Life*—join the team."

She laughed again. "I think George Bailey would be a great addition to any team."

He snorted. "Spoken just like a woman. What's wrong with you, Locke?"

"Nothing," she countered indignantly. "Considering I *am* a woman."

A woman who was lying next to him on his bed, handcuffed to him, her hair spread out on the pillow, her breasts full against her T-shirt . . .

Sam yanked his gaze back to her eyes, forced himself to smile, to keep his voice light despite the sudden five hundred degree temperature increase in the room. "Yeah, I kind of couldn't help but notice."

Too late for keeping things light—the mood had already shifted. And Alyssa wasn't smiling anymore. She was looking at him with those ocean green eyes, with an expression on her face that he'd never seen before. She was looking at his shoulders and his chest, his stomach and . . .

Sam shifted his legs, lying even more on his side. God damn, she was looking at him as if she wanted to touch him. Was it possible . . . ?

"This is really weird, isn't it?" she asked quietly, looking back into his eyes.

He nodded. Cleared his throat. Ached for her. Forced another smile. "Why don't you try closing your eyes again?"

She closed her eyes immediately, and he instantly regretted not suggesting that she kiss him. Would she have done that as obediently, too?

"Good night, Sam."

Maybe it was because she called him Sam. Maybe it was because she looked so young and vulnerable, lying there with her eyes tightly closed. Maybe it was because he was just flat-out insane. But on a complete and total whim, he leaned forward and kissed her gently on the forehead, just like her mother used to do.

It wasn't planned. It wasn't thought out. It just seemed like the right thing to do at that one particular moment in time.

Honest to God, the last thing he expected was for her to reach up with her free hand and catch him. To put her arm around his neck, and hold him there, his face inches from hers, her fingers skimming across his shoulders, her touch impossibly, wonderfully intimate.

"That was nice," she said. "Thank you."

Her mouth was right there, *right* there—that mouth he'd dreamed about for years. And he couldn't stop himself. He kissed her again, just as gently but on the lips this time, brushing his mouth across hers.

"That was even nicer," she whispered, and smiled. At him.

It was all over. Right then and there. Battle lost. Surrender was inevitable and immediate.

She was drunk—drunk enough to handcuff herself to him. He knew that. And he was scum, excrement, toxic waste.

Because he kissed her again, kissed her anyway. Not so gently this time, with his lips completely covering hers. And when she opened her mouth to him, welcoming him, he didn't hesitate. He took all that she offered and more, drinking her in, like a man all but dying of thirst.

She tasted like the best whiskey he'd ever had in his life—sweet and sharp and incomparably intoxicating.

He could feel her fingers in his hair and on his back as he kissed her longer, harder, as she kissed him just as hungrily—hot, deep, delicious kisses that promised heaven was just a few heartbeats away.

She made a sound that was half laughter, half frustration as, when she tried to pull him closer, the handcuffs got in the way.

It was long past the time she should have pushed him over to his side of the bed. It was long past the time she should have gasped and come to her senses, long past the time she should have been using words like *mistake* and *shouldn't* and *stop*.

Instead, she wrapped one of her legs around him, pulling him against her. Tightly. So that there was no way she couldn't notice how completely turned on he was. There was no amount of alcohol that would have kept the hard truth—as it were—hidden from her now.

And it was only then that she stopped kissing him.

Sam was ready to pull back, ready to apologize, ready for damn near anything but the way that she smiled up into his eyes.

"Oh my," she murmured. "Is that for me?"

He laughed at that—he couldn't help himself. And the sound of her laughter wove its way around him, too.

"You are one *amazing* looking man, you know that?" Alyssa told him, pulling his head down so that she could kiss him again.

He knew what he *should* do.

He should put some space between them and make sure she knew what she was doing. Instead, he found her breast first with his hand, filling his palm with her softness, then with his mouth, drawing hard on her, right through both the cotton of her T-shirt and her bra.

She was on fire. She was lightning in his arms, arching up against him, opening her legs. If she hadn't had on her jeans, he could have pushed his way inside of her—just like that, he could have slid home.

"Do you have any condoms?" she gasped. "Please tell me you have condoms."

Okay, so maybe she wasn't quite so completely drunk after all. If she were able to think clearly enough to ask for condoms, she couldn't be *that* drunk, could she?

"Bedside table, top drawer," he told her, and got a beautiful smile in return.

She was struggling to get out of her jeans and Sam tried to help, but the handcuffs made it close to impossible. "Maybe you should get the key."

"What?" she asked, kicking her legs free. "Set you loose and risk having you run off somewhere? No way."

It was a joke. She was making a joke. She knew damn well that he wasn't going anywhere. There was nothing in this world short of a call from his CO telling him to mobilize that would make him leave her right now. Not a million dollars, not all the best friends in the world.

Her panties were white, but there was nothing conservative about them. He slipped one finger under the edge, but she laughed and pulled away, kneeling on the bed beside him.

"Besides," she added, "the cuffs really work for me." She wiggled her eyebrows at him, then reached out to touch him, grabbing hold of him right through his shorts. "This really works for me, too."

She was laughing again, and he caught her mouth with his in a burst of pleasure and happiness that was so intense he was nearly blinded.

He pulled her shirt up over her head, only to realize he couldn't get it past the handcuffs. It hung there on her arm, and she laughed again. She laughed even more as she dragged his shorts down his legs and his erection sprang free.

"Dear Lord," she said, laughter bubbling in her voice. "I think you better get a condom right now because I don't know how much longer I can wait before I flat out attack you."

If she was kidding, she was only half kidding. The look in her eyes was pure desire. She wanted him. She wanted *him*.

Sam dove for the top drawer—and the handcuffs pulled Alyssa with him, right off the bed.

She landed on top of him, laughing giddily at his pratfall as if Buster Keaton were her idea of a dream lover.

She kissed him hard, straddling him as she reached between them to ensheath him with her fingers. He nearly lost it. Just like that, he almost came in her hand.

And she knew it, too. She was laughing *at* him now, but he loved it, loved the sound. He pulled her hips forward so that she had to let go of him, so that she covered him with the heat between her legs instead. And then there was only a small slip of white satin keeping him from paradise.

Dear Holy Father. He wanted her naked and he wanted her now. Her bra had a front clasp that was made out of plastic, and he took it and twisted hard—and it snapped in his hands.

"Shit!"

But, again, she was laughing. He'd broken the damn thing into pieces, and he would have laughed, too, except there she was, so impossibly perfect. He wanted to look and touch and taste all at once—there was no time for him to laugh.

She moved against him, murmuring her approval as he rolled her nipples first between his fingers and thumb and then between his teeth and tongue. Her head went back, and she arched her back, and it was all he could do to keep from tearing her panties off and burying himself inside of her.

He had to get a condom.

But his condoms were in the drawer of the bedside table that now towered above him. He would have to sit all the way up, and even then he wasn't sure he could reach.

He wanted . . . He wanted . . . He slipped his fingers beneath the edge of her panties, finding her slick and hot from desire.

He looked backward, up at the bedside table again, and when he looked back, Alyssa was watching him. She knew what he wanted. She wanted it, too.

She crawled forward, until she could lean even farther across him. Until she could reach the drawer and slide it open. Until she was straddling his chest instead of his hips. Until that white flash of satin was right there, nearly in his face.

He couldn't not do it. He couldn't possibly resist. He shifted down and kissed her, breathing in the sweet muskiness of her perfume.

Her thighs tightened around his face and she gasped. But she didn't pull back. And that was all the invitation he needed.

He reached up and tore her panties free, and then, oh yes, he was in heaven.

The sounds she made were incredible—laughter mixed with pure, desperate pleasure. She wasn't at all shy about letting him know how much she liked what he was doing.

"This isn't fair!"

He didn't bother to answer her. She had absolutely no idea how incredibly, wonderfully fair this was for him. It was stupendously fair. Amazingly fair. Deliciously fair. He held her tightly, so that unless she really tried, she couldn't get away.

She didn't really try.

Her breath came faster and the sounds she made were more frantic, until she gasped, "Sam, please, I want to come with you inside of me."

He let her go.

She had a condom in her hand, already unwrapped, and Sam sat up so that together they could cover him.

She was breathing hard, her hair tumbled down around her shoulders. She was breathtakingly beautiful—he wanted to freeze time so he could look at her and memorize her, so he could have this moment to remember, pure and clean and crystal clear, for the rest of his life.

This moment, this amazing, anticipation-charged, here-and-now moment, was without a doubt one of the very best moments of his life. In a few seconds he would be inside of Alyssa Locke. He would be intimately joined with Alyssa Locke. They would be making love.

He laughed aloud, and she smiled at him as she slowly lowered herself on top of him.

Dear God, she was tight. He thought he saw a flash of pain on her face, and he nearly stopped breathing. "Please don't tell me you're a virgin."

"Don't be ridiculous." She laughed. "Unless virginity is something that grows back after four years."

"Four *years*? Since you've . . . ?"

She kissed him, pushing his shoulders back down to the floor, pushing him all the way home. She made a sound that might've been pleasure, might've been pain.

"Alyssa, I don't want to hurt you," he said hoarsely.

She laughed. "I don't want to hurt you either. How about I settle for making you scream? And you can do the same for me. After four years, I might have some screaming to do—you up for that, Starrett? It sure feels like you are . . ."

Silently, Sam shook his head. Who knew? Not even in his wildest dreams—and his dreams had been extremely wild—had he imagined cool, controlled Alyssa Locke would dare to whisper such things, even in the privacy of a lover's arms.

She began moving on top of him, impossibly slowly, her eyes half-closed, pleasure clearly etched on her beautiful face.

Dear God, he was on the edge. He drew in a deep ragged breath, and she leaned forward and kissed him, her nipples taut peaks against his chest.

"I'm really close, too," she whispered, moving still so slowly, taking the time to completely caress every last inch of him. "But you know, Sam, sometimes I think all you have to do is look at me, and I'll come."

That was it.

It was over for him. Sam felt his release rocket through him in that same exquisite slow motion. "Alyssa!" He heard her name as if torn from his throat, heard her answering cry, like some primal call and response, felt her body tense around him, as she, too, exploded with passion.

Sam held her tightly, long after the last powerful waves of pleasure had faded, long after she'd collapsed on top of him.

"Oh, damn," she said, and he tensed.

Please God, no. No regrets or recriminations. Not now. Not yet.

Not ever.

"The room's spinning again." She lifted her head to look at him, using her free hand to push her hair back from her face. "It wasn't spinning a minute ago." She smiled at him. "At least not this way."

Thank you, God.

Her smile was the smile of his dreams. "Do you think if you took a break," she asked, "if you maybe had a little of that ice cream that's in the freezer to restore your energy, I could convince you to—"

"Yes."

She laughed. "Now how do you know that I wasn't going to suggest—"

"I don't know for sure, but I'm sure as hell hoping," he countered. "Maybe if I'm really lucky, you'll have the bed spins all night long."

Her smile widened. "How about I get you that ice cream? Start getting your energy level back up?"

As he laughed, she climbed off of him, got to her feet. And nearly fell on her face when the handcuffs on her right wrist tethered her to him.

Sam caught her, steadied her, even as he cleaned himself up. God, she was naked. He just wanted to touch her. He just wanted to run his hands, his mouth, his tongue across every inch of her smooth, perfect body.

The hell with the ice cream. He was already half aroused again.

But he let her tug him into the kitchenette, taking the opportunity to watch her walk, naked, across his hotel suite.

The refrigerator was one of those mini ones, low to the ground, and she bent over to open the little freezer section, taking out the dish of ice cream. She handed it to him, but he set it down on the table, far more interested in using his one free hand to touch her. Her back, her shoulders, her arms, her breasts, those incredible legs . . .

She looked back in the main part of the fridge. "What's this?" There was only a bottle of Coke and a quart of milk in there and . . . "Chocolate syrup?"

She reached in and pulled out the squeeze bottle of Hershey's that he'd picked up at the 7-Eleven. "Don't tell me you put this in your milk."

"Okay, I won't."

She laughed as he pulled her closer. "Do you really?"

"Milk, ice cream, corn flakes, you name it." Sam shrugged as he nuzzled her neck. "I'm not proud. I'm a chocolate addict."

She narrowed her eyes at him. "Come to think of it, I have seen you with peanut M&M's on more than one occasion, haven't I?"

"Guilty as charged."

"Want some of this on your ice cream?" She held out the syrup.

He answered her by taking the bowl of ice cream and

putting it back into the freezer. How could he eat ice cream when all he wanted to do was touch her? He pulled her back into his arms, skimming his hands down her body.

"Hmmm," she said.

Oh, he liked the sound of that. He liked the way she was looking at the syrup, looking at him. His body was responding enthusiastically, even though it was still just a little too soon. But give him fifteen more minutes with Alyssa Locke and a bottle of chocolate syrup . . . Oh, baby, he'd be ready for anything.

She opened the top, squeezed some of the syrup onto one finger.

He took her hand, looked directly into her sea green eyes, and slowly licked her finger clean.

Alyssa shivered.

And Sam knew that no matter how much he'd loved chocolate in the past, from now on, it was going to hold an even more special place in his heart.

Eighteen

❧ ❧

"EXIT HERE," MEG said.

Nils glanced at her, and in the dim dashboard light, her face was grim.

This was it.

The moment of truth.

He knew she was going to have him drive down some deserted country road. She'd order him to stop the car, order him out. Probably threaten to kill Razeen if he didn't. Probably mean every word she said. Maybe even do it if provoked.

Nils had known this was coming. He'd figured she'd try to ditch him before dawn, and dawn was on its way. In less than an hour now, the sky was going to start turning light.

He'd done some war gaming in preparation—which was really just a fancy way of playing *what if*. But he'd run a bunch of different scenarios in his head. If Meg did X, then he'd respond with A. If Meg did Y, he'd do B.

And if Meg tried to ditch him in the middle of nowhere, he'd do his damnedest to control the situation. To make sure she dumped him near enough to a place where he could get his hands on a car. He could hot-wire damn near anything and be in pursuit of her—without her knowing—in a matter of minutes.

If he were in control of the situation.

He'd also prepared by taking a nap. While the five minutes he'd caught by the side of the road had helped a little, he'd needed several hours of sleep in a row to erase the ringing in his ears and the radio voices in his head, to make him sharp enough to deal with this or any other situation.

And so had Meg. She was exhausted, too.

She'd been desperate to keep moving south, but he'd convinced her that getting killed in a car accident wouldn't do Amy and her grandmother a damn bit of good.

So he'd slept, right there in the driver's seat, in the shade of a rest area, for three blessed, revitalizing hours.

Nils had awakened to find Meg fast asleep, too, draped across the parking brake, her head in his lap, her handgun on the floor in front of her.

"Don't do this," he said to her now.

"Go right at the end of the ramp," she ordered.

That would take them away from the bright lights of the truck stop and gas stations that were next to the highway. But Nils saw a small sign that indicated the town center was to the right. Five miles.

Where there was a town, there were cars.

He made note of the odometer setting as he quickly took the turn, praying that Meg hadn't seen that sign.

She turned and looked at him now. "I'm sorry, John. This is as far as you can go."

"Meg, please, you've got to trust me." Nils knew that on some level she trusted him enough to move toward him in her sleep. Surely that was a start.

Now that they were here, actually playing out the scenario in which she kicked him out of the car, he didn't want to play along. He didn't want to do it this way.

Christ, maybe he should just overpower her. Take her gun. Tie her up and take her, kicking and screaming, to the authorities. She'd probably be charged with some major felonies, but, damn it, at least she'd be alive.

The moment he stepped out of this car, the moment he left her alone, things could go wrong in a dozen different ways.

Razeen could wake up.

Nils might not find a car in enough time.

Even if he did, even if everything worked perfectly, he could lose Meg. Catching up to her with the kind of head start she was going to have wasn't going to be easy.

He drove as quickly as he could, wanting to get as close to the town as possible before she ordered him to stop the car and get out.

"Why should I trust you," Meg countered, "when you've never trusted me?"

Huh? Nils looked at her. She was serious. "Are you kidding?" he asked. "When have I ever not trusted you? In Kazbekistan—"

"You trusted me not to blow the whistle on Abdelaziz's escape. Big deal."

"Yeah," he said. "It was."

"You know what I remember most clearly?" Meg said. "Out of all the things we did, all the conversations we had, both in K-stan and in Washington—there was only once that you actually told me anything real about yourself. It was when we talked about the Vietnam Wall. Do you remember that day?"

"Yes." He'd never forget it. He'd kissed her, right there on the lawn of the Mall, failing her test.

"You told me that your father and your uncle both served in Vietnam. You told me their lives had been changed by the experience—and that *your* life had been changed by it, too. You told me more about yourself in those few sentences than you'd told me in weeks of nonstop conversation."

"How can you say that?" he countered. "I told you my entire life's story—"

"Except the part about your father serving in Vietnam— oh, you also took some liberties with the part where your mother died. That was pretty different in the version you told me in DC. Which is it, John? Did she die recently, or did she die when you were seven—or was it six years old?"

"Seven," he told her.

"So you either lied three years ago, or you've managed to remember the details of the lie you told me today."

"I altered the truth three years ago because I didn't want your pity," he told her. "I don't want *any*one's pity. That's all I had after she died. Goddamned pity."

"So you lied about your mother. Or—excuse me—you *altered* the truth. How about the rest of what you told me?" she asked. "What other truths did you alter? What other secrets about yourself have you kept hidden?"

He laughed. "Don't be melodramatic. I don't have any secrets. I don't know what else you want me to tell you. My

life was boring. I grew up on eastern Long Island. Big deal.
I went to a private high school, got into Yale, joined the
Navy. There's nothing to hide."

Meg was looking at him with those eyes that seemed to
see into his soul. She didn't say a word, she just sadly shook
her head.

"What?" Nils could see the faintest glimmer of lights
flash through the trees, off to the right. Meg didn't see it because she was looking at him, but the town was out there,
just to the north. He pulled to the side of the road on the pretense that he wanted to give her his full attention. Taking the
car out of gear, he pulled up the parking brake and shifted in
his seat, subjecting himself to the full brunt of her accusing
eyes. "What?"

"You described this near idyllic childhood—except your
father went to Vietnam, and came back a different person.
What did you say about him during that one time the truth
leaked out? That even though he hadn't died, he'd lost his
life over there. Yeah, John, that's what you said. Your life
couldn't have been this episode of *Father Knows Best* that
you pretend it was. Oh, and throw in the fact that your
mother died when you were seven. *Seven*—you were still a
baby. And your poor father—here's a man who's back from
a terrible war, probably just barely keeping it together, and
I'm supposed to believe that his wife dies and your life is
perfect?"

This was so not the time to lose his cool, but Nils felt a
flare of anger. "What do you want to hear, Meg? You want
me to tell you that my father drank too much some of the
time? So what? Four billion other people's fathers drank too
goddamn much. It's nothing new. It's no big deal."

She wouldn't back down. "I don't believe you. I see these
flashes of this incredibly sensitive man peeking out through
this, this . . . slightly bored, macho facade you've put up. I
don't believe you weren't affected by—"

"When he didn't drink, he *was* perfect, okay? *That's* the
way I want to remember him. *That's* the part of my life that I
tell people about. I say what I say, and if they choose to interpret it a certain way—"

"But what about the people who ask for the real story?" she implored him.

"No one asks."

"*I* asked. More than once. But you didn't trust me enough to tell me the truth."

Nils didn't know what to say to that. Because she was right. He rubbed his forehead, trying to banish the worst damned headache of his life.

"You're not the only one who lied," Meg continued softly. "Three years ago, in DC, you asked me if I loved you, and I didn't answer. I lied by omission."

He looked at her. Was she saying . . . ?

"It wasn't just about sex that night," she told him. "It was more than that, and it would've been beautiful, and in the end, that was why I let you go. I was afraid that if you did stay the night, I'd have to face everything I was feeling."

Nils's heart was in his throat. "Meg—"

"Let me finish. Please. I need to tell you this." She drew in a deep breath. "I've thought about it a lot since then." She laughed shakily. "If you want to know the truth, I've analyzed it to death, trying to figure out exactly why I let you leave. The best I've come up with is that even when I first met Daniel, uncertainty and, well, *fear*, I guess, was a part of what I felt for him. I loved him, but I was always afraid—afraid he was going to leave me, afraid I wouldn't live up to his expectations. You name it, I was afraid of it. Then later, when I found out he'd been unfaithful so many times . . ."

She shook her head. "It became a different kind of fear. Fear he was cheating on me again, fear that it was right there under my nose but I didn't see it, fear that the entire rest of the world knew but wasn't telling me. Fear that it was somehow my fault. That I wasn't good enough for him."

"I hear you say things like that and I want to kill him all over again. How could you think—"

"This isn't about Daniel and me," she interrupted. "This is about you and me."

That shut him up.

"I had to explain about Daniel, because before I met you, love meant being afraid. But with you . . ."

She laughed again, and again it sounded so sad. "You had

no expectations, John. You just . . . liked me. I knew you weren't telling me the truth about a lot of things, but I never doubted that you liked me. I could see it in everything you did and said, and I loved the way that made me feel. I knew you weren't perfect—in a lot of ways you're frighteningly similar to Daniel. All those secrets and deceptions. But when it came to our friendship, you had no ulterior motives and that was so refreshing. You know, that's why it shook me so badly when you admitted you sought me out in DC to try to get revenge on Daniel."

"I told you that wasn't *really* what I—"

"I know," she interrupted. "And I believed you—because I had this solid sense that you liked me. You liked me exactly the way I was. You didn't want to change me, you didn't disapprove of me. You were just so sweet and so wonderfully okay with me."

Sweet? "Meg—"

"Just listen, all right?" She looked down at her hands in her lap, at the weapon she still held. "In the end that's why I let you go," she told him softly. "I'd fallen in love with you, and I was afraid that making love to you and admitting to myself how much I did love you—I couldn't have slept with you if I didn't. I was afraid making love to you would be such a . . . I don't know, a joyful, wonderful thing, I guess. Everything I felt for you was so clean and sweet and pure. So untainted. I was afraid of letting myself love you even for only one night—and I had no expectations that you truly wanted anything more than that, honestly. But I was afraid that after experiencing that, it would be torture to go back to the fear and disappointment that came with loving Daniel."

She'd *loved* him. Nils couldn't keep his mouth shut a second longer. "Jesus, Meg, didn't you know that I wanted you to leave him? I didn't want just one night with you. I wanted—"

"All I knew for sure was that I *couldn't* leave Daniel."

"Why the hell *not*?"

She looked up at him, looked him straight in the eye. "Because of Amy. My daughter wanted me to try again, John. She didn't say it in so many words, but I knew. And I'd promised her I'd try. Before she went to England, I promised her I'd give Daniel another chance. She wanted her father back. And I wanted that for her, too."

"So you sacrificed your own happiness—"

"Yes and no," she told him. "I sacrificed *you*. I sacrificed something that I wasn't sure was real. I sacrificed a chance. A promise of something that might've been wonderful."

"It would have been. Jesus, I've always regretted leaving that night. And now . . ."

"Would you have married me?" she asked him. "Or did you just want to sleep with me, John?"

He shook his head. Marriage. Jesus. The idea still scared him. "I don't know. I wanted more than a one-night stand, I do know that."

She gave him a small smile for his honesty. "That was a moot question anyway. If I *had* slept with you, it really wouldn't have changed anything. I wasn't going to leave him. That wasn't an option. And I did love him, too. Please don't misunderstand that."

Nils didn't misunderstand. But he couldn't believe her. He felt sick. Maybe if he'd been honest with her, if he'd given her what she'd wanted and told her the truth about who he was and where he'd come from, maybe if he'd allowed himself to admit both to her and to himself that he was crazy in love with her . . . Maybe that *would* have changed everything.

"Even if you'd told me you loved me," she said, as if she could follow his thoughts, "it wouldn't have made a difference. I went back to Daniel *for Amy*."

For Amy. He'd lost her because of Amy three years ago, and now here it was, happening all over again. Still, he understood. If it had been anything else, he'd argue, try to talk sense into her, try to change her mind. But a mother's love for a child went beyond sense and logic.

Nils didn't say anything. He just watched her, knowing what was coming, powerless to change it.

"You better believe that if I could give you up for Amy's sake three years ago, I would do *anything* to save her now." Meg shifted slightly so that she was facing the backseat. "Including kill Osman Razeen. Including . . ." She shook her head.

She held her weapon now with both hands, aimed directly at Razeen's forehead. "So leave the keys, John, and get out of the car."

Nils didn't move. "No," he said. He laughed. "You can't tell me you love me and then kick me out of the car. That's just . . . it's not fair."

"Loved," she corrected him tightly. "Past tense. That was three years ago."

But she couldn't—or wouldn't—meet his gaze.

"You know, most of the time, you still lie worth *shit*," he told her.

She said it again, louder this time. "Get out of the car, John. I'm *not* taking you any farther."

"I need to come with you," he told her. She wanted the truth? He would give it to her, stark, bare bones. "I need you to let me help you. Because I love you, too. Not past tense, *present* tense—at least as much as you still love me."

Meg didn't say a word, but he knew she wasn't buying any of it.

"Please," he said, "if you stop and think it through, you'll realize that you do need me—now more than ever. Don't sacrifice me again, Meg."

There were tears in her eyes. "Don't sacrifice you? Damn right I won't sacrifice you. That's why I'm doing this *my* way. And yes, that's probably going to get me killed. But as long as there's a chance that I can save Amy . . ." She drew in a deep breath. "But I won't risk your life, too. No way. So get out of the car, or I'm blowing Razeen to hell when I count to three. One."

She looked at him, and time hung as he gazed into her eyes and saw the truth. If he tried to call her bluff, she was going to kill Osman Razeen. Not just to save Amy, but to save *him*, too. Because despite what she said, she loved him still.

"Two." Her voice shook. "Damn you—don't make me do this!"

Nils got out of the car.

Meg slipped behind the wheel and pulled away before she would have reached *three*. She did a yooie, tires screaming on the asphalt as she headed back toward the highway.

And Nils took off at a dead run, bare feet be damned, heading for the glimmer of lights he'd seen just beyond the thicket of trees.

Light.

It was growing stronger, streaming in through the uncurtained windows, penetrating her closed eyes and sending a knifelike shaft of pain directly into her brain.

It was dawn.

Locke kept her eyes tightly shut against both the light and the pain, aware of the fact that her head was drumming nauseatingly, and that her brain felt as if it were sloshing around loose inside her skull.

What had she done?

Her mouth felt as if she'd spent the night gagged, but there was nothing in it now but her own tongue.

Her *own* tongue. Not . . . someone else's . . .

The world seemed to shift, and a vivid memory of Sam Starrett, gloriously naked, kissing her, sweeping his tongue into her eager mouth, as he thrust, hard, into her as she spread her legs wide for him, up on . . . the *kitchen table* . . . ?

Locke opened her eyes.

And shut them fast as the brightness of the day assaulted her.

What had she done?

She opened her eyes just a little, squinting against the light and the pain. Oh, God, she was completely naked, with Starrett sprawled next to her, naked as well, amidst the rumpled sheets of his bed.

She was sticky with something that looked like . . . *chocolate*? With horror, she saw that it streaked the T-shirt that hung off the handcuffs that still connected her to Starrett, too. The shirt she'd been wearing yesterday before *she'd let Sam Starrett undress her*—oh, my God, what *had* she done?

Another flash of memory ripped through her, this one of her gasps of pleasure as Starrett ran his tongue from her breasts to her stomach and then lower, as he licked chocolate syrup from her body. She'd done the same to him, licking him, and taking him into her mouth and . . .

What had she *done*?

All of the whiskey she'd had the night before churned inside of her and she sat up. The movement made the top of her head feel as if it were going to lift off, and she knew that she was, without a doubt, going to be sick. Dear God, could she even make it to the bathroom? It was impossibly far away and she wasn't sure if she could get her legs to work—forget about dragging Starrett.

Beside her, he stirred. He stretched, and winced only slightly as he opened his eyes and the morning light hit him.

"Uh-oh." One look at her face and he somehow knew. It was awkward with the cuffs on their wrists, but he got her off the bed and into the bathroom in record time.

Just in time.

Locke crouched naked on the bathroom floor and leaned over the toilet bowl.

It was violent and vile. Her stomach churned and her throat burned, and vomiting took precedence over all else—including the humiliation.

Although through it she had patches of awareness, a sense of Starrett holding her, murmuring words of nonsensical comfort. *It's all right.* What, was he stupid? This was close to the farthest place from *all right* that she'd ever been in her life.

She felt him wipe her mouth and her face with a cool washcloth. "Go away," she gasped when the sickness subsided enough for the humiliation to take center stage. "Please go away!"

"I can't," he told her softly, as if he somehow knew that talking more loudly than a whisper would split her head open. "I'm sorry, Lys. You're stuck with me until we can make it into the living room and get the key."

The key to the handcuffs.

"Oh, God," she groaned, resting her head against her arm as she still leaned against the toilet. It was going to take a superhuman effort to stand up and walk into the living room, but until she did, she was locked—naked—to Roger Starrett.

Her mortal enemy.

The way she was crouched, she was curled into a ball.

That was bad enough, but the idea of having to stand up in front of him and walk—naked—into the living room was mortifying.

"This is the stupidest thing I've ever done in my life," she moaned. Talk about self-sabotage. Fifty billion men in the world, and *she* had to go and have a one-night stand with Roger Starrett. "Fool," she chastised herself. "I'm such a *fool.*"

"Give yourself a break." Starrett rubbed her shoulders and neck with a familiarity that was chilling. "You're human. You had too much to drink. It's not that big a deal, Lys."

"Don't touch me!" She couldn't bear it another second and pulled away from him, even though the movement made her head explode. She whipped a towel down from a rack and wrapped it around herself. "And don't call me Lys."

Starrett sat on the bathroom floor, much too close, just looking at her. He cleared his throat. "You liked being called Lys last night."

"Yeah, well, I don't like it now." She couldn't meet his steady gaze, couldn't bear even to look at him. He was completely unconcerned about his own nakedness, completely comfortable inside his own extremely bare skin.

And why shouldn't he be? Even hungover, with gold-tinged stubble glistening on his chin, with his hair a mess and his eyes rimmed with red, with streaks of chocolate still on his chest and stomach, he was sexy as hell.

He sighed. "We've reached that part, huh? The part about the regrets and recriminations. The embarrassment part. The light of day, dawning of common sense, morning after part." He laughed, but it was without any humor. *"Shit."*

Locke hauled herself to her feet, and her head managed to stay on her shoulders, but just barely. "Please. I need to get the key."

She needed to take a shower, wash the stickiness of the chocolate from her body, wash away the scent of Starrett—the sweet, faint smell of sex.

If she could, she would wash away the bits and pieces of memories that were coming back, stronger and longer, with remarkable clarity. Condoms. They'd used condoms, at least, thank you, God.

He just sat there, head in his hands, and she tugged on the handcuffs. "Come on."

Starrett looked up at her. "Aren't you afraid I'll run away the minute you unlock me?"

"Please," she whispered. There was no way she could drag him into the living room. She was barely going to be able to drag herself.

He pushed himself to his feet. "Guess not. Guess it's me who's afraid to unlock you. I wish I had more of an appreciation for irony, because—"

"Just don't talk, okay?" Locke held the towel tightly around her as she led him into the living room. Her jacket was on the couch, but . . . "Where's my fanny pack?"

Starrett scratched his stomach, then flopped onto the couch, pulling her down next to him. "I'm not supposed to talk, remember?"

Locke struggled to get free of the soft pillows so that she could look around the sides of the couch, as well as behind and beneath it. She looked under her jacket again. Her head was pounding. "Help me find it, Starrett."

"Gonna be hard to do without talking."

"Please."

He sighed. "Well, where'd you put it down?"

She closed her eyes and pressed her forehead with her un-cuffed hand. "If I knew *that*, then I wouldn't need you to help me find it."

"This place isn't very big. Did you leave it in the kitchen? What color is it?"

"It's aqua. You know, kind of green."

"I know what aqua is. Jesus."

"I'm sorry," she said. She held her head with both hands, hoping that would keep the top of her skull attached. "This is very difficult for me."

"It doesn't have to be," he countered, his voice suddenly gentle. He sat forward. "Look, let's take a time-out, okay? Let's just take a deep breath and start again." He took her hand and gently helped her up, and carefully, gingerly, as if she were an extremely fragile package, led her into the kitchen area.

She couldn't look at the kitchen table.

One of the chairs had been knocked over, probably when they'd . . . Oh, God.

Starrett picked it up, set it upright next to the little refrigerator, and gently pushed her down into it. As she sat there, he took out the bottle of Coke from the fridge, and, using only his right hand, poured her a plastic cupful.

"Little sips," he ordered her as he handed it to her.

From one of the cabinets, he took out a bottle of painkiller—some nonaspirin hangover remedy—and shook two pills out. She took them, unable to do more than glance into his eyes. It was almost harder to deal with this when he was being nice.

"Maybe we should close the curtains, make the room dark, and go back to sleep," he suggested. "When you wake up, you'll feel a little better, and then we can deal with finding the key."

"I want to find it now. It's in my fanny pack," she said. Going back to bed—naked—with Roger Starrett was *not* an option.

"Which doesn't seem to be in the kitchen," he told her. "It wasn't in the bathroom or the living room. Is it possible . . ." He broke off.

"What?"

He was silent.

"If you have an idea, please don't keep it to yourself."

He shook his head. "I was just wondering if maybe you left it in the bar?"

Dear, sweet God. Locke looked at him with horror. If her fanny pack wasn't here, then the *key* wasn't here, either. Oh, God.

She took a deep breath, forcing herself to concentrate. To remember. "I had it on in the bar. No, wait, I had it on in the pool hall. I didn't have it in that other bar, did I?"

He shook his head. "I don't remember seeing it." He laughed. "Oh, shit. I think I remember . . ."

Her dread grew. "What?"

"When we got to the hospital, you threw a bunch of stuff into the trunk of your car."

"Oh, my God!" She had. She remembered now.

The key to these handcuffs was in her fanny pack, which was safely locked in the trunk of her car, which was parked in a garage near her sister's hospital.

All the way across town.

"How old is your daughter?"

Meg jumped, startled. God, she'd almost forgotten about the man sleeping in the backseat.

Except he wasn't asleep anymore.

The way John had tied him, she couldn't see him in her rearview mirror.

"Mine was eleven when she was murdered," he told her. "Her name was Ayesha."

Oh, dear Lord. Meg gripped the steering wheel. "I'm so sorry."

"I have had a taste of your anger and pain." Razeen's voice was gentle, drifting bodilessly from the back of the car. "How old is she? Your Amy?"

"Ten."

"It is a good age," he said. "For daughters. Is it not?"

Meg nodded. "Yes, it is."

Razeen laughed lightly. "Ah, yes. Ayesha had such a smile, you know? As if life held such joy for her—and thus she brought joy to others." He was silent for a moment. "She was shopping with her mother when there was trouble in the market."

Meg didn't want to hear this. She didn't want to know that Razeen had had a daughter, didn't want to hear of his pain and his loss. She didn't want him to be anything other than a terrorist, a villain, a man deserving of death.

"They were rounded up by the Kazbekistani Army," he continued, "simply for being Muslim. Someone protested too loudly, an argument broke out, and the government soldiers opened fire into the crowd. Just like that, Ayesha was gone."

"I'm sorry," she said again—but it was meaningless. What good did her being sorry do him?

"Seventeen people were killed that day, thirty-nine wounded, and the incident was pushed aside by the government. It was forgotten. No one was ever punished. No one even apologized. Of course, that day the casualties were low. Such incidents have happened many times before and many times since then with death tolls of innocents in the hundreds."

Meg was silent. What could she say?

"This is a government that is committing genocide," Razeen continued, "but the world doesn't seem to care. I have tried to make changes politically, but our government cancelled the elections when it looked as if we might take control. I myself was taken into custody and tortured. When I finally escaped, I joined the GIK. And up to the day Ayesha died, I was an advocate of nonviolence. But that day she died, I changed my mind."

In a terrible, awful way, Meg understood. Here she was, with one gun still hidden in her boot, another on the seat beside her, doing things she'd never dreamed she could possibly do—all to protect her daughter.

"I have done some terrible things," Razeen told Meg quietly. "I have done things that are hard to live with. I have taken lives, just as surely taking away someone else's Ayesha. And I know that she would not have understood that. Not at all." He sighed. "No, not at all."

"Why are you telling me this?" Meg whispered.

"I want you to understand," Razeen told her. "If my death can both save your daughter and bring attention to my people's suffering, then perhaps I will be forgiven. Perhaps I will again find peace."

"I received one last letter from Ralph," Eve told Amy and the Bear. "It was some months after he'd joined the British Expeditionary Force, after Hitler had invaded Poland, and the BEF were stationed across the channel, in France.

"He'd taken the time to write out a detailed lesson plan for Nicky," she told them. "His letter was completely impersonal—he mentioned nothing at all of our marriage, nothing of our friendship." She shook her head, remembering how her heart had leapt when she'd received his packet and how hurt she'd been when she'd read his tersely worded note. Compared to his other letters—and she'd kept and read that entire boxful until they were ragged—this one had been written as if by a complete stranger.

"I used that letter to locate him in France." The Bear was scowling, but Eve knew the young man was listening as he cleaned his gun in the early morning light. "He was with the Fiftieth Royal Anti-Tank Regiment, and in the early spring of 1940, I put on my best outfit and my warmest overcoat and I took the ferry across the channel."

She'd used all she'd ever learned from her mother to charm Ralph's commanding officer, who'd bent over backward in his attempt to accommodate her, allowing her to use the privacy of his office to meet with Ralph.

Who was terribly stern as he was led into the room, more like a man meeting a firing squad than a man coming face-to-face with the woman he'd claimed to have loved enough to marry.

His face looked grim, all sharp angles and high cheekbones beneath his military short hair. Of course the chill in his eyes added to the harsh effect.

Ralph waited until his commander left, closing the door behind him, but then he lit into her, his voice low but filled with a terrible intensity. "You must be insane to have come all this way by yourself!"

She was sitting in a chair in front of the commander's imposing looking oak desk, and she crossed her legs with a hiss of silk.

The muscle in his jaw jumped, and he turned jerkily away to look out the window instead of at her.

"You're right," she said, her heart dropping clear down to her fashionable Italian leather pumps. "I'm insane. But I had to see you."

He didn't say a word, didn't look at her.

"How can you still be mad at me?" Eve whispered.

He laughed harshly, turning to face her. "You've seen me." He held out his arms and turned in a complete circle. "All right? So go home. And go quickly. This is no place for a child."

Eve didn't move. "I've been following the news—reading the paper to Nick, and listening to the radio."

He was back to looking out the window. She supposed she had to be grateful that he didn't just walk away. At least he was listening to what she had to say.

Still, his hostility was daunting. This was, without a doubt, the hardest thing she'd ever done.

She took a deep breath and lifted her chin. "Hitler's not going to be content with Poland and Austria," she told him. "I don't care what anyone says. War is coming. And you're going to be smack in the middle of it, here in France."

"And that's what you've come all this way to tell me?" His voice was oddly flat. "Thanks so much for the news."

"I came all this way because I wasn't sure I'd ever get another chance to see you. People get killed in wars, you know." Her voice shook. "I came to tell you that . . ." She closed her eyes and said it. How could he hurt her worse than he already had? "I love you."

He didn't say a word, didn't move, and, as far as she could tell, he wasn't even breathing.

"Maybe that doesn't mean anything to you," she said, her voice suddenly sounding very, very small in the large room. "Maybe you think it doesn't count because I'm so young. But Juliet was barely fourteen when she fell in love with Romeo." She wanted to fall to her knees in front of him and beg him to forgive her, to hold her, to love her again. Her voice broke. "Oh, Ralph, don't you remember Juliet?"

He still didn't move. "Juliet didn't lie about her age to Romeo. What you did was unforgivable. And look at you." His voice shook as he glanced only briefly at her. "You're still pretending to be someone you're not, still *lying.*"

Eve steeled herself as she stood up. She crossed to the window, stood directly in front of him.

"Look at me," she said, forcing him to do exactly that. "I'm sixteen and everyone thinks I'm twenty-one. I can't help how other people choose to see me. I do what I have to to survive in this world—and that includes taking advantage of other people's misconceptions. And I'm lucky that I can do this. I'm lucky that people—including my stepmother—believe that I'm old enough to take care of Nick."

He didn't respond, and she kept going, desperately now.

"You know, if I could wave a wand, I'd magically make myself older, but I can't. I can only wait. Given enough time, though, I win, because every minute that passes I *am* getting older. I know in a few years that I'll actually *be* eighteen and then, yes, twenty-one. And I hope that in a few years you'll be able to let yourself forgive me, and that you'll love me again. And I pray, God, I pray, that in those same few years this war will end, and you'll come safely home to me."

Ralph shook his head. "I won't," he said bitterly. "I can't. How could I ever trust you? Why would I even want to?"

His words ripped her heart open, but Eve refused to flinch.

"You know, half the time you were Nicky's tutor, I dressed in blue jeans and pigtails and didn't wear any makeup," she accused him. "I dressed like a fifteen-year-old girl. But you saw what you wanted to see. And you *wanted* me to be twenty or twenty-five or whatever you thought, so that's who you saw."

Instead of ice, there was guilt in his eyes now. It was almost harder to face. "You're right," he said. "God forgive me."

"Why should God have to forgive you for loving me?" she asked. "I'd think he'd have more of a beef with you for walking away."

He was looking at her, really looking at her now, for the first time since he'd come into the room.

"Please stay safe," she told him desperately. "And remember that I love you. That I'll always love you."

For one heart stopping moment, Eve thought that he was going to reach for her, that he was about to pull her into his arms and hold her tightly. That he was going to whisper that he loved her, too.

Instead he wheeled away from her, nearly running for the door.

It took every ounce of control she had not to burst into tears. Instead she chased after him, out past the commander's secretary, past the commander himself, who looked up, startled, as they rushed past.

She followed Ralph down the stairs and out of the building, her heels clattering on the walkway.

He broke into a dead run as he hit the street, and she had no prayer of catching him. Not in these shoes.

"I'm not just young," she shouted after him, "I'm also a fool! I can't change that about myself either! And fool that I am, I do love you! I'll be there, in Ramsgate, waiting for you. I'll wait for you forever! So you better come home to me! You better!"

Ralph didn't stop running, didn't look back.

"Please, Ralph," Eve whispered, sinking down to sit on the steps of the building. "Just come safely home. It doesn't have to be to me."

Nineteen

STARRETT LAUGHED. "I'M sorry," he said. "I know you don't think this is funny, but—"

"This is *so* not funny." Locke stared at him, amazed and angered that he could be laughing about something so dreadfully serious. "The keys to these handcuffs are locked in the trunk of my car, which is in a parking lot on the *other side of town*! And you think this is *funny*?"

"Well, yeah."

She stood up so fast, she knocked the chair over again. Her brain sloshed hard against the inside of her skull, making her want to scream. "How the *hell* are we going to get the key?" Her own raised voice hurt, and she lowered it, using tone rather than volume to convey her anger and disgust. "I don't even have a shirt to wear. Look at this!" She took her stained shirt from where it was hanging around the cuffs and shook it at him. "I need a shower, I'm covered with this . . . this . . . *chocolate*. But how am I supposed to take a shower handcuffed to you?"

"Actually, I can think of a *number* of ways that would—"

She cut him off. "Are we supposed to just hail a cab wrapped in towels? How are we going to get through the hotel lobby without everyone seeing us—God, without everyone *knowing*?"

"Well, shit," Starrett said. He'd finally stopped laughing. "I guess we've hit on the real problem here, haven't we? God forbid anyone find out that Alyssa Locke is *human*. Well, sorry, sweet thing, you kinda let that little secret slip with me last night."

It was all she could do not to hit him. "Don't you ever, *ever,* call me that again."

"What, *human*?"

Her head pounded and her stomach was churning. She yanked him with her, hard, toward the bathroom. "You know, Starrett, this is a perfect example of how completely stupid it is to drink alcohol. What was I thinking last night? What was I *possibly* thinking? I must've been completely out of my mind, because you're the *dead* last man on earth I'd sleep with if I were sober. But, no, a little too much whiskey, and letting you take off my clothes suddenly seems like a good idea—instead of the biggest mistake of my stupid life!"

He caught her arm, pulling her back toward him, his face taut with anger. "This wasn't entirely my idea," he told her. "You were on board right from the start, babe. And enthusiastically, might I add? In fact, you were the genius who found the chocolate sauce in the kitchen and—"

Locke closed her eyes, remembering the kitchen table. "I know exactly what I did," she told him through gritted teeth. "You don't need to go into detail, thanks."

"You remember. Great. But do you remember if that was the second or the *third* time we made love last night, Alyssa? Or was it maybe the *fourth*?"

She forced herself to meet his gaze. "What we did last night wasn't making love."

He flinched as if she'd slapped him, but he recovered so quickly, she wondered if she'd imagined it. He laughed. "Poor choice of words. Let me rephrase the question. Was it the second or third time we *fucked*? Is that better, sweet thing?"

She didn't answer. She just turned and dragged him the rest of the way into the bathroom.

"You know, you were all over me," he continued, not taking his cue to shut up from her silence. "I would've been fine with doing it once, but you just wanted more and more. I'm actually a little surprised you haven't tried to jump me again this morning."

"I'm going to shower," she told him as matter-of-factly as she could, as she turned on the water. "You can stand out here, outside the curtain. With your eyes closed."

She stepped into the shower and slipped out of her towel, tossing it over the curtain rod, where she could quickly grab it again when she was done. The warm water was just what she needed, and combined with the headache medicine Starrett had given her, she was starting to feel as if her head weren't in quite so much danger of being detached from her shoulders.

"Fuck this," Starrett said, stepping into the shower with her. "I'm not standing out there."

"Hey!" She quickly turned her back to him.

"And I'm not closing my eyes, either. It's not like I haven't seen you naked. Jesus. It's not like I haven't licked chocolate syrup off every inch of your body. I need a shower, too, this is *my* hotel room, so just . . . tough shit, Locke. You're stuck with me for a little while longer."

Locke tried to be efficient and quick, lathering the soap and using her hands to wash herself clean. But her right hand was attached to Starrett's left, and his fingers—intentionally, no doubt—kept skimming her until she wanted to scream. "*Stop* it. God forbid you should start acting like a gentleman at this late stage in your life."

"Pass the soap. I'll wash your back. With pleasure."

With an exhale of frustration, she put the soap down far from him. "Aren't you even the tiniest bit ashamed of taking advantage of the situation last night? You *knew* I'd had too much to drink. You haven't even *tried* to apologize."

"That's because I have no intention of apologizing," he told her. "It was amazing—what we did last night, what we shared. Shit, it was *great*. I refuse to apologize. And I refuse to regret one fucking second of it. Yes, I knew you had too much to drink. And maybe that means I took advantage. But you wanted me, Alyssa. Badly. How the hell was I supposed to turn you down?"

She stepped under the water, letting it flow over her head and her face so that she wouldn't have to hear him. But it was only a temporary respite. They were handcuffed together, and would be, probably for the next few hours, God help her. He was right. She *was* stuck with him for now.

And she *had* wanted him—he was right about that, too. The really stupid thing was that a part of her *still* wanted him. She was trying to pretend otherwise, but it was back there even now, eating away at her, like some kind of sick craving or addiction.

She wanted him to touch her again.

She wanted him to wash her back. She wanted . . .

She squeegeed her hair back from her face with her hands, aware of the weight of his arm next to hers, angry with him for being there, for being too damned sexy, for getting to her, even now when sex should have been the last thing she wanted.

She rinsed out the white T-shirt that was still hanging between them like a sodden and defeated flag of surrender.

"Can we switch places, so I can have a little water now?" he asked.

Silently she moved past him, trying to put as much space between them as possible, but he slipped and caught himself—by grabbing on to her in a full body hug.

"Oh, my God!" Locke yanked herself away from him. He was completely aroused. Extremely aroused. *Enormously* aroused. Suddenly it was very hard to breathe.

She jerked her eyes back to his face, angry at herself, twice as angry at him for making her angry at herself. "What is wrong with you?"

He was indignant. "What's *wrong*? Excuse me, but this is the correct response to this situation. I'm human, I'm male, you're female, you're naked. I'm standing here watching you rub soap all over your body. If I *didn't* have a hard-on, *that's* when something would be seriously wrong with me."

He rinsed himself, his movements jerky with anger. The way they were cuffed together, it was impossible for her to turn her back to him. She was forced to stand there and watch him.

He was male perfection, all hard, sleek muscles, long, powerful legs, narrow hips, and . . .

Oh, God, she remembered . . .

He opened his eyes and looked at her. "You say you remember what we did last night, but how could you remember and not want to do it again? We were smoking, Lys. We were off the charts. How could you not want more of that incredible magic?"

He touched her cheek with his hand, his fingers gentle. She couldn't pull away.

"I could stay cuffed to you for two months," he whispered, "and never once think to look for the key. The hell with the key."

He moved toward her, and she knew that he was going to kiss her. If she let him get close enough, he *was* going to lower his head and cover her mouth with his.

She had to do something. She had to grab her towel and step out of this shower. She had to . . .

But she didn't.

She couldn't.

And so he kissed her.

His lips were so soft and so sweet, but it took only a matter of seconds before what started as a tender kiss exploded into passion.

It was her fault. She was the one who tried to inhale him, who pulled him tightly against her, who nearly ate him alive.

She could taste his surprise for all of a half a second. But then, "Oh, yeah," he breathed, and he kissed her back, just as hungrily.

It happened so fast. How could it have happened so fast? One minute they were fighting, and the next she was wrapping her legs around him.

How could she be doing this? She didn't even like him.

But, God, she wanted him.

She was still nauseous, still had a headache from hell. By all rights she should have been too sick to want anything but the solitude of a dark room and twelve hours of uninterrupted sleep.

Instead she wanted Roger Starrett.

She could feel him, thick and heavy against her. Her shoulders were pressed back against the cool tile of the wall as he kissed her, touched her, his hands everywhere at once. But his hands weren't enough. One shift of her body, and, oh yes, he was inside of her.

"Jesus, Alyssa!" she heard him say, but she drowned him out with her own cry of pleasure, clinging to him desperately, locking her legs around him, moving wildly against him as she lost what little remained of both her control and dignity.

All she'd really needed was to feel him hard inside of her. It was enough to push her over the edge and she exploded.

"Oh, God," Starrett gasped, as if from a thousand miles away. "I can't—"

He was trying to pull away. But she was still being tossed by wave upon wave of excruciating pleasure, and she clung to him. She wouldn't let him go.

He spoke again, his voice a rough rasp through gritted teeth, as if he were lifting a thousand pounds and was more than ready to let it drop. "You gotta let me pull out, Lys, I'm not wearing a—"

Condom.

Locke opened her eyes, all of her pleasure instantly replaced by shocked disbelief. Icy cold, it ran through her veins and she froze—with her legs still tightly around him.

She saw his release. She saw in his eyes the exact moment that he couldn't fight it any longer, as he surrendered to his body's needs and sent his seed deep inside of her.

What had she just done?

She let go of him, pushing him away from her, but it was too late.

Much too late.

"Oh, God, oh, Jesus, I'm sorry," Starrett was saying.

What had she *done*?

Last night she'd had the excuse of too much to drink. This morning she had no excuse at all. And this morning she hadn't even thought—not even once—about protection. What was wrong with her?

Her knees weren't working. She wobbled and Starrett tried to support her, but she pushed him away, holding on to the wall instead. "Don't touch me."

"Alyssa, I swear, I never intended . . ." He was still breathing hard, still shaking. He held on to the wall himself. "It happened so fast. And then you wouldn't let me go and I couldn't pull out—"

"You're a Navy SEAL!" She tried to wash herself clean, but she knew damn well that wouldn't help at all. She was dizzy and sick to her stomach and her headache was back in full force. "You're an expert in hand-to-hand combat. You've got close to seventy pounds on me, and you're telling me you *couldn't* pull out?"

"Not without hurting you. I didn't want to hurt you. I didn't want . . ." He shook his head miserably. "I thought I could hold on. I thought . . . Christ, I'm sorry."

He may well have just gotten her pregnant, and he was *sorry*? God, she was going to be sick again.

"Oh, Jesus." Starrett sat down on the edge of the tub as if he were as dizzy as she was. "Alyssa, look, if you're pregnant, I'll . . ." He took a deep breath. "I'll marry you."

He was serious. He was actually *serious*. As if being chained to him for life would somehow make it all okay.

Yes, she was definitely going to throw up again.

Locke lunged for the toilet, pulling Starrett with her out of the tub. Her stomach should have been empty, but it wasn't. And she managed to be violently ill all over again.

It was worse than before, because this time she couldn't block Starrett out.

"Way to go, Roger," he muttered to himself as he wiped her face with a cool cloth, as he took the sopping T-shirt that was hanging off her arm and wrung it out. "Sex with you makes her hurl. Or maybe it's the thought of marriage. Either way, isn't this just perfect?" He raised his voice just a little. "Alyssa, I am so fucking sorry."

Locke started to laugh. She couldn't help it. Her misery was so intense, so consuming, and yet his apology was completely heartfelt and so totally Roger Starrett.

But her laughter turned almost instantly to first one sob, and then another, and then, horribly, mortifyingly, she was crying.

"Oh, God, I've ruined my life," she sobbed pathetically, giving in to total self-pity. "I've completely destroyed my career."

Starrett knelt beside her, wrapping a towel around her. "What are you talking about? You're not really afraid getting pregnant will—"

"I'm not pregnant!" She looked up at him fiercely. "I'm supposed to get my period any day now. Any minute. I'm *not* pregnant. I can't be. I *won't* be."

He sat back, rocked onto his heels by her ferocity.

"But I don't need to get pregnant to completely screw things up for myself." She wiped her eyes with the heels of her hands, forcing herself to stop. Crying wasn't going to help—in fact it was only making this worse. "I didn't even need to do this—" She lifted her wrist that was handcuffed and raised his arm, too. "—to ruin my life."

He didn't get it.

"I only had to spend the night with you, Roger," she told him. "That's all I had to do. The really stupid part was that it should have been *easy* to keep from messing my life up. Staying away from you should have been a cinch. We don't even like each other."

He still didn't understand. "You're saying that spending the night with me has ruined your career? Get real, Locke—that's just plain stupid."

"You want to hear stupid? Stupid is being the best sharpshooter in the entire U.S. military and being assigned to work a desk. Stupid is dealing with goddamned innuendos and thinly veiled sexual comments day in and day out, and getting so that you're used to it, so that you expect it. Stupid is being recruited for an FBI counterterrorist team because you're the best person for the job and *still* having to face comments about quotas and equal opportunity. Stupid is doing a kickass job and having my supervisor congratulate me while he sneaks a look down my shirt. You have *no* idea what I go up against every single day that I go into work," she told him. "I cannot, can*not* allow my coworkers to see me as a sex object. I cannot have them talking about my sex life. I can't even *have* a sex life!"

"You don't," Starrett pointed out. "You told me last night this is the first relationship you've been in in four years."

"No." She shook her head, wiped her eyes. "This is not a relationship. This is an *accident*. A terrible, terrible accident."

He sat even farther back from her and laughed. "Oh, yeah, that's right. Silly me. It was an *accident*. Of course. Four different times, you accidentally put my dick in your—"

"You're such a jerk," Locke interrupted him hotly. "I

don't know what I'm so worried about. No one's going to believe *you*—go on, you can brag about this all you want."

He stared at her, open mouthed with seeming disbelief. "You think I'd *brag* about . . . ?"

"Cut the insulted act," Locke said, making sure the towel was secure around her as she leaned wearily back against the bathroom wall. "I know you. You like to talk. You'll tell *some*one. WildCard. Or Jenk." She closed her eyes. She could put in for reassignment. Maybe Chicago. Or San Francisco. No, San Francisco was too near the Naval Amphibious Base in Coronado. Maybe Denver . . . "Definitely John Nilsson. I *know* you're going to tell Nils."

And then, forty-five minutes after they got these hand-cuffs off, the entire Troubleshooters squad would know that Roger Starrett had finally scored with Alyssa Locke. Or at least they would have heard the story. Whether they believed it was a different matter entirely.

"I'm not going to tell anyone, Alyssa," Starrett said quietly. "Because you're right. No one would believe me. To be honest, I hardly believe it happened myself."

It was midmorning by the time Meg pulled into the Sea-gull Motel. She'd stopped several times at fast-food drive throughs to get coffee for herself and some water for Ra-zeen. She'd managed to give him the last of the sleeping pills, and he was snoring again, and hopefully would be un-til she could get him inside the motel room.

The Extremist from the parking garage had told her the motel room would be reserved for her under the name Joan Smith. She had been told to check in and wait to be contacted.

Meg parked right outside the office. Leaving the window open only a crack, she locked Razeen in the car and went inside.

The clerk was a tremendously bored, tremendously preg-nant girl of maybe sixteen. She gathered the paperwork for the room with infinitesimal slowness. It was all Meg could do not to leap over the counter and do it herself.

As long as she kept moving, she had the strength to keep going. In the car, she'd kept the radio on, distracting herself

with music. But standing here, waiting, there was nothing to
do but think.

Think about Eve and Amy, who—as John believed—
might already be dead. Her precious baby might not have
been taken from Meg just for these awful few days, but forever. It was too terrible to think about. Too devastating to
consider.

Eve would die protecting Amy, Meg knew that. But even
Eve, despite her sometimes seemingly mythic strength and
determination, couldn't protect Amy from terrorists who
had a reputation, as John had reminded her, for putting bullets into the heads of their hostages.

Meg knew that John had firsthand experience dealing
with terrorists. What he believed was based on a grim reality that Meg herself had come into contact with only very
briefly during her stay in Kazbekistan.

But now she didn't want to think about Amy, and she
didn't want to think about John, either.

Leaving him behind *had* been the right thing to do. She
was probably going to die. She knew that, accepted it. She almost didn't even care anymore. But she did care about John.

She cared too much.

"Joan Smith, huh?" the girl said. "We've been getting
about ten phone calls a day, asking if you've checked in yet."

Meg couldn't breathe. "Really?"

"Is that your car?"

"The white one, yes," she replied.

"How many people are you going to have in this room?
Because we have these rules and . . ." There was a flicker of
something—life maybe—in the girl's eyes and voice that
made Meg turn around and look out the window into the
parking lot.

Five men in long, dark raincoats surrounded her car. A
cargo van, its front door open, stood nearby.

"Oh, my God!" Maybe this was what the Extremist had
meant when he'd said she'd be contacted. Maybe these men
had Amy and Eve in that van.

"What about the room?" the girl asked plaintively. "And
there's a—"

Meg didn't bother to answer, didn't hear the rest of it as she rushed for the door.

The morning sunshine seemed to dance across the surface of her car and make five pairs of mirrored sunglasses shine. One of the men wore a necklace that glistened in the bright light.

It was surreal.

The raincoats seemed oddly out of place under the perfect blue sky, but they hid great, huge guns. The kind of guns John Nilsson and his men had carried when they'd arrived at the Kazbekistani embassy. Assault weapons, John called them. The kind of guns that could cut a person in half with a spray of deadly bullets.

The men kept their guns under their coats as she approached, but they made certain she knew they were there. As if she could possibly miss them.

"Do you have my daughter?" she demanded. "I want to see my daughter, and I want to see her *now*."

Two of the men exchanged a glance, and Meg realized with a sharp surge of dread that the flash of sunlight she'd seen was glinting off stylized Kazbekistani symbols that hung from a thick gold chain around the one man's neck.

Those symbols were the Kazbekistani letters for *G*, *I*, and *K*.

These were not the Extremists. These were Razeen's own men, come to set him free.

Before Meg could move, before she could reach into her pocket for her gun and—God help her!—shoot Razeen right through the car window, two of the men had taken her swiftly by the arms and a third patted her pockets and took her weapon.

Oh, God! She'd come all this way, only to lose now. She could barely stand, barely breathe, barely think.

"You'll see your daughter soon enough." The necklaced man spoke in a heavy accent. "Unlock the car."

Think. *Think,* she ordered herself. If she burst into tears, they'd know she knew they weren't the Extremists. If she just unlocked the car door, they'd take Razeen and be gone, leaving her, probably with a bullet in her head.

Meg could see the motel clerk watching them with un-abashed interest through the big plate glass windows.

One of the raincoats glanced warily toward the clerk, too. And Meg knew they didn't want to create a scene and bring the police into this. They didn't want to break the windows of her car, they didn't want to shoot her, they didn't want screaming or the sound of breaking glass or gunshots.

"We will take him," the necklaced man told her, "and you will stay here for thirty minutes, doing nothing, talking to no one. After thirty minutes, you will get into your car and drive to the McDonald's, four blocks west. Your daughter will be there, in the ladies' room."

Hope and doubt flooded her simultaneously. Maybe she was wrong. Maybe these were the Extremists, and getting Amy back would be as simple as unlocking her car door and waiting thirty minutes before driving four blocks west.

Think. *Think.* "What about my grandmother?" Meg asked. "And my . . . my grandfather?"

"Of course," the man said. "They'll be there, too. You'll have them all back, all safely."

Her hope sputtered and died. All her hope.

No, she refused to accept that the situation was com-pletely hopeless. There had to be another way, another op-tion, another choice.

Escape seemed impossible.

Her only option was to somehow grab one of the big as-sault guns and blast Razeen into hell. Then she had two choices: to kill Razeen or die herself, trying to kill him.

But wait. She had another gun, the one she'd taken from the FBI guard, still hidden in her boot. She could feel it, hard against her ankle. To get it, she'd have to lean over, pull up her pants leg, reach into her boot . . . Impossible. Hopeless.

Or maybe not.

She'd unlock the door, climb into the back to untie Ra-zeen from where John had tethered him to the floor. And while she was doing that, with her back to the raincoats, she would pull up her pant leg, reach into her boot for her gun.

And she'd fire a bullet into Razeen's head at close range.

She *had* to do it. It was Razeen or Amy.

She had to kill Razeen. She didn't have a choice.

Razeen would forgive her. She knew that.

She would die right now, too, because after killing Razeen, the gunmen would kill her. She knew that, without a doubt.

She reached for the keys, and around her, the world had gone into sharp focus. The motel clerk was still watching them through the window. A maintenance man, baseball cap pulled low over his face, was pushing a cart of dirty sheets and towels across the driveway, the wheels rattling noisily on the cracked pavement. He shouted in rapid-fire Spanish up to the maids who were cleaning a room on the second floor, a vacuum cleaner holding the door open, "Ho, Renetta, there's a phone call for you in the maintenance room!"

"He'll need to be untied," she said to necklace man, her voice amazingly smooth. "I'll have to go into the back to reach the ropes."

One of the maids came out of the room and leaned over the railing, shouting back, still in Spanish. "You must be mistaken. There's no one named Renetta here."

"Maybe they asked for Rene. How do I know?" The maintenance man was nearly on top of them with the cart, and the raincoats shifted uneasily, looking to Necklace for direction.

Meg took advantage of the distraction to unlock the front door and to push the button that would release the child restraint lock in the back.

"There's no Rene here, either," came the reply in Spanish. "What are you doing with that cart? I just took that to the laundry room!"

Meg froze. Could it be . . . ? Was it possible . . . ? She didn't want to turn around, didn't want to look at the man. Please don't let it be John, she prayed as she reached to open the back door of her car. Please don't let him be killed, too.

Necklace shook his head at the raincoats in warning, pulling the open front of his own coat closed, murmuring, "Let him go past."

From the corner of her eyes, Meg saw that the maintenance man was paying them no attention at all. He was still pushing the cart, looking up at the maid, shouting angrily back to her. "I don't have time to act as your secretary. Next time the phone rings, you take your big fat ass down the stairs and answer it yourself!"

The maid screeched with outrage, raining an eruption of Spanish down upon them.

Meg opened the back door just as the maintenance man pushed the laundry cart—hard—into the raincoats.

It happened so quickly. One second she was about to step into the back of her car, and the next she was being pushed inside, pressed down onto the floor.

"Nobody moves, nobody *blinks* or Razeen's brains are on the back window!"

It was John.

Meg turned her head to see that somehow he'd taken one of those deadly assault weapons away from one of the raincoats. He held it with an easy familiarity, its barrel jammed right beneath Razeen's chin.

No one moved.

"You okay?" he asked her quietly.

She nodded, unable to speak, trying not to shake. God damn it, she could have done this!

"You still have the car keys?"

She did. She'd slipped them back into her pocket. She managed another nod.

"Good. Get ready to use 'em," he ordered. "When I tell you to, climb over the seat and get us the hell out of here. Can you do that?"

"Yeah." Meg found her voice. He must have followed her here. How in God's name had he managed to follow her here?

"Hands on top of your heads," he commanded the raincoats in a voice that implied dire consequences should he be disobeyed. "Move slowly, keep 'em where I can see 'em. And step back, away from the car."

Meg couldn't see the raincoats. All she could see was John's ear and the tense muscle jumping in his jaw as he waited to see if the GIK terrorists would follow his orders.

Or try to kill him without injuring Razeen.

Meg wanted to shout at him. To ask him why he'd followed her and put himself back into this danger. She wanted to hold him close and thank him, reverently, for coming to her rescue yet again, for making it so that she didn't have to kill Razeen right here and now. She wanted to apologize again, to tell John she really was sorry. She shouldn't have gotten him involved in any of this. She should have executed Razeen in the K-stani embassy men's room, while she had the chance.

She kept her mouth shut, knowing that the last thing she should do was distract him while he was attempting the impossible—and managing their escape.

"Now!" he said to Meg.

Meg went. Out from under him, up and over the seat. But one glance in the rearview mirror reminded her that they were parked in by the cargo van—there was nowhere to go.

"Go, go, go!" John shouted.

She had the key in the ignition and the car in reverse and she braced herself and floored it—slamming them back into the van with a screech of bending metal, pushing it out of their way.

"Keep your head down!" John shouted, and she ducked just as the windshield shattered with a deafening roar.

Necklace was shooting at them.

Meg jammed the car into first and pulled out of the parking lot, tires squealing.

Still alive.

For now.

Twenty

$\backsim$ $\backsim$

ALYSSA LOCKE WASN'T wearing any underwear.

Last night Sam had broken the front clasp and torn the strap off of her bra and damn near shredded her panties, and this morning she'd silently pulled on her jeans commando-style while he'd tried hard not to watch.

Tried and failed.

She'd taken her broken and torn underwear and tucked it carefully into the pocket of her jacket—no doubt to keep him from having a souvenir or material proof that last night had actually happened.

She'd put her T-shirt back on, too. It was wet, but she had no choice. It was that or nothing. It was extremely hard to put on a shirt with one hand cuffed to someone else.

Sam had found a tank top and cut the left shoulder strap, tying it together after he'd pulled it on.

They'd dressed in silence, combed their hair, took turns putting on their sneakers and tying their laces.

After Alyssa had gotten sick for the second time, after the fiasco in the shower where they'd had unprotected sex, neither of them had had much to say.

Sam stared out the window of the taxi that was taking them across town. He couldn't believe they'd had sex without a condom. First time in his entire life he'd done that. He'd tried to stop her, but . . .

Inwardly he shook his head at himself. Like hell he'd tried to stop her.

He'd been so completely blown away by the fact that she wanted him again. And he knew that if he had stopped her to get a condom, she would have come to her senses.

So he hadn't stopped her.

What followed was his fault entirely. He'd assumed he
could handle it, handle her. He'd thought that he could give
her what she wanted, that he'd have enough macho control
to keep himself from losing it and getting her pregnant.

It was a stupid thing to think. Doubly stupid because he
knew, he *knew*, that simply entering her without a condom
put her at risk for pregnancy.

But, oh, sweet Jesus, the way she had felt around him . . .

He sneaked a look at her, sitting as far from him as possible, looking pointedly out the other window. One of his
sweatshirts was draped over the handcuffs that still connected
them, and she held her jacket up to her breasts—hiding
the fact that with her T-shirt wet and nearly transparent, she
looked like a contestant at some low-life frat bar party.

She could be pregnant.

It wasn't as terrifying a thought as he'd expected it to be.
In fact, the idea of his sperm inside of her right now, maybe
connecting with her egg right this very moment, was an un-
deniable turn-on. A piece of him inside of her for nine whole
months . . .

It just didn't happen to be the piece of him he wanted inside of her for nine whole months.

And of course, after nine months, there'd be a friggin'
baby—that was pretty terrifying.

But not as completely mind numbing as he'd thought.

Marry me.

He looked at the smooth line of her cheek, at the way
she'd pulled her hair back from her face in an attempt to
control it, to look professional and cool.

All that ice was just a cover for the volcano that burned
inside of Alyssa Locke.

He'd always thought that a night with her would cure him
of his obsession.

He'd been dead wrong. After last night, he wanted her
more than ever. He wanted her forever.

Marry me.

He could say the words right now. He didn't have to wait
to find out if she was pregnant. *Marry me and I'll fuck you
every night for the rest of our lives.*

Sam laughed out loud. Yeah, that would go over really

well. Women wanted romance. They wanted love. Even women who pretended to be ice cubes like Alyssa Locke.

But Alyssa didn't love him. Hell, she'd made it more than clear she didn't even *like* him despite the fact that she more than liked having sex with him.

She glanced at him, shooting him her disapproval. There was nothing about this situation that she found funny. His laughter was only making things worse.

The taxi pulled up outside the parking garage, saving his sorry ass. He let Alyssa pay for half of the cab fare with a five-dollar bill she had in the pocket of her jeans. No way was he going to start an argument over that.

"Can you wait?" she asked the driver. "He'll be right back—he'll need a ride back to the hotel."

The *he* she was referring to was *him*.

She wasn't going to drive Sam back. They were going to the exact same place, she had a car, but she wasn't going to give him a lift. She hated him that much.

She must have seen something in his face because she said, "I'll pay for the cab," as they started for the stairs that would take them to the level where her car was parked.

"I can pay for my own cab," he told her, careful to leave out the adjectives he was thinking, trying not to sound as pissed off as he felt. Getting into a fight with her now, mere seconds before they unlocked these handcuffs, wasn't going to help.

Although help *what*, he wasn't sure. What did he want from this?

To sleep with her again tonight.

Okay, King of Wishful Thinking, that wasn't likely to happen. Try again, this time keeping it realistic.

He wanted her to be comfortable enough with him so that she'd let him know if she'd gotten pregnant from what they'd done this morning.

Yeah, that was about all he could hope for.

Sam cleared his throat as they climbed the last of the stairs. "If this ends—you know, the situation with Osman Razeen and Meg Moore—in the next few days, I'll, um, call you in about a week, to, um . . ."

"I've got your email address," she cut in. "I'll send you a an email when I know for sure I'm not pregnant."

He could see her car now. Right where they'd left it yesterday. It seemed like a lifetime ago. "And if you are?" he asked quietly.

She wouldn't look at him. "I'm not."

"If you are, please talk to me before you make any decisions," he said. "I deserve at least, you know, to know."

Her face was devoid of all expression, all the light and life of the woman he'd laughed with and made love to last night completely suppressed.

"All right," she conceded. "If I don't email you, I'll call you. But I'm not going to have to call you."

She was, however, going to have to follow him, today and the next day and the next . . . Because she thought he knew where Nils was.

And Sam knew that he wouldn't be able to stand it. Having Alyssa continue to follow him for the next few days was going to drive him completely mad. He didn't want to have to see her, to think about her.

To ache for her.

"I don't know where Nils is," he told her as she unlocked the trunk of her car. "Really."

And there was her fanny pack. Aqua. As he watched, she unzipped it and pulled out a heavy ring of keys.

And then, with a click, they were free.

She pulled on her jacket despite the heat of the day.

"I did know for a while, right after he left," Sam continued. "You were right about that." He told her about Wild-Card's tracking device. "I'm positive Nils caught up with Meg within twelve hours of her being gone. But he hasn't called— at least not me. I seriously doubt Meg killed him, so I've been going on the assumption that they're still together. In fact, I've been expecting Nils to turn up with Meg in tow any minute now, ready to surrender Razeen to the FBI."

Alyssa was silent, just listening to him.

"Nils has a real thing for this woman," he explained awkwardly. "I think he, you know, maybe even loves her. He'll bring her in. Just give him a little more time."

She nodded, rubbing her wrist. "Will you call me if he contacts you?"

"Yes, I will." Was he lying? He didn't really know. Had she been lying when she'd told him she'd call him if she were pregnant? Probably. God damn it. He wanted to cry. There was nothing left to do but walk away from her now. "So now you can stop following me, all right? I think it would be best for both of us if you didn't follow me anymore."

She nodded again and got into her car.

That was it. No good-bye. No *thanks, it was fun*. No see you later.

Because she didn't want to see him later. She didn't want to see him ever again. Not even if she were carrying his baby.

Sam watched her pull out of the parking spot, watched her drive toward the exit.

He savagely kicked one of the enormous concrete pillars that held up the parking garage, but even the pain in his foot didn't take away the pain that was in his heart.

"Damn it!" Meg said. "Damn *you* for following me!"

"Pull in here," Nils ordered her, and she took a hard right turn into the massive parking lot of a resort hotel near Disney World.

The van hadn't followed them.

Meg had hit it so hard, the front axle had broken. Nils had looked back to see the front left wheel listing at an odd angle. Those assholes weren't going anywhere—not in that van. And being amateurs, they hadn't brought a backup vehicle.

Still, he'd had Meg keep driving. They'd gotten on and off the highway until Nils was convinced no one was following them. No doubt they were too busy running for cover after tossing off that shot. The police were probably on the way after *that* genius move. Nils could only pray that the Extremists didn't have anyone watching the place. If they did, Amy and Eve wouldn't be kept alive much longer.

Meg came to a stop with a jerk of the brakes and turned off the car as she glared at him.

She was mad at him. He'd saved her ass, and she was *mad*

at him. She'd been seething while she drove, but now she let it all out. "You could've been killed!"

"So could you have!" he countered. "What was your plan? Shoot Razeen with the handgun you've got in your boot?"

He saw from her eyes that he'd surprised her. She hadn't realized he knew about the backup weapon she was still carrying in her boot.

Her hands were shaking, and she tried to hide it by crossing her arms, tucking them out of sight.

Nils wanted nothing more than to hold her, to reassure himself that she was truly all right, but instead he lit into her the way Senior Chief Wolchonok would've gone after one of the younger members of the team who'd made a stupid mistake.

"What do you think would've happened after you'd done that, Meg?" he asked. "Didn't it occur to you that shooting Razeen might've pissed those guys off? Didn't it occur to you that if you killed him, they'd kill you?"

"Yes," she said just as heatedly, "that *did* occur to me!"

And she'd been ready to do it anyway. She *would* have done it anyway. That was how desperate she was.

"I was minutes from checking in," she fumed. "*Minutes.* And the girl behind the desk told me that someone's been calling—frequently—to see if I had arrived yet. I was *that* close!

"Now what?" she continued. It was getting stale in the car, and she rolled down the window, her movements jerky, filled with fury. "Why are we stopping here? You've got a gun now. You can take me in. What are you waiting for, Nilsson? This is what you wanted, isn't it?"

Nils took the clip out of the little Uzi he'd taken from one of the K-stani thugs in the Seagull Motel parking lot and held it out to Meg. "I'm waiting for you to surrender your weapon *voluntarily* and ask me for help. At which time I'll contact my CO and Max Bhagat, the FBI agent in charge of this investigation. It's possible that the FBI have found out where the Extremists are holding Amy and Eve. Wouldn't you like to know that?"

She snatched the clip from his hands. "If the FBI have located Amy and Eve, it's also possible that the Extremists know it, and have already killed them in retaliation! I wasn't supposed to tell anyone, remember?"

For a moment, Nils was certain she was going to cry, that she was going to crumble and break down, but this time she didn't. She pulled herself together, sat up straighter. Her face pale, she turned to him. "Get out of the car."

Nils reached for her. "Meg, god damn it, let me help you."

She pulled away from him, opening the door and taking both the clip from the Uzi and the keys with her. "Get *out* of the *car*, John."

Christ, she was bending over and taking the little handgun out of her boot.

"You don't need that," he said to her as he got out.

"It's the end of the line." The look in her eyes chilled him to the bone. He wasn't afraid for his own safety. He didn't doubt for one second that she would die herself to protect him. But if he didn't stop her, she *was* going to kill Razeen— and regret it for the rest of her life.

"The Seagull Motel was my contact point with the Extremists," she told him, her voice oddly flat. "I was supposed to check in and wait to be contacted. But I can't go there without being attacked by the GIK. And after what just happened, the place is going to be crawling with police."

"Meg." Nils moved slowly around the car. Why the hell had he given up the Uzi? He should never have let her regain control of this situation. He should have realized how close she was to the edge.

And just how little she felt she had to lose.

It stung knowing that she didn't include what he wanted, what *he* felt, in her equation. It hurt knowing that—aside from her wanting him to be safe—he wasn't a factor that she considered when deciding whether or not she should sacrifice her soul and her life.

And whose fault was that, but his own? He'd never shared enough of himself. All those hours they'd just spent together in her car, and he *still* hadn't told her jack about himself.

Yeah, he'd burped out the fact that he loved her, but she hadn't believed him, and he hadn't made an attempt to convince her it was really true.

So now she didn't have a clue how much she stood to lose.

"I can't go back to the motel. I have no choice," Meg told him dispassionately, as if she'd detached from herself. "Now I've got to kill Razeen, and pray that the Extremists hear about it and believe that it's real, pray that they release Amy and Eve after the news is out."

"Meg, you're not going to kill him. He's not even awake. You promised him you wouldn't—"

"I am awake." Razeen's voice came from the car. "It is okay, Meg. I am ready."

Oh, *fuck*.

"Stay back, John," Meg ordered. "I have to do this. I don't have a choice anymore."

He didn't stay back. He moved in front of the car, between Meg and Razeen.

"There's always a choice," he told her again. "You could do it this way, sure. Murder this man." She flinched at his choice of words, and he ruthlessly used it again. "Murder him and gamble that the Extremists will then release your daughter. *Or* you could let me help. You could let yourself trust me. Let me contact the FBI, let me get us the help we need."

"It is an unnecessary risk," Razeen's voice floated out of the car, "when killing me will get you exactly what you want—your daughter."

Nils raised his voice and talked over him. "In exchange for Razeen, in exchange for your cooperation, because you're under duress, the FBI will drop all charges against you. I'll make sure of that, Meg. Once we locate Amy and your grandmother, I'll make sure my commanding officer, Lieutenant Paoletti, is in charge of the SEAL team that'll do the rescue op. He and Bhagat will work *with* you, Meg, to find and free them."

"Shoot me and save Amy," Razeen urged.

"With the FBI and SEAL task force's help," Nils continued, willing her not to listen to Razeen, willing her to hear him out, to keep looking into his eyes, to stay connected, "we can go back to the Seagull Motel and wait. We'll get the local police and the motel owners to cooperate. You told me yourself that someone's been calling for you—that's good. That means the Extremists probably haven't been watching the place. They probably don't know anything about what just went down. We can go back there, we *can*, Meg, and the FBI will grab any GIK members who show up, attempting to free Razeen. With the FBI's help, we can still get that phone call from the Extremists. And when they do call and tell you where to meet them, I'll go with you. I'll pretend I'm Razeen."

Meg shook her head. "Absolutely *not*."

"I'll use makeup—shading so I look more like him. I'm a little taller, he's a little heavier, but I'll stoop and wear padding. You know I can do it."

"If you go in as Razeen, you'd be putting yourself at tremendous risk," she countered. "They could kill you right away!"

"I'll wear body armor."

"That won't do any good if they shoot you in the head!" Heat was back in her voice. And even though she was arguing with him, it was far better than that near zombie flatness that had scared him to death.

"This is actually a better plan than you going in with Razeen," Nils tried to make her understand, "because if the Extremists have no intention of releasing Amy and Eve, then I'll be in there with you, with *all* of you. You'll have a better chance of survival—Amy will have a better chance, Meg—if I'm there. You *know* this."

"Except if they kill you right when you walk through the door!"

"If we do this right, if we use the Troubleshooters, let them do what they—*we*—have been trained to do, you and I won't even have to get out of the car. Meg, you've got to listen to me—"

"Meg, do you remember what I told you?" Razeen wouldn't shut the fuck up. He was desperate not to be turned over to the authorities, desperate to die as a martyr to his cause at her hand. "My death will save your daughter and bring me peace," he said from the backseat of the car. "It will bring justice."

Nils knew that Meg wanted to believe Razeen. She wanted it to be that easy.

"That's bullshit," he told Meg. "What he's saying is total bullshit. Your killing him won't bring *any* kind of justice. Saving Amy this way won't make up for *any*thing he's done. It will only perpetuate the violence."

Razeen started to say something else, and Nils opened the car door, and got the Uzi from the front seat. He knew exactly how and where to hit the terrorist leader to silence him on a slightly less permanent basis than what Meg had in mind.

It wasn't quite the right punctuation to put on a statement about perpetuating violence, but he had to shut the fucker up and he had to do it now. So he did it swiftly. Efficiently. With a single solid blow. Razeen sagged, out cold and finally silent.

"I know you," Nils said, turning back to Meg, desperate now to make her understand. "Despite everything that's happened, despite everything you've said over the past few days. I *know* you. And killing this man will haunt you for the rest of your life. You'll never be free from it. *Never.* You've got to trust me on this, Meg. Please, God, trust me."

But she didn't trust him. He could see it in her eyes. Once again, it had come down to too little, too late.

Except Nils didn't believe in too late. He didn't buy into no hope. He refused to accept a no-win scenario of *any* kind.

So he kept talking. "Do you really think you can put a bullet in Razeen's head, and not have it destroy you?" he asked her.

She shook her head. "If there's no other way——"

"There *is* another way," he told her. "If there truly were no other way, don't you think that I would shoot him for you? Christ, Meg, don't you know that I would do that for you if there really were no other option?"

She looked startled at that, and he kept going, hammering at her mercilessly.

"I would," he said ruthlessly. "I would die for you, I would kill for you. Let's get that straight right now. I'm telling you that there *is* another way, and you've got to trust me on that, Meg. I'm a professional liar, you know that, and I'll cop to it, too. I haven't been honest with you about where I come from. But that's just the stupid details. You don't need to know that stuff to know me. And you *do* know me." There were tears in his eyes now and he let her see them. "You know—you *have* to know—that I wouldn't lie to you about this. I understand that you want me out of the picture because you think that then I'll be safe, but you're wrong about that, too. It's only when I'm with you that I'm safe. The rest of the time, I am *completely* goddamn lost."

His voice broke and he had to take a deep breath. Jesus, he'd never admitted that before, not even to himself. But shit, why stop there? His lip was trembling and the tears in his eyes were threatening to escape. He was a heartbeat from breaking down and crying like a baby.

"I fell in love with you in that hallway outside of your office in Kazbekistan," he managed to tell her, his voice embarrassingly shaky. "I'm still in love with you. I stayed away because you were married, but that's the *only* reason I stayed away. And you better believe that neither hell nor high water could keep me from you now, Meg. I am in this with you to the end. If you believe nothing else I've said, god damn it, believe *that*."

Ah, Jesus, he was crying. But instead of turning away, he held his ground and let her see. She wanted the truth from him. Well, there it was. Fucking streaming down his face.

"But are you with me?" he asked her. "That's the question that needs to be answered here. Don't you want to cut the crap and give me your gun so that together, *together*, we can go get help to find Amy and bring her home?"

When Meg started to cry, too, Nils knew that he'd won. The relief nearly knocked him to his knees, but somehow he managed to stay on his feet.

She held the side arm out to him. "Help me," she whispered. "Please, John, help me find Amy and bring her back home."

He took the gun from her, took her into his arms. "Thank you," he said, holding her close. "Thank you."

Twenty-one

◦—◦

Locke walked warily into the busy war room that had been set up by the task force in Orlando.

It had happened just the way Starrett had predicted it would. John Nilsson had finally called, telling Paoletti and Bhagat that Meg was willing to surrender Osman Razeen to the FBI in return for a deal.

A major deal.

A deal that included the formation of an FBI task force to locate the Extremists and kick in their door. Max Bhagat was in charge, with SEAL Team Sixteen's Troubleshooters providing assistance. Bhagat was a good leader who knew enough to stand back and let the SEALs do what they'd been trained to do. He respected and listened to Lt. Tom Paoletti.

And Paoletti had specifically requested Locke be part of the team.

She had flown down here with completely mixed feelings. Was she here because Paoletti knew she was one of the best shooters in the Western hemisphere, or was she here because Roger Starrett had been flapping his mouth, and Tom—and the rest of the Troubleshooters squad—wanted to look at her and leer?

It hadn't even been twelve hours since she'd woken up in Starrett's bed. Her head was still pounding—she still felt as if she'd been hit by a steamroller.

She moved carefully, trying not to jar her brain, bracing herself as WildCard Karmody caught sight of her and grinned.

"Hey, Locke. Welcome to the Loony Bin." He turned back to his computer, engrossed by whatever was on the screen.

Locke stood still. Was that it? A simple greeting, no winking, no sneering, no innuendo?

In the far corner of the room, she could see John Nilsson working with a team of FBI specialists to alter his appearance. There were enlarged photos of Osman Razeen on the wall and a big mirror in front of Nils.

Closer to her, PO Mark Jenkins and the new ensign, Muldoon, were have a grand old time, stomping on what looked to be an expensive black suit. They were antiquing it, of course. If Nils were going to pretend to be Razeen, he needed to wear a dark suit similar to the one Razeen had been wearing when he was snatched. Except Razeen had been wearing his suit for days now. So Jenk and Muldoon were making the suit that Nils was going to put on look as if he'd been wearing it for many days in a row, too.

"Good, you're here." Locke turned to find Senior Chief Wolchonok talking to her. "Briefing in three minutes—we've got to take out the GIK members who are watching the motel so their rivals, the Extremists, can contact Meg Moore. Lieutenant Paoletti wants you in with the rest of the team."

Locke nodded. "Thanks, Senior."

He was about to move past, but he hesitated. "Everything okay?"

There was nothing ugly or knowing in his eyes. Just genuine concern. Locke forced a smile. "Headache."

His eyes narrowed. "It's not that flu that's going around, is it?"

"No, Senior Chief, it's not," she said quickly. That would be just her luck—to get kicked off the team before she'd even had a chance to get on it. "Really. My sister had a baby yesterday," she lowered her voice to explain. "I celebrated a little too . . . enthusiastically last night."

Wolchonok didn't smile, but she knew he wanted to. She could see amusement in his eyes. He pulled a bottle of Tylenol from his pocket and gave her three, as if he'd dispensed hangover remedies a time or two before as part of his job.

"Welcome to the human race," he murmured. "Don't worry, I won't tell. Water cooler's in the corner. Briefing's in the room right next to it. Hope you packed your jumpsuit."

She got herself a cup of water, not daring to hope the

senior's comment about her jumpsuit—the black utility uniform the FBI counterterrorist team wore in the field—meant
she was going to see some action with the boys.

Still, it was possible. Lt. Tom Paoletti had put her in
the field before. He knew she was good. He knew she was
reliable.

It was also possible that he knew she'd slept with Starrett
last night, God help her. And if he knew that, that tabloid-
worthy fact could prejudice him and overpower both *good*
and *reliable*.

Locke washed down the pills and crumbled the paper cup,
tossing it unerringly into the trash can next to the cooler.
Squaring her shoulders, she went into the room Wolchonok
had pointed out.

The rest of the team were already present and accounted
for. They sat in rows of chairs that faced the front, where
Tom Paoletti was in deep discussion with his XO, Jazz Jacquette, and the FBI's Max Bhagat.

Sam Starrett was there.

She spotted him immediately, her gaze drawn to him as if
he were some kind of magnet that she couldn't avoid even if
her life depended on it. He was sitting in the back next to
Jay Lopez, who was laughing at something Starrett had said.

Starrett was laughing, too, but he turned to look directly
at her, as if he'd somehow felt her watching him, and instantly both his laughter and smile faded.

For about three seconds, he just stared at her, his eyes
filled with . . . hurt?

No. Couldn't be.

He quickly looked away, looked down at the floor, looked
anywhere but at her.

Lopez greeted her, though. Warmly. "How's it going,
Locke? Long time, no see. Congratulations—I heard you're
with the FBI now."

"That's right," she said. "Counterterrorist. Although I'm
sure Starrett's filled you in."

Lopez looked at Starrett in surprise. "I didn't know you
guys knew each other."

Starrett looked up at Locke, his gaze coolly impersonal

now. "We don't," he said. "Not really." His nod dismissed her. "Nice seeing you again, ma'am."

Starrett hadn't told. At least not Lopez.

Or Wolchonok.

Or Karmody.

Locke sat down on the other side of the room, careful not to jar her head.

And he'd actually called her *ma'am*.

"Okay," Lieutenant Paoletti said from the front of the room. "Here's what we're going to do."

"Someone starts shooting, you get behind me," John murmured as she led him into the office of the Seagull Motel. "Remember?"

"I remember," Meg said. She remembered everything he'd told her over the past few hours. Everything. *I'm still in love with you.*

"Breathe," he told her. "Don't forget to breathe, Meg."

She was leading him. He was pretending to be Razeen, pretending to be heavily drugged and leaning on her, but his arm was warm around her waist. Warm and strong.

He was holding *her* up.

His touch was more than just supportive, though. It was intimate, laced with a warmth of a completely different kind. He wasn't just touching her, he was *touching* her.

"Almost there," he murmured. "Once we get inside the hotel room, it's almost all over."

Almost over.

That was usually what the dentist said right before it hurt the worst.

God, there was so much that could go wrong. The plan was for Meg to go into the office with John just as another car was pulling up. A SEAL who was nicknamed Jazz—the executive officer of John's team, a powerful looking black man—would come into the motel office right behind them, along with a female FBI agent named Alyssa something.

Locke. She'd been part of the team that had taken Meg out of the men's room in the K-stani embassy, too. She was outrageously pretty, despite the fact that she didn't expend much effort smiling—probably not a lot to smile about in her job. Still, she'd taken the time to pull Meg aside and re-assure her that this part of the operation at least *was* going to go off without a hitch.

Meg wished she had that kind of confidence. "Don't you die," she whispered now to John. "Whatever happens, *don't die.*"

He looked at her, straight in the eye, and she knew that if they weren't in public, with twenty-five SEALs and FBI agents and God knows how many GIK terrorists watching them, he would have kissed her.

And she would have kissed him, too—a hot, fierce, des-perate kiss that would have ended from necessity far too soon. She wondered if he could see an echo of that kiss in her eyes as clearly as she saw it in his.

"This is going to go like clockwork," he told her. "We've got the entire squad of Troubleshooters out there. And just as many FBI. This part will be a piece of cake. Trust me, remember?"

Trust him. She had to now. But she noticed that his reas-surances came with no promises or guarantees. Just a lot of unspoken hope.

It was hoped that Jazz and Alyssa's presence would keep the GIK from trying to snatch back the man they thought was Razeen right there in the parking lot, in the late afternoon.

Meg was in disguise, too. She wore a cheap blond wig and a lot of makeup—it was believed the GIK would be sus-picious if she came back without attempting to hide from them by changing her appearance. The wig added that final touch of oddness to an already surreal experience. Like Marilyn Monroe showing up in a Sylvester Stallone movie.

The desk clerk was skinny and balding, an odd stick of a man with more than a passing resemblance to a praying mantis. He was faster than Pregnant Girl had been, thank God. Meg completed the paperwork, paid in cash for two nights in advance, and he stretched out an antenna and handed her the room key.

Jazz and Alyssa were arguing rather convincingly about the best route to Jacksonville and Jazz stormed out to his car to get a map as Meg and John pushed back out the door.

"Keep me between you and the street," John murmured. "You're the target at this point, remember?"

"I just want to get inside the room." They were almost there, and the hard part, the *dangerous* part—at least for now—was almost done.

"We need to make sure we take enough time so they can ID me as Razeen." He tried to make a joke. "Not that I don't appreciate a beautiful woman rushing to get me inside her motel room."

She didn't laugh. None of this was even slightly funny.

He stumbled slightly—on purpose, of course—and the coat he had around his shoulders swung open, revealing the cuffs on his wrists. Meg pulled him up, and he leaned against her, blocking her from the street with his body, as she unlocked the door, and then, thank God, they were both inside.

John locked the door behind them as Meg made sure the window was latched and the curtains tightly closed. The cuffs had never really been fastened, and he tossed them aside as easily as he did the coat. It was too warm for a suit jacket, let alone a coat, and he took that off, too, along with the body armor he was wearing, and in his shirtsleeves, he cranked the air-conditioning.

The room was standard cheap motel. Two double beds with garish spreads, mediocre artwork on the wall, beige telephone on the table between the beds.

John saw her looking at it, and nodded. "Now we wait for the phone to ring."

And Meg knew that she'd been wrong. The danger might've been over for now, but the hardest part—the waiting—was just beginning.

The woman was upset. More upset than usual.

The tension in the old house was sky-high, too, and Eve knew that it was going to have to be tonight. She and Amy—or maybe even just Amy—were going to have to get up to that bathroom and go out that window.

Even if it were raining, even if the roof were slick with water, even if lightning were crackling overhead. It *had* to be tonight.

Because the woman wanted them gone. As in dead and gone.

"What's happening?" she dared to ask the Bear, praying that it wasn't already too late.

He just scowled and shook his head.

Eve gave another piece of butterscotch to Amy, who was trying hard not to flinch every time the woman's voice got louder.

"Where were we in the story?" she asked, hoping to distract her.

"You went to France to see Ralph," Amy said, "but he wouldn't talk to you. He just ran away."

"That's right," Eve told the little girl, smoothing her hair back from her face. Amy could use a good hour in a bathtub. She herself could use a good soak, too, for that matter. Lord, her every muscle ached, every bone hurt. She hadn't felt this bad since she'd tried to run the Boston Marathon back in 1972. "I remember that day as if it were yesterday. I thought it had gotten about as awful as it could get. But that's always a very bad thing to assume."

The Bear had taken his seat. He was listening, as usual. Was all her endless talking doing any good at all? Eve searched his eyes, looking for some obvious sign of humanity, some trace of gentleness and compassion. If it were there, he kept it well hidden.

"It was just a few months later that Hitler invaded France," she told them. "Nick and I were glued to the radio, listening to the news. It was shocking how fast the reports came in of cities that had fallen. It didn't seem possible, this lightning-fast advance of tanks and troops, this *Blitz*. I was scared to death. Because somewhere out there, facing those deadly German panzers, was Ralph.

"I remember I was in town, trying to find information on the whereabouts of his regiment, when I saw ships and boats of all sizes gathering in the harbor. Someone told me that the call had gone out for all available ships and men to meet in Ramsgate, that the Royal Navy didn't have enough ships available to evacuate the BEF from France, so we were going to do it ourselves.

"I drove home as fast I could, and I got the *Daisy Chain*

and sailed her to the harbor. But there were far more boats than able-bodied men. I must've expected it, because I had dressed in trousers and one of my father's old shirts. And I'd tucked my hair up under Ralph's old hat—it was still on board, just where he'd left it—exactly as I'd done when I'd played Romeo nearly a year earlier. And I set off with the rest of the little ships for Dunkirk.

"It was terrifying. The city was on fire, and great clouds of smoke rose like some terrible monster above the French coastline. From a distance—it was the oddest thing! The men, the soldiers lining up on the beaches, looked like rows of sticks. It wasn't until I got closer that I realized just how many men were there, all waiting to be evacuated.

"The German air force—the Luftwaffe—were overhead, shooting at the men on the beach, shooting at *us*. Artillery pounded the beaches—there were bodies everywhere. It was awful.

"It was war."

Eve looked at the Bear again, and this time, there was something in his eyes. Something terrible. Something she recognized from looking into her bathroom mirror.

He'd lived through such a battle himself. He'd known that awful gut-wrenching fear.

She reached for him, taking his hand in hers and squeezing it. Letting him see that she knew he understood.

And then—there! A glimmer of something. She could have sworn she'd seen it in his eyes, right before he pulled his hand away.

Or maybe she'd just wanted it to be there.

"I brought the *Daisy Chain* in all the way to the shore," she continued. "She wasn't as big as some of the other boats, and I could take her almost right up to the strand. I took aboard as many soldiers as I could, asking everyone I saw about Ralph's Anti-Tank Regiment, the Fiftieth.

"No one knew a thing, they barely knew their own names. I heard all kinds of rumors—that the order had come down, 'Every man for himself.'

"For a while I set to work using the *Daisy Chain* as a ferry, taking men from the shore out to the larger ships that couldn't get in close to the beaches. The piers had all been bombed

by the Germans. The entire harbor at Dunkirk was an ob-
stacle course, filled with debris. But then all the larger ships
departed, so I took on as many men as I could—about fifty,
riding low in the water—and headed back for England, too.

"The trip across the channel took about two hours on the
best of days under the best of circumstances. And German
U-boats torpedoing the larger vessels was hardly what I'd
call the best of *any*thing. I returned to Ramsgate, and then
went back again—I was too small to be a target for the submarines, thank God. Too small to do much of anything but
bring back fifty men. And then another fifty men. And another. Asking all the time about Ralph.

"I finally found a man who thought he'd heard that the
Fiftieth was one of the regiments holding the Germans at
bay, making the evacuation of all these men possible. Despite the 'every man for himself' order, the Fiftieth had stuck
quite literally to their guns. They—Ralph among them—
were fighting still.

"I had walked into hell to save Ralph, but apparently he
wasn't ready to come out yet. I heard all kinds of rumors
about the panzer attacks, too—about the terrifying invinci-
bility of those tanks that Ralph and his unit were fighting
against. Some of the men spoke in hushed tones of a secret
weapon that the Germans had—some mysterious force that
caused the British and French guns to be unable to fire." She
laughed. "I think it was called *fear*.

"I heard rumors of the Germans being horribly angry
with the British soldiers who resisted their advance. It was
said they were taking no prisoners, that they were lining up
their captives and shooting them as punishment. The word
had gone out among the BEF not to surrender, but instead to
fight to the death.

"And each time I returned to Dunkirk, there were more
bodies. Bodies *every*where. Littering the beach, floating in
the ocean. They were stepped over, stepped on, pushed aside.
And still the evacuation went on.

"I crossed the English Channel more times than I could
count, through that day and the following night. And the
only reason I stopped was that one of the soldiers I had rescued realized that I was a girl. He put me out at Ramsgate,

wouldn't listen to my arguments, and took the *Daisy Chain* back to Dunkirk himself.

"I went to work in Ramsgate then, helping the wounded off the ships that came in, searching, always searching, for anyone who knew or might have seen Ralph.

"Hundreds of thousands of men returned to England by that armada of little ships and boats. We fed them, and held them in our arms while they cried. We welcomed them back home, back to life, and put them on trains sending them farther inland, so they could regroup. Many of those poor battered souls went home first, before reporting back for duty. I left a note on the door of the estate—everyone, even Nicky, was in Ramsgate helping as best they could—hoping that Ralph would somehow make it there."

"But he never did," Amy said. "Did he?"

"No," Eve told the little girl, told the Bear. "He never did. I searched for him for days. I even phoned his mother to see if he might've gone there. But he didn't make it out of France. The Fiftieth Anti-Tank Regiment stuck to their guns until the bitter end.

"338,226 men were rescued from Dunkirk between May 26 and June 4, 1940," Eve told Amy and the Bear. "It was a miracle so many had been saved—a miracle that Ralph and the Fiftieth had helped to come about by holding off the German advance. It was every man for himself, but the Fiftieth and the other antitank regiments weren't fighting to save themselves. They had to have known they'd be left behind. Surely they knew, and yet they held fast to their hills, keeping the Germans from those beaches and those virtually defenseless ships and men. *They* were the true heroes of Dunkirk.

"For a while I was really mad at Ralph for that," Eve admitted. "For being so blasted heroic. I didn't want a hero, I wanted him back in England and *safe*." She could smile about it now—just barely, still wistfully. "At sixteen years of age, I'd already faced so many hardships in my life, but nothing, by far, was as hard to bear as this."

"What did you do then?" Amy asked softly.

"I did what everyone else did," Eve answered. "I fought on. *We* fought on. We British—and oh, yes, I was one of them now—we dedicated our lives to making darn certain that the sacrifices that Ralph and the other men of the BEF antitank regiments had made were not in vain. Winston Churchill made a speech right after the miracle at Dunkirk—we called it a miracle and a victory even though it really was a crushing defeat. But we'd saved so many men at such impossible odds, it was hard not to feel triumphant. *We shall defend our island,* Churchill said to all of England, to all of the world, *whatever the cost may be.* But oh, what a cost had already been extracted from my very heart and soul.

"Dunkirk was just the start," Eve told them. "But it was the first act of defiance in a long and bloody war filled with defiance in the face of seemingly insurmountable odds. It wasn't until 1945 that the Nazis were finally completely defeated, but I know that their defeat started in 1940, at Dunkirk. I know that I helped save the world. Or rather, I helped Ralph and his brave fellow soldiers save the world. His sacrifice was not in vain—I was convinced of that. But it didn't make it any easier to bear late at night when I missed him so terribly."

Amy held Eve tightly. "I miss Mommy terribly," she said.

"I know, sweet." Eve looked at the Bear. "I miss her, too."

It was going down as if it had been choreographed.

The GIK, despite their pricey costumes—the raincoats and shades, at twilight for crying out loud—were standard issue dumbfucks. They came creeping out of their van like a pack of kids playing ninja, as if the setting sun made them invisible.

Sam was right next to WildCard, who was having trouble not laughing aloud. Sam would've had the same problem if it weren't for Alyssa Locke.

Despite his efforts to stay as far away from her as possible, she'd somehow ended up right beside him. She didn't want to be there anymore than he did—he could see that news bulletin clear as daylight in her eyes.

When the order came to go, to move stealthily forward and out-ninja the ninjas, he was more than ready for some action.

But it was unsatisfyingly easy. The GIK tangos were totally outmatched by the team of SEALs and FBI. They were down on the ground, their weapons taken from them, in a matter of seconds.

And somehow—Jesus Christ, give him a break, *please*—Alyssa was right beside him again. Close enough to catch a whiff of her clean-smelling shampoo.

Apparently one of the tangos caught a whiff of it, too. The son of a bitch no doubt took one look at Alyssa's pretty face and slender physique, and pegged her as the weak link in the chain.

Lopez had grabbed the bastard's Uzi out of his hands, and Muldoon had delivered a blow that should have sent him face first onto the driveway, but the fucker bounced. He was up again in an instant, hitting Alyssa hard, with a bone-jarring crunch, right in the chest.

She went down, and Sam turned fast. They'd taken the dumbshit's Uzi, but Jesus, he could have a hunting knife or a switchblade. Or he could be one of those commando wannabes who'd managed to learn to break a neck with a single swift twist of an opponent's head.

Alyssa hit the pavement with another solid-sounding thud and a muffled, pain-filled shout.

If he'd stuck her with a knife, this fucker was going to *die*.

But Sam didn't have a chance to extract revenge. Alyssa took the tango down with her, despite the fact he was nearly twice her weight. It only took a heartbeat, a few short seconds, tops, and she was straddling the guy, shouting for him not to move, her side arm jammed neatly up beneath his chin.

It was difficult for the bastard to *not* move seeing that he was writhing in pain. Seeing that Alyssa had kicked him in the balls so hard he was going to need a doctor to pull 'em back down from where they'd lodged near his spleen.

Sam faded back, fast, so that she wouldn't see he was one of the men who'd leapt to her aid.

The FBI cleanup team was fast. They had those assholes searched, cuffed, Miranda-ed, and loaded into a properly nondescript van in record time. Another agent impounded the tangos' vehicle, driving it swiftly away.

Alyssa didn't look at him as they got themselves the hell out of there, too. She was breathing hard, she'd torn the elbow of her jacket, and she was trying to hide a limp.

It took every last ounce of willpower he had to keep his distance. But he knew he was the dead last person she'd want checking up on her right now. As he watched, she shook off Lopez, the team medic—just brushed right past him.

"Man," WildCard said in admiration. "Did you see that? Let that be a lesson for us all. Don't ever, *ever*, get Locke mad at you."

Too late.

Twenty-two

NILS PACED AROUND the motel room, double-checking the fact that the room had only one entrance.

No, there wasn't a window in the bathroom. There was actually a small coin-operated machine attached to the wall that sold condoms—classy place—but no window.

He went back into the other room, where Meg looked ready to jump out of her skin.

In fact, she did jump when Nils's cell phone rang. He flipped it open, turned it on. "Nilsson."

"Yeah, it's Paoletti. We just bagged seven GIK terrorists in the parking lot. So far there's been no sign of any more of 'em, but we'll be out here watching for as long as it takes."

"Thanks, L.T."

"We've got surveillance set up to record and trace any phone calls that come in, and we're continuing to keep watch, but that's it."

In other words, this room didn't have any cameras or listening devices.

"I thought you'd appreciate that information," Paoletti continued. Lieutenant Tactful.

"Yeah," Nils said. Meg was watching him, dying to find out what the phone call was about. She was sitting on the edge of the bed that was farthest from the window, her body pointed toward that beige telephone.

Please, Jesus, for her sake, let the Extremists call this evening. Let them call *now*.

The phone didn't ring. And then it still didn't ring.

"Thanks, L.T.," Nils said again. "Look, Lieutenant, I know I owe you an explanation for—"

"You do," Paoletti interrupted. COs could get away with

331

interrupting whenever they wanted. "After this is over, you *will* be spending a good long time in my office. With the door closed. While I go down a list. A very long list."

"L.T., I *am* sorry—"

"Yale, right, Nilsson?"

"Uh, yes, sir, I went to Yale."

"In that case, Ivy League Genius, do you really need me to define *after* for you?"

Nils closed his eyes. This was going to be okay. He was going to get yelled at. Or even worse—he'd get Paoletti's quiet "I'm disappointed in you" speech. It would be hard to stand through, but he could endure anything short of getting kicked out of the Troubleshooters squad. And as long as the CO was calling him faintly insulting names, he was still at least slightly beloved. "No, sir, you do not."

"Good." Paoletti was silent for a moment, and then he sighed. "You do know, Johnny, that in the next twenty-four hours you could well be facing the ultimate no-win scenario. That little girl could be dead. She probably is. And I know you're good—you're one of my best officers. I know you've got this 'nothing is impossible' mentality, and I applaud it, you know I do—even when it gets you into trouble. But even you can't bring a child back to life."

"I know that," Nils said. "I'm counting on luck and maybe even a miracle, sir. I'm counting on getting there before she's harmed."

The lieutenant didn't argue. He just sighed again. "Tell Meg my prayers are with her and her daughter and grandmother tonight."

"I will, L.T. Thank you."

Paoletti cut the connection, and Nils snapped his phone shut. "They got all the GIK out of the way," he told Meg.

"That fast?"

"Yeah. We can relax a little bit." He sat down across from her, on the other bed. She looked like the poster girl for high stress. "It might be a good idea to try to get some sleep."

She glanced at that beige motel telephone. "You can turn out the light if you want."

And leave her sitting bolt upright on the other bed, strung

too tight even to close her eyes? No way. As bone tired as he was, he wasn't going to do that.

"If the phone rings, I'll hear it," Nils told her gently. "Even if I'm asleep. I promise."

She had her arms crossed in front of her as if she were cold, or as if she were holding on to herself for dear life. She looked at the phone again.

"They'll call," Nils told her. "They will. They want Razeen. They'll definitely be in touch with you."

"I know that." Meg nodded. "I understand that. I just . . ." She shook her head. "What if they don't? What if they just never do? How long are we going to wait here? A day? Two? A week? A *month*?"

She was starting to shake, and she tried desperately to stop, tried holding herself even more tightly.

"What have I done?" she said. "What if the Extremists find out I've turned Razeen over to the FBI? They'll kill Amy and my grandmother right away. This is a mistake, John. I don't think I can do this."

Nils crossed the little aisle between the two beds and sat next to her. "Yes, you can," he told her. "Don't start thinking about worst case scenarios. Don't do that to yourself."

"I can't help it." She was trying hard not to cry and her breathing was ragged. "I just keep thinking, what if they don't call? Or what if they *do* call, and God! What if they kill *you* then, too?"

"They're not going to kill me. There are a lot of people working with us, Meg, making sure the Extremists aren't going to kill me. Or you. And as for the Extremists finding out about Razeen—there are very few people who know he's been taken into custody. Max Bhagat and about two other FBI agents. My SEAL team knows, too—I trust those guys with my life all the time. I'd trust them with your life, too. And Amy's."

Nils wanted to touch her. He was dying to take her into his arms and hold her, to try to soothe her, calm her down. But she'd set up this invisible boundary around herself with those crossed arms, and he didn't want to trespass over the line, didn't want to move into the realm of potentially inappropriate.

They were locked together in a motel room, trapped in wait mode, sitting on a bed with not a whole hell of a lot to do.

He didn't want her to think he had a list of ways they could entertain themselves quite nicely in the course of the next few hours.

Even though, damn it, he did.

"You've got a whole pack of highly trained experts on your side, Meg," he told her instead of reaching for her. "And you've got me, for what it's worth. I'm here. I'll be here—whatever happens—whatever we have to deal with."

"You think they're dead." She looked at him searchingly, as if trying to prove her own statement wrong.

Nils gave her what she wanted. It was the least he could do. "No," he said. "I don't. Not really. I think Amy and your grandmother are still alive."

She both laughed and cried at that, her tears finally escaping. "You are such a liar."

She reached for him then. She unwound her arms and reached out for him, giving him all the permission he needed to take her into his own arms. He held her tightly, glad she'd chosen to let him in, to lean on him, to share her fears and apprehension with him this way.

"I want them to be alive," he told her, stroking her hair. "And as long as there's a chance, I'm choosing to believe they *are* still safe."

"Is there really a chance?" she asked. She pulled back slightly to look into his eyes again. "I need you not to lie to me, John."

"Yes, there's a chance." It was a slim chance, but there *was* a chance. He wasn't lying. Nils took her hand and placed it on his chest. "There's always a chance. Cross my heart and ..." Hope to die. Wrong thing to say tonight. "Cross my heart."

"What are the real odds here?" she asked. "Truthfully. In terms of going face-to-face with the Extremists and coming out alive?"

"I don't know about odds," he admitted. "I'm not much of a gambler so I don't think in terms of odds. Is it going to be dangerous? Yes, it is. Is there a chance we might be killed?

Zealots and weapons are a bad combination, Meg. Bullets tend to fly when the two get together. And whenever bullets start flying, yes, death is a possibility. This is why I'd like to send in a female FBI agent in your place and—"

She put her hand over his mouth. "No. No more replacements. No more lies and no more replacements. Okay?"

He nodded. And when she took her hand away, he leaned forward and kissed her. It wasn't a real kiss—just a brief touching of his lips to hers. Still, he knew it startled her.

"No more lies," he agreed.

He didn't give her a chance to respond or react. He pulled her with him, so that they were sitting on the bed, leaning back against the pillows and the headboard, his arm around her, her head against his shoulder.

"Tell me about Amy," he said. "Tell me about what she's been up to in the last three years."

He could feel her surprise at his question. It was the last thing she'd expected him to say.

"Tell me all the good stuff," he continued. "Does she still like to draw? She's ten now, right? Does she still wear her hair long or did she get it cut? Is she in middle school yet— or is she going to start that next year?"

Meg exhaled—just a brief burst of air. Nils just held her and waited. Come on, Meg. Talk about Amy.

"Actually," she said, her voice breathless, "I've been . . . I've been thinking about taking Amy out of the public school and enrolling her in an all-girls school in September. I want to move out of the city—I know she does, too, and . . ." Her voice trailed off.

"What does she want to be when she grows up?" Nils asked, trying to keep her in the here and now, trying to keep her out of *what if* land.

Meg tipped her head to look up at him and smiled. It was shaky, but it was a smile. "She's ten. She wants to be an astronaut. Or the next Britney Spears."

"Astronaut or . . . pop star? I'm not sure I get the connection."

Another smile. "The connection is that she's *ten*."

"Ah." Nils smiled back at her, loving the life that was coming back into her eyes, into her face.

Meg's smile faded, but her eyes stayed warm. "Thank you," she whispered. "For talking about her as if she's got a future. As if she's going to have a September."

"She is," he told her. No lying. He corrected himself. "She probably is. And right now—tonight—she definitely is. Tonight she's still alive. Even if she's not, Meg, we don't know it yet, so we can give her one more night of life. One more night with a future. You know?"

Tears were back in her eyes, but she smiled at him again, reaching up to touch his face. "Thank you." She settled back against him, resting her head on his shoulder, holding him tightly, her arms around his waist. "She still wears her hair long," she said. "Although she's been talking about getting it cut for the summer. The humidity makes her curls go wild." She laughed. "Oh, God, did I tell you that she's taking karate?"

Nils ran his fingers through her hair, loving the way it slipped through his fingers. "No way!"

She smiled. "She just started, but she loves it."

"That's so great." Please, God, keep this child safe.

"She's still really small for her age," Meg explained. "She's pretty annoyed about that. I think she wants to be able to pull a Jackie Chan and beat up the boys who tease her for being flat chested."

Nils had to laugh. "Give me a break—she's only ten. I hope she's still flat chested."

"That's what I tell her," Meg said. "That she's got plenty of time to . . ." She stopped.

"She's got plenty of time to be a teenager," Nils finished gently for her. "Does she like boats? After this is over, maybe the two of you could come out to California. I'll take you out on my boat. Bet she'd like that."

Meg didn't answer. She just held him tightly. Just breathed.

Nils talked about his boat, talked about California, talked about the places they could go, the things Amy might want to do and see when they visited. When. Not if.

And finally, slowly, her death grip on him loosened. Her breathing slowed.

She was asleep.

Nils stared at the beige phone as he held her.

Come on, god damn it.
Ring.

"Yo, Locke!"

Alyssa turned to see WildCard Karmody waving to her from the other side of the hotel lobby.

He was with Jenk and Muldoon. And Sam Starrett. They must have come in the other entrance. Karmody bore down on her now like a heat-seeking missile. He had a mad scientist look to him even when he wore black BDUs. It might've been the way his dark hair stuck out in all directions—as if he'd been pulling it while he sewed together some monster made with various body parts. Or maybe it was the gleam of near-crazed intelligence in his eyes. He'd been blessed with a brain that most men would kill for, but unfortunately for him, it came with a piss poor lack of judgment and an inability to keep out of trouble.

Karmody caught up to her by the elevators. She pushed the up button, praying that she wasn't going to have to ride up to the twentieth floor in an elevator with Starrett, who was straggling behind with Jenk and Muldoon.

"Good job out there today," Karmody said.

"Thanks." She gave him a purposely cool nod. "You, too."

"Nice defensive moves," Karmody said. "I think that guy's going to be singing soprano for about a week." He winced in sympathy. *"Ouch."*

Ouch was right. Her elbow was bleeding, and she'd wrenched her ankle pretty badly when she'd been knocked over. She stared up at the elevators' lights, willing one to go on, signaling her escape.

"We're heading over to the restaurant," Karmody told her. "We're starving and it's still early, barely even eighteen hundred hours. Wanna come?"

"I've got a roast beef sandwich and an ice cream sundae with my name on it," Jenkins chimed in.

Ice cream sundae. Oh, God.

Locke looked up to find Sam Starrett watching her.

And just like that, she was hit by a vivid memory of Starrett looking into her eyes that very same way as he . . . as they . . . Oh, *God.*

She quickly looked away. She had to clear her throat before answering Karmody. "Thanks, but no." She held up her elbow as an excuse. "I need to get cleaned up, and . . . Thanks, anyway."

Ding.

The elevator doors opened, and she jumped inside.

"What's up with Locke?" she heard Jenk wonder as the doors slid closed.

She closed her eyes. God help her. She needed a shower and about twelve hours of uninterrupted sleep.

She needed to stop thinking about Sam Starrett.

It was absurd—how difficult could it be to stop thinking about the man? She didn't even like him.

Meg awoke with a start. "Is that the phone?"

The room was silent and dark. Nothing rang. Nothing moved. Except for John's heart, which was racing beneath her hand.

He finally exhaled. "You must've been dreaming." His voice was thick and warm from sleep.

Somehow she'd fallen asleep. Somehow she'd moved from sitting up against the head of the bed and waiting for the phone to ring, to lying here in the darkness, with John's arms around her.

Oh, God, it felt so good. It was a freakish combination of her worst nightmare and her ultimate fantasy. She was in bed with John Nilsson—because Amy had been kidnapped.

He was solid and warm against her, but he shifted as he checked his watch.

"What time is it?" she asked.

"Twenty-oh-nine." He translated, "About ten minutes after eight." She could hear him smile in the darkness. "Congratulations. You slept for about two and a half hours. I don't suppose I can talk you into sleeping a couple hours more?"

This was weird, and yet at the same time it felt so natural. Lying in the darkness beside this man, listening to his sleepy voice as it wound its way around her, through her, inside her.

"You should go back to sleep if you want to," she told him. "I know you're still tired."

He laughed softly. "Yeah, while you do what? Lie here and worry?"

"Just because I can't sleep doesn't mean you shouldn't."

John shifted onto one elbow, leaning on her slightly as he reached across her to turn on the lamp. His body was heavy against hers. Muscular and completely solid. Capable of pinning her down—probably with one arm tied behind his back.

It was funny, but she hadn't realized until that very moment exactly what John had done. Oh, she'd guessed it, but she hadn't truly known until now.

All those hours in the car . . . He'd had countless opportunities to overpower her. He could have gained control of her gun nearly any time he'd wanted to.

But he hadn't. He'd used words and compassion instead of physical strength, reason and kindness over violence. He'd used *love*.

His hair was rumpled and he squinted a little as his eyes got used to the light. He smiled at her, completely at ease with her scrutiny of his face.

"You want to talk more?" he asked, propping his head up in his hand, elbow bent. "About Amy? Or how about your grandmother? I'd love to hear about her. Eve, right?"

Meg touched him. His shoulder, his face, his hair. She'd always loved his hair, even in Kazbekistan when it was shaggy and long. Even after she'd given him a Marine-style, square-topped crew cut. It was such a pretty shade of brown, so thick and soft to the touch.

She ran her fingers through it. She'd always wanted to do that. There'd been way too many times she'd wanted to touch this man, but hadn't. Couldn't.

But there was nothing stopping her now. In fact, this would probably be her last chance.

Before she'd fallen asleep, they'd played at normal. Pretending that Amy and Eve were unharmed, that she and John were going to survive the violence that was still to come. Talking about September, talking about the future.

When in truth, her future was down to these few final hours of existence.

And, no, she didn't want to spend that time sleeping.

John's smile faded as she gazed up at him, and the look in his eyes, on his face, was a heart touching mix of uncertainty and desire. Apprehension and need. Meg knew that he was afraid of reading her wrong.

So she gave him a message he couldn't possibly misread. She kissed him.

Meg kissed him.

Nils heard himself make a low sound in the back of his throat. She wasn't just being friendly. This was no sweet thank-you kiss. This was a *kiss*, complete with her tongue swept into his mouth, complete with her arms around his neck, complete with her leg thrown up and over his.

Her mouth was so soft, so warm, so what he wanted.

He pulled back to make sure this was really what she wanted, too.

And found heat in her eyes.

"If the phone rings," he started.

"I'm answering it," she finished for him fiercely. "No matter what."

"Of course," he said.

She kissed him again, pushing him completely onto his back, straddling him, just the way she'd done that day on the Mall lawn. It was as if three years hadn't passed, as if they were right back there, almost where they'd started, white hot desire primed and ready to erupt given half a chance.

What she was doing was way more than half of anything.

She unbuttoned his shirt as she kissed him. She swept her hands up and across his chest, pushing his shirt off his shoulders. He wanted to take her shirt off, too, and he tugged it free from her jeans. Her skin was like silk beneath his fingers. After one touch, he just wanted to stay there for an eternity, kissing her and running his hands up and down her back.

But she sat up, positioning herself more exactly on top of him, pulling out of his reach.

"Last chance," she whispered, with the kind of smile he'd only dreamed about. Except in his dreams she hadn't had such sadness in her eyes. "You want to say no or throw on the brakes, you've got to do it now."

He had to laugh. "You honestly think I'm going to stop this?"

"You stopped us three years ago."

"You were married," he countered.

"That really mattered to you?"

"Whoa," he said. "Haven't you been listening to anything I've told you? I was in love with you, Meg. I didn't want just one night. I wanted . . . a lifetime." Jesus, he couldn't believe he'd actually said that aloud. But he had. And in retrospect he knew it was true. He *had* wanted a lifetime. He'd just been too stupid, too scared to know it.

He looked up at her now, praying that she wouldn't laugh at him or fall over in a dead faint from shock.

Her eyes were even more sad. She gave him a tremulous, beautiful smile.

"When you say *whoa*," she said, obviously trying desperately to keep things light, "does that mean you're putting on the brakes?"

So okay, she wanted to skip the lifetime comment. She clearly didn't want to go there now, and Nils wasn't about to make her. Instead he followed her lead.

He answered her question by lifting her up and flipping them both over so that he was on top of her. He managed to get both her shirt and her bra off in the process—no small feat—and she was laughing breathlessly as he kissed her breasts.

She was impossibly beautiful, and he wanted to spend another eternity just looking at her. But he couldn't look without touching, couldn't touch without wanting to taste.

Her laughter turned to a sigh as he did just that, drawing her into his mouth, using his knee to push between her legs so that he could settle against her, cradled there by her softness and heat.

She was touching him, running her hands across his back and shoulders as if she, too, couldn't get enough of him.

"Please," she said. "John . . ."

She wanted out of her jeans. Which was perfect, since he wanted her out of them, too.

Together they pulled them off her, peeling down her panties as well.

She was naked and beautiful—the most beautiful, incredible woman he'd ever known—and she was lying back on that bed, waiting for him.

Nils let himself look at her as he stood back and unfastened his belt. "I'm not putting on the brakes," he said. "FYI, I'm just taking my time."

"I know." Meg watched him as he stepped out of his pants. Her gaze shifted down to his briefs, lingering there. She looked up at him and smiled. "I can tell."

Yeah, okay. Now he was completely on fire. "You wouldn't happen to have two dollars in quarters, would you?"

She laughed. "Wow, you're a real bargain."

He loved that she could make jokes, that she could tease. He hoped it meant that she'd decided to go on living, that no matter what happened over the next few hours or days, that she'd take the time she needed to get past it and keep on breathing.

He sat down next to her on the bed, unable to keep from touching her legs, running his hands down the softness of her skin. "There's a machine that sells condoms in the bathroom."

"Really?" She laughed. Shook her head. "I don't know whether to be impressed or appalled."

He grinned. "This place is four star all the way, baby."

"I didn't pick it," she objected.

"I know, I'm just . . ." Shit, the mood had shifted. All fun was erased. She hadn't picked this place. No kidding.

Her eyes filled with tears, and he reached for her and gathered her into his arms.

"I'm sorry," she said, clinging to him.

"Shhh." He stroked her hair, wishing that he could somehow hide the fact that he was completely aroused, hoping she'd understand that what he needed right now had nothing to do with him and everything to do with her. That sex was secondary to everything. That putting his clothes back on and holding her in his arms was more than he'd expected, more than he'd ever dreamed possible. "You don't need to—"

She lifted her head and kissed him. Hot, wet, and passionate. A tongue down the throat, every nerve cell jangling, every pleasure center up and completely online kind of kiss.

It was a take-me-now kiss. A throw me back on the bed and give it to me hard and fast kiss. She reached into his briefs and wrapped her fingers around him—no doubt just in case he hadn't gotten the message from her kiss.

He came up for air, gasping. "Meg—"

"Please," she breathed between more frantic kisses. She'd straddled him again, pushing him back on the bed, yanking down his briefs and freeing him completely from their confines. "I need you, John. *Now.*"

She shifted her hips and would have driven him hard inside of her if he hadn't caught her and held her in place. Jesus! He started to sweat. "We need one of those condoms."

She gazed down at him, breathing hard, a vision of female arousal. She needed him. Now. Hoo, baby. He was either a saint or an idiot.

"Why?" she asked.

He could see in her eyes that she honestly didn't think it would matter. Birth control. Safe sex. What did any of it matter if they were going to die?

Shit. She still expected to die.

"What if we live?" he asked her, shifting her back so she was sitting on his thighs, still holding her securely in place. "I want to live. And I'm going to die myself before I let *you* die."

Emotion flared in her eyes. "I don't want you to die!"

"Good, that makes two of us," he countered. "So let's decide right now. We're not going to die, okay?"

She shook her head. "Please," she said.

Great, now the gorgeous naked woman who needed him desperately was begging. Both an idiot and a saint would have long since caved in—the idiot discovering some brain cells that worked, and the saint throwing over his sacred vows. But Nils was neither. He was just a man—who loved her.

"Do you *want* to get pregnant?" he asked gently. "Will you please just consider for a second what could happen if—shit, not *if, when*—when we live. When this is over and—"

"Yes."

"—we're still alive," he finished. "Excuse me?"

"I would love that more than anything," she whispered, her eyes filling with tears. "As long as we're pretending we're going to live happily ever after, let's pretend that, too, can't we?"

"If we don't use a condom, Meg, that's not pretend anymore. That's *real*. That's—"

"Please," she said. "If I live and Amy doesn't, if we find out tomorrow that she's already dead, I'm going to want to die. Give me something, John—some*one* to live for. Please."

Oh, shit, *that* hurt.

"How about me?" he said, all but slicing himself open and laying his beating heart out on the table. "Couldn't you maybe live for *me*?"

She didn't answer. Whether she wouldn't or couldn't, Nils didn't know.

All she could do was whisper, "Please, John."

It was all over. He could refuse her nothing she asked for. Not even this. Maybe especially not this.

And maybe he *would* get her pregnant. Christ, he hoped he did. Then he'd have her forever. She'd stayed with Daniel for Amy's sake; surely she'd marry Nils if he got her pregnant.

And maybe, in time, it wouldn't matter so goddamn much that she didn't really love him as much as he loved her.

He lifted her up and lowered her down on top of him slowly, watching her face as she moved to receive him.

She held his gaze as he filled her, as she surrounded him. He knew she could see the tears in his eyes, knew he was unable to hide the crazy mix of emotions that crossed his face.

Anger, hurt, relief, need.

Love.

He pushed it all aside, all except the love.

He was here, right where he'd wanted to be for too many hundreds of nights. Meg loved him on some level—he knew that to be true. He wouldn't be inside of her right now if she didn't.

He let all the other bullshit escape, let nothing remain but the sweet pleasure of her body around him and the liquid heat of his love for her. Let her see that. He wanted her to see that.

She sat there, atop him, intimately joined with him, for several long seconds, just looking into his eyes.

But then she fell forward and kissed him hungrily, moving in a rhythm that was much too fast, too soon. Nils caught her hips again, slowing her down, wanting and needing them to take their time, refusing to give in to the part of him that wanted her hard and fast and three years ago. He took control of her kisses, too, turning them languorous—deliciously, wickedly slow.

She moaned her approval as he filled his hands with her breasts, and he swept his fingers across her bare skin, kissing and touching as much of her as he could.

Without a condom, the sensation as he moved inside of her, as they moved together, was impossibly intense. Each stroke brought him dangerously closer to his release. Each stroke was heaven, each withdrawal ecstasy. And the knowledge that when he came, he would send his seed deep inside her, was a total turn-on. He loved her. Forever. What better way to show that to both Meg and the entire world?

She was impossibly sexy, riding him the way she was, with her head thrown back, her breasts tightly peaked with desire. She was killing him, completely killing him.

He reached between them, desperate to take her with him. She was soft and slick and touching her was nearly enough to take him over the edge.

He lifted her up, turning her so that he was on top, so he could be in complete control.

She smiled up at him and spread her legs even wider, and he knew it was hopeless. She was sexy as hell on her back, too. Sexier, looking up at him like that.

She moved her hips up to meet him, faster now, still holding his gaze. He was supposed to be in control now, but he wasn't. It wasn't even close. He was completely under her spell, completely unable to slow her down, to do anything but give her all she wanted.

And right now, she wanted him hard and fast.

Nils kissed her, taking her mouth possessively, claiming it, claiming her as his own.

Or maybe—and far more likely—claiming himself as hers.

He belonged to her. Completely. He had since the day they'd first met.

"I'm going to come inside you now," he breathed. "Are you ready for me to do that?"

Meg nodded. "Yes. *Yes.*"

She wanted that as much as he did. And she was with him.

His release was like being hit by a train. It slammed into him, through him, not slowing down but instead building in intensity as he crashed into her. And she was right there, with him, beneath him. Part of him. Crying out his name as she exploded around him.

It was beyond pleasure—and knowing she was feeling this, too, transcended anything he'd ever experienced in his life.

He lay on top of her, completely spent as the motel room began to reappear around him. He realized he was crushing her and he would have rolled off, but she stopped him. She clung to him, holding him tightly in place.

He would have spoken, would have told her that he loved her, but she must have felt him take a breath.

"Shhh," she whispered. "Not yet. Please, let's not talk yet. Let's just stay right here a little bit longer."

He was still inside of her and content to stay right there until the end of time, if she wanted.

There was no reason for him to withdraw, no need to worry about a condom leaking—there was no condom.

Disbelief shot through him. But it wasn't followed by fear. It was followed by warmth. By certainty. By an intense surge of pleasure. Right now, maybe right this very second, a miracle could well be occurring.

Another miracle.

Nils breathed in the sweet scent of Meg's hair as he closed his eyes and let himself drift, giving thanks for the miracle he'd already been given, and putting his list of requests for additional miracles right out on the table, for whoever might be up there to see.

In the past, he'd used a lot of different tactics when facing potential no-win scenarios. He wasn't afraid to ask for outside help if the situation called for it.

And this situation called for all the help he could get—including divine intervention.

He wasn't asking much—just that Meg's little girl be kept alive until he could get there. That's all he wanted.

He and his team would take it from there.

Twenty-three

$\curvearrowright$ $\curvearrowleft$

Alyssa kept the chain on as she opened the door to her hotel room. She didn't speak, she just looked at Sam, her face expressionless.

She was wrapped in a terry cloth robe, her hair still wet. He'd caught her coming out of the shower. Which meant that she was probably naked under that robe.

And Sam no longer had to fantasize about what she might look like naked. After last night, he knew.

He had to clear his throat before his vocal cords would function. "Sorry to bother you. I know I'm probably the last person you want knocking on your door."

She didn't say anything. She just looked at him, somehow managing to do it without ever quite meeting his eyes.

He cleared his throat again. "Yeah, well, I just . . ." Shit, Starrett, just say it. "I wanted to make sure you were all right. I saw you limping, and—"

"I'm fine. I twisted my ankle. It's no big deal. Nothing a little ice and rest won't fix."

She started to shut the door, but he leaned against it. "How about your elbow?"

She met his gaze at that, but only briefly. Just a flash, and then she quickly looked away. "Scraped. I've done way worse."

"Did you get it cleaned out okay?"

"Yes."

"It's hard to do that yourself. I mean, a knee, sure, no problem. But an elbow . . . If you want I could—"

"It's clean." Impatiently, she pulled back her sleeve and showed him.

"Shit." She'd taken off nearly the entire top layer of skin.

348

It wasn't deep. It was just raw. And Sam knew from experience that it had to hurt like hell. Someone in the team was usually always scraped up like that and whining about it far more than Alyssa ever would. It was really no big deal, but seeing it on her otherwise perfect arm somehow made it seem worse.

"I'll put peroxide on it," she told him. "It'll be fine."

Yeah, and that was going to make it sting like a bastard. Wisely, Sam didn't volunteer to come in and hold her hand. He suspected that would get the door shut in his face, fast.

"How's your sister and the baby?" he asked, wishing she would take that chain off the door and let him in. Knowing she wasn't going to.

That question actually surprised her, and she looked at him again. She even almost smiled. "Fine. They're both doing fine. Thanks."

"Good," he said. "I'm glad." Quick, think of something else before she made her excuses and closed the door. "Are your ribs okay?" he asked. "You got hit pretty hard and—"

"Did I miss something here?" That almost smile disappeared fast. "Like the part where you suddenly got your medical degree?"

"No," he said. "I'm just . . . I'm . . ."

"Feeling nervous?" she asked. "Don't be. I just got my period. I already sent you an email about it. Pressure's off."

She wasn't pregnant. "Oh," Sam said. "Wow." He waited for the relief to hit, but it didn't come. Instead, he felt . . . *wistful*?

"So now if you don't mind, I'm exhausted and I really—"

"I didn't tell anyone," he told her. "About last night."

She finally met his gaze and held it. "Yeah," she said. "I know. I was . . . I wasn't expecting that. I thought . . ." She shook her head. "Thank you."

Despite his reassurances back in DC, she'd actually thought he was going tell everyone on the team what he'd done last night. She'd probably even expected him to give some kind of locker room account, maybe even a blow-by-blow replay.

Christ.

"You know, Locke, I'm a decent man," he told her, anger

making his voice tight and louder. "Some people even consider me to be an *exceptional* man. I made it through BUD/S—which is more than most men—and any woman—can say. I passed all the moral and psychological requirements, too, and I got my ass assigned to Team Sixteen. I'm not this spawn of Satan that you seem to think I am."

"Look, I said thank you." Her voice got louder, too. "But that's all I'm going to say—or do—so you might as well—"

He laughed in outraged disbelief. "Fucking perfect! What, do you really think I expect you to go down on me in gratitude or something? Jesus!"

Now she was thoroughly pissed, too. "I think you expected me to let you in, that's what I think. Coming up here, pretending to give a damn about my *ankle* . . . ? Get real. You're here because you want a replay of last night."

Okay, so maybe she was right about that. Shit, he'd wanted a replay four minutes after she drove out of that parking garage in DC this morning. But that comment about pretending to give a damn was going too goddamn far. "I came up here because I wanted to make sure you were okay. I came up here because I fucking care, all right?"

Her laughter was decidedly derisive. "Yeah, right. You're a real prince. Give it up, Roger. I'm not letting you in. I'm not too drunk tonight to know that you are nothing but one big, dumb, rednecked mistake."

Dumb? No one called him dumb. He may have gone to college late, but once he got there, he was Phi Beta Fucking Kappa.

"Fuck you," he shot back at her. "No, wait a sec, I've already done that, haven't I?"

She slammed the door in his face.

Sam kicked it, hard.

Shit.

He limped away, cursing her, cursing himself.

That hadn't gone quite as well as he'd hoped, but about as well as he'd expected.

Considering he was a fucking idiot and she hated his guts.

Impending death was a freeing thing.

Meg lay naked in John's arms, gazing up at the ceiling as

he ran his fingers from her shoulder down to the curve of her hip and back. It was soothing and hypnotic.

It would have been easy to fall asleep. He was probably hoping she'd do just that. But her life had come down to hours, and sleep seemed a waste of precious time.

"Do you trust me?" she asked John.

His hand stilled for a moment before continuing its endless journey up and down her back. "Yes, but I know you don't think I do."

Navy SEALs were known for their high levels of intelligence. There were no stupid men in the teams. John *had* to know what was coming next.

Meg wanted to know who he really was, where he really came from—she'd made that clear to him before.

And now they were almost out of time. If he didn't tell her now . . .

"How bad was it really?" she asked, surprising herself a little by her ability to be so direct. But that was one of the pluses of impending death. It was now or never, so damn it, she had to ask—now.

He pretended not to know what she was talking about. "How bad was what?"

"Okay," Meg said. "I'll tell you, and you can just kind of nod if I get it right, okay?"

He laughed. "Meg—"

"Your father drank and when he drank he beat the crap out of you—"

"No," John said. "Not true. My father wasn't that kind of drunk, not like—" He shut his mouth fast, as if he realized he'd just given too much away.

"Not like your uncle?" she finished for him. She lifted her head to look at him, her heart in her throat. "Oh, John." She hadn't really believed it. She hadn't actually thought . . .

"Shit." He closed his eyes.

He had a beautiful face, all clean lines and strong jaw. A perfect nose, and eyes that would have made him a fortune had he gone to Hollywood instead of Coronado.

She waited for him to open those eyes and look at her, but he didn't. He tipped his head back and looked up at the ceiling. "Shit," he said again, this time on a sigh of air.

And he *still* wasn't going to tell her. Meg fought the urge to cry. "I've trusted you as much as any human being can trust another," she told him, her voice sounding very, very small to her own ears. "I've put Amy's life into your hands. And we just made love. That implies a certain amount of trust, too. Can't you trust me enough in return to let me inside of you? Just this little bit?"

He was silent, and her heart broke for him. How badly had he been hurt, how bad had it been that he'd had to create an entirely different version of his life?

"I've already guessed a lot of it," she told him. "I figured you grew up poor. Not just middle class, but hand-to-mouth poor. Food stamps. Evictions?"

He nodded, still not looking at her.

"You're really from Amagansett," she continued. If you're going to lie, he'd told her once, use as much of the real truth as possible. "Just not the wealthy part of town."

Another nod.

"You said your father was in the food industry." That had to be another part of the truth. "Where did he work—in a restaurant?"

John nodded again and finally spoke. "He was a short-order cook for a while. Before that, before he went to 'Nam, he and my uncle Al owned a fishing boat." He cleared his throat. "I'm not sure if he drank because he couldn't keep up the payments on the boat, or if he lost the boat because he drank. All I know is that he loved that boat, loved that life, and he lost it. He lost everything—our house, everything. You name it, it was gone."

He looked at her as if he were angry she was making him talk about this, as if he didn't want to remember. As if by not talking about it all these years, it had somehow disappeared or ceased to be. As if her need to know was resurrecting his pain.

"We moved into a shitty apartment with my uncle and his wife, my aunt Debbie. She drank too much, too. It was pretty much up to me to take care of them. I was seven the first time a neighbor called to say that my father had passed out in the parking lot. It was oh-two-thirty, and I had to go out there and find him and bring him inside."

Meg could imagine him at seven years of age far too

easily. Too serious for his years, with sad brown eyes, still raw from missing his mother. "Oh, God."

"Are you sure you really want to know this? Because it's pretty ugly—not just the stuff I had to live with, but the things I did. You know, there were times I got so hungry, I stole food. I got good at shoplifting, so I used it to get other stuff, too. I was a thief, Meg. My father would have died of shame if he knew. He was the most honest man I've ever known."

"Except he didn't manage to take care of you," Meg pointed out. "If you were the one taking care of him when you were *seven*—if he was unable to keep you from going hungry—how does that make him *honest*?"

John shook his head. "Why do you want to know all this?"

She touched his face. "Because I want to know *you*."

He kissed her. "Meg, you know me better than anyone in the world. What does it matter where I came from? It sucked, all right? And it got worse before it got better." He shook his head. "It didn't get better until I joined the Navy. And by then I'd gone to both Milfield and Yale, and everyone who met me after that thought I'd been raised at the yacht club alongside Ashley and Chip Moneybags."

What does it matter? he'd asked. "It doesn't matter to me at all," Meg told him. "Why does it matter so much to you?"

"Because I don't have any room for pity. Poor Johnny Nilsson," he said mockingly. "His mother died, and his father's too much of a drunk to notice that his bastard of a stepbrother kicks the shit out of his kid every chance he gets. And believe me," he added hotly, "the son of a bitch didn't get a lot of chances. I learned to be fast on my feet. I learned to move around the house without making any noise. I learned a lot of valuable skills that I should probably thank him for now."

She couldn't keep her disagreement in—it escaped in a soft sound of protest.

He looked her in the eye again. He forced himself to. She could tell this wasn't easy for him. "See why I like the story I made up better?" he asked. "Can you understand why I didn't want to be *this* John Nilsson? I didn't tell you about any of this because, you're right, I didn't really trust you. I was afraid you wouldn't like me if you knew. I'm still afraid that some of the things I could tell would be too hard for you to hear."

"How could you think that?" she asked.

"How could *you* be so certain we're going to die?" He looked at her intently. "How could you be so *willing* to die?"

Meg sat up. "See, this is what you always do. The conversation gets too personal or intense, so you turn it around, throwing it back on me. Well, right now I don't want to talk about me! I want—"

"I don't want to talk about me, either," he cut her off. "If you want to hear all my bullshit, all my pathetic poor-me stories about stupid things I've done that I regret, you're just going to have to live through the next few days, Meg. Because I'm not going to talk about it anymore. Not now. Not until we get Amy back. Then you can have at me. You can rip open all my emotional baggage with a crowbar if you want. But you can't do it until this is over."

He was serious.

"So," he said. "The way I see it, we could either make love again, or talk about something else."

She couldn't believe it. "This could be our last chance to—"

John shook his head. "No," he said. "It's not our last anything. It's our *first*. It's the start—of something that's going to last a very long time. What do you think of *Edward*?"

She blinked at him. He was gazing at her with that intensity that could practically knock her over. And he smiled—a hot, quick smile that warmed his eyes—at her confusion.

"Or maybe Julie, if it's a girl?" he continued. His smile softened, and the warmth in his eyes turned to something else, something tender, something a little uncertain. He reached for her, covering her stomach with his hand. "That's what *I* want to talk about. Names for our baby." He kissed her, sweet and lingeringly, on her mouth. "Unless you want to double our chances at procreation and make love to me again?"

Meg couldn't breathe. "You think . . . ? You want . . . what?" His hands were exploring her body, making it even more impossible to make any sense of his words. *Baby.*

"One thing we've got to discuss," he told her between long, slow kisses, "is the best way to tell Amy. I mean, it's gonna be a shock for her. She gets kidnapped, and when she comes home, her mom's going to get married and—"

Meg pulled away from him, out of his arms and off the bed. "Don't," she said. "Don't! I don't want to do this anymore! I don't want to play your stupid pretend game! It's not funny anymore! I'm not going to marry you, we're not going to have a baby! So just *stop*."

He followed her over to the sink that was outside the bathroom door, catching her arm and pulling her back to him. "Pretend? You think this is *pretend*? We didn't use protection, Meg. That means it's not pretend."

"Yes, it is!" She couldn't help it, she started to cry. "I have no future! Oh, God, he told me . . . He said . . ." She couldn't get the words out. She wasn't even sure she wanted to.

John pulled her to him and wrapped her tightly in his arms. "Jesus, Meg. What haven't you told me yet?"

She shook her head. If he knew . . .

"He," he repeated, trying to tip up her chin so that she'd have to meet his gaze. "As in the Extremist who first approached you in the parking garage. What'd he tell you, Meg?"

She tried to pull away, but he wouldn't let her go.

"How am I going to know what we're up against if you don't tell me everything?" he asked. "How the hell can I figure out how to beat this if you don't come clean with it all? And I mean *all*."

"Promise me you won't stop me from going to wherever it is they have Amy!"

She could see from his eyes that he didn't want to do that. Still, he was reading her pretty damn accurately, too, and he knew she wasn't going to move on this. "I promise. *Fuck*. What did he tell you?"

"That they're going to kill me." She managed somehow to get the words out. "That even if I bring them Razeen, that part of my payment to get Amy back is my death. That even if I killed Razeen myself, that they would come after me and kill me, too. That one of us is already dead—it's either going to be me or Amy. And I'm *not* going to let Amy die."

"The son of a bitch," John said. He laughed, but there wasn't much humor in it. "Meg, he was lying."

"No, he wasn't." She knew liars, and this man had been telling her the gospel truth.

But John held her chin and looked into her eyes. "Yes. He was. He was pushing your buttons—playing mind games with you, Meg. If you killed Razeen the way they wanted you to, what possible reason would they have to come after you? Why would they take that risk? Think about it. It doesn't make sense."

God, she wanted to believe him. But, "Does *any* of this make sense?"

"Yes. They want Razeen and—" John cut himself off. "Look, Meg, whether this guy is telling the truth or lying doesn't matter. If he's telling the truth, we're going to prove him a liar anyway, do you understand? If for some reason their intention really is to target you for death, we can take measures to protect you. And we *will* protect you."

"Even after it's over?" Meg asked.

"Yes," he told her.

"How?" she asked.

"However we need to," he said absolutely. "Whatever it takes."

She wanted to believe him. Hope flickered. God, she wanted so much to have hope again. She'd gone far too many days without any hope at all.

Meg looked into John's eyes. He stood there, looking back at her, meeting her gaze steadily, clearly trying to infuse her with his hope and his strength and his . . . love.

He'd said he loved her. He'd said it often over the past few hours—maybe too often.

She'd assumed it meant nothing, assumed it was simply something he said to help convince her to trust him.

But now he was talking about . . .

Naming their baby.

Meg had to sit down. She'd made love to him just a short time ago. She hadn't given a damn about protection—at the time it seemed ridiculous and useless—because she knew she was going to die. She'd told him she wanted his baby, but when she'd said that, she'd thought it was so far out of the realm of possibility. But John . . .

For John, it hadn't been impossible. When John had made

love to her, he hadn't believed she was going to die. He'd thought there was a very definite chance that he could get her pregnant—and he'd made love to her anyway.

He wanted her to have his baby.

He wanted a lifetime—he'd used that very word, and he'd actually meant it.

He *loved* her.

"Is that finally everything?" he asked her now. "No more secrets?"

She didn't get a chance to answer him.

Because the phone rang.

Meg leapt for it as John scrambled for his clothes.

"Hello?" Her heart was pounding so hard, it almost drowned out her own voice.

"Sorry to bother you," a very American-sounding man said, "but this is the front desk?"

The disappointment that hit Meg was nearly physical. She had to sit down on the bed.

It wasn't the Extremists who had Amy. It was the insect-man from the motel.

"My wife just came back in," he told her. "Apparently there's been a package here, waiting for you. I'm sorry—it was under some newspapers and I didn't see it when you checked in."

A package. For Joan Smith. The hope was back with a surge of power through her veins.

"Can you send it up to this room?" Meg asked. "Immediately?"

"I'm on my way," insect-man said.

The Bear was arguing with the woman with the dead soul.

Eve put her arm around Amy, who nestled more closely at the sound of the raised voices.

This didn't sound good.

The Bear gestured to the windows, gestured to the watch he wore on his left wrist.

"Not tonight," Amy whispered. "That's what he's telling her. *Not tonight.*"

Eve looked at the little girl in astonishment. "You understand them?"

"Just a little." Amy's brown eyes were so like her mother's. A grandmother wasn't supposed to have favorites, but she and Meg had always had a special bond. "She's upset. Something about a phone call. Someone's supposed to call, but they haven't so she's mad. Something about being ready to leave quickly. Something about a boat to . . . somewhere. Cuba, I think. Something about you and me. Bear keeps telling her yes. Yes, but not tonight." She frowned, worried. "I can't understand a lot of it. It's been a long time since I lived in Kazbekistan."

Not tonight was all Eve had to hear. Yes, but not tonight meant yes, in the morning.

When the sun came up, the Bear was going to take them into the swamp and shoot them.

He followed the woman out of the room, still arguing, and Eve heard the woman stomp up the stairs, clearly angry at not having gotten her way.

The Bear stomped back into the room, scowling.

Eve gave him time to sit down, time to cool off. He was mad at the woman, mad at *them*, too. Mad at the world.

She knew what that felt like.

She waited nearly forty minutes, forty *endless* minutes, before she spoke.

"I wonder, young man, if you could arrange for Amy and me to have some soap and a towel so that we might wash?"

He scowled at her, but she didn't let her gaze waver. She just kept on looking him straight in the eye.

"Allow us at least the dignity of clean hair," she said quietly.

He didn't speak, didn't move—aside from the muscle jumping in his jaw. He just gazed back at her for what seemed like another forty minutes.

Finally he stood up and left the room.

She heard the TV go on in the kitchen, blaringly loud. Was it possible the Bear had turned it on that loudly? He was always shouting at the others to turn it down. And what did that mean? For him to walk away, leaving them unguarded while he watched *Who Wants to Be a Millionaire?*

But she heard his footsteps returning, and when he came back carrying a gray towel and a bar of soap, Eve knew it was true. They had been scheduled for execution. The soap and towel was to be their final request.

"Thank you," she said, as in the other room the audience applauded a contestant who'd decided to use his lifeline.

Her heart was pounding as he led them upstairs to the bathroom. This was it. They had to go out that window tonight.

Right now.

If one of their captors saw or heard them, they would probably be killed on the spot. But that was a chance they'd have to take. If they didn't leave, they'd be dead tomorrow for sure.

The Bear stopped outside of the bathroom door, pushing it open and gesturing for them to go inside. As Eve did, a breeze pushed the shower curtain up and out, revealing the open window.

The Bear glanced at it and Eve's heart nearly stopped.

But then she saw her reflection in the cracked and grimy mirror. She was seventy-five years old, and after being held hostage for all these days, she looked every single minute of it.

She limped across the small room to hang the towel on a rack to further drive home the point. She was old and half lame. See? She could barely even walk—let alone escape out a second-story window.

"Be fast," the Bear said. He touched her arm with a hand the size of a catcher's mitt. "Be as swift as you possibly can."

She looked up at him in surprise, but he was already out in the hall, shutting the door behind him.

Amy was already with the program, already in the bathtub, over by the window. "We'll have to be quiet," she whispered to Eve. "Even if we slip and fall and hurt ourselves."

Eve smiled at her. "That's my brave girl."

She turned on the water in the sink, letting it run, masking the sound as she took out the screen.

She had two last pieces of butterscotch left, and she took them from her pocket, giving one to Amy and opening the other herself.

"For a little extra courage," she said.

The sweet taste gave her a little bit of Ralph, too, whose ghostly spirit was with her still. He'd done what he'd had to do all those years ago, in the French countryside just south of Dunkirk. And she and Amy would do what they had to do tonight.

They *could* do this. And they would.

"Hold tightly to my hand," Eve told the girl, and they went out the window and into the humid Florida night.

Despite Meg's impatience, the package was opened by an FBI bomb squad. It had been wrapped in brown paper, and addressed in slanty handwriting.

To Joan Smith, c/o The Seagull Motel.

Beneath the paper had been a priority mailing box. And inside was a cell phone and a slip of paper with a phone number—a number that had Kazbekistan's country code.

As an FBI agent disguised as a delivery man returned the package, along with a large cheese pizza, to their room, Nils knew they were in the home stretch.

They no longer had to wait for the Extremists to call them. They could call the Extremists.

Meg took the phone and dialed.

It was dark.

That was good.

Eve's eyes grew accustomed to it as she held tightly to the waistband of Amy's pants. They moved as soundlessly as possible across the roof, toward the back porch.

In theory, she'd figured they could climb down using the porch rail and the corner beam.

Reality was far more, well, *real* than theory.

In reality, the ground was very, *very* far away. In reality, a slip and a fall would not result in her landing on her feet like one of those X-Men that Amy enjoyed reading about.

Reality involved brittle, seventy-five-year-old bones. Reality also had the possibility of men with guns sitting out there on that porch. Men they could well come face-to-face with as they attempted to climb down from the roof.

Reality also ranked "as soundlessly as possible" as a six

on a scale from one to ten, with one being soundless and ten being as noisy as a fox in a chicken coop.

Still, the TV was blaring in the kitchen. With luck it was up too loud for anyone to hear the scraping and skittering sounds coming from overhead as they crossed the roof on their bondoons.

Amy was a trouper. Eve could hear the little girl trying to slow her ragged, fearful breathing, obviously conscious of the noise she was making.

You would be so proud of her, Meg.

Climbing down onto the porch railing was both easier and more difficult than Eve could have imagined. She went over the edge of the roof legs first, wrapping them around the corner beam, risking getting splinters in places where splinters had no right to be.

But right now she would be willing to sit on a porcupine if it meant saving Amy.

Eve's feet finally found the railing, and still holding on to that beam with all her might, Amy slid down into her other arm.

The child was part monkey—thank goodness for tomboys! Once her feet hit the railing, she was out of Eve's arms and quickly down on the ground.

Eve hadn't been part monkey in years—it took her a little bit longer.

But then—alleluia!—they were both on the ground.

"I'm not going without you," the little girl whispered. "I know your leg hurts, but we'll just go as fast as you can, and hide if we have to."

Eve didn't take the time to answer. She just took Amy's hand and took off at a sprint, not on the road, but through the woods. If they kept going long enough and far enough, they'd eventually reach another house. And another house would have a telephone where they could call the police, the FBI, the National Guard—*anyone*—for help.

And they'd need that help, in spades. It wasn't going to be much longer before the Bear and his friends discovered they'd escaped.

And they *would* come after them, Eve had no doubt about that.

Amy was dragging, and Eve slowed her pace. The girl's shorter legs would naturally make it hard for her to keep up. And, chances were, Amy hadn't recently trained for a marathon.

When Eve was fifteen, she'd fooled the world into thinking she was twenty because she looked twenty, and because people expected her to *be* twenty. That had taught her a thing or two about people's expectations.

When people saw a seventy-five-year-old with white hair and a wrinkled face, they expected to see old, to see weak, to see a limp.

They didn't expect to see a strong woman—with her share of age-generated aches and pains, yes—who'd done rather well in a twenty-kilometer footrace raising funds for cancer research just a few weeks before leaving to visit her favorite granddaughter in America.

The underbrush was thick, and it smacked and scratched against them like reaching arms with claws. Spanish moss dripped like tendrils, and Eve tried very hard not to think about snakes.

After several long minutes at a brisk trot, they finally hit a road.

But there were no lights, no cars, no other houses.

They were in the middle of nowhere.

Twenty-four

THEY WERE IN the middle of nowhere.

It was as if they'd gone back in time, to the days before Florida had become the mecca of vacationing families, to the days before the interstates, before the multitude of 7-Elevens and McDonald's.

Meg was driving. Nils was in the backseat—just in case they were being watched.

The Extremists kept calling on the cell phone that had been in that package sent to the Seagull Motel, giving them further instructions in bits and pieces.

Meg had called the K-stani phone number. She'd been told to hang up and wait for a call.

When that call came in on that cell phone, they were ordered to get into Meg's car and start driving south. Immediately. The Extremists—in their own amateurish way—were attempting to make sure Meg would have no time to contact the authorities and get help.

But the FBI and most of the Troubleshooters squad were already prepped and ready to go.

Nils had a miniature receiver in his ear and a microphone attached to his coat. When activated, it connected him via secured radio line to Paoletti or the senior chief. He kept it open, relaying the information that came in in bits and pieces from the Extremists.

He'd been talking pretty much constantly since they'd gotten into the car. As a result, the entire task force was now aware of the death sentence Meg believed that the Extremists had given to her. Not that it made that much of a difference. One of their top priorities already had been to keep her safe, at any and all costs.

The task force was already moving in station wagons and minivans instead of military trucks—to keep a low profile. Paoletti had also told Nils that the agents and SEALs who were off duty were being rousted to form a support team. A van and a camper of men were being readied right now. They'd follow a parallel route instead of trailing along behind.

Nils turned off his microphone.

"You okay?" he asked Meg from the backseat.

"Yeah." She didn't sound okay. He could see only the back of her head and her shoulders—and her shoulders looked pretty tight.

"You want to go over the plan?"

"Right before we get there, we stall until your guys get a chance to check the place out. We let them handle it. I don't get out of the car." Meg's voice was tight. "There's not much to go over."

She was right. When she put it that way, it didn't sound like much. But she didn't know Tom Paoletti. She didn't really know what the Troubleshooters were capable of with even just a few minutes of prep time.

"You know, John, back at the motel you asked me if I had any more secrets," she said, and Nils's heart sank. Ah, Jesus, what was she going to tell him now? "I haven't had time to breathe since you asked that, let alone tell you—"

"Meg, just say it, okay? Just put it out on the table so that we can—"

"I love you," she said. "Too. I love you, too."

"—deal with it and—" Nils shut himself up and the silence in the car was complete for several long seconds.

"Wow," Meg said with a shaky laugh. "That was effective. Are you still alive back there?"

"Yeah," Nils said. "I'm . . ." He had to clear his throat. "I'm hoping to hell you're not just saying that because you think you're going to die."

"Well." Her voice was very small, and he knew he was right. "I'm saying it because I mean it—and because I *am* afraid I'm going to die without it being said. I've loved you for a long time. I'll love you forever. I'm just afraid that forever's not going to be too—"

"You know, you left out the part of the plan where after we get Amy and your grandmother out, you come back to California with me, and—after Amy's had time to get over the shock of having such a handsome stepfather—we get married and make love every night and twice during the day while Amy's in school," Nils interrupted her, his chest feeling tight and full. But it was a good feeling, a wonderful feeling. She loved him. Not just past tense. Present tense. And, please, Jesus, future tense. "I think that's a damn good plan. How about you?"

Meg laughed softly. Sadly. "If we do get through this, I'm not going to hold you to that or anything else you've said over the past few days."

"*When* we get through this," Nils countered, "I owe you the rest of my pathetic story. I'm not going to hold *you* to anything until you've heard *that*. Every single stupid word. You know, I used to sell term papers for three hundred dollars. I think of that now, and I wonder how I could have been so stupid."

"If you'd gotten caught, you would've been in trouble," Meg agreed.

"No, I was thinking, how could I have been so stupid to set my price so low—I could've gotten at least five hundred a pop."

Meg laughed again. "There's nothing you could tell me that would make me stop loving you," she said, and he knew he was the closest to winning that he'd ever been in his life. Happily ever after was hanging right there, just in sight.

Come on, God, keep the girl alive until we get there.

"How could this have happened? The old woman could barely walk! How could she have gone out a second-story window?"

Maram was furious. She'd finally gotten her phone call. Osman Razeen was finally on his way. She should be happy. Victorious. Triumphant. Instead she was about to pop a vein.

Umar was terrified and looking for someone besides himself to blame. He glared at the Bear. "This is *your* fault. You let them go upstairs."

The Bear glared back. "This is *my* fault? When I asked you to stand guard at the bathroom door? What did you do, shitbrain? Fall asleep?"

Umar was about three seconds away from charging him, and the Bear refreshed his grip on his AK-47, holding the other man's gaze, daring him to try.

"Find them," Maram ordered Umar and Khatib. "They can't have gone far." She looked at Bear, too. "You, too. Find them and kill them. It's just as good to get them taken care of and out of the way now that this is almost over."

Umar and Khatib clattered down the steps of the front porch and headed out toward the road. They knew enough to stop arguing and complaining as they left the house. In silent agreement, they each went a different direction on the road, each breaking into a quick trot.

No doubt they'd reasoned that the old lady would stick to the road. After all, the underbrush out here was dense. Or swampy.

The Bear didn't follow the two men. Instead he went back behind the house. He looked up at the open bathroom window, looked at the roof, looked at the back porch.

He moved closer to the porch, then crouched down to look at the ground.

Yes.

There were definitely two sets of footprints—one large, one small—there in the softness of the earth.

He looked up toward the thick brush at the edge of the yard, following the direction those footprints pointed. They weren't heading toward the swamp. Somehow the old lady had known to steer clear from the swamp.

Or maybe it was just good luck.

She'd had her share of luck in her long life—both bad and good. It made sense in the scheme of things that after being kidnapped and held hostage, her luck was now once again running clean and pure.

Because it was also good luck that Umar and Khatib had gone on the road and in the opposite direction from those tracks. Of course, it would be the best of luck for *them* if either were able to find their own buttocks—even in broad daylight.

He straightened up with a sigh. Using his foot, he kicked the sandy soil over the footprints, erasing them all the way to the edge of the yard.

Sometimes even the very best of luck needed a little extra help.

He'd gone into this thing because of his religious beliefs. He'd get out of it for the very same.

Without another look back, the Bear shouldered his weapon and ambled toward the swamp.

How had this happened? Two different vehicles filled with SEALs and FBI agents, and Locke managed to climb into the one with Sam Starrett.

She'd had to do some fancy footwork to avoid sitting next to him. But now she was sitting dead across from him, his long legs stretched out, his big feet invading her personal space.

They were part of the backup team. Another separate convoy of unmarked vehicles—mostly minivans and SUVs—were trailing about a half mile behind Nils and Meg.

These vehicles—a van and a camper—however, were taking a different route. They were taking the instructions that Meg Moore was receiving from the Extremists in fragments, and they were attempting to predict a final destination. They were navigating a parallel route, hoping they'd circle around and come at the terrorists' location from a different direction.

Luck and guesswork played heavily into this strategy.

And because of that, there was a strong chance they were just going to drive around all night, too far from the action to provide any kind of backup or support at all.

"I would kill for a cup of coffee," WildCard muttered.

Starrett shifted in his seat.

Locke didn't let herself look at him. He was the reason she was so blasted tired. If she'd fallen right asleep the moment she'd gotten into bed, she would've had a healthy hour's nap. Instead, no. Instead she'd stared at the ceiling, fuming, furious with Starrett for coming to her room, furious with herself for losing her temper and letting him see how upset he made her.

She should have played it cool. She should have remained aloof. Yes, she'd slipped when she was drunk, but now reason and sanity had returned. Slamming the door in his face wasn't the answer. Freezing him out was a far better strategy.

She let herself look at him now, practicing her iciest gaze. He looked about as exhausted as she felt, but somehow on him exhausted was attractive. Didn't it figure?

He pointedly didn't look back at her, as if he were still angry at her, too.

As if he had a right to be.

"I'm getting carsick from riding in this Kleenex box on wheels, and if I don't get some caffeine," WildCard said, "I'm seriously going to hurl."

Around Locke, the SEALs sprang into action, digging into their pockets. Apparently the petty officer wasn't kidding—and they all knew it.

"I've got a candy bar," Jenkins reported, opening the wrapper. "That's got a little caffeine in it, doesn't it?"

"I've got caffeine gum." Jay Lopez tossed a piece toward WildCard.

"Bless you," Starrett drawled. He leaned forward to look at WildCard Karmody. "You mainline that gum if you need to. Do the Technicolor yawn, and you're a dead man."

"Ditto," Jenk said. "We've got a potential chain reaction situation. Sometimes it helps just to put something in your stomach. I don't have a lot, but if anyone wants a piece of chocolate, help yourself."

Chocolate.

Locke looked up and directly into Sam's blue eyes.

Chocolate.

Heat flooded through her at the memory. Chocolate all over her body. His voice, soft and smooth as velvet, murmuring about how good she tasted. His mouth gliding across her as he took his sweet time and licked her clean. She'd finally broken down and begged him to give her what she really wanted, and then he'd done that, too.

Exquisitely.

She could see an echo of that night in the heat of his eyes, and despite her intentions, despite herself, she stared at him, mesmerized, horrified, hardly able to breathe.

Finally, *finally,* Sam jerked his gaze away, freeing her.

God help her.

"Lopez, you got another piece of that caffeine gum?" Starrett asked. "I'm feeling a little digestively challenged right now myself."

A car was coming.

Eve could see the headlights approaching from way down the road, lighting up the fog that hung in the air long before the car was in sight.

She pulled Amy—or maybe it was Amy who pulled her—into the underbrush.

The bugs were intense and they were probably hiding up to their noses in poison ivy. No doubt they were going to itch and scratch for days. But scratching was far better than not being alive enough to itch.

Amy was scared to death. She was trying to pretend that she wasn't, but all these days of staunch bravery were starting to wear, and she was fighting tears.

"They'll probably drive right past," Eve said. "But if they do stop, don't look at them. Do you know that sensation that you sometimes get—that someone's watching you?"

Amy nodded.

"That's why we want to keep our eyes down. Or closed. If they stop, we don't move and we keep our eyes closed, all right?"

"What if it's a trick?" Amy asked. "I saw in a movie once where these people were looking for these kids, and they drove past in a car, and the kids thought they were gone, only the bad guys were also walking around, searching for them, and when the kids came out, the bad guys grabbed them."

"Then we'll stay hidden," Eve said. "We'll stay right here after this car goes past."

It was moving slowly, and it was still way down the road.

"Is that a plan?" Eve asked.

Amy nodded. "Will you tell me again about Dunkirk?"

"I will if you want," Eve said, "but I haven't finished the

rest of my story—the part that happened after VE Day. After the war in Europe officially ended. VE stands for Victory in Europe, you know."

"There's more to the story?" Amy said.

"There is," Eve said. "Remember, I was married—again—in May 1945."

"That was when you met Grandpa, right?" Amy asked.

Eve smiled. "Shall I tell the story?"

"Yes, please."

"With the war—at least *our* war—finally over, Nick and I didn't spend much time celebrating. Like many people, we spent those first few days and weeks reading the newspapers, searching the lists of names of war prisoners returning to England."

"Nick?" Amy asked. "Reading the newspapers?"

"Absolutely," Eve said. "It had taken five years, but he learned to read—using the method Ralph had sent to me in his final letter. It *was* a miracle, but it wasn't the particular miracle I was hoping for.

"But then, on May 27, five years after Dunkirk, we found it." All these years later, she could still feel the dizzying thrill. She'd never lost hope. She'd never given up, but after five long years, that hope was burning awfully low. But then, just like that, with eight little letters printed in the London *Times*, it blazed aflame. "R. Grayson," Eve told Amy. "The name R. Grayson was there, on one of those lists of returning British soldiers.

"I couldn't get any further information from the war office. I didn't know if R. stood for Ralph or Ronald or Richard. But they did tell me which ship this R. Grayson would be on. And I was there on the dock as the ship pulled in and the men began to disembark."

It was a day she would never forget. Not ever. The crowds were intense. The atmosphere one of a carnival. The sky was a shade of blue she'd never seen before.

She'd anticipated the crowds and brought a sign with Ralph's name on it. If he were on that ship he'd see it, see her.

The men came off that ship in droves, most of them moving slowly, thin and malnourished beyond belief. Eve stood there, holding her sign until her arms ached. Until the crowd dissipated. Until she was nearly alone on the dock with that sky turning pink from the setting sun. And then there were only stragglers coming down the gangplank, and her hope again had nearly gone out.

Nearly.

He'd found her first. She hadn't recognized him. Not until he stopped, about five feet away from her.

He was terribly thin—frighteningly thin—his face gaunt. But his beautiful eyes were exactly the same.

He had both of his arms and both of his legs. Not that she would have cared. Not that it would have made any difference at all.

"Hi," she'd said. What a stupid thing to say to the love of your life returning home from five years in hell. She supposed it was better than collapsing on the ground, overcome with relief. But not by much.

Ralph did much better. "I never stopped loving you," he said. "I want you to know that. Not a single day has passed since you came to see me in France that I haven't thoroughly, *completely,* regretted the fact that I didn't tell you I loved you, too. I've kicked myself one thousand nine hundred and seven days for that."

Eve couldn't help it. She started to cry. She just stood there, clinging to her sign and crying.

"That trip you made to France saved my life," he told her, his voice so matter-of-fact. "Knowing that you loved me enough to come all that way was something I could cling to. It kept me sane through some pretty terrible times. I think it's important that you know that, too."

He didn't reach for her. And she was too afraid to reach for him. He looked so fragile, and he was taking such care to keep his distance.

"You're even more beautiful than ever," he told her. "How old are you now?"

"Twenty-one." She laughed at that, right through her tears. She couldn't help it.

Ralph laughed, too. "How convenient." But then he stopped laughing, stopped smiling. "That is . . ." He cleared his throat. "It's been a long time, Eve. Five years. That's . . .

very long. Are you . . . Do you need my signature? Didn't my solicitor send those papers? Is that why you're here?"

"He thought I was looking for him because I needed to finalize our annulment," Eve told Amy. "He thought I needed his signature so I could get married. He thought I'd found someone else."

"Did you?" Amy asked.

The car was almost upon them. "Hush now," Eve said. "Eyes down. Silence until we're sure there's no one out there on foot."

"What's Grandpa's first name?" Amy whispered.

"Ralph," Eve whispered back.

"I knew it!" Amy said. She kissed Eve. "I *knew* it! You lived happily ever after!"

"We certainly did. Shh now!" She pulled the little girl close, holding her tightly, both of their heads down as the car slowly approached.

Go past. Just go past, she ordered it silently, watching it only in her peripheral vision.

But it didn't go past. It slowed to a stop right out on the road in front of them.

And it wasn't a car. It was a van. Just like the one their captors had driven.

"We're almost there," John reported to Lieutenant Paoletti over his radio as Meg approached the house. "Go slowly," he told Meg. "And remember, whatever happens, don't get out of the car."

From the car the place looked run-down and deserted—except for all the lights. "This has got to be it," John continued into his microphone. "The house is dark but the yard is lit up like the surface of the sun."

"Tell them not to try to get close." Meg's heart pounded. God, if the Extremists saw even just one commando type crawling across their lawn, Amy and Eve would be killed immediately.

If they weren't already dead.

She was going to find out soon if her daughter was dead or alive. Please, God, if something was going to go wrong, if she *were* going to die here tonight, at least let her find out that Amy was still alive. At least let Amy escape.

She wanted to hold her daughter so badly, her hands shook.

Meg's cell phone rang.

"This is it," John told her from the backseat. "Meg, I need you to continue to stall. Our team is getting into place."

Stall. *How?* He was still talking on his radio, still describing the place in complete detail to his CO.

The phone rang again. "I can't pick up until you're quiet," she told him.

He shut his mouth.

Meg took a deep breath and answered the phone. "Yes."

"Bring him inside."

Stall. "Please," she said. "I want— I'd like to talk to them first. To my daughter and my grandmother. I want to hear their voices, to know they're alive and—"

The line went dead.

"They hung up," she told John. "They just—"

Boom. The sound was impossibly loud, even from inside the car.

"*Shit!* Yes, confirmed," John said into his radio. "We've had a single gunshot from inside the structure. Meg and I are unharmed."

Meg couldn't breathe. A gunshot. From inside. "Oh, my God."

The cell phone rang.

"Oh, my God." She couldn't even say hello, could barely hold the phone to her ear, her hands were shaking so hard.

"It's too late to talk to the old lady," the voice on the phone said, "but if you want to talk to the little girl, you should bring him inside. Now."

Meg got out of the car.

"*Shit!*" Nils said. "*Meg—*"

She opened the back door. "They killed Eve," she told Nils. "Oh, my God, John—"

"Get back in the car, Meg," he ordered her, trying to infuse her with his calm. This situation wasn't out of control—not yet. But it would be if she didn't get back into the car. "I'll go in there, but you—"

Shit.

She was already moving toward the house, and he scrambled to follow her, to make it look as if she were pulling him with her.

"What the *fuck* . . . ?" came Wolchonok's voice over his headphones. "Get her out of there!"

Nils couldn't. She was just out of his reach, and then she was out from behind the car, and a clear target, easy to pick off by a terrorist shooter aiming from one of the darkened windows of the house.

And then there was nothing to do but keep moving forward, pray, and try to shield her with his body.

His MP-4 was locked and loaded. He kept it concealed under his coat—Razeen's coat. "When the shooting starts, stay down, stay behind me," he told her.

She was crying, and his heart clenched. Those bastards. Those goddamned sadistic bastards. If wouldn't surprise him one bit to find out that they'd kept Eve and Amy alive all this time—only to kill them now, in front of Meg.

"When?" she asked as she led him up the brightly lit path toward the house.

"If. I meant if," he corrected himself, even though he knew damn well he was probably lying to her—for the very last time.

Sam couldn't believe it.

The genius who was driving this camper was convinced they'd taken a wrong turn. He'd been arguing with the genius who was driving the van for about ten solid minutes. And then—even more brilliant!—they'd stopped the frigging things right there in the middle of the road and got out so that he and genius number two could both look at the same map.

As highest ranking naval officer in both vans, Sam pushed his way out into the night. Was this how they trained 'em to keep a low profile at the Bureau?

"What'dya say we just keep moving?" Sam suggested in his friendliest-toned good-old-boy—just in case any tangos were out there in the woods, listening in. They were just a bunch of stupid campers, lost as shit. "We're bound to find our *campground* sooner or later. There just aren't that many roads out here. What'dya say we get back into the vans before we start getting unwanted attention from the wildlife?"

He gave them each a pointed look, praying that they'd catch his drift. Crap, nothing like standing around making a lot of noise.

It rubbed even worse knowing that Nils and Meg were out there somewhere, about to walk into a nestful of K-stani terrorists, and here he was with Huey and Dewey, wasting time.

"How about we give the map reading job to one of the Boy Scouts in the back," Sam suggested. "I bet we got *someone* who's got a navigation merit badge."

He heard the sound before Huey and Dewey did—something big, something human-sized was out there in the underbrush. He leapt in front of the FBI drivers, pulling his handgun free from his shoulder holster, ready to fend off an attack . . .

From Little Red Riding Hood and her granny.

They blinked at him as they emerged from the bushes, blinked at his handgun.

"I guess scouting is much more intense now than it was back when my brother was a boy," Granny said. "You *did* say you were the Boy Scouts, didn't you? The Boy Scouts of *America*?"

Sam looked at the old woman, looked at the little girl. "Amy?" he asked, hardly daring to hope as he lowered his weapon. It was. It had to be. And what was the old woman's name? "And Mrs. Grayson. I'm Lt. Sam Starrett, ma'am, U.S. Navy SEALs. Please step into the camper. You'll be even safer there."

Sam banged on the side panel. "Someone get on the radio to Lieutenant Paoletti. We need to get word to Nils, pronto, to abort, repeat, *abort*. The hostages are safe and sound! He should get Meg the hell out of there!"

"We're going in," Nils announced over his radio, and the door to the house swung open.

A man and a woman stood there, AK-47s in their arms. Both were dressed in desert print camouflage pants and jackets—the sleeves torn off. Desert print. Here in the middle of the Florida jungle.

They were amateurs—the way they held their assault weapons verified that. Neither of them had had military training. But neither of them needed more than a heavy trigger finger to use that AK-47 to make Meg and Nils extremely dead.

He was in front of Meg as they went into the house, and he hung his head, keeping his face in shadows, wishing he could stay right there, shielding her from them until this was over.

There was no one else in the entryway, no one in the room off to the right. He'd expected the place to be crawling with Extremists. Was it possible . . . ?

There was no sign of Amy or Eve. No bloodstains, no bodies, nothing. Just a nearly empty house with two tangos.

The woman had her gun up and on them as the man shut the door. "Put the gun on the floor, and kick it over here," she ordered Meg, who obeyed.

The man shouldered his weapon, and at a nod from the woman, he pushed Meg onto the floor to search her.

He wasn't gentle and Meg cried out.

Nils clenched his teeth. It took every ounce of willpower in him not to react. He was Osman Razeen right now. Meg wasn't his lover, his friend, his *life*.

The woman was looking at him, her eyes narrowed, and he shifted slightly, hiding his face even more while he let her see a glimpse of the cuffs on his wrists.

"Where's Amy?" Meg asked, and got a backhand across her mouth for the trouble.

But she was tough. She'd come this far, and she wasn't going to quit now. She struggled to sit up. "Where's my daughter? I've done as you've asked. I've brought you Razeen. We had a deal and I've upheld my end of it!"

"She's dead," the woman said harshly. "They're both dead." Oh, God, no.

As Nils watched, Meg died. The life left her face, the fight left her body. She went completely still.

He looked at her, willing her to look back at him. Willing her to move back and out of the way, or at least down flat onto the floor. He was going to shoot these motherfuckers and get Meg safely out of there, but he couldn't start firing and hit them both—not with Meg right there in the kill zone.

"Osman Razeen," the woman said in a Kazbekistani dialect. "I sentence you to death."

She shifted her grip on her AK-47, split seconds from firing as Meg came back to life. She dropped to the ground and rolled out of the way.

Nils had his weapon up and firing, shouting for support from the rest of the team.

It was over in seconds. He'd pulled back and into the other room, shielding her with his body. If there were any other tangos in this building, they were going to come running at the sound of the gunfire.

The door was smashed in with a crash, and Wolchonok and Muldoon were the first inside, checking the fallen Extremists—making sure neither was going to pop back up, shooting.

Meg was crying and he dropped his weapon and held her tightly, crying for her, too. And for himself.

Her daughter was dead, but she'd chosen life. He knew it would've been easier for her simply to give up. To let herself be killed, instead of living with the pain and loss.

Nils knew she would never get over it. Not completely. But with his help and his love, she would get through it.

"I'm here," he told her. "Whatever you need, I'll get it for you."

"Nilsson, report." Lieutenant Paoletti's voice came over the receiver in Nils's ear.

"I need Amy," Meg cried.

"Nilsson, dammit—"

"He's here, L.T.," came the senior chief's familiar growl. "Both he and Ms. Moore are here and alive. They're sharing a, ahem, private moment."

Nils looked up to see Senior Chief Wolchonok standing in the doorway. "They killed them, Stan," he told him quietly. "Both Amy and Eve."

Wolchonok swore. "L.T., we've got some bad news. The hostages are dead."

"Someone's wrong," Paoletti's voice came back. "I've got Starrett in one of the backup vehicles saying he's got Amy and Eve with him right now and they are very much alive. Hang on . . ."

There was a buzz and a click and then a very sweet voice came loud and clear over the line. "Hello, Mommy?"

Nils yanked the miniature receiver free, held it right up to Meg's ear, leaning close so that he could hear, too.

"Mommy, this is Amy. Nana and I are all right. Are you all right?"

Meg gasped and looked up at Nils. "Oh, my God!"

He switched on his microphone. Held it close to her mouth.

"Amy?" she said. "Oh, my *God*!"

"Mommy, we're okay. Nana and I climbed out of the window and onto the roof and we ran and ran and I'm so hungry and I knew you would be so worried."

Meg laughed through her tears. "It's Amy," she told Nils.

"Are you all right?" Amy asked again.

Meg touched Nils's face and smiled at him. "I am so totally all right, honey," she told her daughter. "I am fabulously all right."

She kissed him and he got his very first taste of happily ever after.

It was enough to convince him that he definitely wanted more.

Twenty-five

$\backsim$ $\backsim$

$\mathbf{A}$MY SAT IN the camper next to Eve, eating a chicken salad sandwich that one of the FBI agents had packed for a snack.

The child's hands were filthy dirty, but there was nowhere to wash, and Eve was too hungry herself to care.

First food, then Meg would arrive, then they'd be taken somewhere safe to wash and to sleep in the beautiful softness of a real bed.

"What about Ralph?" Amy asked with her mouth full.

Eve laughed. Ah, yes, they'd left poor Ralph standing there, on the dock. "He'd tried to be so casual," she told Amy, "asking me if I'd come to get that annulment. As if I had traveled all that way and dressed up in my very best clothes to greet him as he set foot in England for the first time in five years because I wanted an *annulment*?"

Amy laughed. "Boys are dumb."

"Boys sometimes are," Eve agreed, "very dumb. I told him I had a box of over two thousand letters waiting for him, back in Ramsgate."

Letters she'd written to him over the past five years. Letters she'd written even though she didn't know if he were alive or dead.

She'd looked him in the eye then. She'd done this before, in France, but still, it hadn't gotten any easier. "I love you," she told him. "There never has been and never will be anyone else."

He started to cry. Right there on the dock, Ralph broke down and wept. He took a step toward her. Just one move in her direction was all she needed. She threw down her sign and launched herself at him, and into his arms.

379

He wasn't as fragile as he looked. He might've been thin, but his arms were still strong.

"He kissed me," Eve told Amy, "and kissed me and kissed me, right there for all the world to see. It was glorious and I knew that no matter how hard the past few years had been, the future was going to be *wonderful*.

"He told me that I'd saved his life in Dunkirk. He said that his unit was finally captured, and the Germans who took them prisoner were ready to kill them right then and there. He was on the ground, on his knees, with a Nazi gun to his head when he started talking—about me.

"He spoke in German, telling the man who was about to kill him all about this girl back in Ramsgate, an American girl named Eve whom he loved with all his heart. He told the German soldier that although it was probably hard to believe, this girl loved him, too, and that she'd be distraught at the news of his death. He told this German all about how we'd met, about Nicky getting sick, about the warm feeling in his heart whenever he saw me.

"He told me that he was convinced that by talking about me that way, he'd forced the German to see him not as a nameless, soulless enemy soldier, but as a human being. As a man—who loved and was loved."

"It worked," Amy said. "Because they let him live."

"That's right." Eve smiled, remembering how through the years Ralph had told her time and again of the way his stories of her light and life had served to entertain his captors—and to make him an individual in their eyes.

"He asked me to marry him," she told Amy. "Right there on the dock. I told him that I already had married him, that I'd never signed or sent back those annulment papers. But I told him, if he wanted me to, I'd marry him all over again."

"And he wanted to, right?" Amy said. "Because you got married again."

"We did."

The back door of the camper opened, and the strikingly beautiful FBI agent named Alyssa Locke stuck her head in. "Your mom just pulled up," she said to Amy with a smile.

Amy was up and out of the door in a flash.

Eve sat for a moment, letting the little girl have some time alone with her mother, content to rest.

And remember.

"I'll marry you again," Eve told Ralph as she stood on the dock in his arms. "But what I *won't* do is delay our wedding night another day longer."

He'd laughed at that, his laughter rich and warm. It wrapped around her, and she knew her words were a lie. She'd wait for him forever if she had to.

Still. He was English, after all, and it was possible he'd need a bit of a push. "What are your plans?" she asked him. "Are you going to teach?"

He shook his head. "I haven't thought much about it. I haven't thought much beyond fresh eggs and a rare steak for years. And you, of course," he added with a smile. "And not at all in that order."

She kissed him, long and sweet. "You always were a fabulous teacher." She kissed him again, longer and a little less sweetly. "As a matter of fact, there's something very specific I was hoping you could teach me tonight."

He shouted with laughter at that. But as he looked at her, the warmth in his eyes shifted to something potent. Something hot. "Oh, yes," he murmured. "Count on it."

His kiss held a promise of something achingly wonderful.

He pulled back to look into her eyes. "Promise me," he said.

"Yes," she said.

He laughed. "Now how do you know I'm not going to ask you to promise me something ridiculous?"

"I don't care. I'd promise you *any*thing."

His smile softened as he touched her face. "I am the luckiest man on this planet. The war didn't break your spirit, did it?"

She shook her head.

"I'm not sure whether to be grateful or terrified about that," he told her with a laugh. "Just . . . promise me that you'll never withhold the truth from me again. Promise you'll never again pretend to be something you're not. Because you're perfect, Eve, just the way you are. No more lies, all right?"

"I promise," she told him. She kissed him again, and

he took possession of her mouth, slowly, deeply. It was exquisite.

And so were the words he spoke when he pulled back to look into her eyes. "I'll never leave you again," Ralph told her. "From this moment, Eve, until the day that I die, I'll be with you, right by your side."

Fifty-five years later, Eve sat in the camper all alone, remembering those promises they'd made.

The door was still open a crack, and she could see outside, see the other vehicle that had pulled up, see Amy, held tightly in Meg's arms.

She'd delivered the child safely into her mother's arms. She'd done it. Or rather, *they'd* done it. She and Ralph.

Although he'd been gone from this world for these past two years, he'd been with her in spirit throughout this entire ordeal.

Eve smiled and sent him a silent apology for pretending to have that limp that fooled her captors so successfully. Yes, she'd promised him all those years ago that she would no longer pretend to be something she wasn't, but he would have to admit that there were times when pretending did have its usefulness.

She could almost hear Ralph's rich, warm laughter wrapping around her.

Still filling her heart.

Meg held Amy on her lap. Since she'd turned ten, she'd claimed to be too old for that. But not today. Today, she was parked there pretty darn permanently.

Meg held her daughter close. Amy's hair smelled like a bad mix of wet paper bags and soggy dog, but she didn't care.

She had a lifetime to get Amy clean.

Eve sat next to her, holding her hand. "Thank you," Meg kept telling her grandmother.

She still couldn't believe they'd gone out a second-story window.

She still couldn't believe that in a single heartbeat, her life had turned from tragic to perfect.

She knew what Lazarus's mother must've felt like.

The door opened, and John came inside the van.

Meg felt Amy shrink slightly. John was big, she realized. Tall and broad and . . . He smiled at her and her insides melted.

"Amy, this is Lt. John Nilsson. Do you remember him from Kazbekistan?" Meg said. "He saved my life about twenty different times these past few days."

Eve was looking from her to John, and Meg knew she hadn't missed the message he was sending her with his eyes. His love for her was written all over his face. He didn't even try to hide it. Eve squeezed her hand and when Meg turned to look at her, she made big eyes and a completely approving face.

Meg laughed. "John, this is Amy, and my grandmother, Eve Grayson."

John sat down, shining the warmth of his smile on them both. "I'm honored to meet you, Mrs. Grayson. You should be proud of what you did out there tonight."

"I am," Eve said.

John's smile widened. "Well, good. The FBI's going to be taking both you and Amy to a safe house where you can get cleaned up and where a doctor will come in and check you both out." He turned to Amy. "This must've been pretty scary, huh?"

"I do remember you," she said. "Your hair was shorter. You're a language specialist, right? Like Mom?"

"Yeah," John said. "Like your mom. I have a lot in common with her."

Amy smiled. "You colored with me. And you taught me to say *shit* in Kazbekistani."

Meg laughed. She had to feign outrage. "You did *what*?"

"Oops."

"You also taught me to say—"

"Thank you *very* much," John said to Amy. "I clearly made a lasting impression. Wow."

"You did," she told him, laughing at the face he made. "You always made me laugh, even when I didn't feel much like laughing."

John looked up at Meg and the expression in his eyes was priceless. He'd been scared, she realized. This big, strong, capable man who didn't know the meaning of the word *quit*, this man who'd gone fearlessly into battle for her today and had taken two lives to protect her, had been scared to death of meeting a ten-year-old girl.

"We're going to be seeing a lot of John from now on," Meg told her daughter.

"You and me, Amy," John added, "we're going to be really good friends. We have a lot in common, too, you know. Starting with the fact that we both love your mother."

Amy looked from John to Meg to Eve. And she smiled at her great-grandmother. "This is so cool."

"So of course I get down here *after* the action is over," Jules complained.

"You didn't miss all that much," Locke countered. As she watched, Sam and Lopez came out of the house with the forensics team, who were carrying one of the body bags out of the house.

Jules watched, too, as the FBI team went back into the house. "How many are in there?"

"Just two. Two others are in custody—they were picked up on the road. Mrs. Grayson says there were five that she knew about. One's still at large."

The second body bag came out. Sam and Lopez were still standing next to the truck. As Locke watched, Sam turned away. He leaned down, alongside the wheel, and threw up.

Holy cow.

"I heard there's some kind of bogus death threat," Jules said, "that Meg Moore's going to be under protection for a while."

"Just until the word gets out," Locke told her partner.

Lopez touched Sam briefly on the shoulder. Sam shook his head rather vehemently as he straightened up, wiping his mouth with the back of his hand.

Locke turned away before he looked over and caught her watching. "We think the threat was just a mind game. Just more psychological warfare. But the Extremists—and all of the other fringe groups in K-stan—are going to get a very explicit message," she said. "They go near Meg Moore or her family, and they will be crushed. They stay away, and we use our embassy to open up lines of communication between them and their government."

"Ah," Jules said. "The old threat combined with dangling a little of what they want most in front of them. That should do the trick."

Locke glanced back at the trucks. Sam was gone.

"I heard from Max Bhagat that we've announced to the media that the so-called hostage situation at the K-stani embassy was just a training operation." Jules laughed. "Everyone saves face—except CNN and all the other networks who're made to look like fools for having reporters standing outside a training op for all these days."

Locke spotted him. Sam had moved over to the house, where he sat on the front steps, head in his hands.

Who would've thought . . . ?

"Excuse me for a sec," she said to Jules.

"Sure."

Locke approached Sam cautiously. Slowly. Carefully.

He heard her coming, though, and he looked up. And laughed derisively. "Great, you saw that, huh? Perfect. Have at me, Alyssa. My night hasn't been painful enough."

"Are you okay?" she asked.

"Fucking perfect," he said. "I'm not sure which it was that did it to me—the thought of how close that little girl and her grandmother came to getting a bullet in their heads or catching a glimpse of the forensics guys shoveling pieces of a human being's brain into one of those body bags. Either way, it still makes my stomach churn."

"I wanted to apologize," she said. "For some of the things I said to you before, you know, back at the hotel."

He was surprised and working hard to hide it. He reached down onto the step beside him and picked up a dead twig that was lying there. "*Some* of the things," he repeated, snapping the twig into two. "Only some?"

She gave him the smallest of smiles. "That's right. You know you were there dogging me."

He looked her dead in the eye and the world tilted slightly. "Can you really blame me?"

She couldn't respond to that. "I really appreciate your not

giving in to your anger and, you know, your not talking to anyone about what we, um, did that night."

"Okay," Starrett said. "We're a slow learner, huh? Let me see if I can say it so you'll understand. I'm not going to talk about it to anyone. It's not their business. What we did is between you and me. No matter how mad you make me— and, shit, you can make me mad!—that's not going to change. You want me to say it again, more slowly this time?"

Locke shook her head. "No, I'm ... I got it. I'm ... Thank you."

He tossed the pieces of twig into the dust, one at a time. "Forget about it."

"Yeah," she said. "That's not a bad idea. In fact, I was thinking ..."

He looked up at her in silence, waiting for her to go on. How was it that he could have been so good, so gentle and kind with Amy and Eve out there in the woods just a few hours ago? She'd been impressed with the way he'd taken charge of the situation. He was good at what he did. She couldn't deny that.

So why did he always treat *her* so badly?

Locke cleared her throat. "You know, Starrett, since you're in the most elite SEAL team in the country, and I'm in the FBI's top counterterrorist unit, well, there's a really good chance we're going to run into each other with a certain frequency."

He nodded. "There is."

"I'm assuming you're not going anywhere in the near future—"

"No, I'm not."

"And *I* would rather not have to transfer and ..." She took a deep breath. "In an attempt to make things as least awkward as possible, I think we should both simply pretend that night never happened. You know, forget it ever took place."

Sam nodded, still just watching her. "Is that really what you want?" he asked quietly.

As she looked into his eyes, she felt a flash of uncertainty. "Yes," she said, trying to feel as sure as she sounded. "From this point on, we don't talk about it again, all right?"

Sam still watched her steadily. Finally he nodded. "All right."

Locke nodded, too. "Good," she said. "Thank you." She backed away from him. "I'm going to . . . go find Jules and . . ." Her voice trailed off as she looked at him. He looked even more green than he did before. "Are you sure you're okay?"

"Perfect," he said. "I'm abso-fucking-lutely perfect."

"See you around, then," she said.

"Right. Later." His soft laughter followed her as she walked away.

The sun had been up for hours before Meg came out of the room in the safe house where Amy was sleeping.

"I'm going to sleep in there," she told Nils. "I hope you don't mind. I just . . . I need to be with her for a while."

He nodded. "I didn't expect anything less."

She sat next to him on the couch, slipping into his arms as if she belonged there.

"Okay," he said.

She looked up at him. "Okay?"

He nodded. "I'm ready."

She put her hand directly on top of him. "Hmm," she said, "that can't be what you mean . . ."

Nils laughed and moved her hand. He kissed her palm and placed it over his heart. "Don't try to distract me. This is hard—I mean, *difficult*—enough, Ms. Dirty Mind."

She kissed him sweetly then pulled back to gaze into his eyes. "John, you don't have to do this right now."

He shook his head. "I've got something I need to ask you, but before I can do that, I have to talk to you about a couple things. You know, about tonight—"

"Ah," Meg said. "I was wondering when we were going to talk about what you had to do tonight to save my life. Are you okay?"

"Actually, it's not an issue for me," he told her. "But I thought the fact that it wasn't might be an issue for you. I eliminated two targets tonight. To be honest, I don't think about them as people. I know that probably sounds cold to you, but . . . I don't gain anything by giving names and homes and families to terrorists. They were threats, Meg. To you and to me. And I took them out. It was fast, it was clean, and if I'd only wounded them, they would have kept shooting until one of us was dead. I did what I had to do and I refuse to feel bad about it."

"Really?" she asked.

"After something like this happens, I have to go in for a required number of sessions with a shrink," he explained. "He seems convinced I'm doing okay—at least for a guy who's a liar, a killer, and a thief."

"Liar, killer, and thief I can handle. What *I'm* having trouble with is the fact that you never taught *me* to say *shit* in Kazbekistani."

He laughed. "Sorry about that. She asked, and . . . well, I told her."

She leaned her head back against his shoulder. "You're forgiven. I'm feeling very forgiving today."

Nils took that as his cue. "When I was fifteen," he told her, "my father got a job working as a janitor at Milfield Academy."

"He was the janitor. Suddenly it all makes sense."

"He was treated like crap by all those rich kids," Nils said. "He hated it, I know he did, but he wouldn't quit. He said it was good, honest work and there was no shame in that. But you see, part of his salary was my tuition. He was doing it for *me*."

She was listening, so he kept going, telling her things he'd never told anyone. Things he'd never managed to forget. Things he'd tried for years to keep hidden. Things he didn't want to hide from her. Not anymore.

"So I went there—this poor-as-shit kid, jammed in with all those rich assholes. And it got to me, Meg. What they did and what they said and what they thought. It started to matter. And I . . ." He choked it out. "I pretended I wasn't related to that weird old janitor who shuffled around the campus. God forbid anyone find out he was my father. Yeah, even though I wasn't rich, I got the asshole part down pretty well, pretty fast."

Meg took his hand and interlaced their fingers. "I did

some terrible things in high school, too, John. Nobody judges other people on that kind of ancient history."

"I judge myself," he told her. "I live, every day, with the memory of the look in my father's eyes . . . It was the afternoon I got the highest score on some test—I don't even remember what it was anymore. All I remember was that I was a freshman, and I got the best grade in the school—it was posted for everyone to see. And, Jesus, he was so proud of me. He waited for me outside of one of my classes after he got the news. I saw him there—he knew I saw him. And I walked right past him without even saying a word. I didn't want to stop and acknowledge him in front of my friends." Just thinking about it still brought tears to his eyes. "From that day on, he never approached me during school. Never again."

Nils shook his head. "I swear to God, Meg, until the day I die, I will never forget the look on that man's face as I walked away. He was a good man. He was one of the most honest, intelligent, *kindest* people I've ever known."

"Yet he drank." Meg sat up, kneeling on the couch to face him.

"That doesn't make him a bad person," Nils told her. "He was a good person who made mistakes."

She was looking at him with those eyes that could see right through him, past all the bullshit and pretense, right to his heart and soul. "Why can't you cut yourself the same slack?"

Nils nodded. "That's what I'm trying to do—what I'm hoping you'll do. Cut me some slack and . . ." He laughed. "I don't know how to do this, how to say it, so I'll try to imagine what my father would've done, okay?"

He got down on the floor, in front of her, on one knee.

Meg laughed. "Oh, John . . ."

"Will you marry me?" he asked her. He couldn't keep from laughing either. "I'm serious. I know I don't look or sound it, but, Meg . . ." He lost himself in her eyes. "I want to spend my life with you."

She smiled at him. "I like your father's style. And I love your father's son, despite all the mistakes he might've made."

His heart leapt. "Is that a yes?"

"Yes," she whispered.

She smiled into his eyes, and he knew he'd found the ultimate win-win scenario.

Nils kissed her, grabbing hold of his happily ever after. It had been a long time coming, and he was never going to let it—or Meg—go.

Read on for a sneak peek
of *Gone Too Far,*
the breathtaking new novel
from Suzanne Brockmann

Roger "Sam" Starrett's cell phone vibrated, but he was wedged into the rental car so tightly that there was no way he could get the damn thing out of the front pocket of his jeans.

At least not without causing a twelve car pileup on Route 75.

He had the air conditioning cranked—welcome to summer in Florida—and the gas pedal floored, but the subcompact piece of shit that was one of the last cars in the rental company's lot was neither cool nor fast.

It was barely a car.

Feeling trapped in an uncomfortable place had been pretty much SOP for Sam ever since he rushed into marriage with Mary Lou nearly two years ago, and he waited for the familiar waves of irritation and anger to wash over him.

Instead, he felt something strangely similar to relief.

Because the end was finally in sight. And Sarasota was only another few minutes down the road.

Sam knew the town well enough—he'd hitched down here from his parents' house in Fort Worth, Texas, four summers in a row, starting when he turned fifteen. It had changed a lot since then, but he had to believe that the circus school was still over by Ringling Boulevard.

Which wasn't too far from Mary Lou's street address.

Maybe he should make a quick stop, pick up a few more Bozos, turn this thing into a bonafide clown car.

On the other hand, one was probably enough to qualify for clown car status.

His phone finally stopped shaking.

What were the chances that it had been Mary Lou, finally calling him back?

Nah, that would be too damn easy.

Although, in theory, this should have been an easy trip. Pop over to Sarasota. Pick up the divorce papers that Mary Lou was supposed to have sent back to him three weeks ago. Put an end to the giant-ass mistake that was their marriage, and maybe even try to start something new. Like a real relationship with his baby daughter, who after six months probably wouldn't even recognize him, then pop back home to San Diego.

Fucking easy as pie.

Except this was Mary Lou he was dealing with. Yes, she was the one who'd filed for this divorce. Yes, she'd been compliant right up to this point. But Sam wouldn't put it past her to change her mind at the zero hour.

And it was, indeed, the zero hour.

And, true to form, Mary Lou was surely messing with him.

Had to be.

Why else wouldn't she have sent the papers back to the attorney after receiving them four weeks ago? Why else wouldn't she return Sam's phone calls? Why else would she not pick up the phone even when he called at oh dark hundred, when he knew she had to be there because the baby was surely sleeping?

Sam reached for the stick to downshift as he took the exit ramp for Bee Ridge Road, and came into contact with the stupidass automatic transmission.

Six months ago, this entire suckfest scenario would have made him bullshit. Everything sucked. This car sucked, the fact that he had to come all this way for something that should have cost the price of a first-class postage stamp sucked, and knowing that Haley was going to look at him as if he were some stranger *really* sucked.

But along with that weird feeling of relief came a sense of readiness. Maybe this wasn't going to be easy, but that was okay. He was ready for it. He was ready for anything.

Like, Haley was probably going to cry when he tried to hold her. So he wouldn't hold her at first. He'd take it slow.

And Mary Lou, well, she was probably going to ask him to get back together. He was ready for that, too.

"Honey, you know as well as I do that it just wasn't working." He tried the words aloud, glancing at himself in the rear view mirror, checking to see if he looked apologetic enough.

But, shit, he looked like roadkill. His eyes were bloodshot behind his sunglasses, and the flight out of Atlanta had been weather delayed for so damn long that he desperately needed a shower.

And he definitely shouldn't start out by calling her honey. She had a name, and it was Mary Lou. Honey—and every other term of endearment he'd ever used like sugar, darling, sweetheart, *sweet thing*—was demeaning.

He could practically hear Alyssa Locke's voice telling him so. And God knows Alyssa Locke was the Queen of Right.

She'd hated it something fierce when he'd called her *sweet thing*. So he'd called her Alyssa, drawing the S's out as he whispered her name in her perfect ear as they'd had sex that should've been listed in the World Record Books. Best Sex of All Time—Sam Starrett and Alyssa Locke, Champions of the Simultaneous Orgasm.

Ah, God.

What was Alyssa going to think, when she heard about his divorce?

Sooner or later the news was going to get out. Up to this point, his commanding officer, Lieutenant Commander Tom Paoletti and the SEAL team's XO, Lieutenant Jazz

Jaquette, were the only ones who knew that Sam and Mary Lou were finally calling it quits. He hadn't told Nils and WildCard yet—his best friends in Team Sixteen. Shit, he hadn't told his sister, Elaine. Or even Noah and Claire.

And he sure as hell hadn't told Alyssa Locke.

Who was probably going to think, "Thank God I'm in a committed relationship with Max so Roger Starrett doesn't come sniffing around my door looking for some play." Max. The fucker. Even after all this time, Sam was still insanely jealous of Max Bhagat. Despite his new sense of relief and hope, he was feeling neither when it came to thoughts of Alyssa and Max.

"How could you fuck your boss?" he asked.

Alyssa, of course, because she wasn't in the car, didn't answer him.

It wasn't too tough of a question. Sam could come up with plenty of answers without Alyssa's help. Because Max was handsome, powerful, brilliant and, yes, probably great in bed.

Yeah, and who was he kidding with that *probably*? Max was no doubt *definitely* great in bed. Sam knew Alyssa, and she wasn't about to spend over a year of her life with someone who couldn't keep up with her sexually.

And as far as the fact that the man was her boss . . .

She and Max were incredibly discreet. In fact, they were so discreet, there were some people in the Spec Ops community who refused to believe that they actually had an intimate relationship.

But Sam knew better. He'd gone knocking on Alyssa's hotel room door about six months ago. And yeah, it was a stupidass thing to do. He and Mary Lou hadn't even separated back then. He had no business knocking on anyone's door.

But an FBI agent matching Alyssa's description—a woman of color, in her late twenties—had been killed that day, and until the news came down that Alyssa wasn't on the casualty list, Sam kind of lost it.

Except who had opened that hotel room door that he'd knocked on? Well, gee, hiya Max. Sorry, I woke you, man.

And that was it. Game over. It was looking into Max's eyes that did it. The fucker cared deeply about Alyssa—that was more than clear.

And every day since then, Sam tried—he really honestly tried—to be happy for her.

And as for his own elusive happiness . . .

Well, he was done feeling sorry for himself. And he was done letting this divorce take place on Mary Lou's timetable, with Mary Lou running this freak show.

Sam and his expensive new lawyer had worked out a schedule of visits—dates and times that he could see Haley. He wasn't looking for joint custody—that would be crazy. As a SEAL he went out of the country at the drop of a hat, sometimes for weeks or even months at a time.

He just wanted to be able to see his kid a couple of times a week whenever he was Stateside. Surely Mary Lou would agree to that.

To make it a no-brainer for her, Sam was prepared to give her the deed to their house back in San Diego—free and clear. He'd take care of the mortgage and continue to pay the taxes. Now that Mary Lou's sister Janine had split up with her husband, Sam's plan was to talk all three of them—Mary Lou, Janine and Haley—into moving back to California.

Where he *would* be able to see Haley every other weekend and once a week on Wednesday nights—instead of some pathetic twice a year bullshit.

So, yeah, Sam was hopeful that he and Mary Lou were going to be able to work this out.

Traffic in the city was light at this time of the morning. He was literally four minutes from Mary Lou's door.

Please be home.

Sam had tried calling his soon-to-be ex-wife from a pay phone at the airport, right after his flight had gotten in. It had occurred to him that she was screening her calls, and that maybe she'd pick up if her caller ID gave her a number other than that of his cell phone.

Not a chance.

He didn't leave a message on her machine. He was just going to head over to the house and wait. Sooner or later Mary Lou or Janine would scoop up Haley from day care and come home.

And then he'd do whatever he had to do to get Mary Lou to sign those papers and move back to San Diego.

Hell, if she didn't want to live in that same house they'd once shared, they could sell it and she could buy another. It didn't matter to him as long as she lived in the San Diego area. He was going to move into the BOQ on base either way.

Sure, the bachelor officers quarters were tiny and there was no privacy to speak of. But since it was highly unlikely that he was ever going to have sex again, privacy wasn't something that he needed.

Sam laughed at himself. That really sounded pathetic—never having sex again—like he was such a loser that no woman would want him.

Truth was, women went for him in a major way.

In fact, the girl at the car rental counter couldn't have been more obvious about her interest if she'd used semaphore flags.

"Where are you staying?"

"Are you in town alone?"

"If you're looking for a good hangout, you might want to try Barnaby's, down by the dock. I go there all the time after work."

Hint, hint.

She was hot, too. A strawberry blonde with a lithe, athletic body and a cute little ass. But hot wasn't enough for him anymore. No, thank you.

Sam was finished with casual sex. He was keeping his pants zipped, which actually wasn't as hard as it seemed, even after he'd gone for well over nine months without getting laid.

It sounded like a really pansy thing to say, but he wanted more from life than a fast fuck with an empty-headed stranger.

He wanted sex to mean something. He wanted to be fucked for more than his blue eyes and his muscles and the fact that he was a lieutenant with the U.S. Navy SEALs.

Unless, of course, Alyssa Locke called him up and begged him to come over, get naked, and light her world on fire.

If that ever happened, all bets were off.

Alyssa was neither empty-headed nor a stranger, but during the few nights they'd spent together way back before Sam married Mary Lou, she'd definitely thought of him as only a temporary plaything, which still stung.

Sam leaned over to look at the numbers on the houses as he turned onto Mary Lou's street. 458. 460. 462.

Bingo.

462 Camilia Street was a tiny little single story Florida-style house with a carport that sat empty. There wasn't a car in the driveway either, nor one parked out in front.

A tired looking palm tree provided the only shade out front. The door was tightly shut behind the torn screen, and the dark shades on the windows were pulled all the way down and—

What the fuck . . . ?

Sam turned off the engine and got out into the sweltering heat, staring across the roof of the rental car.

Were his eyes playing tricks on him, making those window shades seem to shift and move, or . . . ?

He moved closer to the house.

Holy Lord Jesus Christ Almighty, those weren't dark shades, those were *flies*. There were so many of them, they almost seemed to cover the windows.

Oh, *fuck!* That many flies inside a house could mean only one thing.

Whoever was in there was dead.

Sam went around the back of the house, looking for the

kitchen door and praying that he was wrong, praying that Janine, Mary Lou and Haley had gone to visit Mary Lou's mother in Northern Florida, and that an animal—a raccoon or a skunk—had gotten into the house and, trapped there, had died.

But Jesus, there were flies covering every window, even in the back of the house. Especially in the back. Whatever was dead in there was bigger than a skunk.

Sam knew he shouldn't touch the doorknob in case there were fingerprints on it. He had to call the authorities.

Except, he didn't know for sure that anyone was dead.

Yet the fact that Mary Lou hadn't returned his call for three weeks—three *long* weeks—suddenly seemed telling. He'd assumed that she wasn't calling him back—not that she *couldn't*.

Please God, don't let her be dead.

He lifted the clay flowerpot that sat on the back steps— Mary Lou's favorite hiding place—and sure enough, there was a key beneath it.

The lock on the kitchen door was right on the knob, and he knew he could unlatch the door by inserting and then carefully turning the key. He didn't need to touch the knob and therefore wouldn't add to or subtract from any fingerprints that might be there.

The lock clicked as it unlatched, and he gagged. *Jesus.* Even just the inch or two that he'd opened the door was enough to make his eyes water from the unmistakable stench of death. Sam quickly pulled the collar of his T-shirt up and over his nose and mouth and swung the door open.

Oh God, *no*.

Mary Lou lay face down on the linoleum floor— although, Christ, she'd been lying there so long in this heat, she probably didn't have much of a face left.

Sam couldn't bring himself to look more closely.

He saw all he needed to see. She was undeniably dead, her brown hair matted with blood and brains and, shit, maggots. She'd taken what looked like a shotgun slug to the back of her head, probably while she was running away from whoever had come to the kitchen door.

Sam stumbled outside and puked up his lunch into the dusty grass.

FBI Agent Alyssa Locke answered the phone in her partner's office. "Jules Cassidy's desk."

There was a pause before a voice that sounded remarkably like Sam Starrett's asked, "Where's Jules?"

No, it didn't sound remarkably like Sam. It sounded pathetically like him.

Because *she* was decidedly pathetic.

What in God's name did she have to do to get that man out from under her skin for once and for all? She saw and heard him everywhere. She couldn't so much as see a blue jeans ad in a magazine without thinking about his long legs and . . .

"Who's calling please?" she said, scrambling to find a piece of paper and a pen on Jules's black hole of a desk. Her fault for coming in here in search of a file, her fault for picking up the phone instead of letting Jules's voice mail take the message.

There was the sound of air being exhaled, hard, then, "Alyssa, it's Sam. Starrett. Can you please put Jules on the phone? Right now?"

Holy God, this time it really *was* Sam.

"Oh," she said, temporarily startled into silence. Why on earth was Sam calling *Jules*?

"Look," he said in that Texas drawl that she'd always found either infuriating or sexy as hell, depending on her state of mind. "I'm sorry if this sounds rude, but I've got a fucking bad situation here and I need to talk to Jules right fucking now. So put him on the fucking phone. Please."

Whoa. A triple *fucking*. Even in the best of situations, Sam had a sewer mouth, but something definitely had him rattled to make him *that* profane.

"He's not here," Alyssa told him. "He's out of the office and he won't be back until Friday."

"Fuck!"

"What's happening?" she asked, sitting down behind Jules's desk. Aha, there was a brand new legal pad buried among his junk. She pulled it free. "Is this call business or . . . ?"

She uncapped a pen as Sam laughed. It was the laughter of a man who didn't find anything particularly funny right now. "God *damn* it. Yes, it's business."

"Where are you?" And no, she refused to let her heart beat harder at the thought that he was here in DC. That was just indigestion from drinking too much coffee on an empty stomach.

"Sarasota," he said.

"Florida."

"Yeah. I'm at Mary Lou's sister's house. Alyssa, I'm really sorry, but I need your help. I need you to call someone in the Sarasota Bureau and have them get over here as quickly as possible."

"What's going on?"

Another loud exhale. "Mary Lou's dead."

It was a good thing she was sitting down. As it was, she had to hang onto the desk. "Oh, my God. *Sam!* How?"

"A shotgun slug to the head."

Oh, dear Lord. Oh, Sam, no. Alyssa had suspected that things weren't particularly good between Sam and his wife, but . . . "Was anyone else hurt?"

"I don't know," he said. "I came outside to . . . Well, shit, you know me well enough . . . I got sick. Big surprise. But I . . . I have to go back in there to look for Haley and . . . " His voice broke. "Jesus, Lys. I'm pretty sure Haley's in there."

"Whoa," Alyssa said. She leapt to her feet, pulling the phone as far as it would go as she went to the office door. "Wait. Just wait a second, okay, Sam? Don't move."

Laronda was in the hall. Alyssa covered the mouthpiece of the telephone. "Has Max left for lunch?"

"About an hour ago. He should be back in about fifteen minutes."

"*Shit.*" Fifteen minutes wasn't good enough. "Is Peggy in her office?"

"She's gone, too." Laronda was eyeing her with curiosity. "Everyone's out but George. You want George Faulkner?"

George was still new to the team and had even less experience in this type of situation than Alyssa did. She shook her head. It was up to her to talk Sam down from whatever emotional ledge he was on. "Get me the head of the Florida office in Sarasota."

"Yes, ma'am."

Alyssa went back to Jules's desk, speaking into the phone. "Sam, are you still with me?"

"Yeah."

"Good," she said. "Don't go anywhere. Don't go back inside. Just . . . Just sit down, okay? Are you sitting down?"

"Yeah," he said.

"Where's the shotgun?" she asked.

"I don't know. It was so bad in there, I didn't think to look—"

"Sam, I'm going to call and get you help, all right? But you cannot go back into that house. Do you hear what I'm saying?"

"Yeah, I do, but—"

"No buts. You sit still and you talk to me. I need you to make sure that you are nowhere near that weapon when the authorities arrive. Is that clear?"

On the other end of the phone, Sam was silent.

"Sam?"

Nothing. Oh, God, please don't let him have put down the phone.

The intercom buzzed. "Manuel Conseco from Sarasota on line two," Laronda's voice said.

"Sam, you're going to need to give me the street address."

Sam laughed. "You think *I* killed her," he said. "That's really nice, Alyssa. Jesus."

"Are you saying you didn't . . . ?"

"Fuck, no. What kind of asshole do you take me for?" He laughed again in disgust. "Apparently the kind who would shoot his soon-to-be ex-wife and leave her dead in the kitchen. Thank you *so* very much."

Soon-to-be *ex-wife* . . . ? "I thought it was an accident . . . "

"With a fucking *shot*gun?"

"Well, I'm sorry, but you said—"

"462 Camilia Street," Sam said flatly. "Sara-fucking-sota. Mary Lou didn't return my phone calls for three weeks so I finally came out to see her—to finalize our divorce. I'm pretty sure she's been dead all that time, and I haven't searched the rest of the house, so I haven't found Haley's body yet. Call whoever you need to call so that the feds get here first. I don't want the local police fucking up the investigation."

"Sam," Alyssa said, but he'd already cut the connection.

GONE TOO FAR $5.00 REBATE COUPON

Buy one copy of **GONE TOO FAR**
by Suzanne Brockmann
and receive a **$5.00 rebate**!

Name: _____

Address: _____

City: _____

State or Canadian Province: _____ **Zip:** _____

Country: _____